PRAISE FOR

Mary Kay Andrews and *The Fixer Upper*

"This authentic tale of cleaning up life's messes and self-discovery is bright, engaging, and thoughtful, enlivened by Andrews's quirky characters and lovely backwoods setting." —*Publishers Weekly*

"A summer read that's guaranteed to satisfy your thirst for Southern fiction at its best." —*Daytona Beach News-Journal*

"Entertaining. . . . Delightful." —*Library Journal*

"An expert balance of warmth and compassion, terrific supporting characters, a little steamy sex, and just enough suspense to keep you from guessing how it will all go down. . . . As ever, Andrews injects a brisk tale with generous doses of her sassy trademark humor." —*Atlanta Journal-Constitution*

"Andrews serves up a tempting and satisfying dish." —*Booklist*

About the Author

MARY KAY ANDREWS is the *New York Times* bestselling
author of nine novels including *The Fixer Upper*, *Deep Dish*,
Blue Christmas, *Savannah Breeze*, *Hissy Fit*, *Little Bitty Lies*,
and *Savannah Blues*. A former journalist for the *Atlanta
Journal-Constitution*, she lives in Atlanta, Georgia.

www.marykayandrews.com

The Fixer Upper

Arlene

The Fixer Upper

MARY KAY ANDREWS

HARPER

NEW YORK • LONDON • TORONTO • SYDNEY

HARPER

A hardcover edition of this book was published in 2009 by HarperCollins Publishers.

THE FIXER UPPER. Copyright © 2009 by Whodunnit, Inc. All rights reserved. Printed in the United States of America. No part of this book may be used or reproduced in any manner whatsoever without written permission except in the case of brief quotations embodied in critical articles and reviews. For information, address HarperCollins Publishers, 195 Broadway, New York, NY 10007.

HarperCollins books may be purchased for educational, business, or sales promotional use. For information, please e-mail the Special Markets Department at SPsales@harpercollins.com.

FIRST HARPER PAPERBACK PUBLISHED 2010.
REPRINTED 2012.

Designed by Jessica Heslin

The Library of Congress has catalogued the hardcover edition as follows:

Andrews, Mary Kay
    The fixer upper / Mary Kay Andrews.—1st ed.
        p. cm.
    ISBN 978-0-06-083738-9
    1. Young women—Fiction.   2. Dwellings—Conservation and restoration—
Fiction.   3. Family—Fiction.   I. Title.
    PS3570.R587F59 2009
    813'.54—dc22   2008048241

ISBN 978-0-06-083739-6 (pbk.)

17 18 19   WBC/RRD   20 19 18 17 16 15 14 13 12 11

Dedicated with love to my favorite aunt,
Alice Barchie, from her favorite niece

Acknowledgments

As always, I'm indebted to others for invaluable advice and support given during the writing and research of this novel. Any errors or misstatements of fact are due to my own bumbling. Huge thanks go to James Van Camp, of Pinehurst, North Carolina; Beth Fleishman of Raleigh; William L. McKinnon, Jr., and Sharon Douglas Stokes of the U.S. Attorney's Office, Northern District of Georgia, who shared legal expertise; FBI Special Agent Greg Lockett in Atlanta; Chrissie Shoemaker, DVM, who helped save Shorty; the Scribblers, including Diane Chamberlain, Margaret Maron, Katy Munger, Sarah Shaber, Alex Sokoloff, and Bren Witchger; the Weymouth Foundation for the Arts and Humanities of Southern Pines, North Carolina, where the early germ of the book was hatched; and Diane Kaufman of Mermaid Cottages and Ron and Leuveda Garner who gave me shelter on Tybee Island, Georgia.

On the professional level, I've had the best of the best with the wonderful Carolyn Marino and the rest of the HarperCollins gang, and Stuart Krichevesky and "the girls" at Stuart Krichevsky Literary Agency guiding me at every step of the way.

On the personal level, without my family, Tom, Andy, Katie, and Mark, nothing would be possible. To them I send oceans of love and thanks.

At the end of the very worst day in my life up until that point, my roommates and I sat in a back booth at the Filibuster, a crappy bar on a crappy street on the outskirts of Georgetown, as the endless news footage of my public demise played itself out again and again on the television set mounted on the wall directly in front of us.

I'd commandeered the remote control for the television as soon as we'd scurried into the Filibuster's darkened back room, but it seemed that every broadcast outlet in D.C. had decided to lead the day's newscasts with the story they'd already dubbed Hoddergate.

Stephanie and Lindsay stared, goggle-eyed, at the television as I poured my first beer of the day.

"God, Dempsey," Stephanie said. "You never told me your boss was an *old man.*"

I glanced up at the television. They were showing the footage of us leaving our office for a business meeting earlier that day. My boss, Alexander Hodder, strode forcefully down the sidewalk, the vents of his charcoal gray suit jacket flapping in the stiff March breeze, his head up, eyes directed straight ahead, resolutely ignoring the dozen or so reporters and cameramen who'd been lying in wait for us. Alex hadn't even bothered to give them a "no comment" as we ran the gauntlet of reporters waving mikes in our faces and shouting questions about bribes and junkets. Meanwhile, I trailed a few yards behind, clomping clumsily along in my too-high black suede pumps, my steps constrained by the pencil skirt I'd stupidly chosen to wear to work that day.

"Alex isn't old," I snapped. "He's just fifty. Anyway, nobody would ever guess he's not in his early thirties."

"Fifty!" shrieked Lindsay, putting down the beer pitcher in midpour. "Jesus, Dempsey. The way you always talk about him, I just assumed he *was* in his midthirties."

"Fifty's, like, prehistoric," Stephanie agreed, gazing at the screen. "Although, yeah, I see what you mean about his looks. He's got the whole chiseled chin, high cheekbones, broad shoulders thing going on. Is that his own hair? Or do you think it's a weave or something?"

"Would you all stop?" I begged. "My life is going down the toilet— even as we speak—and all you guys can think about is how old Alex Hodder is."

Stephanie, always the analytical one, sat back in the booth and tapped her fingertips on the scarred wooden tabletop. "You don't think they'll really indict him, do you? And anyway, it seems to me that his life is the one going down the toilet, not yours."

"They've already indicted Congressman Licata," I pointed out. "And now they're after Alex. And me. All because of that damned trip we took Licata on in the Bahamas. You guys just heard what those reporters are saying— 'Unnamed sources claim that prominent Washington lobbyist Alexander Hodder is under investigation for bribing a congressman.'"

I nodded in the direction of the television, and the girls swiveled their heads to watch. Now CNN was showing grainy footage of Representative Licata, Alex, and me, all of us dressed in formal wear, for a thousand-dollar-a-plate charity benefit headed by Licata's wife, Arlene. Our firm, Hodder and Associates, had bought a table for ten at the dinner, and all the young associates had been instructed to attend.

"Nice dress, Demps," Lindsay murmured.

I blushed. "I would have asked to borrow it, but you were out of town."

A gleeful-looking CNN reporter was declaring Hoddergate "the biggest influence-peddling scandal of the decade," adding that "unnamed sources report that Hodder's firm, which represents major petroleum interests, among other things, entertained Representative Licata with a golf outing to the exclusive Lyford Cay resort in the Bahamas, where Licata and Hodder were allegedly spotted romping with call girls on the resort's nude beach."

"Eeeww," Stephanie said, shuddering and wrinkling her nose. "A nude beach? With those two old men? That Licata dude must weigh three hundred pounds. And he's as old as my grandpa!"

"Forget the nude-beach part. What about the call girls!" Lindsay said, her eyes widening again. "Demps, did you actually hire prostitutes for a congressman?"

"No!" I protested. "Alex asked me to have the hotel arrange for a wakeboard instructor for Congressman Licata. Nobody ever said anything about prostitutes. I would never—"

"Isn't Licata, like, sixty or something?" Lindsay persisted. "Why would an old geezer like that want wakeboard lessons?"

"I don't know," I said, moaning. "I'm an idiot. It never occurred to me that there was anything like that going on."

"What about the condo in South Beach they say your boss bought Licata?" Stephanie asked. "That's not true, right?"

"It wasn't Alex's money," I said, slumping down in the booth. "Alex told me it was supposed to be some kind of loan thing. The condo belongs to one of the senior executives at Peninsula Petroleum and Licata was supposed to be making payments—"

"Ooh, look," Lindsay interrupted, pointing at the television.

CNN was showing the footage of us fleeing from the reporters earlier that morning. "Sources within the Justice Department say they expect more indictments as the investigation continues," the reporter said solemnly.

"Shit," Stephanie said.

"Yeah," Lindsay agreed, nodding her head sadly.

"You need a plan." Stephanie whipped a notebook out of her omnipresent red leather satchel.

"For staying out of jail?" I asked, sipping my beer.

"A life plan," Stephanie said. "You know, what's the next step, that kind of thing. We analyze your career path up to now, examine your strengths and weaknesses, likes and dislikes—"

"She likes older men," Lindsay broke in. "Much older men."

"Not funny," I snapped.

"Sorry," she said unconvincingly.

Stephanie began writing as she recited, "Hates mushrooms on her pizza, salt on her margaritas, cheap shoes, cheap wine—"

"Cheap old men," Lindsay crowed.

"Give it a rest, will you?" Stephanie said. "Dempsey needs us."

"I appreciate it," I said. "Really. But I think you're jumping the gun—"

My cell phone rang, and I glanced at the digital readout. "It's Ruby, the office manager. Sorry, I better take this."

I scrambled out of the booth. A crowd of men had gathered near the front door, their gazes all turned toward the television, where now, thankfully, the channel had been changed to a college basketball game. I walked rapidly toward the rear exit, pushed the heavy steel fire door open, and stepped into the alley, which smelled like stale beer, pee, and cigarettes.

"Ruby?"

"Where are you?" she snapped. "I've been trying to reach you all afternoon."

"I'm in Georgetown," I said, feeling instantly guilty. "After what happened . . . you know, with Alex, he canceled our meeting and said he was going to see his lawyer, and it was so late in the day, and I was sorta afraid the reporters might still be hanging around outside the office. I didn't think there was any point in going back so late in the day. But if you need me—"

"I needed you at two. When FBI agents swarmed the office and cleaned out all our files and the hard drive to your computer and Alex's."

"What? My hard drive? Why? What are they looking for? Is this about Licata? I mean, Alex asked me to draft some notes on the new energy bill for him, but—"

"Goddammit," she said quietly, in a very un-Ruby-like way. In fact, this whole conversation was very unlike Ruby Beaubien. In her early sixties, and a graduate of the Mississippi College for Women, Ruby was the personification of a sweet Southern belle. She rarely raised her voice or got flustered, and I'd never heard her use a curse word stronger than "daggum."

"What a mess," she went on. "Did Alex copy you on his e-mails to and from Licata, or from any of the guys over at Peninsula?"

"Sometimes," I said, my heart sinking. "Not all the time. But yeah, he said I should be in the loop since—"

"I don't suppose you dumped those e-mails once you'd read them?"

"No. It never occurred to me. I'm so sorry, Ruby."

"Well, it can't be helped now," she said. "Alex had hoped you'd deleted everything."

"You talked to him? What did he say? Is he all right?"

"He's fine," she said, cutting me off again. "Listen, Dempsey, you've got some vacation time coming to you. Alex wants you to go ahead and take it. Immediately."

"Now? I can't just go off on vacation in the middle of all this. I've got meetings on the hill almost every day this week and next. I'm writing a speech for David Welch to give at that breakfast in Houston, and we've got the pipeline people coming in at the end of the month—"

"Never mind all that," Ruby said. I could hear phones ringing in the background, and the drone of a television. She was watching the news too, I realized, on the set in the break room. Or maybe in the conference room where we had a bank of televisions so we could all keep up with breaking news in D.C.

"Alex was very specific," Ruby said. "You'll have four weeks of vacation pay coming. I've already cut your check."

"But I don't have four weeks of vacation time," I said. "I don't even have a week. Remember? I used four days to go to a wedding in Boston."

"This is per Alex," Ruby said. "Are you still living in Alexandria? The same address on LeConte?"

"Yeah, but—"

"I'll have your things boxed up and sent out today. There's no need for you to come back to the office at all."

"Why would you box up my stuff?" My heart was racing. Things were going very wrong, very quickly. "Ruby—what is this? Am I being fired? You said Alex said it was vacation."

"I can't go into it right now," Ruby said, her tone suddenly formal. "Mr. Hodder has decided to streamline the operation at Hodder and Associates, to concentrate on his core interests. If you need the name of an outplacement consultant, I can get that for you. It'll be best not to call here, though. You can reach me at my Hotmail address."

"Ruby," I cried pitifully. "You're firing me? What is this? Does Alex know about this? Where is he?"

"Mr. Hodder is in meetings with his attorneys," she said. "I have to go now, Dempsey. Good luck."

The phone went dead. I redialed Ruby's number, but my call went immediately to voice mail.

My legs suddenly felt like overcooked spaghetti. I sank down on a stack of empty wooden wine crates. I flipped my phone open again and scrolled down my list of contacts until I came to Alex's name. I punched the connect button. It rang once, and then I was hearing Alex's voice, with that unmistakable deep, refined Virginia accent.

"This is Alexander Hodder of Hodder and Associates. If you're getting this message, I'm either on another line or out meetin' and greetin'. Leave a message and I'll get back to you just as soon as I possibly can. Oh? And in the meantime? Have yourself a great day."

"Alex?" I was biting back the tears. "It's Dempsey. Ruby just called. And she said you said . . . well, it sounds like I've been fired. I don't understand. Call me please, Alex. So we can get this straightened out. And I want to know what's going on with you. Okay? So call me the minute you get this—"

The machine beeped to let me know I'd run out of time. I was starting to call back when I heard the rusty scrape of the fire door opening. Lindsay's head popped out.

"Demps? Are you all right? We're getting worried about you. Thought maybe you were kidnapped by aliens."

I stood up slowly. "Not kidnapped. Just fired."

Lindsay's deep blue eyes widened. "For real? He fired you? Just like that?"

I nodded. "At first Ruby said I should just take vacation time. Four weeks. I don't get that much vacation. I only have, like, three days left for the whole year. Then she said they were shipping all the stuff in my office back to the apartment. The next thing I knew, she was saying good-bye and good luck."

"For real?" She put her arm around my shoulders, and I realized I was coatless and shivering in the cold, the fingertips clutching my cell phone tinged with blue. "Is Alex okay with this?" she asked.

"Dunno. She said it was all on his instructions. I left a message on his cell phone asking him to call me right away."

I felt a tear slide down my cheek.

"Come on back inside," she said, moving me toward the door. "We'll get this all worked out. Don't worry. There's nothing the three of us and a pitcher of margaritas can't solve."

3

I'd been out in the alley for only about twenty minutes, but in that time, every cubicle geek in D.C. seemed to have wandered into the Filibuster. The jukebox was playing some '90s Madonna song, and the guys standing around watching the basketball game were jeering and cheering. With my red-rimmed eyes and snotty nose—and sudden status as a virtual untouchable—I felt unbearably self-conscious.

"Let Dempsey sit in the middle," Lindsay ordered Stepanie. "We don't want people staring at her." Stephanie got up and let me in and I squeezed her hand in gratitude.

"We've got a little problem," Lindsay said quietly. "Dempsey just got fired."

"They can't do that," Stephanie said. "It's illegal. Isn't it?"

Lindsay and I shrugged. Although we'd all met in law school, none of us had taken any classes in employment practices.

"I'm through in D.C.," I said, drawing circles with my fingertip in the wet glass ring on the tabletop. "You guys better start looking for another roommate."

"Oh stop," Stephanie said. "Don't be so dramatic. Hodder and Associates is one of the top public relations firms in town. People know that. They'll be climbing all over each other to sign you on. Alex will give you a good reference, right? I mean, they won't say you were fired. They couldn't. Right?"

"Ruby said something about referring me to an outplacement consultant. I guess that's like a headhunter firm. But she didn't say anything about paying for it. And I think those places charge big money."

"You know tons of people in D.C. And so do we," Stephanie said. She pulled out her BlackBerry and started scrolling down her list of contacts. "We'll just get busy and network."

A round of boos went up from the front of the bar. We looked up. The game had apparently ended badly and the channel had now been turned to Fox News. There I was again, clomping behind Alex in HDTV, headed straight to doom.

"Everybody in town is seeing that right now," I said, looking away. "They're hearing the words 'Hodder' and 'scandal.' I'll be tainted goods."

"That's crap," Stephanie said. "Alex will ride this out. And so will you. You know what this town is like. You wait. Tomorrow another scandal du jour will come along. Some congressman diddling some intern or page, or a minor war in East Bumfuck, and suddenly Hoddergate will all just be a dim memory."

"She's right," Lindsay said. "It's not as if you did anything wrong. You weren't indicted. Right?"

I tried a smile. It felt fake. "According to Ruby, the FBI has my hard drive. With all my e-mails from the last six months."

"Oh my God!" Stephanie cried. "All that stuff about me missing my period back in October. You deleted those, right? And the ones about my bitchy boss?"

Lindsay's face had taken on a faintly green sheen. "Oh Christ. I e-mailed you about asking Alex to get Licata's chief of staff to talk to my cousin about a job. Oh shit. The FBI's going to think I'm mixed up in this mess."

"Shit." The three of us said it in unison.

My cell phone rang again. I stared down at the readout. The phone number had a California area code.

"It's Lynda," I said glumly. I let the phone ring five times. It stopped and then started ringing again. "I can't deal with her right now."

"You're not going to take a call from your mom?" Lindsay asked. "That's kinda cold, isn't it?"

"You guys all met my mom at graduation," I reminded her. "Did she strike you as the kind of person you want to chat with in the middle of a crisis?"

The ringing stopped and then started again.

"Either turn the phone off or take her call," Stephanie said, stepping out of the booth to let me by again.

Out in the alley, I took a deep breath and pushed the connect button. "Lynda?"

"Sweetheart!" she cried. "I'm looking at you on CNN. Now, don't be mad at me for telling you this, but I really, truly think you should fly out here and let my stylist do something about your hair. Maybe some layers to soften things up around your cheekbones. You do have those unfortunate Killebrew cheekbones that tend to make you look like Hiawatha. And the color. What have you done with your color?"

Without thinking, I put my hand to my cheek and then pulled out a strand of hair to see what was wrong with it. My hair was what I thought was a perfectly nice deep shade of brown. Chestnut, an old boyfriend with a flair for the poetic had called it.

"Mom, this is my natural color," I said. "I haven't done anything to it."

"Nonsense," she said briskly. "Anyway, there's no reason you have to stay a brunette for life. From what I'm seeing on television right now, you're going to need some kind of makeover, and your hair is the perfect place to start. And don't get me started on your clothes. Tell me something. Do they make all you girls in Washington wear those straight skirts and heels as a uniform? They make you look like a prison matron."

I closed my eyes and tried to visualize my mother, out in San Jose, watching me on the tiny television in her jewelry studio. She'd be dressed in the bright blues, greens, and yellows she called her trademark shades, probably a flowing silk flowered top and yoga pants. Her feet would be bare, the toenails in a French pedicure, with a ring—of her own design, of course—on the second toe of each foot. It was nearly six in D.C., which meant it was three in California, which meant she'd be sipping a Perrier and lime with vodka—low-carb vodka.

"In Washington women are expected to dress like professionals," I said. "Which means no toe rings and no visible tattoos." Lynda had gotten a butterfly tattooed on the small of her back a dozen years before.

"All the more reason to get the hell out of there on the next flight west," Lynda said. "Does this mean you're really in some kind of serious trouble?"

"I don't know," I admitted. "I haven't done anything wrong. Not intentionally anyway. I'm just a tiny little minnow. The feds are probably really just after the big fish—Congressman Licata."

"Fucking Republicans," Lynda said. "No senses of humor."

"Not when it comes to bribery," I agreed.

I heard the faint tinkle of ice, and I knew she was fixing herself another drink.

"I'll be all right," I said bravely. There was no way I was going to admit to my mother that I'd already been fired and that even as we spoke, the FBI was poring over my best friends' e-mails about bitchy bosses and skipped periods. "Hodder and Associates is one of the top firms in D.C. And I've got a little money saved."

"Of course you do," Lynda agreed. "You were always the most practical child I ever saw. You were born competent. Practically came out of the womb clutching your Day Runner. You used to tell me what to pack in your own diaper bag. I have no doubt that you'll be fine. There's just one thing I'm dying to know. And you *can* tell me, you know. I mean, we both know I'm not exactly the garden-variety little soccer mom in polyester sweatpants, right?"

That did give me a laugh. The thought of Lynda in polyester. And elastic. "Right. So go ahead. What do you want to know?"

"This Alex Hodder," she said slowly. "I'm looking at him right now. And I must say he is a fine-looking piece of man. I have always had a weak spot for a man with a firm chin and a Southern accent. That's how your daddy got me into bed on our first date, the rascal. You are sleeping with Alex, aren't you? I mean, if you're mixed up in this little mess, that must mean he's taking care of you. Right?"

"No, Lynda," I said. "I'm not sleeping with Alex Hodder. He's married."

"Mmm," she purred. "He doesn't look all that married to me."

"I'm hanging up now," I announced. "Good talking to you, Lynda."

"Wait," she said quickly. "Think about what I told you. About your hair, I mean. I'll have Leonard send you a plane ticket. We could have a mother-daughter spa weekend. Wouldn't that be delicious?"

"Yum," I said dully. I flipped the phone shut and started back inside. It was full dark now, the temperature seemed to have dropped ten degrees, and it was starting to sleet.

My phone rang again. "Damn," I said. It was parents' weekend in D.C.

Dutifully, I punched the connect button.

"Hi, Daddy," I said, forcing a smile into my voice.

"This is all your mother's fault," he said.

"I take it you've seen the news."

"Pilar called me at the office. The boys were wrestling with the remote and it accidentally switched to CNN, and there you were, being hounded by a pack of reporters, like a common criminal. They started hollering, 'Dempsey! Dempsey!' the minute the camera panned to you. Pilar told them you'd won a spelling bee, and that's why you were on the news."

"I wish," I said weakly.

"This thing sounds pretty serious, Dempsey," my father said. "This Hodder fella, is he a stand-up sort?"

"Yes," I said, wondering if he really was.

"Does the Justice Department really have the goods on him? Wait. Where are you? Don't answer that."

"I'm in Georgetown, at a bar," I said. "Or, outside a bar."

"Drinking? Is that a good idea?"

"It seemed like an excellent idea an hour or so ago," I said.

"You don't sound like yourself. Is there something else going on that I should know about?"

I bit my lip. I'd lied to Lynda, but my father was different. I'd never been good at lying to him. Anyway, what was the point?

"I've been fired," I said finally. "Well, the office manager didn't put it that way. She said Alex is restructuring the firm. To concentrate on his core business. And they did give me a month's vacation pay."

"Bastard," my father said. He sighed. "Do I need to hire you a lawyer?"

I felt the tears welling up in my eyes again. "I don't know. The FBI has my hard drive, and all my e-mails for the past six months, but, Daddy, I didn't have anything to do with this mess. Honestly, I thought the wakeboard instructor down in the Bahamas really was a wakeboard instructor. How did I know she'd end up in a hot tub with Congressman Licata?"

I shuddered at the thought of it, Licata, with his bulbous vein-streaked nose and hairy potbelly, naked with a twenty-year-old hooker at the Lyford Cay Resort.

"This is all your mother's fault," Daddy repeated. "You've always been insanely naive, just like her. No street smarts at all. I really thought when you got into law school at Georgetown you would outgrow that unfortunate tendency. Toughen up. Make your way in the business world."

I sniffed. "I thought I *was* making my way in the business world. I was in the top ten percent in my class. Hodder and Associates could have hired anybody, but they hired me. Alex told me I was his first choice."

"Doesn't mean jack now," Daddy said. "Christ! Listen, what are your plans?"

My most immediate plan was to go back inside the bar, thaw out, and switch from beer to margaritas. After that, my agenda was pretty open.

"I'm not sure," I said. "They're going to hook me up with an out-placement consultant."

"A lot of bullshit," Daddy said. "All right. Here's what we'll do. I'll have my assistant book you a flight down here. Tomorrow. Pilar and the boys will pick you up at the airport, we'll have a nice family dinner, and then you and I will strategize."

"Strategize," I said dutifully. "About what?"

"Your future," he boomed.

"I've got a month's pay coming," I started. "I just thought I'd lie low for a little while, polish up my résumé, maybe call some of my law school classmates . . ."

"Screw that," Daddy said. "See you tomorrow."

"Tomorrow," I repeated. I closed the phone and pulled my suit-coat collar up against the chill wind blowing through the alley. Hell, I was apparently going to Miami tomorrow to visit my father and stepmother and my twin four-year-old half brothers. Surely the sun would come out tomorrow in Miami.

4

I'd been to Alex Hodder's house in northwest Washington exactly once before, when Trish, his wife, had thrown Alex a surprise fiftieth birthday party. Now, emboldened by the pitcher of margaritas we'd slurped down at the Filibuster, I sat in the back of the cab parked at the curb in front of his town house and dialed his cell phone one more time. One more time, the ringing went straight to his voice mail.

"Alex," I pleaded. "Please pick up. I'm leaving town in the morning, flying down to Miami to see my dad, and I really, really need to talk to you."

Nothing.

It was still sleeting, and the windows of the three-story white brick town house glowed a golden yellow. Through an opening in the thick drapes I could see the glittering crystals of the Hodders' dining room chandelier on the right side of the house, and on the left, I could just glimpse the book-lined shelves of Alex's study. Maybe that's where he was right now, sitting at the simple pine table that served as his desk, sipping from a tumbler of Dewar's, pondering his future the same way I was pondering mine.

"What's it gonna be, ma'am?" the cabbie asked, half-turning in his seat. We'd been sitting there a good five minutes while I tried to figure out if I was really drunk—or brave—enough to ring Alex's doorbell.

"Give me a minute, please," I said.

"It's your dime," he said, turning back around and picking up the neatly folded sports page he'd just put down. "But the meter's running, you know."

The mention of money gave me all the courage I needed. The meter was running on my life. I needed some answers, fast.

"Wait for me," I said, hopping out of the cab and buttoning up my coat. A thin sheet of ice coated the high, white marble stoop at the front door, and I had to cling to the iron handrail to keep from sliding off in those damned black suede stilettos.

I punched the brass doorbell and could hear it buzzing from inside. A moment later, I heard footsteps approaching the door. The brass lanterns on either side of the door flickered on. "Who's there?" a woman's voice called.

"Mrs. Hodder?" I'd only met Alex's wife that one time. It didn't feel right calling her Trish. "It's Dempsey."

"Who?"

"Dempsey Killebrew. From the office. I work for Alex, I mean, Mr. Hodder."

I heard her mutter something under her breath, and then the click of the lock tumblers. The door opened a few inches. Trish Hodder obviously wasn't expecting callers. Her dark auburn hair was pulled into a knot on top of her head, her pale smooth face scrubbed clean of any traces of makeup. A long, pale blue mohair robe was belted loosely around her waist, and her feet were encased in thin, monogrammed leather slippers in the exact same shade of blue.

All the other previous sightings I'd had of Trish Hodder had been at charity functions where Alex had purchased tables or tickets for the office, or in photographs of her in the society pages of the *Washingtonian* or the *Post*. Always, she was exquisitely dressed and groomed. Annabeth, one of the other women in the office, told me that Trish dressed exclusively in Carolina Herrera for evening and Michael Kors and Zac Posen for daytime. But tonight, she seemed dressed mostly for bed.

She looked me up and down, as though trying to place me. "Oh yes, Dempsey," she said finally. "It's pretty late, you know."

"I know, and I'm terribly sorry for disturbing you," I said eagerly. "But I really need to talk to Alex, please."

"A lot of people need to talk to Alex," she said. "But as you might imagine, he really isn't seeing anybody tonight. I'm sure if you call Ruby tomorrow, she can work something out."

"I've already talked to Ruby," I said, feeling my cheeks flush hot from the memory. "According to her, Alex has terminated me."

Trish shrugged. "Then there's probably not much more he can say to you, is there?" She started to close the door.

"Just like that?" I said shrilly. "I've worked for him for two years, and he fires me the same day we're implicated in a federal bribery case? Doesn't even tell me in person—just has his assistant tell me to buzz off?"

She cocked one eyebrow. "What would you have him do? Look, um, Denise—"

"Dempsey," I said. "My name is Dempsey Killebrew. I've been an associate for two years. I'm the one he told to hire that wakeboard instructor down in the Bahamas. I'm the one who was standing right behind him today when this whole mess exploded. The FBI is going over my e-mails right this minute. I don't know what do. I really, *really* need to speak to your husband. I need to figure out what to do next."

"Alex doesn't have a clue about what you should do next," Trish said. "And I'm damned sure not going to wake him up to let you ask him. He doesn't even have a clue about what he's going to do. It's his ass on the line, sweetheart, not yours. I can assure you, the FBI doesn't give a good goddamn about any of the silly little girls my husband has been having do his dirty work. And neither does Alex. You want to know what to do next?"

She leaned out the door and saw the cab parked at the curb, its motor—and meter—running. "Go home, Dempsey. Sober up and start polishing your résumé. And stay away from men like my husband."

Trish stepped back inside the house. She closed the door gently. Then the lights flickered out, and I was standing outside on that icy stoop, watching the lights in Alex Hodder's town house switch off, one by one.

5

A s usual, the minute I stepped out of the Miami airport, I began to have regrets. My black slacks and cashmere sweater set had seemed like a good idea that morning, when temperatures in D.C. hovered in the upper twenties. I'd stripped off my jacket the minute I got off the plane, but now the sweater clung to my back, the tight turtleneck choking my windpipe, and my ankles, encased in high-heeled black leather boots, were swimming in perspiration. My thick hair hung limply around my shoulders. Everywhere around me, people swept by in their shorts and sandals, chattering in Spanish and English. I felt like a polar bear trapped in the flamingo exhibit at the zoo.

"Dempsey!" I heard childish voices cry. I looked up, and a white Mercedes SUV zoomed up and over the curb, barely grazing the suitcase I'd just set down. One of the twins hung out the rear window, waving madly at me.

My stepmother hopped out of the car, leaving the motor running. "Come on, for God's sake," she said breathlessly. "This is the fourth time I've come around looking for you. The cops will give me a ticket if they see me stopping here again."

She gave me a quick peck on the cheek, then popped open the rear hatch, leaving me to heft my bag up and inside. I slammed the door, then ran around to get in the front seat.

"Oh," Pilar exclaimed, "Get in back, will you? I promised the boys you'd sit with them."

"Fine," I said, slightly annoyed. I hopped into the backseat and glanced over at the preschoolers strapped into their car seats. Garrett was sound asleep.

"How are you, Gavin?" I asked, smiling broadly at the child on my left.

"No!" he exclaimed. "No Dempsey." He clapped both hands over his eyes.

Pilar jerked the car off the curb and we sped away from the airport.

"Sorry," Pilar said, weaving in and out of the thick traffic. "They seem to be in a holding pattern from the terrible twos. Whatever Garrett wants, Gavin wants the opposite. After lunch, they were so excited about coming to pick you up, they refused to go to play group. Now, as you can see, Gavin is in his negative phase."

"No Dempsey!" Gavin said, as if on cue. "Go away!"

Pilar handed me a small bottle of apple juice and a plastic Baggie of animal crackers. "Here. Give him these. His blood sugar gets low and he gets cranky." She turned halfway around in the seat and fixed her son with a dazzling smile. "See what Sissy has for you?"

Gavin took his hands away from his face long enough to swat the bottle out of her hand, spilling juice down the front of my sweater.

"Now look what you've done," Pilar cried. "Apple juice on the leather seats I just had cleaned. Papí will be very angry! Mommy is very angry."

Dempsey was soaked in apple juice and not feeling especially perky herself. I helped myself to an animal cracker and chewed in silence.

"Is Dad working today?" I asked.

She sighed deeply. "It's Saturday, but yes, of course, he had to go into the office to finish some paperwork. Then golf. Client golf, he calls it." She muttered something else under her breath in Spanish. She glanced at the thin gold watch on her deeply tanned wrist. "Four now, if we hit traffic right, maybe we're home by five. Maybe he's home then too."

For the next hour Pilar gave me a running update on her tennis game—really showing marked improvement, according to her doubles partner—and progress on the house they were building in Coral Gables.

"I have to keep Mitch away from the contractor. *Ay Dios Mio!* When he got a look at the invoices last night, I thought he would have a heart attack. I went over there Wednesday, and the idiots had installed the marble for the boys' bathroom in the maid's bathroom. Can you believe it? I made them rip it all up, and of course, most of it was ruined. The light fixtures for your dad's study came, and they were all wrong. French bronze, I tol' them, like a million times. What do they send? Brass!"

Finally, we pulled into the driveway at the house, a low-slung white stucco ranch that Pilar told me they were renting while the new house was being built. Pilar punched a button and the double garage doors slowly slid open. A gleaming black Porsche was parked on the right side, a set of golf clubs poking out over the open convertible top.

"Good," Pilar said, cutting off the engine. "He's home." She glanced over at Garrett, who was still asleep, and back over at Gavin, who'd drifted off too. "Can you help me get them into the house? Mitch is having lower back spasms, and I don't want to bother him."

Somehow, we managed to get the sleeping boys out of their car seats and into the house, where we dumped them down in their beds in a bedroom just off the back hallway.

"The place is a mess," Pilar said, leading me and my suitcase into the kitchen, past a pile of plastic toys and a basket of unfolded laundry. "I can't wait till we get into the new house. I tol' Mitch, if I have to cook one more Thanksgiving dinner in this place—"

"You'll what?" my dad asked, turning around from the sink with a full martini glass in each hand.

"Kill you," Pilar said, taking a glass and giving him a lingering kiss. "I'm full on Cuban, you know. We're a very hot-blooded people."

He kissed her back, handed me a martini, and slid an arm around his wife's waist. "That's why I married you. That, and your cooking."

"Hi, Daddy," I said, giving him a peck on the cheek. I set the martini glass down on the kitchen counter. Gin and I don't really get along. "How was golf?"

"Fine," he said. "Was the flight okay? What'd you think of your little brothers? Aren't they the biggest little ballbusters you've ever seen?"

"Gavin threw apple juice on her," Pilar reported. "Now I'm gonna have to have the car detailed again."

While my father and Pilar caught each other up on their day's events, I excused myself to clean up for dinner.

"You're on the pull-out sofa in the television room," Pilar informed me. "You can put your suitcase in your dad's study, but you'll have to share the boys' bathroom. Sorry about that. I can't wait to get out of this dump. In the new house, we'll have a guest suite . . ."

I left her detailing all the fine points of the new house. I pulled a pair of jeans and a top out of my suitcase, along with my cosmetics case, and headed for the shower. I unzipped the case, set it on the bathroom counter, and pulled out my shampoo and conditioner. My hair was already a ball of frizz from the Miami humidity.

When I stepped out of the shower, Garrett was sitting on the commode, naked except for his *Pirates of the Caribbean* T-shirt, which was how I knew he was Garrett. Gavin had been wearing a white-and-orange Miami Dolphins T-shirt. Garrett looked me up and down. "Boobies," he pronounced. "Boys like boobies."

"I know," I said, reaching for a towel and wrapping it around me. "Are you almost done here?" I asked politely.

He grunted loudly. "Uh-uh. I make poops."

"Good for you," I said.

I grabbed my clothes and made a run for the study, where I quickly toweled off and dressed.

Pilar's cooking, as my dad had promised, was spectacular. She'd pulled out all the stops at dinner, starting with a scallop seviche, then romaine salad with avocado and pink-grapefruit sections, pan-seared grouper, and a vanilla bean flan for dessert.

They made a good couple, I thought, watching them from my end of the oval table. Pilar was much younger, of course, only four years older than me, which made her thirty-two. She'd been a flight attendant, but had stopped working when she and my dad married. Her straight black hair was cut in a short bob. She had a long neck, and huge brown eyes that seemed focused most of the time on either her boys or her man.

Daddy was worth looking at. I was taken by surprise with that realization. He wasn't movie-star handsome or anything. But he took good care of himself. He was tanned, with an unlined face, those wide Kille-brew cheekbones, and only a touch of gray around the temples marked his otherwise dark hair. He did have, as Lynda had pointed out, a firm chin. I wondered, idly, if that had gotten Pilar into bed with him on *their* first date.

After Pilar brought in coffee, the boys started fussing. "Isn't it their bedtime?" Dad asked pointedly.

"Story time!" Garrett cried, throwing his plastic sippy cup into the middle of the table.

"I want *Olive the Reindeer*," Gavin said. "Read that, Papí."

"That's a Christmas book," Pilar said. "But Papí will find you an-other good story."

"Not tonight," Dad said, pushing back from the table. "Dempsey and I have some things to work out." He gave each of the boys a kiss on the top of his head. "Be good boys and give your mommy a short story tonight, all right?"

Pilar shot him a dirty look. "I did story time last night. You promised you'd take them tonight." She turned toward me. "Mitch is a very in-volved father. He reads to the boys every night. It's their little ritual."

"That's sweet," I said, standing up and starting to gather the dishes. I didn't tell her that in all my own growing-up years, the only thing Mitch ever read to me was the list of house rules he'd posted on the refrigerator door when I went to live with him at the age of eight.

Funny, it had been twenty years, but I still lived by those rules. I could even see the neat block letters he'd written them in. Make bed. Tidy room. Clean bathtub and sink each morning. Sweep kitchen floor. Put dishes in dishwasher. Fold and put away clothes. No whining.

Mitch ignored Pilar's pouting and picked up his own plate and hers. "You go ahead with the boys. Dempsey and I will clean up the kitchen."

We'd gone into Mitch's study, which consisted of his scarred old ma-hogany desk and leather chair, and two leather club chairs facing the desk, one of which held my open suitcase.

When my dad's eyes flickered meaningfully over the suitcase, with a bra hanging out of it, I quickly tucked the clothes inside, snapped it shut, and stuck it in the corner.

Dad sat behind the desk, picked up a remote control, and pointed it at the small portable television sitting on the bookcase behind me. "You don't mind, right?" he said. "It's the Doral open. I just wanna see how Tiger's doing.

"So," he said, putting the remote down. "Let's talk about your future."

I shifted uncomfortably in my chair. "Well. Right now, things aren't so good. But one of my roommates dates a guy who works for a firm that does a lot with environmental issues. It's something I'm interested in—"

"Damn," he said, staring up at the television. "Double bogey." He looked over at me without missing a beat. "Environmental issues? I thought you were a lobbyist, not a tree hugger."

"Green issues are a hot button right now," I said. "That doesn't mean I'm a tree hugger. I happen to care about this planet. After all, I've got two half brothers."

He frowned. "Don't call them that. They're not half of anything. Is that how you think of them? Only half related to you?"

"No," I said quickly. "I was just saying I care about the world they'll grow up in."

"Good," Dad said. He picked up the remote and pushed the mute button. "The guy at this firm. Do you know that they have openings? What the pay scale is like?"

"No, but—"

"Would there be anything wrong with your practicing law?" He tilted back in his chair. "You do have a degree from a very expensive law school."

"Yes," I started. "But I've been working on policy since I got out of school. Even my internships were with trade associations and public relations firms."

"Which, if you remember, I was against at the time," Dad said. "You're a lawyer, dammit. Go for the big bucks, none of this dicking around with politics."

"Well, I'm done with politics for now," I said ruefully. "Thanks to Congressman Licata."

"Don't get me started on that asshole," Dad said. "Anyway, that's all water over the dam, right? So, what's your plan?"

He was staring at the television again.

"I haven't managed to save a lot of money," I admitted. "Everything's so expensive in the district. My share of the rent alone is two thousand a month—"

"Two thousand a month?" Pilar walked into the room and handed Mitch another martini. "To share a closet with two other girls? One bathroom? A kitchen the size of my bathtub? You need to move down to Miami, Dempsey. Enough!"

"Pilar," Dad said, a note of warning in his voice.

"Ridiculous!" she said, waving her hand to signal that she'd had her say.

I forged ahead. "My share of the rent's paid up for this month, and the girls have offered to let me stay for at least another month, since we did that for Lindsay last year after she was out of work."

"But long term?" Dad asked.

"I just got fired yesterday," I pointed out. "It's not as if I was planning on my boss being investigated by the FBI."

"Failure to plan equals planning to fail," Dad intoned. I gritted my teeth. How many times had I heard that little maxim over the length of my lifetime?

A diabolical thought occurred to me.

"Lynda called, right after it happened," I said innocently. "She wants to fly me out to L.A. to stay with her for a while. She has a lot of contacts—"

"Contacts!" Dad slammed his martini glass so hard the contents sloshed over the edge of the glass. "By contacts, she means that boyfriend of hers has plenty of money—and rich friends."

"Leonard has a lot of clients in the film business," I said, deliberately twisting the knife. "I don't know that I'd want to do entertainment law forever, but it might be interesting for a while—"

"How long has your mother been living with that character, anyway?" Mitch demanded.

"About four years," I guessed. "Leonard is really good to Lynda. And let's face it, they get along way better than she ever did with anybody she was ever married to."

Pilar helped herself to a sip of the martini. "Did she offer to help you financially?"

"No," I admitted. "But if I asked—"

"Forget it," Mitch said. "We don't want you owing money to that slick Hollywood character. No telling what kind of shady deals he'd get you involved with. Your mother always was a terrible judge of character."

I gave him a long look. He missed the point entirely.

"California's out," he said, as if that settled it.

I decided to seize the moment. "What I'd really like to do is stay in D.C. I went to school there, that's where all my contacts are. Dad, if you could just help me out. It would only be three months. Six months tops. I've got a month's severance pay coming. And I really think I could get by on three thousand a month. And it would be a loan. I'd pay interest and everything. I've been adding it all up. With rent, utilities, food—not that I spend that much on food, mostly I have business lunches with clients who pay, and most nights there's a cocktail party, or a reception or dinner the girls and I can go to. There's my Metro card, and of course, I've gotta keep up with my law school loans."

Mitch drained his martini. "That's another thing. Georgetown! You could have gone to any law school in the East. Not to mention Chicago and Denver. Goddamn Jesuits. They'll be into you your whole life. If you'd listened to me and gone to Florida State, with in-state residency—"

"I wasn't a resident of Florida," I pointed out. "And I got my own scholarships and took out the loans, and I haven't asked you for anything since I got out of undergrad school."

Pilar had whipped a calculator out of the pocket of her sundress and was punching the keys and shaking her head. "Three thousand dollars? Tha's, like, eighteen thousand." Her eyes bulged from their kohl-lined sockets.

"*Ay Dios Mio!* Do you wanna know what I run this house on?"

I didn't. And I certainly didn't want her in on this discussion of my finances with my father. And I didn't want to hear her usually normal accent deteriorate into a cartoon version of Ricky Ricardo either.

"We got two lil' guys runnin' around here. You know what a box of pull-ups costs? And I buy generic at Costco, so don' start on that with me, Mitch. Groceries, gas, utilities, you should see the power bill—this dump got no insulation at all. Preschool? Our Lady of Angels is sixteen hundred a month. Multiply that times two." She was standing now, her hands on her hips. "By the time my boys get to high school, Gulliver Prep is gonna be six thousand a month. Again, times two, pray to the baby Jesus we get Gavin potty trained by then. And what about the new house? You think that's gettin' built for free?"

"Pilar," Mitch said. He nodded gently. "Nobody said the boys would have to go to public school. Or that we'd have to stay in this house."

"Fine," she said, sitting back down. "I'm jus' sayin'."

Mitch opened the bottom drawer of his desk and took out a manila file folder. He opened it, read the top sheet, nodded his head in approval.

"I've got another idea," he said.

Pilar rolled her eyes. "I can't wait."

6

My father slid a yellowed black-and-white photograph across the desk in my direction. I picked it up and studied it. The picture was of a huge old house, antebellum, I guessed, with tall white columns marching across a wide front porch. It was set back behind a hedge of tall flowering shrubs, and a woman dressed in a hoopskirt and a 1950s-looking hairdo was posed prettily on the porch, waving, as if to a tour bus.

"What's this?"

Pilar took the photo out of my hands and frowned. "Yeah. Wha's this?"

"Birdsong," Mitch said smugly. "My maternal grandmother's family homeplace."

"Your grandma lived on a plantation?" Pilar asked. "You never said anything about a plantation to me."

"This is the house south of Atlanta?" I asked.

"Guthrie, Georgia," he said. "Sixty-two miles south of Atlanta, if you want to be precise." He smiled nostalgically. "I wasn't born there, but my mother and father did take me there from the hospital. I guess I spent every Sunday of my life there until Dad and I moved when I was six."

"When your parents split up?" I asked. I knew Mitch's parents had divorced when he was young, and that he and his father had moved from Georgia to Nashville before he started first grade, but he'd never talked much about those early years of his life.

"That's right," Mitch said. "I guess I went back half a dozen times after we moved, to visit my mother and grandparents, but I don't think I've seen the place since I was twelve. To tell you the truth, I'd forgotten it even existed until I got this letter from the lawyers." He tapped the file folder.

"My great-uncle Norbert was the last of the Dempseys," he said. "An old bachelor farmer. Never married, never had kids. He died several months ago at the ripe old age of ninety-seven. And it seems he's left Birdsong to me."

Pilar turned to me. "So, you're named after them? I kinda wondered how you got such an unusual name."

"It was Lynda's idea," Mitch said dryly. "She bought into all that romantic Southern crap about old family names. While she was pregnant, she got hold of an old family Bible and went through it looking for names for the baby. I told her I thought Dempsey was a terrible choice for a baby girl, but she was dead set on that name."

Pilar turned to me and rolled her eyes again. "No offense, but your mama sounds like a nut."

For some reason, I felt the need to defend Lynda, and her choice of baby names.

"I hated my name when I was in grade school. I always wanted to be named Katelyn or Tara or Brittany. But when I got to boarding school, it was kinda cool to be the only Dempsey."

I turned to Mitch. "I always wished you'd had some family photos of your mother's side of the family. So I could see the people I'd been named for."

"My father wanted nothing to do with the Dempseys after the divorce," Mitch said. "He never talked about them, so it wasn't what you would call an amicable split."

"But now they've left you a plantation house," Pilar said excitedly. "How many acres? How many bedrooms?" She grabbed the photo again and stared down at it. "A place like this must be worth a lot of money."

Mitch shook his head. "Not according to the lawyer." He picked up a pair of horn-rimmed reading glasses and took a letter from the folder.

"Carter Berryhill, he's the attorney representing my great-uncle's estate, says Birdsong conveys with point eight acres of land. At one time,

I think, the property consisted of a couple hundred acres, but I imagine the Dempseys sold off that land over the years, and the town kind of grew in around the house."

"No plantation?" Pilar's face fell.

"Sorry," Mitch said. "By the time my grandparents lived there, there were maybe five or six acres. When I was a boy, it seemed like a huge place, with a barn where they'd once kept horses, and a small pasture where my granddaddy did keep a cow, along with a chicken coop and a big flower and vegetable garden, but of course, to a kid everything seems huge and magnificent."

He ran his finger down the typed lines. "Berryhill says the property was recently appraised for ninety-eight thousand."

"That's all?" Pilar got up and went around behind the desk to read over Mitch's shoulder, just to make sure he hadn't gotten the number wrong.

"That's next to nothing," she complained.

"It does seem low to me," Mitch said. "Birdsong was a showplace. When I was a kid, it was the biggest, fanciest house in town. Berryhill does say old Norbert was in poor health the last few years, and that the house is in pretty bad disrepair, so maybe that explains it."

I'd picked up the picture and was examining it more closely. The Southern belle on the porch had a familiar look about her. I held it up for my father to see.

"Who's this?"

He put the reading glasses on again and squinted down at the photo. "It's such a grainy old print, it's hard to tell. Could be my mother, I guess. Or maybe just some pretty girl who lived in town. Guthrie was the kind of place that always had aspirations to be like something out of *Gone With the Wind*. There was some kind of festival they had every spring, and all the women in town would get themselves up in hoop-skirts and other costumes like this. I think it was something the mill people and the business owners came up with to try to bring tourists in off of the interstate."

Pilar looked at my father with astonishment. "You don't even know if this is your own mama?"

"She died when I was nine," Mitch said quietly. "Anyway," he added, pushing the file across the desk to me, "this is what I've got in mind for you."

"What? Dress up in a hoopskirt and wave to tourists?"

"Birdsong," he said briskly. "My first thought was to tell this Berryhill fella to go ahead and put it on the market, sell it and be done. That's what I intended, until you called and said you'd been fired."

I winced.

"Look," Mitch said. "You're out of work. Out of money, basically. No place to live—"

"The girls said I could stay—"

"Until your savings run out. After that you're freeloading."

"Not if you loan me the money—"

"Never loan money to family," Mitch said quickly. "That's my policy. Anyway, how do you plan to pay me back? There's no guarantee you'll get a job with this mess hanging over your head."

"You're saying you want me to move to Guthrie, Georgia? A place I've never been? Move into a house I've never seen?"

He tapped the photo with his glasses. "You're seeing it right now."

"I'll bet it's a dump," I said flatly.

"Now, maybe. But not when we're done with it."

"We?" I said.

"I thought we could form a little partnership."

"What kind of partnership?" I asked warily.

"I think we can flip the place," Mitch said. "You and me. I don't care what some country-bumpkin lawyer thinks, I know the old home place has to be worth more than ninety-eight thousand. A lot more. When I was a kid, Atlanta seemed a world away. But now, with all the urban sprawl, Guthrie's got to be almost a suburb of Atlanta. I've done some research, and real estate in Jackson County has been skyrocketing in the past few years. Birdsong, fixed up, would be the perfect 'estate home' for some Yankeee corporate executive. Or a country retreat. Hell, the house alone has sixty-eight hundred square feet. A historic property like that, fully restored, ought to be worth around half a million."

Pilar nodded vigorously. "At least. You can't even get a chicken coop in Miami for that much money."

"I'm not asking you to stay down there indefinitely," Mitch said.

"Yeah," Pilar put in. "You can't expect your dad and me to give you a free place to stay forever. We got bills too, you know."

"Are you talking about flipping? Like all those reality television shows?"

"People do it all the time. Make a lot of money at it," Mitch said.

"People who know what they're doing. And I don't," I started.

"What are you talking about? I remember when you were just a little girl. We got you a Barbie dream house for your birthday. You threw out the plastic furniture that came with it and spent weeks painting and redecorating it with scraps of wallpaper and fabric from a sample book your mother had lying around the house."

He turned to Pilar. "This was during Lynda's 'I want to be an interior designer' phase. Which came after the fashion-model phase, but before the sculptress phase. If I had a nickel for all the art lessons and books and crap that woman bought—"

"Stop making Lynda out to be such a flake," I said angrily, tired of his criticisms. "She's actually a very talented artist. She's been doing the jewelry for years now, and several of the hottest boutiques in Hollywood sell her stuff."

"Hollywood!" Mitch said. "Where else could you sell a necklace made out of pieces of broken taillights and beer can pop-tops?"

"For a couple thousand dollars," I added. "That's what one of her pieces sells for, you know."

"If you say so," Mitch said, his expression telling me he found it unlikely. "Anyway, the point I'm making is, you don't have to be a rocket scientist to fix this place up and make a nice profit on it."

"Maybe." Now I was the one who wasn't buying what he was selling.

"Tell you what," Mitch said, turning his attention back to the golf tournament. "Hang on. I gotta check to see how Tiger's doing now. That kid from Australia's been breathing down his neck for the past three holes."

"Dad?" I said.

"Oh yeah. You go on down to Georgia. Get yourself settled in the house, then get busy fixing it up. I'll set you up with a credit card to buy supplies and food and whatnot. Shouldn't take you more than a month or two to whip the place into shape, right? Then we'll flip the place and split the profits. How's that sound?"

"What?" Pilar screeched. "That sounds like some kind of fabulous sweetheart deal to me. How 'bout Dempsey stays here with the boys, and I'll go up there and get the place ready to sell. It won't take me any month, I'll tell you that right now."

"Damn!" Mitch cried, slapping the desktop. "He shanked it. Son of a bitch has been six under par all day, and he shanks it on the seventeeth hole." He flicked the television off and stood up. He stood up and put his arm around Pilar.

"Now, baby, you know you don't want to be messin' around with some old house in some dinky little town in Georgia. What would the boys do without you? Hell, what would I do without you?"

"You'd get along," Pilar said darkly.

"Dempsey?" Mitch said, looking over at me. I was staring down at the picture of Birdsong, at the mystery woman in the hoopskirt, waving to a carload of passing tourists.

"What do you say? Is it a deal?"

I sighed. "Deal."

7

My mother was just as thrilled with Mitch's project as my step-mother. "Guthrie, Georgia!" Lynda cried when I called to tell her of my impending change of address. "Precious, you can't move there. Why, the place is a flyspeck. I bet they don't even have a Starbucks."

I was packing up the last of my belongings from the apartment in Alexandria. Not that there was much to pack besides my clothes and books. Lindsay had furnished the place before Stephanie and I moved in. And the girls quickly lined up a third friend to sublet my room on a month-to-month basis.

"Fix up the old Dempsey place?" Lynda went on. "What on earth can your father be thinking? You're a lawyer, sweet pea. You don't know the first thing about real estate."

"Dad says I used to love to redecorate," I said huffily. "Remember that Barbie dream house you guys gave me when I was little? And I made my own furniture and repainted the whole place? Dad said it was really something."

"It was ghastly," Lynda said. "You took Magic Markers and scribbled giant orange flowers on the outside of it, and then you glued scraps of hideous striped purple wallpaper over all the windows and the front door. But then, that's how you dressed too, at that stage. I used to worry that you were color blind or something. Thank God you grew out of all that."

The door to my bedroom opened and Stephanie plopped down on the bed. "My mom," I mouthed, pointing to the phone. She nodded that she understood, but pointed at the watch on her wrist.

My plane was due to leave at noon, and it was getting close to ten.

"Look, Lynda," I said, struggling with the zipper on my suitcase. "It's not like I'm moving to Outer Mongolia or something. Guthrie is only an hour south of Atlanta. Remember Becky—my roommate from junior year at St. Catherine's? She lives in Atlanta, well, Decatur, actually. She does something with computers. She's going to pick me up at the airport and give me a ride down to Guthrie."

"So does that mean you'll be stuck down there without a car?" Lynda asked, even more horrified.

"Dad says I can pick up a used car cheap once I'm down in Guthrie," I said. "Who knows? I may even get a pickup truck—wouldn't that be cool?"

"Don't even joke about something like that," Lynda said. "It's not funny. In fact, this whole bizarre undertaking has me worried sick. I still don't see why you don't just come out here and stay with us for a while. Leonard has so many friends in the film business. And you wouldn't have to live in some backwoods hamlet and work like some field hand just to prove to your father that you're not a failure."

"Dad doesn't think I'm a failure," I lied. "And it's sweet of you to want me to come out there, but I don't know anything about the movie business. And I'm not licensed to practice law in California. It would take months and months before I could get to that point."

"You could work with me," Lynda said impulsively. "Learn to make jewelry. I'm about to hire an assistant. I could teach you instead."

"I'll be fine," I told her for the tenth time. "It's just for a couple of months. It'll be an adventure! And in two months, after everybody in Washington has forgotten about this whole Hoddergate thing, I'll come back, get another great job, and pick up the pieces of my life again. Which is what I really want to do, you know."

"What about your boss?" Lynda asked. "Have you heard from him? What does he think about this whole crazy idea?"

"I haven't heard from Alex," I admitted. "According to Ruby, the office manager, he and his wife are in the Grenadines, on vacation. I sent him an e-mail, telling him where I was going and how he could reach me."

"On vacation with his wife," Lynda mused. "That can't be good news for you."

Stephanie stood up and tapped her watch again. "It'll all be fine," I repeated. "I'll call you when I get down to Guthrie. And I'll take pictures of the house, so you can see what it looks like."

"Oh, I've *seen* Birdsong," Lynda said. "Of course, it was a wreck twenty-five years ago, when your father's family was living there, so I can only imagine how awful it must be now."

"You've been to Guthrie? Seen the house? But when? Dad said he hadn't been there since he was a kid."

"He hasn't, as far as I know," Lynda said airily. "Your father had absolutely no interest in anything like that. But before I married Mitchell Killebrew, I made it my business to see the town he'd come from and meet the people in his family. On *both* sides of his family," she emphasized. "Why do you think I was so determined to name you Dempsey? I'm not surprised his uncle Norbert left him the house. Such a sweet old man! And he always doted on Mitch, God knows why."

"Demps?" Now Lindsay was at the door, jingling her car keys. "Let's roll, girlfriend. Traffic on the beltway's gonna be a bitch."

8

G UTHRIE, GEORGIA, THE LITTLE TOWN WITH BIG IDEAS. POP.
2,200. The roadside sign showed a stylized skyline featuring a
clock tower and some towering trees. Becky slowed the Honda
down to thirty-five miles an hour as the four-lane county road narrowed to two lanes at the approach to the edge of town.

"Wow. Only twenty-two hundred." Becky glanced over at me. "Did
you know it was this small?"

"No idea," I said. "My father hasn't been here in, like, forty years. I
guess I'm surprised it's this big, considering what he's told me about the
place."

My flight down from D.C. had been unremarkable, and when I looked
out the window of the plane and saw clear blue skies, sunshine, and
green trees on the ground below, I decided to take it as a good omen.

The trees were one thing that surprised me about this part of middle
Georgia. I'd lived in Atlanta for a short time after my parents' divorce,
and thereafter had been under the distinct impression that everything
outside Atlanta was mostly red mud and tall Georgia pines.

There were plenty of pines down here, yes, but other trees too, many
of them already budded out or in full leaf. I recognized oak trees and
poplars, and as we got closer to the center of Guthrie, we began to see
blooming azaleas along the side of the road, and bright patches of yellow daffodils.

"It's actually kind of pretty," I told Becky.

"What did you think?" she said with a laugh. "It was some kind of
wasteland?"

"Honestly? Yes."

The county road had segued into something called simply Boulevard, although it bore no resemblance to any of the boulevards I'd seen in other places. There were a few strip-mall shopping centers on either side of Boulevard. The businesses didn't look exactly thriving; I saw a Bi-Lo grocery store in a shopping center alongside a dollar store, a tanning salon, and a car wash.

"Look," I told Becky, pointing out the window. "An Ace hardware store. Thank God. Hopefully I can buy paint and stuff there."

After a block or two of shopping centers, the commercial district petered out and we began to see houses—big ones, with rolling green lawns and huge magnolias and boxwood hedges. Oak trees marched along both sides of the street, their branches meeting overhead to form a leafy tunnel. The road changed names again, this time to Colquitt Street. Most of the houses were redbrick, mostly built in the early 1900s, I thought, although there were two or three that appeared to be older, even Victorian, and there were a smattering of large Craftsman bungalows. Maybe, I thought, with a glimmer of hope, Guthrie wasn't as dinky as Lynda remembered.

"Is Birdsong on this street?" Becky asked, slowing down.

I checked the MapQuest directions I'd printed out back at home. "Nope. Looks like you go another couple of blocks into town, and then take a left onto Poplar. The house number is 375."

The next street sign we spotted was for Mill Street.

"I guess that's where the bedspread plant used to be," I told Becky. "According to my dad, nearly everything in Guthrie used to revolve around the Dempsey bedspread mill. Everybody in his family worked there, and I think maybe his mother's grandfather or uncle or somebody founded it. At one time, Dad said, the mill ran three shifts a day, seven days a week, and a couple thousand people worked there. The town must have been a lot bigger back then."

"Is the mill still operating?" Becky asked.

"Dad said it closed for good in the eighties, but he thinks it had probably kinda started dying out as early as the seventies, after it was sold to some big conglomerate in New Jersey. His mother's family was mostly long gone by then. Except for good old great-uncle Norbert. He's the one who left the house to my dad."

As we passed Mill Street, a long, sharp, high-pitched whistle punctuated the otherwise quiet of the late afternoon.

"Holy crap!" Becky laughed. "What was that?"

I looked around. "No idea. Maybe a train?"

"We crossed some railroad tracks back at the city limits, but I haven't seen any since then," she said.

I looked at my watch. "It's exactly five. Maybe that's the town whistle for curfew. Dad said they roll up the streets pretty early in Guthrie."

We both laughed at the notion of a five o'clock curfew.

"Here's Poplar," I said, spotting the white concrete street marker up ahead.

Becky made the turn.

Poplar seemed only slightly less prosperous a street than Colquitt. The lots were large and leafy, although somewhat narrower, with houses set closer to the street. An elderly woman bundled up in a bulky quilted jacket, knit scarf, and cap, despite what seemed to me the fairly mild sixty-degree weather, walked a biscuit-colored cocker spaniel along the sidewalk, pausing to let him lift a leg on a shrub. She turned and stared at the Honda, which was creeping rather suspiciously down the street. I gave her a friendly wave, which she returned, in a lukewarm version.

"This is 373," Becky said, rolling to a stop at the curb. "And I see 377, there, with the picket fence out front, but I don't see a 375."

"Mitch said it was a huge house," I told her, staring at the two houses, with a large, overgrown patch of trees and shrubs in between. The house on one side was a prim white Victorian clapboard affair, with a wide front porch and a row of upended rocking chairs. The house on the left was pale yellow brick, with arched second-floor windows that made it look perpetually surprised. In between the two houses was a veritable jungle, dominated by a hedge of six-foot camellia bushes near the curb, which in turn was punctuated by a hulking magnolia tree whose roots were pushing through the cracked concrete of the sidewalk.

"Number 375 can't have just disappeared. Maybe there's another Poplar Street, like maybe this is West Poplar and there's an East Poplar."

I leaned my head out the window of the car to call to the old lady, who was now studiously avoiding making eye contact with us. "Excuse me."

She looked down at the dog, and nudged its butt with the toe of her rubber galosh.

"Ma'am?" I called again, afraid she might not have heard me.

She whirled around, fire in her rheumy blue eyes. The dog barked a short, sharp warning.

"What you want?" she demanded.

"Excuse me," I said, giving her my friendly lobbyist smile. "I'm looking for number 375 Poplar Street." I spoke in a deliberately slow, distinct voice.

"What's your business?"

"Pardon?"

"What do you want on this street? What's your business in Guthrie? I seen those Atlanta plates on your car."

"Uh-oh," Becky said under her breath. "I think we just found Guthrie's version of Boo Radley."

"Well, uh, I'm here to see about 375 Poplar Street. It, uh, belongs to my father," I stammered. "And, uh, I've come down here to uh—"

"I knew it!" the old lady exclaimed, stepping closer to the car. "Knew it the minute I laid eyes on you. You're Killebrew, all right. Ain't ya?"

"Uh, yes, ma'am," I said, smiling uncertainly. The way she said Killebrew made it sound more like a contagious disease than a name. "I'm Dempsey Killebrew."

"Dempsey!" she shrieked, taking a step backward. "He's got some nerve."

The cocker yipped and lunged toward the Honda, snarling and hurling itself against the tires.

"Holy crap," Becky said. "Boo Radley and Cujo on the same street."

The old lady reluctantly reined in the cocker, and continued to glare daggers at me.

"Do you know this street?" I asked. I held up the folder of papers

Mitch had given me before I'd left Miami. "The house is called Birdsong. The lawyers gave us the address as 375 Poplar Street. But I don't see—"

Before I could continue, the old lady wheeled around and marched rapidly away, crossing the street in midblock.

"Oooh-kaaay," I said, watching her retreat. "That was kinda weird."

"Hey, Demps," Becky said. She'd opened her door and stepped out of the car. "Look here."

She stood in the shade of the magnolia. With the toe of her shoe, she'd kicked away a patch of the dense carpet of pine needles and fallen leaves, revealing what looked like a cracked and crumbling concrete driveway leading into the overgrown lot.

I got out of the car and walked around to join my friend.

"Hey," Becky said, pushing aside a low-hanging tree limb. "Demps, I think there's a house back in here."

I ducked under another branch draped with a luxurious fringe of kudzu. "You're right. I see something pink."

After another five minutes of ducking and batting away at vines, branches, and brambles, and cursing myself for not changing out of the high-heeled boots and Theory pants suit I'd worn on the flight down to Atlanta, we found a clearing in the underbrush.

Looming up before us was an enormous wreck—a tottering wedding cake of a house painted an improbable shade of Pepto-Bismol pink.

"I think we found your Birdsong," Becky said.

"Bird droppings is more like it."

I picked up a stout tree branch lying at my feet—not sure whether I would use it as a walking stick or a weapon—and walked closer to the house.

The concrete steps leading up to the front porch were as cracked as the driveway, and laced with more kudzu, which seemed to be making a determined advance against the house.

Now, standing at the edge of the porch, looking up, I could start to see that this was, indeed, the house that had once been Birdsong.

The grand columns that had marched across the front of the house were still here, but their faded pink paint was now blistered and peeling, and in places I could see where their plaster plinths had started to crumble.

I poked my stick on the wooden planks of the porch, afraid they might suddenly give way beneath my feet, but, mercifully, they seemed solid.

Becky stood at the edge of the porch, looking distinctly uncomfortable.

I walked over to the front door. It was heavily carved, and painted a faded gray, with leaded-glass sidelights and a fanlight overhead. I found the doorbell, a cracked plastic button, and pushed it. I heard a shrill ringing inside.

I tried the doorknob, expecting nothing, but when it turned in my hand, I let out a surprised gasp.

"What?" Becky rushed to my side.

I pushed the door open, its hinges screaming a protest.

"Holy crap," she whispered.

9

At first glance, the interior of Birdsong wasn't much of an improvement over the exterior. The large room before me was the foyer, although that seemed too grand a word for this dump. A single bare lightbulb dangled from an extension cord that snaked its way up a wall with faded brocade-patterned wallpaper and into the center of an elaborate plaster ceiling medallion. The rest of the ceiling's plaster either hung in clumps or lay in chunks on the floor of what had once been an elegant center entrance hall.

The floor itself was made of alternating diamonds of black and white marble, and it was littered with a bewildering assortment of random items—a wooden nail keg full of rakes and brooms, a plastic bucket full of faded plastic flowers, stacks of paperback romance novels, their once-vivid colored covers dulled to a uniform violet. There was even a large dressmaker's dummy that wore a multilayered assortment of ratty sweaters, jackets, and scarves. Leaned against a corner was a huge bag of dog food.

"Holy crap is right," I said, stepping gingerly over the threshold. My voice echoed in the high-ceilinged room. "The lawyers told Mitch that good old Uncle Norbert died back in September. When do you think the last time was that anybody lived here?"

Becky's patrician nose quivered as she sniffed dramatically. "I don't smell anything like a corpse."

"How do you know what a corpse smells like?" I asked, leaning down to examine the label on the dog food bag. The colors on the label seemed bright and clear, and the price tag showed that it was from one of those big-box pet-supply stores.

"I was a candy striper one summer in high school," she said smugly. "You learn these things." She sniffed again and wrinkled her nose. "Mildew. Gross. Also dog doo."

I looked down at the floor, and then at our feet, and laughed. "Check your shoes. I think you must have stepped in Cujo's calling card."

"Gross!" She darted out the front door and when she came back inside, she was cleaning her shoes with a wadded-up newspaper.

"I think somebody's living here," I told her in a quiet voice, pointing to a pair of worn tennis shoes that had been left in a corner. "One of those shoes is still damp."

She shuddered. "Did the lawyers say anything about a tenant? Or maybe a caretaker?"

"Mitch didn't say anything about either one," I told her. "He just said I should go right to the lawyer's office to pick up the key. The place was supposed to be locked up tight."

Becky took a step toward the door. "Okay. I'll admit it. I'm a scaredy-cat. Let's just go. All right?"

I looked around the hallway. There were closed doors on either side, plus another partially ajar door that looked like it led toward the back of the house. Now that I was inside Birdsong, I wasn't quite ready to leave yet.

"There's nobody here," I assured her. "I rang the doorbell." I held up my stout stick. "Anyway, if any skeletons or beasties jump out of a closet, I'll be ready. Come on. Let's take a look around."

"You first," Becky said, tugging at the collar of her coat. "It's freezing in here. I hope for your sake this place has heat."

I put my hand on top of a radiator in the corner of the room. "Radiator isn't working. But the place has to have fireplaces, right? Anyway, you saw those azaleas and daffodils blooming. It's almost spring."

"Last year we had an ice storm the last week of March," Becky said, letting her teeth chatter for effect. "Don't think that because you're in Georgia we don't have winter. It gets plenty cold down here."

"And hot," I reminded her. I pushed on the door on the right side of the room and stepped into another century.

A long mahogany table draped with a yellowing lace cloth sat squarely in the middle of the room, which, though covered in dust and cobwebs, managed to retain its elegant proportions.

Massive Chippendale dining chairs sat on each side of the table, their faded maroon needlepoint seat covers each adorned with a different flower. A floor-to-ceiling bay window dominated the right side of the room, and through its dust-streaked glass I could see that Birdsong's side yard was just as overgrown as its front. Standing in the bay window was an Empire mahogany sideboard, its top covered with stacks of gilt-edged floral china. On the facing wall, a glass-fronted china cabinet seemed full to bursting with more china and dusty cut glass.

The oriental rug on the floor was threadbare in spots, but its jewel-like reds and blues made a splash of color in the dimly lit room.

"Spooky," Becky said, drawing a fingertip through the dust on the top of the sideboard.

"Like everybody got up from some swell dinner party fifty years ago and just . . . disappeared," I agreed, holding up one of the delicate porcelain plates.

"This is hand painted," Becky said, picking up another plate and tracing the design of pink roses and forget-me-nots in the center of the dish. "My great-grandmother had a lot of this stuff in her house when she died. My mother's supposedly saving it for when I get married."

She sighed. "My mother never gives up hope."

We put the plates back and moved across the hall to the door on the opposite side.

This time we found a formal parlor, in more or less the same condition as the dining room.

The parlor walls were covered in a faded floral-stripe wallpaper, which seemed to be molting from water-stained plaster walls. The fireplace had a surround of elaborate flower-printed tiles and a highly carved dark oak mantelpiece. Over the mantel hung a large oil portrait of a brooding woman in a sleek 1920s flapper-era bobbed haircut. The woman was dressed in a gold off-the-shoulder gown and wore a long strand of pearls and dangly pearl earrings.

"Think she's a relative?" Becky asked.

"Maybe." I shrugged. "Mitch hasn't exactly been forthcoming with the Dempsey family genealogy. I think his father was pretty bitter after their divorce."

"One thing we know," Becky said. "At one time, they had some bucks."

"They did," I agreed, looking around the empty room. "Wonder what happened to all the furniture in here?"

She rubbed her arms to ward off the gloomy chill. "Maybe they burned it to stay warm."

My cell phone rang, startling both of us. I plucked it from my shoulder bag and checked the caller ID anxiously. It had been two weeks since I'd been fired from my job, and I still hadn't heard a word from Alex Hodder.

"Unknown caller," I said, hesitating before punching the connect button.

"Hello?"

"Is this Dempsey Killebrew?"

"It is."

"Good. Hello. This is Carter Berryhill."

"Yesss," I said cautiously.

"Of the law firm Berryhill and Berryhill? We represent the estate of Norbert Dempsey?"

"Oh yes," I said. "I was just on my way over to see you."

"So I gather," he said. His accent was deeply Southern, with that faint aristocratic tinge and formal diction you hear in men of a certain age from a certain social strata. Alex Hodder had an accent like that.

"My informants tell me you've been by to see Birdsong?"

"How did you know that?"

He chuckled. "Oh, Miss Killebrew. You really don't know the first thing about Guthrie, now do you?"

I walked over to the window and peered out, just in case Carter Berryhill happened to be standing in the side yard, peering in at us. All I saw was a tangle of bare branches and vines.

"Guess not," I said. "As a matter of fact, my friend and I are in the house right now."

"Really?" He didn't sound pleased.

"The front door was unlocked," I said. "I rang the doorbell, but there was no answer. Mr. Berryhill, has somebody been living in the house recently?"

There was a long silence on the other end of the line. "We can discuss that in my office, if that's all right with you. Were you heading over here anytime soon?"

"We'll leave right now," I told him.

"Excellent. Would you do me a favor? Lock the door behind you? We don't really have much of a crime rate in Guthrie, but you can never be too careful about these things."

I agreed, he had me repeat the directions to his office, and we hung up.

Becky raised an inquiring eyebrow.

"Carter Berryhill. He's the lawyer representing the estate. Mitch must have given him my phone number."

"And he already knew you were here? This place gets spookier and spookier, Demps. Are you positive you're up for living here and dealing with all . . . this?" She gestured at the decrepitude surrounding us.

"I'll be fine. It's just small-town stuff. Probably somebody in the neighborhood saw your car with the Atlanta license tags parked at the curb and called him to make sure we weren't burglarizing the joint."

"Hardly." She sniffed again and tugged at one of the faded deep blue velvet drapery panels hanging from the window. "Scarlett should have made a ball gown from those things."

I reached over to touch the velvet, which seemed to crumble under my fingertips. "This was expensive fabric, back in the day. In fact, everything I've seen, what's left of it, looks like it was pretty costly."

"Speaking of which," Becky said. "This place is falling apart. I don't see how you're going to be able to do all this work by yourself. It's not just a matter of a new paint job, you know."

"I know," I said ruefully. "Crumbling plaster, peeling wallpaper. God knows about the heat or the wiring or the plumbing. And we haven't even checked to see if the place has an actual kitchen or bathroom."

"Did your dad give you an idea of how much of a budget you'd have? Does he have any idea of the shape this place is in?"

"Not yet," I said. "But he will."

10

"So this is greater metropolitan Guthrie," Becky said as we approached the courthouse square. She turned and wrinkled her nose. "Kinda bleak, Demps."

I couldn't argue with her. The town's main street, called Confederate Avenue, was a short, two-block strip of tired storefronts, about half of them empty. It faced the courthouse square, where a granite plinth held a bronze statue of a Confederate soldier. The courthouse itself was a hulking dark brown brick affair that looked like it dated from the late 1800s. An awkward yellow-brick boxy building that screamed '70s had been tacked onto the side of the courthouse. Two police cruisers were parked at the curb in front of the courthouse.

"Mr. Berryhill said his office is half a block down from the courthouse," I told Becky. "Look for a dark green house with a red front door." She nodded and drove down Confederate, while I scanned the street for signs of life. It was still cold and windy, but late in the day. There were cars parked along both sides of the street, but I saw only a couple of shoppers, who hurried out of the stores to their cars.

"At least there's a restaurant," I said, pointing to a storefront window painted with pictures of pies and steaming cups of coffee. "The Corner Café. But it isn't even on a corner."

"Semantics," Becky said. "It's a restaurant. And they obviously have pie. So, bonus points for Guthrie."

She slowed the car in front of a dark green house with a front porch that had a signpost swinging from its gable: BERRYHILL AND BERRYHILL, ATTORNEYS-AT-LAW.

"You coming in?" I asked. She shook her head no. "I'll just stay out here. Give you some privacy." She hesitated. "I hate to bring it up, but

I'll have to get going pretty soon. I've got a dinner meeting tonight. I tried to weasel out of it, but this is a new client, so it's kind of a command performance."

"I understand," I told her. "Let me just talk to Mr. Berryhill and get the key, and I'll be right out. Fifteen minutes okay?"

"Fine. Hey—what are you going to do about a car down here? I know you didn't have one in D.C., but this is Georgia, honey. You're gonna need a car."

"I know. Mitch says he'll pay for me to buy some kind of secondhand junker so I can get around. Maybe even a pickup truck!"

She hooted. "Dempsey Killebrew in a pickup truck? I want to see that."

"I'm going native," I assured her. "Pickup truck, blue jeans, boots, the works."

"I bet you don't even own a pair of jeans."

"Do too. They cost a hundred and seventy-five dollars. Guess maybe I'll have to get something a little cheaper to work in."

"Have to go back to the hardware store and get you some Carhartts," Becky said. "That's what every well-dressed redneck wears for chores."

I stood on the porch of the Berryhill law office and wondered what to do. In D.C., you just walk into a lawyer's office. But this was Guthrie, and the office was in a house, and I'd already walked into one house today, and the spies had notified the authorities. There was no doorbell to ring, so that was out. I knocked. Three demure raps with my knuckles.

No answer. I pounded with the flat of my palm. Still no answer.

I turned the doorknob and stepped inside. I found myself in a small outer office, furnished with a desk and chair, a bank of file cabinets, and a couple of worn chintz-upholstered wing chairs. The chairs faced a small fireplace with a gas-log fire merrily burning away. Cozy, but empty.

"Hello?" I called loudly.

"Coming," a male voice called from the back of the house. I heard footsteps on the wooden floors, and then a tall, angular man with a thick mane of silver hair and a neatly trimmed goatee popped into the office.

"Miss Killebrew?" He stuck his hand out. "Sorry about that. I was in the kitchen getting a cup of coffee. Scott, my secretary, left early to take his dog to the vet, so I'm just minding the store until my son gets back."

I shook his hand. Carter Berryhill had long thin fingers and a firm handshake. "No problem," I said. "I was a little uncertain about the etiquette of visiting a home office."

"Home office?" He laughed. "Good Lord, no. I don't live here." He gestured toward the hallway he'd just come through. "Come on back and let's chat."

I followed him past two closed doors and into a large book-lined room with a desk overflowing with papers and files.

He gestured for me to sit in a high-backed leather armchair.

Carter Berryhill pushed his own chair back away from his desk. He looked me up and down. I did the same to him. He looked to be in his mid to late sixties, with sharp brown eyes, a longish nose, and reading glasses pushed up into his hair. He was casually dressed in brown corduroy slacks and a camel-colored sweater worn over a white dress shirt, a loosened burgundy necktie around the shirt's collar. A brown tweed sport coat hung on the back of his chair, and he quickly slipped it on over the sweater.

"You look like a Dempsey," he said finally. "Course, I can see some of your daddy's family looks in you too, the cheekbones especially, but the eyes, that odd slate blue, and those dark eyebrows and lashes, that's Dempsey through and through. Norbert had amazing eyes, even in his late nineties. How is your father? Haven't seen him since he was just a little thing."

"He's fine," I said politely. "People always say I have my mother's eyes."

He shook his head. "They don't know the Dempseys. You rummage around enough over at Birdsong, you're sure to find some old family photos. You'll see."

"About Birdsong," I started.

"You gave Ella Kate quite a start, driving up there like that," he said. "I guess maybe we should have warned her you'd be coming to town. She burned up my ears about it, let me tell you."

"Ella Kate?"

"Ella Kate Timmons. She's some kind of kin to you. Second cousin maybe?"

I shrugged. "Don't know her."

"Sawed-off little thing, gray hair, white Supp-Hose? Always bundled up, even in the summertime? She was walking Shorty when you pulled up to the house. Ran off and called me and ripped me a new one, if you know what I mean."

"The old lady at the house? She's the one who told you I was there?"

"That's right," Berryhill said. "Ella Kate Timmons. She sort of took care of old Norbert these last years."

"Why was she upset with you?" I asked. "In fact, why was she upset with me? As soon as I told her my name, she had some sort of fit, and then she just ran away."

I heard a door open somewhere in the house, and then footsteps. The office door opened, and a younger version of Carter Berryhill stepped inside.

"Dad—" He stopped short when he saw me. "Sorry. Didn't know you were with a client."

"Come on in, son," Berryhill said. "She's actually your client. Miss Dempsey Killebrew, meet my son, T. Carter Berryhill the third."

"It's Tee," the younger man said, shaking my hand. "And I'm pleased to meet you. By the way, my sympathy on the loss of your great-uncle. Mr. Norbert was an institution around Guthrie."

Tee Berryhill stood a shade over six feet tall, which was just a shade under his father's height. His hair was reddish blond, and he was clean shaven, but other than that, he looked remarkably like his father. He was dressed in a dark pin-striped suit, with a red-and-blue-striped rep tie stuffed in the breast pocket of his jacket.

"Thank you," I said. "I'm sorry I never met him. This is my first trip to Guthrie."

"Miss Killebrew went by Birdsong and got Ella Kate all stirred up," Carter Berryhill told his son. "I was just about to explain Ella Kate when you came in."

"It's Dempsey," I said quickly.

"You met Ella Kate?" Tee asked. "I can't wait to hear Dad explain her to you."

"She was walking her dog in front of the house when my friend and I pulled up," I explained. "We didn't see the house, not at first, with all the trees and overgrowth. So, I just asked her where 375 Poplar was, and then, when I told her my name, and she got a good look at me, she just sort of freaked."

"Burned up the phone lines calling me and cussing me out," Carter told Tee.

"Why is she so upset?" I asked.

The two men exchanged looks. Carter shrugged and looked away.

"Uh, Dempsey," Tee said. "Ella Kate took care of your uncle for a long time these last years. She just sort of assumed he would leave the house to her when he died. And when we told her about Norbert's will, and how he'd left the house to your daddy, well, she just went off."

"Went off? How do you mean?"

There was that look again.

"She's really pretty harmless," Tee said. "Hell, I don't think they even make ammo for that shotgun of Norbert's anymore. Really, once you get to know her, I think the two of you will get along just fine."

"She has a shotgun?"

"It's a lot cheaper than a burglar alarm," Carter said with a laugh.

My own look of alarm let them know I wasn't amused.

A thought suddenly occurred to me. "She's living at Birdsong? I could tell someone had been there recently. So it's Ella Kate?"

"That's right," Carter said. "Tee's been working on getting her used to the idea of moving."

"Not making a lot of progress," Tee admitted. "The last time I went over there to talk to her, she set Shorty on me."

"Son, that dog is downright elderly," Carter said. "He probably doesn't have a tooth in his head."

Tee pulled up the right leg of his pants and displayed a nasty oval-shaped bruise on his shin. "You think not?"

Now it was my turn to be upset. "You're telling me there's a shotgun-toting, dog-siccing, crazy old lady living in my house? Essentially squatting there? What am I supposed to do about that? I can't live with somebody like that."

"Live?" Carter said. "You weren't planning on living at Birdsong, were you? I mean, we just assumed you'd get a room at the Econo Lodge, or maybe rent a little place in town. Birdsong's all right for Ella Kate. She's used to it. But now, you don't want to be living in that place. It hasn't exactly been kept up so well."

"It's a disaster," I told him. "I only saw a couple of rooms inside, but the place is a total derelict. Crumbling plaster, exposed wiring, mildew. We had no idea. But yes. I am planning on living there while I get the house rehabbed and ready to sell. Didn't my father tell you that?"

Tee looked at Carter, who looked away.

"I meant to tell him about Ella Kate, and about Birdsong," Carter said. "But we just never actually had a conversation about the fine points. He called to tell me you were coming down, and that the plan was for you to get the house ready to sell." He gave me a sad smile. "It never occurred to me that you might plan to try to live there."

"Well, I am," I said, standing up. "In fact, I'll be moving in today. As in, right now. My friend is waiting outside, and she needs to get back to Decatur. I'll just get my things out of her car, and maybe one of you can call me a cab to take me back over to Birdsong? I want to get moved in and take a look around before it gets too dark."

"I'll take you over there," Tee said quickly. "I'll have a talk with Ella Kate too, while I help you with your stuff. If you're sure that's what you want to do?"

"I'm sure."

Carter shook his head sadly. "The Econo Lodge would be better. Satellite television. Free continental breakfast. They've got heat too."

"Birdsong," I repeated. "I'll be staying at Birdsong."

11

B ecky was talking on her cell phone when I came out of the law
office with Tee Berryhill in my wake.

"Sorry for the delay," I said, making the introductions.

"Tee is going to give me a ride back over to Birdsong and help me
get moved in," I said. "That way you can get on the road before traffic
gets too terrible."

Becky gave Tee a friendly smile, and I knew she was sizing him up.
"That's really sweet of you," she told him, getting out of the car.
"Dempsey's going to need a friend down here."

"He's the lawyer handling the estate," I said quickly.

Tee flashed a grin. "I'm fairly friendly—as lawyers go. Look here. I'm
parked in the back of the office. I'll pull around and we'll get you
loaded up."

A couple of minutes later, Tee pulled his car to the curb in back of
Becky's Honda.

"Oh, a Mini Cooper," Becky said. "How do you like it?"

"I love it," Tee said. "Course, you take a lot of ribbing in a town like
Guthrie when you show up driving a hybrid."

But when Becky opened the trunk of the Honda and he got a look at
my large rolling suitcase his smile disappeared. "Oh," he said, blinking
owlishly. "Man. I'm not sure that puppy will fit in my car."

Before he could stop me, I'd pulled the suitcase out of the Honda.

"Go on," I told Becky. "I don't want to make you late for your dinner."

"I hate leaving you like this," Becky said. "And I really hate the idea
of you staying alone in that spooky old flophouse."

"I won't be alone," I said cheerily. "Remember the old lady walking
the dog? We're going to be roommates."

"Huh?"

"I'll call you later and explain everything then," I said. "And I'll be fine. Really. It'll be like camping out."

"You never camped out in your whole life," she reminded me. She stuck her head out of the car and called to Tee.

"Hey. Can't you talk some sense into this girl? Make her check into a motel for a few days?"

He shrugged. "My dad tried to tell her it'll be pretty primitive at Birdsong. I got the impression your friend has her mind made up."

"Damned straight," I said briskly. I pounded her car door. "Shoo! Move along."

"Call me," she repeated. She drove off, and I immediately started having doubts. But it was too late. Tee Berryhill had dragged my suitcase over to his Mini Cooper and was busily wedging it into the minuscule trunk.

"Your friend seems nice," he said when we were ready to leave.

"Becky's a sweetheart," I said. "We've been friends since boarding school days. I was the new girl—my parents had split up and my dad had taken a job in Orlando, and I didn't know a soul at St. Catherine's. Her parents had gotten a divorce too, so she knew what that was like."

"St. Catherine's," he murmured. "Is that in Georgia?"

"Richmond, Virginia," I said quickly. "Mitch moved a lot for his job, and he just thought it was better for me to be in a school where I'd have some sense of stability."

He nodded. It was dusk now, and as we passed the darkened shops on Confederate, I felt a deep chill sink into my bones.

"Where do people shop?" I asked. "Is there a Target or anything like that?"

"No such luck," he said. "We had a Wal-Mart out on the bypass, but that closed down a couple of years ago. For groceries, you've got Piggly Wiggly or Bi-Lo. There's a Family Dollar store, you passed that on the way into town. Anything more than the basics, you've gotta head down to Macon, or up to Peachtree City."

"Oh." It was starting to sink in. I was really and truly in the sticks.

He must have seen the depressed look on my face. "Guthrie's not such a bad place," he said quietly. "The economy could be better, but the folks down here are the real thing. Most of 'em, anyway."

"I'm sure it's a wonderful place," I said. "I don't mean to downgrade your hometown. It's just . . . I've been living in D.C. It'll be an adjustment, I'm sure."

"You mind if I ask what you're doing, moving down here? I mean, Dad told me you're a lawyer, been working as a lobbyist. Seems like a pretty high-flying life to give up and move to Guthrie."

I grimaced. "My job ended. Sort of . . . unexpectedly. And I thought I'd take a little time, maybe reevaluate my career path, before I just jump into another job. Mitch told me about Birdsong, and it seemed like an interesting opportunity."

While I was speaking, my inner voice was editing: Talk about major lobby-lingo double talk. Interesting opportunity? Face it, Dempsey, you're outta work, no prospects, no money, no home. Guthrie's your only shot.

"Interesting?" Tee said. "Yeah, it ought to be interesting, at the very least. What do you plan to do for transportation?"

I gave him a pretty smile. "That's where you might help me out. I guess I'll be buying something to drive. But I've been living in D.C. for so long, I can't even remember the last time I owned a car. Any thoughts about where I can pick up a set of basic wheels?"

"Well . . ." He pondered the matter. We'd arrived at Birdsong. It looked even gloomier at nightfall. From the curb I could see one tiny light shining through the underbrush.

"There's the Catfish," he said finally. "Ella Kate used to drive it, but I think the sheriff finally sweet-talked her into giving up her license after she drove up over the curb trying to park at the courthouse. It ain't pretty, but it runs."

"The Catfish?"

"Your uncle Norbert bought it at a government-surplus auction. It's a Crown Victoria—you know, like a police cruiser? I'm guessing from the mideighties. It's about the size of the *Queen Mary*. Probably gets roughly the same gas mileage."

"A police cruiser?"

"Well, to be specific, I think it was a Georgia Highway Patrol car. But Norbert had it painted. Bulldog red, of course. He was a big UGA fan."

"Oh." I sat there looking at that dim light shining through the tangle of weeds and trees. What had I gotten myself into?

"Hey," Tee said softly. "Why don't you just let me take you over to the Econo Lodge? Just for tonight. I could pick you up in the morning, bring you over here, give you a proper introduction to Ella Kate. It'll all look better in the morning, I promise you."

I bit my lip, sorely tempted to accept his offer. But no, I decided. Now or never.

"That's very kind of you," I said, my hand on the door. "But I really just need to get myself established here. You know, dig in my heels and get started?"

He laughed. "You're tougher than you look, aren't you?"

"We'll see."

He half-carried and half-dragged my suitcase up what was left of the driveway, cursing softly as branches and vines slapped at our faces and snagged on our clothes. "You're going to have to get a bush hog in here first thing," Tee muttered, holding a thick branch aside to let me pass.

"First you'll have to tell me what a bush hog is," I said, standing at the foot of the front steps and staring up at the house.

"It's kind of like a tractor," he explained, stopping beside me. He glanced down at his wristwatch.

"It's after six. Full dark. According to my dad, Ella Kate goes to bed with the chickens."

"She keeps chickens?" I had a visual image of hens roosting in the rafters of my new bedroom.

He chuckled. "You really are a city girl. She goes to bed really early. Gets up early too. With any luck, Ella Kate's already tucked in her bed, fast asleep. And the two of you can have a proper meeting at breakfast."

When we got to the front door, I took out the key and fitted it into the lock. The doorknob turned, with some effort on my part, but the door wouldn't budge. I gave Tee a worried look. "Is there a dead bolt?"

"Don't know," he said. "Maybe. If Dad told Ella Kate you were coming over tonight, she just might have rigged up something to keep you out. I wouldn't put it past the old turkey."

Another poultry reference. Unsettling.

"Is there another door?"

"In the kitchen. Around the back of the house. Are you absolutely positive you want to do this? The Econo Lodge has a cocktail lounge. It's still happy hour . . ."

I pushed a strand of hair behind my ears. "This is my family's property. I have every right to be here. Your father said so himself. You can go. But I intend to stay. You don't happen to have a flashlight in the car, do you?"

He sighed and held up his key ring, which held a tiny penlight.

We left the suitcase and haltingly made our way around to the back of the house. The shrubbery was sparser on the side of the house, but our way was littered with all manner of junk—old garbage cans, garden equipment, wooden crates full of empty Coke bottles, beat-up bicycles, even the rusting carcass of an ancient Volkswagen bug propped up on concrete blocks and draped with kudzu vines.

"Hey," Tee said, waving the penlight over the bug. "This looks just like my dad's old VW. I wrecked it when I was seventeen—"

"Who's out there?" A high-pitched voice pierced the darkness, startling both of us. "I hear ya, you know. I'm old, but I'm not deaf. Speak up now, or I'll get my shotgun. I can use it too."

The dog started barking, staccatolike.

"Christ," Tee said, under his breath. "Miss Ella Kate! It's me, Tee Berryhill."

"Who's that? Shorty, hush!"

The dog stopped barking.

Tee grabbed my hand and began pulling me toward the back of the house, where a yellow light shone down on a small porch stoop.

Ella Kate Timmons held up a withered hand to shade her eyes from the glare of the porch light. Her white hair stood up wildly around her head, like a barbed-wire halo. She was dressed in oversize men's blue flannel pajamas, with an old green army fatigue jacket as a bathrobe. In one hand she held the cocker spaniel's leash, and in the other she held what looked like the shotgun Carter Berryhill had mentioned.

"Miss Ella Kate," Tee said breathlessly. "It's me. Tee Berryhill. Carter's son. We didn't mean to wake you up."

"Well, you did," she said waspishly, jerking on the dog's leash. The dog whined and strained against it.

We'd been edging slowly toward the back porch. The old lady took a step backward when she caught sight of me.

"Hello," I said. "I'm Dempsey. Remember?"

"What's she doing here?" she demanded, turning toward Tee. "I don't want her here. I told your daddy that."

"Now, Miss Ella Kate," Tee started. "We've been over this already. Dempsey's father is Mitch Killebrew. He's Norbert's great-nephew. Remember Mitch?"

"Little pissant," the old lady retorted. "Pulled the cat's tail. If he'd a been mine, I woulda wore his britches out."

"I'm sure he regrets bothering your cat," Tee said soothingly, still inching his way toward her, with me in tow. "That was a long time ago. He was just a little boy back then. He's a grown man now. And this is his daughter, Dempsey."

"Hi." I gave her a friendly little finger wave, keeping my eyes on the shotgun.

"You were in my house," she said flatly. "I seen you. You and that other girl."

I hesitated. This was no time to argue property rights. Not with an old lady who had both a firearm and a mean dog on her side.

"I'm sorry," I said. "I rang the doorbell and knocked. And the door was open. I didn't realize anybody was living here. It's a, uh, beautiful old home." Surely God would forgive me for lying to an old lady.

"It's a mess!" Ella Kate said sharply. "It's a mess. And I'm a mess." Her face crumpled. She turned and fled inside the house, leaving the dog sitting on the porch, eyeing us warily.

"Now what?"

Tee walked haltingly up to the dog, his right hand extended, palm up. "Hey, Shorty," he crooned. "Good old Shorty. How ya doing tonight, Shorty?"

The dog eyed Tee suspiciously. He backed away an inch, and then stopped. Tee got a little closer, then dropped down on his knees, at eye level with the dog. He kept his hand held out, and after a moment, the dog began licking it.

"Good boy," Tee murmured, scratching the dog's ears tenderly. "Good old Shorty. You like ol' Tee, don't you?" The dog wriggled, then flopped onto his back, rolling deliriously back and forth as Tee scratched his belly.

"How do you think Shorty feels about Yankees?" I asked, still keeping my distance.

Tee looked up. "Oh, I don't think it's Yankees he hates. If he's anything like Ella Kate, it's the Killebrews he hates."

Despite the warning, I bent down and gave Shorty my hand to consider. He gave it a friendly lick.

Tee stood up. "Come on, then," he told me, holding the kitchen door open. "She didn't shoot you and Shorty didn't bite you. That's about as warm a welcome as you're apt to get tonight."

12

"Ella Kate?" I peered around the dimly lit room to make sure she wasn't standing there, about to brain me with a frying pan. But the room was empty. And bone-chillingly cold.

"Damn," Tee said, closing the door behind us and fumbling around for a light switch. He took a step, stumbled over something, swore, fumbled some more. He made his way to the far wall and turned on the light.

What I saw made me want to run right back out the door. The kitchen was like something out of a movie. A horror movie. The walls were painted a dingy hospital green. There was a wall of cabinets—sagging wooden cabinets with peeling white paint. The wall closest to the kitchen door held another cabinet, with a gargantuan chipped white porcelain sink—the old-fashioned kind with the built-in drainboard. The countertops were of faded yellow Formica, the floor of cracked green linoleum tiles. There was a stove, roughly the size of an aircraft carrier, and a refrigerator—in an incongruous pale pink—crouched like a dejected pig, in a corner of the room. The overhead fixture was another naked lightbulb, which showed, all too clearly, a room that apparently hadn't been cleaned—or modernized—since the Nixon administration.

"Oh my," Tee said, looking around at the battered saucepans stacked on top of the counters.

Shorty whined, as though in sad agreement.

I walked over to the opposite wall and opened the door to what turned out to be a broom closet. I found one dog-eared broom, a dustpan, and an enamelware bucket. And what looked like a year's supply of discarded plastic bags.

"Cleaning supplies," I said briskly. "Gonna need a lot of cleaning supplies."

"Not tonight," Tee said, his voice sounding alarmed.

"Tomorrow," I said firmly.

He stood in the middle of the kitchen, his arms crossed over his chest, afraid, apparently, of coming into contact with the decades' worth of accumulated grunge.

"You really don't have to stay," I told him. "I'll be just fine. Let me figure out where I'm going to sleep, and get my suitcase into the house, and you can take off. All right?"

"We'll see."

He followed me into the hallway, turning on light switches as we went. There were three more doors leading off Birdsong's center hall. One turned out to be a bathroom, with fading pink-and-blue-flowered vinyl wallpaper. Another was a large room that had probably been a bedroom at one time. At first glance, I thought the room had been painted school bus yellow. But on closer examination, it turned out that the walls were merely lined, from floor to ceiling, with stacks of *National Geographic* magazines. Aside from the magazines, the only other thing in the room was a heavy wooden schoolhouse desk with a brass study lamp and a rickety chair pulled up to it.

"I guess this was the study," I said, walking from stack to stack, leaning in to read the print on the magazine spines. "They're arranged chronologically."

"Norbert was a little eccentric," Tee said. "Especially later in life."

"A little? There must be fifty years' worth of *National Geographics* in here."

"My grandfather collected Jim Beam bottles," Tee said. "The figurals? Like, bourbon bottles in the shape of a bust of Elvis, or Robert E. Lee? We must have found a couple hundred in the basement of his house after he died. And you know what? He was a teetotaling hard-shell Baptist. So a roomful of magazines doesn't seem that crazy to me."

"At least you can drink bourbon," I said darkly, trying to repress a sneeze.

We walked out into the hallway, and as I was closing the door, a shrill voice echoed in the high-ceilinged hallway. "That's Norbert's study, you leave that alone now!"

Ella Kate stood at the top of a flight of stairs I hadn't even noticed, glaring down at us.

"Sorry," I said, quickly stepping away from the door. "I was just trying to figure out where I could sleep—"

"Not there," she said. Inserting two fingers in her mouth, she whistled sharply. "Shorty! Come!" The cocker scrambled up the stairs, stopping at her feet. Ella Kate turned, and with the dog following right behind, she stomped off, slamming a door behind them.

"I'll get your suitcase," Tee said. "I've never been on the second floor. I don't know if anybody other than Ella Kate has, since Mr. Norbert died. But according to the tax records, there should be four more bedrooms and a couple of bathrooms up there."

"Hopefully, one of them has a bed," I said meaningfully.

A moment later he was back with my luggage, dragging it up the stairway. The suitcase hit each of the worn wooden stair treads with a thud. As I followed behind, I scanned the dozens of framed black-and-white family photos that had been nailed, willy-nilly, to the stairway wall.

Tee stopped in front of a large family portrait in an elaborate gilt frame. The photo showed a stiffly posed couple in Victorian dress. The wife had dark hair piled on top of her head, and a high-necked frilly white blouse fastened with a large jeweled brooch. The husband had one of those scary mad-scientist beards, slicked-down hair parted in the middle, and a pair of pince-nez perched on his beaklike nose. The wife held a fair-haired toddler on her lap, and a little boy dressed in a sailor suit, with a toy boat clutched in his hand, stood at attention with his papa's hand on his shoulder.

"The Dempseys," Tee said. "Dad would know everybody's name, but I think the little boy in the sailor suit would be Augustus." He tapped the image of the child. "He's the one who started the bedspread factory. I guess he'd be, what? Your great-great-grandfather?"

"Don't know," I admitted. I gestured at all the photos. "I've never seen or heard of any of these people before."

Tee started back up the stairs. "You will. Guthrie's that kind of town. You won't have to bother to look up your family tree. Everybody in town will be more than willing to explain how they're related to you through your third cousin twice removed."

"Like I care," I muttered under my breath.

We walked quickly past the room Ella Kate had gone into, and down the wide stair landing. Tee paused in front of the last door at the end of the hall.

I opened the door. The room was tiny, with sloping walls, faded blue-sprigged flowered wallpaper, and a jumble of old suitcases and broken furniture. "This was probably a nursery, or maybe a trunk room," I said, turning to go out.

"How can you tell?" Tee asked.

"The way the walls slope, you couldn't get an adult bed in there," I pointed out. "And a lot of old houses had rooms like this. Sometimes they called them cradle rooms."

"Never heard of that before, but it makes sense," he agreed.

The door on the other side of the hallway from the trunk room turned out to be a large, high-ceilinged bedroom. I found the light switch, which revealed a big brass bed standing in the middle of the room. The bed held a lumpy, naked mattress, and the floor, though dusty, was covered with a frayed and faded pale pink hooked rug in a floral motif. The only other furniture was a huge mirrored mahogany armoire, and an Empire mahogany dresser with round glass knobs. Faded chintz curtains hung limply at a double window.

"Home sweet home," I said briskly, walking around the room.

Tee looked dubiously at the bed. "You're going to sleep on that?"

"For now," I said, walking back out into the hallway and opening more doors. I found another bathroom, to my great relief. It was old-fashioned and in dire need of paint and bleach, but at least, I thought, there was a bathtub, and running water. I'd begun to have my doubts. Next to the bathroom I opened a narrow door and was thrilled to discover a linen closet.

The closet smelled of mothballs, but its shelves were loaded with linens—heavily starched and pressed—yellowing sheets and pillowcases, wool blankets encased in cracked-plastic zipper cases, and stacks of threadbare pastel towels. On the top shelf of the closet I found a couple of sad-looking feather pillows in age-stained ticking cases. The next-to-top shelf held a stack of neatly folded white chenille bedspreads. I pulled one out and unfolded it. A slip of paper floated to the floor. I picked it up and read out loud, " 'Martha Washington Model. Finest Quality. Dempsey Mills. Guthrie, Georgia.' "

Tee rubbed a corner of the spread. "This one feels like it's never been used. My grandmother had a spread just like this in her guest bed-room. Probably everybody else in town had one too."

I gathered the pillows, a set of sheets, pillowcases, a blanket, and the spread into my arms and headed back toward my new bedroom.

Tee followed me. "Need a hand?" he asked, leaning against the door-jamb and watching as I tucked the starchy linen sheet around the mat-tress.

"Nope. I'm good," I told him. "I've got a bed, and a blanket to keep me warm. That's all I need for tonight. I'm going to unpack, and then do like Ella Kate. Go to bed with the chickens."

"If you're sure then," he said. He reached inside his jacket and brought out a business card. "My cell number is on there," he said. "Feel free to call if you need anything."

I thanked him and walked him downstairs and to the front door. "I will call you tomorrow, if you don't mind," I said. "I've got to see about transportation—whether it's my great-uncle's car, or whatever. And I'll need directions to the store."

"Anything at all," he assured me.

When he was gone, I locked the dead bolt, then walked through the downstairs rooms, at a more leisurely pace this time, making mental lists of all that needed to be done. First, I promised myself, I would get the front yard cleared. And give the place a thorough scrubbing. Once some of the layers of grime were removed, I'd be better able to tell the full extent of the repairs that Birdsong needed.

As I shut off the lights in those cold, dusty rooms, I was surprised to find myself excited, rather than depressed, by the job ahead of me. In Washington, I'd spent my workdays attending meetings and hearings, drafting documents in arcane legalese. Rarely, if ever, did I get to see any real concrete evidence of how I'd spent my working days—and evenings. But here, at this old wreck of a house, one swipe of a wet mop would make a remarkable difference.

By the time I got to the kitchen, I realized, with a start, that I hadn't eaten anything since the bag of peanuts I'd been handed on my flight hours earlier. My stomach growled.

I opened the refrigerator door, half afraid of what I would find there. But the contents, though sparse, seemed surprisingly normal. There was a quart of milk, a pint of half-and-half, some bowls with aluminum-foil toppers, a half-empty package of lunch meat, a packet of plastic-wrapped cheese slices, and the usual condiments; pickles, mayonnaise, mustard.

After retrieving a plate from one of the cupboards, I helped myself to a slice of the lunch meat and a slice of the cheese. Another cupboard revealed a small stash of pantry staples—saltine crackers, a box of oatmeal, cans of generic-brand soup, tuna, beans, and Spam.

In five minutes, I had a pan of tomato soup heating on the stove, while I devoured a hastily made plate of cheese and crackers. When the soup was ready, I sat at the enamel-topped kitchen table and slurped it down happily.

Upstairs, I climbed quickly into my warmest flannel pajamas and got into the bed and under the blanket and bedspread I'd heaped on top. I reached for my cell phone and dialed.

"Dempsey?" Mitch answered on the third ring. "Is something wrong?"

"Not really," I said. "Just wanted to let you know I'm in Guthrie. I met Mr. Berryhill, the lawyer, and I'm actually staying at Birdsong tonight."

"How is it?" he asked anxiously.

"Well, it's, uh, sorta run down," I said slowly, remembering Ella Kate's assessment. "In fact, Dad, to tell you the truth, it's a big mess. Much worse than I expected."

"How much worse?"

"It's got a roof," I said. "And plumbing. And wiring. If it has heat, it's not currently turned on. The kitchen's pretty bad. Bathrooms are going to need major updating. I haven't been able to take a good look around the outside yet, but I can tell you that the front-porch columns look pretty rickety."

"Oh."

"I guess we're going to need to talk about a budget," I said, rushing on. "Because a coat of paint and some new wallpaper aren't going to do the trick. And there's one more thing, Dad."

"What the hell else could there be?"

"Do you remember an old lady named Ella Kate Timmons?"

"No. Why should I? I was only a kid when we moved from Guthrie."

"She's some sort of cousin, according to Mr. Berryhill. She remembers when you were a little boy. You pulled her cat's tail."

"Dempsey, what's this about?" Mitch asked. "Pilar and I are at the boys' school for parent-teacher night. I'm supposed to be looking at Garrett's art portfolio. I told you, I don't remember anybody named Ella Kate."

Wow. Parent-teacher night at the preschool. I couldn't remember Mitch ever going to any meetings at my school. Ever.

"Dempsey? I really need to get back in there."

I took a deep breath. "It's just that Ella Kate is living here."

"Where?"

"Right here. In Birdsong. She and Shorty are living upstairs. She doesn't like me. According to the lawyer, she really, really doesn't like the Killebrews. She's mad that your uncle Norbert didn't leave the house to her, because she took care of him when he was sick."

"And?" I could hear children's voices in the background. And Pilar. "What's she sayin'?" Pilar asked. "What's goin' on up there?"

"The thing is, Dad, Ella Kate Timmons is kinda squatting here at Birdsong. And it doesn't look like she's going to get out anytime soon."

"For God's sake, Dempsey," Mitch said irritably. "It's just an old lady. If she's living there, she's doing it illegally. Talk to the lawyers. Get them to draft something and make her get out. For that matter, you're a lawyer. File an injunction or something. All right? We'll talk later about the budget."

He hung up. I got out of bed, turned off the light, and buried myself back underneath the covers. An injunction. Against a shotgun-toting old lady who had some kind of vendetta against me and my father's family.

Things, I thought, were going to get interesting.

13

"My" bathroom had a high ceiling, a yacht-size bathtub, and an old-fashioned pedestal sink. Those were the pluses. The minuses were lengthy. The fluorescent light over the cloudy mirrored medicine cabinet winked on and off as though tele-graphing an ominous message. The tiny hexagon-shaped tiles were cracked and yellowed with age. The sink, the commode, and the tub bore decades' worth of rust stains, and their porcelain coatings were pock-marked with chips. But when I stepped into the tub and turned on the hot-water faucet, I got the nastiest surprise of all.

The old pipes groaned and knocked behind the cracked plaster. A thin trickle of lukewarm brownish water finally came sputtering out of the showerhead. It was the fastest shower I'd ever taken. A new hot-water heater would definitely be on my shopping list.

When I got downstairs, there was no sign of Ella Kate. But there was a note, in crabbed handwriting, Scotch-taped to the refrigerator door.

Actually, it was more of a bill than a note.

1 can tomato soup—67 cents
2 slices American cheese—(Borden) 42 cents
1 package saltine crackers—(Best-Maid) 80 cents
Cash only. Miss Ella Kate Timmons.

"Caught red-handed," I muttered, tucking the note in the pocket of my jeans. As I heated water for a cup of instant coffee, I wondered how the old lady would amortize the price of a tablespoon of Piggly Wiggly coffee. Deciding to err on the side of generous, I found a pencil in one of

the drawers and made an addendum to her note—"Cup of coffee—$1."
I taped three dollar bills to the note, and put it back on the door of the
pink fridge.

As I sipped my coffee, I made my first list of the day. It consisted
mostly of every kind of cleaning supply I could think of, plus enough
basic groceries to get me through the week without dipping into Ella
Kate's larder.

The kitchen was still chilly, but sun streamed in through the window, which I took to be a good sign. After rinsing out my coffee cup, I
zipped up my fleece sweatshirt and stepped outside. A squirrel perched
on the limb of a nearby oak tree chattered at the sight of me, and I
heard rustling in the underbrush. A cardinal made a bright splash of
red as it darted from the handlebars of one of the rusted bicycles I'd
seen last night, and two or three small bright-winged birds hopped
about on the ground, pecking at a sprinkling of bread crumbs. So. Ella
Kate had established her own nature preserve at the aptly named Birdsong.

I picked up another stout stick, and beat back the undergrowth as I
began my exploration of the grounds. A few yards from the kitchen I
came up against a dilapidated outbuilding of weathered gray clap-
boards. I'd passed right by it the night before, but hadn't even noticed
it in the dwindling light of day.

With effort, I managed to pull the double wooden doors open. Rusting hinges screamed a protest, and the doors scraped against the concrete floor of the building as I yanked them open.

The shed was more barn than garage, but resting inside I was thrilled
to find a dark red American-made sedan. "The Catfish, I presume," I
said aloud, walking around the car to appraise its roadworthiness.

The Crown Vic's paint job was faded to a dull maroon, and the car
was covered with a thick film of dust, but I noted that the tires seemed
fine. The doors were unlocked, so I slid into the black-vinyl-covered
driver's seat. "Keys," I muttered, "where are the keys, Ella Kate?" I
flipped down the sun visor, but no keys fell out. Checked under both
floor mats, unsuccessfully. Dejected, I got out of the car and walked
around the shed.

A workbench at the back of the building held ancient, rusting cans of paint; a jumble of tools; and jars of nails, screws, bolts, and other hardware. Finally, on a Peg-Board rack nailed to the wall above the bench, I found a ring of keys. Most of the keys looked like house keys, and a few were large, old-fashioned latchkeys, but finally, I found one that looked like a car key.

The Crown Vic's motor coughed politely when I turned the key, and then died. "Damn!" I tried again, gave it a little gas, and the engine roared to life. I wanted to cheer. Instead, I gave it a little more gas, and the engine hummed agreeably. I checked the gas gauge. There was a quarter of a tank! None of the other gauges was issuing any alarming levels, and no warning signals flashed on the dashboard.

Barely able to suppress my excitement, I hopped out of the car, found a rag on the workbench, and wiped off the windshield and rear window. Back in the driver's seat, I adjusted the mirrors, and slowly backed the car out of the shed, my heart thumping a mile a minute. I managed to make a three-point turn, wincing as tree branches slapped and scraped at the paint.

Despite my initial impression that the old driveway was impassable, I discovered that by going slowly and steering the car down the center of the cracked concrete path, I could barely, and with more scrapes, make it out to the street without the use of a machete, or even the bush hog that Tee Berryhill had recommended.

Once I was on Poplar Street, I felt another rush of exhilarating free-dom that reminded me of my first time behind the wheel, after I'd passed my driver's exam at sixteen. I had to stop and think to remember when the last time was that I had actually driven. Had it been over a year ago, when Pilar had pressed me into car-pool duty for the twins?

Retracing the route Becky and I had taken the day before, I made my way back to the business district. The Catfish's engine was surpris-ingly powerful, and I had to make an effort to stay under the speed limit.

I found the hardware store again with no trouble. Once inside, I steered my shopping cart up and down the aisles, loading it with mops and brooms, plastic trash bags, window cleaner, Pine-Sol, Comet, rubber gloves, paint scrapers, steel wool, and every other implement I could find to help in my cleaning project.

I studied the paint chips in the paint department for nearly an hour, debating the merits of white versus cream, sage versus celery, tan versus taupe. I was so lost in my own mental rainbow that I realized, with a start, that a man was standing right beside me, peering over my shoulder at the cards I held fanned out in my hand.

"Aww, no," he drawled, plucking the taupe card from my hand. "You don't wanna go with that color. Every yuppie in Atlanta is painting their media room Bennington. I swear to God, it's the Pottery Barn influence. Everybody wants their house to look like the goddamn Pottery Barn catalog."

I blinked. "I happen to love Pottery Barn."

He was unfazed. "Baby, that's all right for one of those minimansions up in Alpharetta or Dunwoody, but you're living in a nineteenth-century Greek Revival mansion in Guthrie, Georgia. Why would you wanna junk it up like that?"

I took a step back. My unpaid paint adviser smiled, revealing a set of brilliant white teeth. Despite the weather outside, he was deeply tanned, with light brown hair having just a touch of gray at the temples. His eyes were a brilliant green, with laugh lines etched into the corners, and he had a cleft chin. He was dressed for a day on the greens, albeit a winter day, in khaki golf shorts, a long-sleeved pale yellow V-neck argyle sweater, and well-worn Top-Siders. His calves were muscular, and his legs were just as deeply tanned as his face.

"Do I know you?" I asked.

He stuck out his hand. "You do now. Jimmy Maynard. And you're Dempsey Killebrew, right?"

I took his hand and shook it. "I am. How did you—"

"Saw you drive up in the Catfish," he said. "Carter Berryhill was telling me about you just last night at the country club. Doesn't take a rocket scientist to figure out that the pretty lady driving old Norbert's car must be his niece."

"Great-great-niece," I corrected him. I looked down at the paint chips in my hand. He plucked one in a warm white, and another in a deep black-green, and held them up. "This one, this white, for the outside. And then, the window casings, you wanna do them in this Charleston green. Give 'em some depth. The rest of the trim, you wanna find a medium espresso tone. I'd do the front door in a barn red. Benjamin Moore's got one I like, but you'll have to drive to Macon for that. You'll do oil—not latex, right? A primer, then at least two coats. The paint guys, they'll tell you all you need is one coat, but take it from me, it's gonna take an ocean to cover up that puke pink ya got now. I know, I know, oil's a pain in the butt to work with, but Dempsey, honey, Birdsong is a historic property. You don't wanna go muckin' it up with cheap paint."

"Are you an interior designer?"

"Me?" He hooted derisively. "An interior designer? No, ma'am, not on your life. Here." He pulled a money clip from the pocket of his golf shorts, and handed me a business card.

MAYNARD & ASSOCIATES, it read. JAMES R. MAYNARD, PRINCIPAL. There were two phone numbers, and an address.

"Real estate sales," he prompted. "I do a little consulting, a little insurance work, some property management. But it's mostly real estate that pays the bills."

"I see."

I started to hand back the business card, but he gently pushed my hand away. "Keep it. You're gonna need it. You ask around. Ask ol' Carter, or Tee, or anybody else. Buyin' or sellin' let Jimmy do the tellin'. That's my motto. Corny, huh? But you'll remember it. I guarantee."

"Uh, thanks."

He laughed. "Aw, now. Did I come on too strong?"

"Well," I began. "I just got here. I'm still feeling my way around. It's my first time in Guthrie."

"Carter mentioned that," Jimmy said. "And he did say your daddy is Mitch Killebrew. I used to know some Killebrews, when I was at Auburn. You any kin to them?"

"Uh, I'm not sure. My father was an only child, and he and his dad moved away from Guthrie when he was a little boy. Mitch only came back here a couple of times after that. He barely remembers his time here."

"I gotcha," Jimmy said. "Well, it's not a bad town. Not once you get used to small-town life." He cocked his head. "From your accent, or lack of one, I'd say you didn't grow up in a small town. Not in the South, anyway."

I realized I was being grilled, but Jimmy Maynard was such a skilled practitioner, I found myself giving in to his unabashed charm.

"We lived in Atlanta until my early teens, but after my mom remarried and moved to California, Mitch and I moved around a lot. Nashville, Orlando, places like that. I went to boarding school in Richmond."

"And you're a lawyer, I hear tell."

"Does everybody in this town already know all my business?"

He laughed again. "Not all of it. Not yet, anyway. But give us a few days."

"From the look of Birdsong, I'm going to be here for quite a few days," I told him. I started to push my cart toward the cash register, intending that to be a signal that our paint consultation was done.

But Jimmy Maynard didn't shake that easily.

"You're not gonna try and tackle that place all by your lonesome, are you?" He looked me up and down. "Expensive jeans, I can't see the label, but I'm guessing those are Nine Lives. They run, what, a hundred and fifty bucks? Suede boots, North Face parka. You studying to start painting dressed like that?"

"These are Nine Lives," I said, "but actually, they cost more like a hundred and seventy-five. And thanks for reminding me. My girlfriend told me to buy myself some Carharrts."

"Next aisle over," Jimmy said. "Don't think I'm a pervert or anything, but it's a shame to hide a cute little butt like yours in a pair of them big ol' baggy Carharrts."

My eyes widened, and I felt myself blushing.

"Aw, damn," Maynard said. "There I go again. My second wife used to tell me, 'Jimmy, you need a filter between your brain and your big mouth.' Guess that was maybe one of the few things she was right

The Fixer Upper ⟶ 75

about. I'm sorry, ma'am, for being so forward." He bowed deeply. "Please accept my heartfelt apologies for such a boorish comment."

I giggled despite myself.

"You do forgive me," Maynard said. "Now, you gotta let me make it up to you. How 'bout lunch? I know, it's early yet, but Tuesday's pot roast day at the Corner Café, and you gotta get there no later than eleven thirty, because they'll run out, just as sure as shooting, and you'll be stuck with the shepherd's pie."

My stomach growled at the mention of food, but I refused to give in to temptation.

"I do forgive you," I said. "But if you've seen Birdsong, you know the kind of job I've got facing me. I don't dare stop for lunch. Not today."

"All right," he conceded. "I can see you're a lady with a mission. But would it be all right if I stopped by someday, to check up on your progress? Birdsong used to be a hell of a place. I'll be anxious to see what you do with it."

I made a wry face. "The first thing I'm going to do is scrub it, from top to bottom. Then I'll start thinking about paint and all the rest of it. And sure, stop by anytime." I flashed him a grin of my own. "But be forewarned, if you do come by, I might just put you to work."

He grinned back. And at that moment, I realized, I'd just engaged in my first, official, small-town flirt. And it felt pretty darned good.

made a quick stop at the Piggly Wiggly for groceries. Not that I intended to do much cooking. Moving around with Mitch, and then through college, law school, and my life as a lobbyist, I'd never had the time or the inclination to become much of a cook. On the hill, my roommates and I managed to subsist on coffee, bagels, business lunches, and cocktail receptions.

Now, I realized, things were about to change. As Lynda had pointed out, there was no Starbucks in Guthrie. And unless I intended to let Jimmy Maynard treat me to lunch on a daily basis at the Corner Café, I was going to have to learn to feed myself. Quick and cheap would be my bywords. I bought some frozen casseroles, canned soup, lots of yogurt, cereal, and salad fixings. And a big bag of French roast coffee beans. One thing I couldn't do was deal with instant coffee.

At the checkout counter, the cashier, a middle-aged woman with long, beribboned braids, gave me a bright smile. "You're Mr. Norbert's niece, aren't you?"

Did everybody in Guthrie know me by sight already?

I smiled back. "Well, I'm his great-great-niece. Dempsey Killebrew."

"And I'm Chellie. Chellie Tighe. My husband, Dave, is kin to the Dempseys on his mama's side, I think, but I can't keep all that stuff straight. Anyway, welcome to Guthrie. How are you settlin' in over there at Birdsong? Is Ella Kate cutting up something awful over having you there?"

"She didn't exactly roll out the welcome wagon," I said. "But we'll get along. There's a lot of work to be done."

Chellie rolled her eyes. "Honey, that's the understatement of the year. At least when Mr. Norbert was alive, he kept up the yard. He used to have the prettiest camellias in town. Buttercups too. And roses. He'd cut roses and bring 'em in here, to Delores over at the bank, and church, of course. After Norbert passed, I think Ella Kate tried for a little while, but it all got to be too much for her. She's gotta be eighty if she's a day. Anyway, you're young. And you're skinny, but I reckon you're probably strong too. You'll do just fine, long as you don't let Ella Kate mow you down."

"Thanks," I said, handing her my money. "I'll try to keep that in mind."

When I got back to the house, I was surprised to see a pickup truck loaded with rakes and mowers and other lethal-looking implements parked at the curb. A tall mound of tree limbs and vines was stacked there too, and I could hear the high-pitched whine of a chain saw.

I grabbed a bag of groceries and followed the racket up the driveway. A young man in jeans and a flannel shirt was flailing away at a sapling with the saw. When he saw me, he cut the saw's motor.

"Hi," I said. "Did I hire you to clear the property?"

"No'm," he said. "Mr. Carter sent me over. He told me to tell you it'll be billed to your daddy."

That was fine by me.

When I let myself in the kitchen door, I found, to my relief, that Ella Kate seemed to have decamped.

Upstairs, I paused outside Ella Kate's bedroom door. I tapped lightly, but there was no answer. As I'd expected, her door was locked.

But the next door down was unlocked. This one was another large, square bedroom, approximately the same size as the one I'd claimed for myself.

The wallpaper was peeling, but charming, with a floral stripe of blue morning glories. A narrow bed with a tall iron headboard and footboard was covered by an old army blanket, a worn quilt folded at the foot. The tall oak dresser had a delicately embroidered linen runner with what looked like hand-crocheted edging. Set on top of it was a tarnished silver comb and hairbrush set with a few white hairs still clinging to the bristles. Beside the brush sat a hinged double tintype portrait of the couple I recognized from the picture on the stair landing. I peered closely at them, trying to recognize my Dempsey ancestors. Was there something in the set of the chin? The woman's was narrow, making her face nearly heart shaped. Her lips were thin and unsmiling, but the upper lip had a hint of a cupid's bow. I'd spent a lot of time trying to get lip liner around my own cupid's-bow upper lip.

I opened a narrow closet door. Apparently, I'd found great-uncle Norbert's bedroom. Six white dress shirts hung stiffly from their hangers, their collars and cuffs yellowed with age and blotched with brownish rust stains. Four or five faded flannel shirts hung beside those, telling me that Norbert favored utility over formality. There was a rusty black suit with narrow lapels in a plastic dry cleaner's bag, and on a nail hanging from the back of the closet door I saw three silk neckties in sober maroon and navy stripes. A hook held two pairs of denim overalls, softened from what must have been hundreds of hours of work and washings. On the floor of the closet were a pair of dusty black lace-up dress shoes, a pair of work boots, and a pair of paint-spattered high-top Chuck Taylor Converse sneakers.

Chucks! I picked them up and sniffed. They smelled like red clay and turpentine. I set the shoes down gently.

Back in my bedroom, I undressed and slid my legs into the Carharrts. They were as stiff as a board and ugly as mud. I surveyed myself in the age-clouded dresser mirror and frowned at what I saw. They were big and boxy, and though I'd used the size chart at the hardware store as a guide, they were four inches too big around the waist, and at least six inches too long. Not to mention the fact that they felt like sandpaper long johns. I could roll up the hems of the pants and cinch them with a belt, but until they'd been washed at least a couple of times, they just wouldn't do.

But Uncle Norbert's clothes might. I hurried down the hall, dressed only in my panties, bra, and socks, and helped myself.

Norbert had been tall, but thankfully, what my mother would have called a "string bean." I pulled one of the flannel shirts over my head and rolled up the cuffs four times. The overalls, soft as an old blanket, were several sizes too long too, but I managed to adjust the straps, and with the pants legs rolled up, I judged them perfect. And what about shoes? The work boots were stiff and mud caked, but I took another look at those Chucks.

Uncle Norbert had been tall and slender, but his feet were surprisingly small for a man, maybe only a size larger than my own. With another pair of socks for extra padding, I decided, the Chucks would work like a charm.

I rummaged around in Norbert's dresser until I found a stash of neatly washed and ironed handkerchiefs, including a large blue bandanna, which I folded and knotted over my head, kerchief style.

I was ready to do battle with Birdsong.

Although it was still chilly, not even fifty degrees, the day was sunny. I lugged a broom, a mop, a bucket of hot sudsy Pine-Sol, and my iPod out to the front porch. I slipped the iPod into the front pocket of the overalls, put in my earbuds, and got to work.

I'd downloaded the rereleased Michael Jackson *Thriller* album before leaving D.C., and now, with Michael and his celebrity buddies moonwalking in my head, I rocked it hard.

Starting at the front door, I swept my way up and down the porch, knocking down spiderwebs, desiccated insect carcasses, long-abandoned birds' nests, and a forest of dead leaves as Michael sang "Wanna Be Startin' Somethin'." Three times, because I kept punching rewind. But even after an hour of sweeping, dirt and mildew clung stubbornly to the worn wooden floorboards. I sloshed Pine-Sol all over the porch, and attacked with the mop, and "Beat It," smiling with satisfaction as the water in my bucket grew grimy with the accumulated grunge. Four changes of water and two hours later, I decided the floor was done. I'd scrubbed down the old boards so hard that I could see bare wood shining through the faded battleship gray paint.

The windows, and "Billie Jean," were next. The panes were so caked with grime I didn't even attempt to start with the Windex. Instead, I hooked up a garden hose and splashed water all over the old wavy glass, sending a dirty river seeping down over my previously pristine floorboards. Damn. I'd have to give the porch another rinsing later. But for now, I washed and polished and spritzed the eight tall windows that ran across the front of the house, inside and out, until they sparkled like crystal in the afternoon sunshine.

I'd saved the front door for last. I scrubbed away layer after layer of dirt and dust, finally revealing, to my surprise, a faded red paint job where I'd thought was previously a dull gray one. Jimmy Maynard had been right. Birdsong was meant to have a red front door. And a handsome door it was. From the look of the bare wood peeping from underneath the old paint, I decided it must be heart pine. There were six finely detailed raised panels, with a beveled-glass insert and beveled-glass sidelights, along with a fan-shaped transom above the door that I couldn't reach without a ladder.

With an old toothbrush I'd found under the kitchen sink, and "PYT" blasting into my ears, I worked brass cleaner into the large elaborately worked doorknob and faceplates, the knocker, even the faceplate around the cheap, splintered plastic doorbell. That doorbell would be my first rehab project, I decided. A door as grand as this one deserved better. I didn't know where I'd get something like a reproduction doorbell in Guthrie. This might take a little research. Fortunately, research was my forte. And at least, I knew, Guthrie had a public library, because I'd passed it earlier in the day.

With the porch rinsed off again, the windows clean, and the brass shining brightly, I decided to step back to take it all in. The iPod was playing "Thriller" as I moonwalked down the wet concrete steps, and a few steps away into the yard.

I stood there, bobbing my head and singing along, thrilled with my results. Once the top layer of dirt was removed, I could see, for the first time, that Birdsong really could be something fine.

But my elation was mixed with the overwhelming realization of all I still had to accomplish. It had taken me an entire day just to get this far. The yardman and his chain saw were gone now, and three head-high piles of vines and tree limbs were stacked at the curb. The good news was that the house was actually visible from the street now. The bad news was that I could see the full extent of Birdsong's state of decay. Ivy and kudzu crept over the side of the house, and had covered what little foundation plantings remained. My hands itched to start yanking at vines and limbs, but my arms were already screaming from the unaccustomed punishment I'd given them that day. No Pilates workout had ever left me this sore.

And the inside of the house. My God, I hadn't even started there. Did I have enough energy left to at least open the front door and start sweeping my way from the front of the house to the back?

A tap on my shoulder made me jump nearly a foot. I whirled around, wild eyed, to see a bemused Tee Berryhill standing there, holding a lethal-looking machete in one hand and a pair of long-handled tree clippers in the other. He was dressed in a navy blue suit, and once again, he had a necktie stuffed in the breast pocket of his jacket.

"Jesus!" I exclaimed. "Where did you come from?"

He reached over and tugged at my earbuds. "I've been standing here for five minutes, watching your dance routine. I called your name, but you didn't hear me. What the hell are you listening to?"

My cheeks burned with embarrassment. Had he seen the whole thing? The whole hip-swaying, finger-popping routine I'd done to "Billie Jean"?

"It's *Thriller*," I said lamely. "The rerelease."

"Wow," he said, walking up toward the porch. "It must work for you. The porch looks great. How long have you been working like this?"

"Hours?" I shrugged. "I lost track of the time."

And I had. The sun had slipped below the tree line, and the air had gotten chillier.

"It's after five," Tee said. He held up the machete. "I meant to bring these over earlier today, but I got caught up myself with a hearing in Milledgeville. Anyway, I see you beat me to the punch. You got the yard cleared out yourself? You're Wonder Woman!"

"Not really," I admitted. "I was wondering how I could ever tackle this disaster, but when I got back from the supermarket and the hardware store, there was already a guy here with a chain saw. Your dad sent him over."

"You got the Catfish running? Man, you don't waste any time, do you?"

"No time to waste," I said. "I did a walk-through this morning. And it's even worse than I expected."

He gave me a stiff pat on my shoulder. "Well, from the looks of things out here, you've made a good start. Are you ready to knock off for the day?"

"Yeah," I said, already feeling the energy seep from my body. "My mind wants to keep going, but my body says, 'Hell no.'"

"I vote for hell no too," Tee said. "Now, what about some food? I know for a fact that Ella Kate doesn't keep much in the way of food in the house. So Dad sent me over to bring you back for supper."

"Oh, no," I said quickly. "I'm a mess. And—"

"Come along," Tee said, gently taking my arm and tugging me toward the front door. "Day shift is over. I guess you didn't hear the mill whistle blow?"

"I haven't heard anything but Michael Jackson for the past few hours," I admitted. "Anyway, isn't the mill closed? Why would the whistle still blow?"

"It's a long story," he said, heading up the front steps. "We'll fill you in over supper."

15

After I'd showered and was changing into some respectable clothes, I could hear voices downstairs. At one point, I heard a dog's sharp bark, then a woman's voice, and Tee's, and then a door slamming.

He was sitting on a bench in the hallway when I rejoined him.

"Was that Ella Kate?"

He jerked his head in the direction of the front door. "It was. I invited her to join us for dinner, but she politely declined. I believe she had a previous engagement."

I raised an eyebrow. "Politely?"

"Her exact words were 'I'd rather choke than eat with her and you two ambulance chasers.'"

"Oh dear."

"At least she didn't throw anything at me this time."

Tee filled me in on Guthrie's social strata on the drive over to his house.

"That house there," he said, pointing to an imposing brick Colonial Revival mansion a few doors down the block, "belonged to one of the Dempseys. Dad could tell you exactly which one. Local gossips say that what money he didn't blow on wine, women, and song, he lost speculating on the stock market. It's changed hands a bunch of times over the years. Now it belongs to some dot-com genius. She's not even thirty."

"Nice house," I said, pressing my face to the car window. "And I bet she didn't even have to kill any spiders to get it that way."

He showed me the mayor's house too, a gray-shingled bungalow with a huge old oak tree in the front yard. A tire swing hung from the tree's lowest branch, and an assortment of brightly colored plastic toys lay on the ground around the tree. "He's got triplets, all girls, four years old," Tee said. "Poor guy, I don't think he knows what hit him."

I nodded sympathetically. "I know the feeling. My dad has twins that age."

"You've got brothers who are four?"

"Half brothers. My stepmother is quite a bit younger. They're little devils too."

Finally, he pulled up to a charming white-frame cottage encircled by a low boxwood hedge and a dark green picket fence. A discreet wrought-iron sign hanging from the mailbox told me we'd arrived at BERRY HILL.

"Oh!" I said with a sigh. "I love it already. Berry Hill. That's adorable."

He made a wry face. "The name was Mama's idea. She even planted raspberry vines to grow on that fence, and there's a patch of rabbit-eye blueberries out back. The birds eat up most of 'em now, but when she was alive, she put up enough jam to feed pharoah's army."

"How long has she been gone?"

He got out, came around, and opened my door, a true Southern gentleman. "Let's see. She was diagnosed with breast cancer right before I took my bar exam, and six months later she was dead. So that's, what? Ten years, I guess."

"And your dad never remarried?"

He laughed. "Not for lack of trying. Every woman in this town under the age of eighty has done her level best to save 'poor ol' Carter' from his pitiful life as a bachelor. He goes along and allows himself to be fixed up, but I don't think he's had a second date in all these years."

I was about to ask about Tee's own marital status, but now Carter himself was standing in the doorway, a clean dish towel wrapped around his waist and a glass of wine in his outstretched hand.

"Dempsey!" he said, giving me an impromptu hug.

"This is for you," he said, handing me the glass. "I don't figure you for a teetotaler."

"You figured right," I said, taking a sip. "And although I went to the grocery store, I totally forgot to hit the liquor store."

Tee and Carter laughed at my ignorance.

"Honey, you can't buy liquor in Guthrie," Carter said. "We're dry as dust. You'll have to drive over to the next county to BJ's Bottle Shop if you want a drink of anything stronger than Coca-Cola. Or come over here to Berry Hill."

He walked me into the living room, and I stood for a moment admiring my surroundings. With its walls of horizontal pine paneling, muted chintz-upholstered sofas and chairs, worn oriental rugs and gold-framed paintings, the Berry Hill living room looked like a room that was lived in and enjoyed. The fireplace was surrounded by bookshelves crammed with leather-bound books, and a leather club chair pulled up beside the fireplace held a folded-up copy of *The New Yorker*.

"What a nice room," I said, pausing in front of a surprisingly good oil landscape.

"All of this was Sarah's doing," Carter said. "Tee and I just try to keep it from looking too much like a fraternity house."

"You've done a good job," I said, warming my backside in front of the fire.

"You should see what Dempsey's done over at Birdsong, Dad," Tee told his father, emerging from the other room with his own glass of wine. "It's the first time since I can remember that you can tell what color the front of the house is painted."

"And that reminds me," I said. "Thank you so much for sending over your yardman. I had no idea how I was going to tackle that jungle. He worked wonders. Unfortunately, now you can actually get a good look at that paint Tee mentioned. Pink. Ugh."

Carter handed me a polished silver tray. Perched on top of a paper doily were an assortment of warm miniquiches. I took one and tasted. "Nice," I said, not bothering to hide my surprise.

"Don't be too impressed," Tee warned. "We've got a freezer full of this kinda stuff from the discount store over in Macon."

We sat by the fire and chatted for a while, doing that practiced little dance you do when you're sizing up new acquaintances for their potential as friends. The Berryhills, father and son, were easy to be around. I could tell by their verbal sparring that they were genuinely fond of each other.

After a leisurely cocktail hour, during which time Carter disappeared several times to "check on my masterpiece," as he put it, he decided everything was ready.

"Hope you like salmon," Carter said, again tucking my arm into the crook of his elbow to escort me into the dining room.

"Love it," I said. "But then, anything you serve me will be a treat. I'm not much of a cook myself."

"Neither is he," Tee said, taking my other arm and steering me toward my chair as Carter went back to the kitchen. "But that never stopped him. Salmon, little dinky roasted potatoes, and poached asparagus with dill sauce, which is what's on tonight's menu, is his company dinner. The rest of the week, it's strictly by the book. Monday is rice and beans, Tuesday's baked chicken, Wednesday is Hamburger Helper, and Thursday's some kind of casserole made with the leftover chicken."

"Are you complaining about my cuisine?" Carter asked, coming in from the kitchen with a platter of food.

"Not me," Tee said, standing up and serving me a slice of the salmon, along with the aforesaid potatoes and asparagus.

While the men served themselves, I took the time to look around the dining room. The walls were painted a soft robin's-egg blue, and cream-colored linen curtains hung from a bay window that looked out onto a back garden. A large crystal chandelier hung over the table, which was covered with a floor-length damask tablecloth. The chairs were Sheraton, with seat covers in a blue chintz. All the artwork was of large tropical birds—parrots, macaws, flamingos, and egrets—framed in heavy gilt-edged frames.

I got up to look at the largest print. "Is this a Menaboni?" I asked.

Carter looked pleased. "Yes, ma'am," he said. "You know art?"

I sat back down. "Not a lot. But I've seen Menaboni prints in magazines. These are really lovely."

"Sarah's doing," Carter said. "I'm just an old country lawyer. You could put what I know about art and antiques and all that mess in your hat. But she just loved that kind of stuff. Went to symposiums at the High Museum in Atlanta, read books, and when we traveled, she always made it a point to go see the art museums and antiques shops. She loved to go to auctions best of all. She'd study the catalogs, read up on the history of anything she was interested in, and go in there ready to do battle. I told her she should have been a horse trader."

I looked over at the sideboard, a massive, dark oak piece that held dozens of pieces of blue-and-white transferware china. "Is that Canton ware?" I asked. "It looks like the real thing."

"It surely is," Carter said. "Those plates were Sarah's pride and joy. She bought them at an auction in New Orleans when we were down there for a bar association meeting. Never would admit to me what she paid. Not that I would have cared." His face grew serious. "They were the last things she bought before she got sick."

Tee raised an eyebrow. "How does a lobbyist-slash-lawyer happen to know about all this stuff?"

I blushed. "I'll tell you my dirty little secret. I'm a closet interior designer. When I was in law school, stressed out over studying or finishing a research paper? While everybody else was out getting sloshed at the bars, I'd hole up in my apartment and read decorating magazines. I've got stacks of them, everywhere. Mario Buatta is my idol."

Carter looked puzzled. "The race-car driver?"

Tee snickered.

"No, I think that's Mario Andretti. Mario Buatta is a famous interior designer. The prince of chintz, they call him. But I'm also a fan of Charlotte Moss and Bunny Williams. Pretty silly, huh?"

"No sillier than a lawyer wasting billable hours running a small-town newspaper," Carter said mildly.

Tee's smile looked forced. "Here we go again." He stood up and started clearing our plates, mercifully ignoring my half-eaten salmon. "Coffee, Dempsey? We're brewing Starbucks tonight. We buy the whole beans in Macon."

I got up hurriedly. "Only if you let me help with the dishes."

"Absolutely not!" Carter exclaimed. "I'm looking forward to hearing all about your budding friendship with Ella Kate."

"Not until I've at least loaded the dishwasher," I said.

He followed Tee and me into the kitchen. It was a small room, probably last modernized in the 1960s, but with its yellow-and-white checkerboard linoleum floor and white-painted wooden cabinets it exuded warmth and cheer.

Tee was filling the kitchen sink with soapsuds. "No automatic dishwasher at the Berryhills'," he told me. "We kick it old school around here."

"I happen to like doing dishes old school." I picked up a dish towel and handed it to him. "How 'bout I wash and you dry, since I don't know where anything gets put away."

"Scandalous," Carter harrumphed, sitting down on a red metal step stool in the corner of the room. "Letting a guest do the dishes."

"Start the coffee, Pop," Tee instructed.

In a matter of minutes, we'd washed, dried, and put away the dishes, and the three of us were gathered around the enamel-topped kitchen table sipping coffee.

"Now, tell me about Ella Kate," Carter said, stirring another spoonful of sugar into his cup.

I held my mug under my nose and inhaled happily.

"Not much to tell. I think she's avoiding me. Last night, she only opened her bedroom door long enough to tell me where I couldn't sleep. By the time I got up this morning, she was gone. Although she'd taped a bill to the refrigerator door."

"A bill?" Tee asked.

"I helped myself to some of her groceries," I admitted. "But I paid her back."

"What's this about telling you where you can or cannot sleep?" Carter asked, frowning. "Dempsey, I assure you, I have made it quite clear to Ella Kate—both personally and in writing—that Birdsong belongs to your daddy. Not to her."

"It's no big deal," I said. "There are three bedrooms upstairs. Four if you count the trunk room. I'm perfectly comfortable in the room I chose. Although," I said wryly, rubbing my lower back, "I think my first big purchase is going to be a new mattress. The one on my bed might have come to Georgia by covered wagon."

"I wouldn't be surprised," Carter said. "All the Dempseys were tight as ticks when it came to money. And old Norbert, he was so tight he squeaked when he walked."

"I still can't help but wonder why Ella Kate took such a strong and immediate dislike to me," I said.

"It's not you, per se," Carter told me. "I think she just flat out resents anybody named Killebrew. She and your grandmother Olivia weren't just distant cousins. They were best friends, from back when they were little-bitty girls. I think they were roommates at one of those women's colleges, Tift, or maybe it was Wesleyan, or Agnes Scott. Anyway, they did go off to school together freshman year, but then Olivia met your grandfather Killebrew, at a party, and the next thing anybody knew, they'd run off and gotten married."

"Sounds romantic," I said.

"The Dempseys didn't think so," Carter chuckled. "They were fit to be tied. And poor old Ella Kate was left out in the cold. Olivia was always the live wire. Without her at school, I think Ella Kate was just a lost soul. She came home to Guthrie and never did go back to school."

"But that's what? Fifty or more years ago? I didn't have anything to do with that. And neither did my dad."

"Maybe she'll warm up to you," Carter said.

"And maybe pigs will fly," Tee retorted. "Look, Dad, maybe we need to be more proactive with this Ella Kate thing. If Mitch Killebrew intends to sell Birdsong once it's been fixed up, she'll have to leave eventually anyway."

Carter sighed heavily. "You're right, I know. But I honestly don't know where she'd go. She's got no close kin around here anymore."

"Didn't Norbert leave her anything?" I asked. "After all those years she took care of him? God! No wonder she hates us."

He reached across the table and patted my hand. "Calm down, my dear. I didn't say she didn't have the means to leave. I can't discuss another client's financial affairs, but don't you fret about Ella Kate. Between the investments she made with her own little pension money, and what Norbert left her, that old lady is sitting pretty. She just happens to like sitting in somebody else's house. And Tee's right. It's time we had a serious talk with her about the future. She's got to face up to facts."

I put my cup down and stretched. "Well, there's no big hurry. I don't know how long it will take me to get the place shaped up. There's so much to do! I guess I'm going to have to start seeing about getting some bids for things like wiring and plumbing."

"Not to add to your worries," Tee said, "but I'm pretty sure you're gonna need a roofer and a carpenter too. When I was driving down your street the other day at dusk, I happened to look up. There were bats flying into holes up under the eaves on the side of the house."

"Bats!" I shivered. "I guess I won't be exploring the attic anytime soon."

"I'll give you the name of our exterminator," Carter said reassuringly. "And you probably need to meet Bobby Livesey. Actually, Bobby can take care of pretty much anything that needs doing over there. He's as honest as the day is long."

"Good idea," Tee said. "I didn't think about Bobby."

"I'll have to talk to Mitch before I commit to spending that kind of money," I said warily. "Guess we'll have to come up with some kind of budget for the project." I put a hand over my mouth to cover the yawn I'd been trying hard to suppress. "So much for slapping a coat of paint on the place and hanging up the For Sale sign."

16

When we got in the Mini Cooper to go home, Tee turned the car in the opposite direction from the way we'd come to his house. "Is this a shortcut I need to know about?" I asked.

"Nope." He kept driving.

"Part two of the Tee Berryhill tour of Guthrie?"

"You could say that."

At the four lane, Tee headed east. When we whizzed past the Guthrie city limits sign, I began to feel a little alarmed. As far as I could tell, there was nothing on either side of the road except for pastureland or woods. All was darkness.

"You want to tell me where we're going?" I asked.

He turned on the radio and fiddled with the controls until he found a station he liked. Country. I should have known.

"You think I'm taking you across the county line for immoral purposes?"

"Are you?"

"Nope."

After another five miles or so, signs of life started to appear. We passed an all-night gas station, a used-car lot, and a small strip-mall shopping center. Finally, a street sign told me we were entering Griffin city limits.

At the first traffic signal, Tee turned left, and into the parking lot of a brightly lit restaurant called the Burger Chef. The parking lot was full, and teenagers lounged around at picnic tables in front of the entry-way.

"We're here," he announced, parking the car.

"The question is, why are we here?"

"To eat," he said, getting out and coming around to let me out of the car.

"But we just had dinner back at your house," I said.

"You're not hungry?" He raised one eyebrow.

"Okay. Yeah. I'm a little hungry."

He steered me into the restaurant, which looked like something out of a rerun of *Happy Days*. The place was all chrome and Formica, with half the restaurant given over to booths with red leatherette seating, the other half to a long counter where every stool was occupied.

It smelled like hot grease and chocolate cake. My stomach growled in appreciation.

We took a seat in a booth near the front window. He handed me a huge laminated menu.

"You do eat meat, right?"

"Of course," I said, hungrily scanning the offerings.

"Don't get me wrong," Tee said. "Dad's a great guy. He's an excellent litigator, plays scratch golf, is widely read on any number of subjects, including history and philosophy. But his cooking sucks, as you've just seen. I couldn't help but notice that you managed to hide most of your salmon in your dinner napkin."

I blushed to the roots of my hair. "Was I that obvious?"

"Only to me," Tee said. "Dad truly believes he's a great chef. He's always oblivious to the fact that our dinner guests only pick at his salmon, which I cannot convince him not to keep making. Hence, our trip to Burger Chef. We roll up the streets at eight P.M. in Guthrie on weeknights. It was either this or the Canton Buffet out on the county highway."

"This'll do," I said quickly.

He nodded and closed his menu. "So. Burgers or chicken fingers?"

"Burgers."

"French fries or onion rings?"

"French fries."

"Chocolate shake or malted milk?"

I hesitated.

"Don't tell me you're watching your weight," he said.

"That's not it. I like 'em both, but I haven't had a malted milk in years."

"I recommend the shakes. They rock."

The waitress came over, took our orders, which were identical, and left.

He folded his arms on the table and smiled enigmatically.

"What?"

"I'm trying to figure out a way to tactfully ask you what the hell you're doing in Guthrie, Georgia."

"You already know the answer to that. My father inherited Birdsong. He sent me down here to get it fixed up and ready to put on the market."

"You're a lobbyist with one of the biggest law firms in D.C. Your boss has been implicated in a public-corruption case involving the alleged bribery of an influential congressman," Tee said.

My face fell. "Who have you been talking to?" I whispered.

"We do get CNN down here," Tee said matter-of-factly. "Plus, I Googled you. And then I ran a Nexis search. I found out you'd left Hodder and Associates. The blurb I read said you'd left 'to pursue new interests.' "

"I was fired," I said flatly. "You want to know the rest?"

"If you feel like telling it. I told you I was trying to be tactful."

"You're not very good at tactful, are you?"

"I've been told I'm a straight shooter."

"That's one way to put it. Okay. Since you asked so nicely. After I was fired from Hodder and Associates, it was clear that no other firm in town would hire me until this thing with Alex is settled. I couldn't afford to pay my share of the rent on the apartment I shared with two other girls. My father has remarried and doesn't need any more complications in his life. My mother lives in California and makes jewelry out of smashed-up headlights and I really don't care for her boyfriend. So that's what the hell I'm doing in a place like Guthrie."

"Alex?"

"Alexander Hodder. My boss. I'm . . . that is, I was, sort of his protégée. So, to an outsider, it might look as though I'm involved in this mess. But

I'm not. Not really. I mean, yes, I made the arrangements for the senator to hire that wakeboard instructor, and for him to get a massage, but I totally had no idea that anything, you know, fishy, was going on."

Tee nodded. "And was anything fishy going on?"

"No," I said quickly. "Okay, well, in hindsight, it has since dawned on me that a sixty-something-year-old with two knee replacements might not have been entirely interested in taking up wakeboarding. Or that the massage the congressman wanted was not therapeutic. I was naive."

He tapped his fingertips on the tabletop.

I sighed. "Okay. I was incredibly stupid. But that doesn't automatically mean I'm a criminal."

"Hopefully not," Tee said. "What does your lawyer say?"

I looked away.

"You don't have a lawyer?" He looked incredulous.

"Do you know what a criminal-defense attorney in D.C. charges? My dad has offered, but I haven't been charged with anything. Anyway, I was afraid if I hired a lawyer, it would look like I'd done something wrong. And I haven't. Not deliberately. I'm a policy wonk," I said, feeling my lower lip start to tremble. "Not a pimp."

He smiled. Tee Berryhill had very nice eyes. Kind eyes. With very long curly lashes. "What does this Alex guy say? Does he think you need a lawyer?"

Unbidden, tears started to well in my eyes.

Just then, the waitress arrived at our table. She set my cheeseburger platter, all the way, down in front of me. I picked up a French fry and dabbed it in the little white paper cup of ketchup, and took a bite, and burned the devil out of my tongue.

I gasped and reached for my milk shake. Tears streamed down my face.

"Hey!" Tee said. "Are you all right?"

I sucked a mouthful of cold chocolate and let it sit on my blistered tongue. I nodded miserably. "Burned my tongue."

He busied himself arranging the lettuce, tomatoes, and purple onion rings just so on top of his hamburger patty. He splurted mustard and ketchup generously on top of the bun, closed the sandwich and took a bite. He chewed energetically. Swallowed. Took a sip of his own milk shake.

"This Alex guy," he said finally. He paused and ate a French fry. "I guess it would be pretty tactless of me to ask if you were sleeping with him?"

"I wasn't!" I blurted out. "He's married. I'm not that kind of person."

"I didn't think so," Tee said. "I mean, you don't strike me as someone who would, uh, well, anyway, that was a bad question. Forget I asked."

I took a bite of my own cheeseburger. It was delicious. But now my tongue was starting to throb. I took a long sip of the milk shake.

Tee ate and I sipped. People ebbed and flowed around us. Somebody put some money in the jukebox. Country music. God, hadn't they heard of rock and roll out in the boonies?

My shoulders were starting to throb. My back ached and my calf muscles were screaming. I was suddenly drained of energy.

Tee finished his burger, signaled for the check, and paid for both our dinners. I didn't even bother to offer to pay for mine.

He turned the radio off, and we rode in silence for a while.

"Since we're asking personal questions," I said. "What was that thing your dad said at dinner? About it being a waste of billable hours running a small-town newspaper?"

"Oh that. It's just his way of needling me about the *Citizen-Advocate*."

"That's a newspaper?"

"The *Guthrie Citizen-Advocate*. It's a weekly. Founded in 1908. Which we now happen to own, and which I now happen to be the publisher of. It pisses Dad off mightily."

"Why would you guys buy a paper if your dad doesn't want you to run it?"

"We didn't exactly buy it," Tee said with a chuckle. "We represented the wife of the former owner in her lengthy and highly entertaining divorce. Hammond, that's the guy who owned the paper, decided to get foxy and try to hide assets from Veronica, who was our client. It took us nearly two years to run him to ground, but we eventually did it. Luckily for us, the divorce judge had just been elected in our circuit, and he didn't give a rat's ass about Hammond's social standing. He was very annoyed that Hammond tried to hide a couple million dollars' worth of marital assets. So he awarded half the assets, including the *Citizen-Advocate*, to Veronica. Who, when it came time to pay our legal bills, balked at all the hours we'd worked on her behalf. We took it to arbitration, but long story short, the Berryhill law firm is now the owner of the *Guthrie Citizen-Advocate*. And you are looking at the publisher of record."

He grinned.

"You look pretty pleased with yourself," I observed. "Even if it does annoy your father. Do you actually know anything about running a newspaper?"

"I'm learning. We took over about eight months ago. It wasn't much of a paper, to tell you the truth. What people in the business call 'a shopper.' Which means most of the revenue—and content—was generated by advertising. It helped that we were the legal organ for the county, so we're guaranteed all the legal advertising."

"It makes money?"

"Not a lot," he admitted. "I've hired a new editor, who is also the sole reporter, and we've got a new sales staff—actually, the sales staff consists of Sally, who I hired away from a weekly down in Perry, Georgia. They're young, and enthusiastic. And don't tell anybody, but I'm having a ball. I've even written some editorials. Running a small-town newspaper is way more fun than doing trusts and estates."

"If you say so," I said, shaking my head.

"Dad thinks the paper is a total waste of my time, and the firm's resources," Tee said.

"I've heard that line before," I told him. "My dad never could understand why I went to all the trouble of going to law school, and then went to work as a lobbyist. He's just dying for me to cross over to the dark side and sue somebody."

Tee laughed out loud. "The dark side. Yeah. That's a good one. The dark side." He chortled, and I giggled, and pretty soon we were riding along in the night, laughing our collective butts off.

We were still laughing when we pulled up in front of Birdsong. I could see a single light burning in an upstairs window. Ella Kate's room. The porch light was off. I'd deliberately turned it on before leaving a few hours earlier, so I wouldn't have to navigate the perilously cracked driveway in the dark.

Tee saw me looking at the front of the house. "I'll walk you to the door. You should get that front-porch light fixed."

"It works just fine," I told him. "I think Ella Kate turned it off on purpose."

"Old bat," he muttered.

He trained a penlight on the ground and we picked our way slowly up the cracked and broken pavement.

"Thanks for dinner," I said, when we'd reached the front porch. "Both of 'em. I can make it from here."

"You sure?"

"Positive," I said, feeling awkward. I was too tired to invite him in, and anyway, I didn't want him getting any ideas.

"Okay, then. Well, good night," he said.

He was a couple of steps down the driveway when I called out impulsively.

"Hey, Tee?"

"Yeah?" It was so dark I couldn't see his face, which was a good thing.

"You know how I told you I wasn't sleeping with Alex? The thing is, he never asked. We were probably working up to it though. There was definitely something there. I'd be lying if I denied it."

"Oh." His voice was soft, disembodied sounding.

"He won't return my calls," I said. "I even went to his house. His wife wouldn't let me in."

"Dempsey?" He was walking back toward me again, but stopped when he was two feet away. "Why are you telling me all this?"

"I don't know," I said. "I guess . . . you seem like somebody I don't want to lie to. And you said I don't strike you as being that type of girl. But the thing is, I probably am that type of girl."

He shook his head. "No you're not." His face was pale and serious. I heard a soft hoot coming from the top of the camellia bush at the edge of the driveway, and then the fluttering of wings. Tee turned and walked away.

17

I awoke Wednesday to the slow, excruciating drip of rain, and the sensation that I'd been beaten with a stick. Apparently my twice-a-week gym regimen in D.C. had failed to properly tone my housework muscles. A glance at my travel alarm clock told me I'd overslept. It was closing in on eight A.M. "Damn," I said, with a yawn. So much for my plans to spend the day working in the newly cleared yard. It wasn't until I finally managed to drag my aching bones out of bed that I made the depressing discovery that it was raining inside Birdsong, as well as outside. The dripping sound that had awakened me was actually coming from a spot on the ceiling only a foot or two from the window that overlooked the street. Water was already pooling on the floor, and an ugly brown mark stained the cracked plaster ceiling. And now that I was looking for it, I could see other, similar damp brown stains on the ceiling, close to the window. And yes, once I pulled up the edge of the braided bedroom rug, I could see that the worn pine floorboards also showed signs of water damage.

"Damn." I stumbled around the room, searching for something to catch the drips, finally coming up with a wide-mouthed china bowl, decorated with a delicate tracery of blue vines, that had been stashed on the top shelf of the closet.

While the rain fell softly outside, I hastily pulled on the work clothes I'd left folded on a wooden chair the night before, and ran around the house to perform a thorough rain check. The news was not good. I found a leak near the back door, in the kitchen, and another in the trunk room. I placed a couple of battered tin saucepans under each leak, and went back to the kitchen.

I was pouring water into the coffeepot when I heard a bedroom door open, and then the tip-tapping of a dog's paws coming down the hall-way. Shorty pranced into the kitchen, and without giving me so much as a sideways glance began pawing at the back door. I looked around for the dog's mistress, but when Shorty's pawing turned to urgent whines, I unlatched the door and let him out. "Don't run away, okay?" I said nervously, poking my head out the door to watch him relieve himself on a tree trunk a few feet away.

"Shorty ain't goin' nowhere." The voice startled me so, I nearly jumped out of my skin. I whirled around to find Ella Kate standing in the doorway with her customary peeved expression. She was dressed in another of her odd ensembles. Over her flowered, pink, calf-length housedress she wore a moth-eaten black cardigan sweater that sported a large gold *G* on its right breast. She wore thick, white-cotton tube socks, and over those, a pair of worn, brown-leather house shoes. Her fine, white hair had been scraped into a topknot that looked for all the world like a whale's waterspout.

Ella Kate shuffled over to the kitchen counter. She filled a teakettle and set it on the stove's front burner, which she ignited with a wooden kitchen match. From the cupboard by the sink she took a sturdy white porcelain coffee mug into which she spooned some of the Piggly Wig-gly instant coffee.

"I'm brewing fresh coffee," I said, in what was supposed to be a friendly gesture. "You're welcome to some, if you'd like."

"Hmmph," she enthused.

"The ceiling leaks," I offered. "In my bedroom, and the trunk room, and even in here, right by the back door."

"Hmmph," Ella Kate chirped.

"I guess I'll have to get a roofer over here, right away, for an esti-mate."

She shuffled over to the back door and held it open. "C'mon, Shorty," she called. "Get your bidness done and be quick about it. I don't need you tracking mud into my clean kitchen."

I cocked an eyebrow. *Her* kitchen? And a *clean* one, at that?

Shorty ran into the kitchen and sat expectantly at her feet. "Good boy," she said, pouring dog food into a cereal bowl she took from the cupboard—the same cupboard that held the dishes I'd been eating from.

I poured myself a cup of the French roast coffee, and sat down at the kitchen table. Ella Kate stood and watched the dog eat. When the tea-kettle whistled, she poured boiling water over her own cup, stirred it with a spoon, then disappeared back down the hallway, cup in hand, the dog in her wake again. Seconds later, I heard her bedroom door open, and then close.

So much for our cozy little coffee klatch.

While my own coffee cooled, I dug the Guthrie telephone directory out of a kitchen drawer. It was only slightly bigger than a pamphlet. I found the number for Bobby Livesey, the handyman Carter had recommended, and dialed it, but got only a recording, promising that if I'd leave a number, Bobby would call back, "just as soon as I possibly can."

"Yeah, right," I muttered, chin in hand, listening to the hollow chink of raindrops meeting saucepan.

After I'd finished my bowl of cereal, and placed the rinsed-out bowl on the highest shelf of the kitchen cupboard, where Ella Kate presumably couldn't reach it, I decided to mount a frontal assault on the inside of Birdsong.

I plugged in my iPod, and thumbed it to a selection of songs I'd listened to back in D.C., during my infrequent stints of jogging. When Sheryl Crow started singing "All I Wanna Do Is Have Some Fun," I knew I'd found a tempo to work with.

By noon, and with the help of some serious dance tunes from Fergie, Gwen Stefani, and Madonna, I'd mopped, dusted, and scrubbed my way through the kitchen and the rest of the rooms downstairs, discovering, along the way, two more threatening dark patches in the ceiling.

When I got to the foyer though, I suffered a serious loss of momentum. The bare light bulb cast a gray gloom over the assortment of junk arrayed around the room. Sweeping up the plaster chunks and thin layer of dog hair did little to improve the room's look. What this room needed, I decided, was a total and complete clean sweep.

I knocked purposefully on Ella Kate's door.

"Who's that?" Her voice was muffled.

I rolled my eyes. Who else would it be?

"It's Dempsey. I need to speak to you, please."

"Me and Shorty are busy." I could hear canned laughter from a television set in the background.

"It's important, Ella Kate."

Footsteps. She opened the door a crack and poked her head out. Her pale blue eyes narrowed and her thin lips pursed. "What's so important it can't wait until *Golden Girls* is over?"

I took a deep breath. "I wanted to let you know that I'm getting the house cleaned up and cleared out. What would you like me to do with all the stuff in the foyer?"

"What stuff?"

"All that junk," I sputtered. "A barrel of rakes and brooms? Buckets of fake flowers, all those old paperback books? And that dressmaker's form? I need to know what you'd like me to do with all of it?"

Her nostrils flared. "Junk? That happens to be my property, missy. You just keep your mitts off of that stuff and leave it be." She slammed the door to announce the finality of her decision.

I took another deep breath. Was I going to let an octogenarian squatter get the better of me?

"Ella Kate!" I rapped on the door. "I'm sorry, but this is my father's house, and he's asked me to get it cleaned up and ready to sell. You can't leave that junk in the foyer. If you don't get rid of it, I will."

The door swung open. She stalked down the hallway with Shorty at her heels. A moment later, she was dragging the fifty-pound sack of dog food back toward her room. It was nearly as big as she was.

"Here," I said, coming to her aid. "Let me help you with that."

"Leave me alone!" she said, slapping my hand away. "You've done enough already. Those tools are perfectly good gardening tools. I was gonna put 'em in the shed myself, once the weather cleared and my bursitis quit acting up."

"I'll be happy to move them to the shed," I said. "Now, what about the books? And the flowers? And the dummy?"

She continued to drag the dog food sack toward her room. "I save the flowers to put on graves in the family plot over at Greenlawn. Put 'em out in the shed too, if you wanna be like that. That dressmaker's form is a real antique. Norbert's mama used it, and her mama before that."

"Could it go up in the attic?" I asked gently. "Or would you like me to move it to your room?"

"Do what you want," she muttered. "It ain't my house, so I guess it ain't for me to say."

I sighed. "I'll take it up to the attic and try to find a nice dry spot for it. Now, what about the books?"

"The books are for the ladies over at the nursing home. I can't lift 'em, and since the sheriff took my license away, I can't tote 'em over there myself."

"I'll load them into Uncle Norbert's car and drop them off if you'll give me the address of the nursing home," I promised.

"I guess that would be all right," she said reluctantly. A moment later, she slammed the door in my face again.

I smiled despite the rebuff. Score one for Dempsey in this round.

I borrowed a plastic rain scarf from the dressmaker dummy, picked up the barrel of rakes, and made a dash for the driveway. It took three trips, but soon the boxes of books had been safely stowed in the enormous trunk of the Catfish.

Now, I thought, grimacing, it was time for a trip to the attic. I couldn't help but remember what Tee had told me about bats emerging from Birdsong's eaves. I decided to leave the rain scarf in place—just in case.

The dressmaker form wasn't heavy, but it was bulky. It bumped along behind me as I dragged it up the stairs to the second floor. I'd found the door to the attic on an earlier exploration of the house. It was narrow, and the steep stairs up to the attic were narrower still. The dummy barely fit through the door.

As I climbed the crude wooden stairs, the attic's smell wafted down to me—a mixture of decay, mothballs, and dust. I was out of breath when I reached the top step. In the half-light filtering through the room's grime-covered windows, the attic reminded me of an elephants' graveyard, with the hulking, dust-covered carcasses of cast-off trunks and furniture and wooden crates arrayed about the space.

I found a frayed cord, and a yellow lightbulb bathed the old wooden roof timbers with a weird amber glow. I scanned the room nervously, on the lookout for marauding bats. Thankfully, I saw none. What I did see were the sources of several leaks, with rain drops steadily dripping through the ceiling and down through the floorboards. I trundled the dressmaker's form to a corner of the attic that showed no signs of water damage, and then scurried around placing every container I could find under the leaks.

When she was high and dry, I looked around the room. Another time, I might have spent the whole afternoon exploring the attic. I'd been a bookish little kid, and as a preteen, had gone through a serious Louisa May Alcott period, when I longed to be like Jo, of *Little Women*, scribbling away in some cozy rooftop garret. In an earlier time, I'd gobbled up stories of pirates and treasure chests. The kid in me longed to start rummaging through all those mysterious crates and trunks.

Today, though, I had work I needed to get to. And a roofer to track down. Just as I was turning to go back down the stairs, I caught a glint of light from the far corner of the room. As I got closer, I saw that the source of the glint was an elaborate, triple-tiered crystal chandelier, which seemed to be hanging from the roof rafters by some sort of pulley.

I gazed up at it in admiration. Three tiers of crystal arms protruded elegantly from its center shaft, and ropes of dusty crystal beading festooned each of the arms. This, I thought, had to be the missing light fixture, either from the foyer or the dining room. It would come downstairs soon, I vowed. But not today. Not until I had a handyman with a strong back and a knack for old wiring.

With the foyer cleared of Ella Kate's junk, I could finally get a good look at the room's graceful lines. For the first time, I noticed the wedding-cake ceiling moldings, and the detailed wooden wainscoting. On either side of the door I discovered a pair of crystal-drop wall sconces that I hadn't noticed before. There was even a deep coat closet, which had been hidden behind the stacks of book boxes. Its door was solid mahogany, and the handle, like all the other door handles in the house, was crystal, with a finely etched brass back plate.

Under all those layers of junk and grime, I was discovering that Birdsong truly was a gracious old lady of a house.

After I removed each of the crystals, soaked them in a sinkful of ammonia water, and replaced them on the sconces, I screwed new forty-watt bulbs into the fixtures and held my breath as I flipped the light switch near the front door.

Magic! It was still rainy and gray outside, but now, with the front door's glass inset and sidelights cleaned, the floor mopped and the sconces functioning, the foyer looked positively elegant. I stood there, turning slowly, grinning like an idiot, soaking up the immensity of my accomplishment.

"Hmmph."

I hadn't even heard Ella Kate leave her bedroom. She stood in the doorway to the foyer, holding a squirming Shorty in her arms, a cracked patent leather pocketbook tucked in the crook of her right elbow.

"It's pretty, isn't it?" I asked.

She shrugged, setting Shorty down on my newly mopped floor. "Better than a poke in the eye with a short stick, I reckon," she said.

I decided to take it as a compliment.

She stood there, her hands on her hips now, waiting.

"You coming, or what?" she said finally.

"Coming?"

"The nursing home," she said. "You said you'd tote the books over there. I'll show you where it's at. Then, I need to get some things at the Piggly Wiggly. Need to get my heart medicine pills refilled at the drugstore. And I need to go to the bank too."

"Oh," I said weakly. I *had* promised to take the books for her. I went in search of my purse and the keys to the Catfish. Score one for Ella Kate.

18

T hursday dawned so bright and sunny it almost made me forget the wet gloom of the previous day. I walked around the downstairs rooms, coffee cup in hand, trying to decide where to start the day's work.

I'd had a serious money talk with Mitch the night before. "The roof is probably shot," I told him. "And the kitchen is positively prehistoric. If there's heat in the house, I can't tell. We need to come up with a budget before I get in too deep down here."

"Damn," Mitch said. "Hang on." Over the phone I could hear the tapping of keys. A calculator. "Damn," he said again. "What about the plumbing?"

"The toilets flush," I reported. "But there's barely enough water pressure to rinse out a glass."

"Old pipes," he said. More tapping. "Damn."

"Eighty thousand," he said finally. "That's it. As it is, I'll have to move some money around, make up some story for Pilar about why we can't buy a new car this spring. Eighty thousand, Dempsey. I mean it. Not a penny more."

I had no idea how far eighty thousand dollars would go. But I had a strong idea that it wouldn't go nearly far enough, and that I'd need to invest plenty of my own sweat equity in the project at hand. Right now, the parlor's peeling wallpaper seemed to be calling my name. I cleared some porcelain doodads off the mantel and set my cup down. One firm tug brought a whole sheet of the paper gratifyingly—and cleanly—off the wall. Fine flakes of plaster rained down on Norbert's borrowed sneakers.

With a fingernail, I pried up the edge of another strip of the paper, but no more. "Come on," I muttered, moving on to the next strip, whose edge seemed to be glued securely.

Somewhere, in all those magazine articles that made home renovation seem as charming and effortless as a summer picnic, I remembered reading a how-to article about wallpaper. Something about soaking the old paper off with some kind of chemical solvent.

I went to the kitchen to survey my arsenal of cleaning products. Window cleaner in a spray bottle. Pine-Sol. Furniture polish. A squirt bottle of concentrated tile cleaner. Bleach. Green-apple-scented dish detergent. Scouring powder. Surely, one of these would do the trick. I dumped half a cup of the Pine-Sol in a plastic bucket and filled it halfway up with hot water. Then I carried everything back to the parlor. I spritzed the window cleaner on the edge of the wallpaper and waited a moment, to give the ammonia time to work its magic.

I blinked back tears from the fumes, then attacked the paper with my fingernail. The top layer dissolved into a gooey mess, leaving behind a stubborn layer of yellow backing, clinging tenaciously to the plaster.

Okay, no window cleaner. I dipped a sponge into the bucket of water, sprinkled it with scouring powder, and scrubbed hard on the backing. I managed to rub my fingertips raw, but the backing stayed intact.

Pine-Sol? I dunked the sponge in the soapy, pine-scented water, and dabbed it on the same patch of wallpaper.

A shrill ring echoed from the hallway, startling me so much that I dropped the soapy sponge on the floor. *Brrinnnnggg.* It sounded like an old-fashioned bicycle bell. For a moment I thought it might be a telephone. But the ring was coming from the hallway.

Brrinnnggg. I trotted out to the hall, and could see, through the now squeaky-clean glass in the door, that the ringing was coming from the doorbell, which was being rung by a man.

I opened the door. My visitor was an older black gentleman, medium height, trim build. His hair was hidden under a red ball cap, but his thin mustache was graying, and he wore thick-lensed eyeglasses. He was dressed in work clothes, but not like any work clothes I'd ever seen before. His pale blue denim shirt was pressed, and LIVESEY CONTRACTING was embroidered in red over the shirt pocket. His blue jeans were spotless, knife creased, and his work boots had a dull polish.

"Hello?" I said cautiously.

"Hello. I'm looking for Miss Dempsey?" he said, glancing down at the clipboard he held in his right hand.

"Yes," I said, wiping my own hand on the seat of Norbert's overalls. "That's me."

He eyed me quizzically. In baggy overalls worn over a faded Redskins jersey, my hair held off my face with Norbert's oversize handkerchief, I probably didn't look like Miss anything. "You're the Miss Dempsey called lookin' to have some work done on your house? Roofing, like that?"

"Yes," I repeated. "I'm Dempsey Killebrew. I'm the one who called you."

"Ohhh," he said slowly. "Killebrew?"

"Dempsey Killebrew. I live here."

"That so?" He tugged at the bill of his cap, and looked around the porch, then back at me. "I was thinking Mr. Norbert's family still owned the house. You the new owner?"

"It's confusing," I said, with a laugh. "My father is the new owner. Mitch Killebrew. Norbert Dempsey was his great-uncle. My father's mother was Olivia Dempsey Killebrew. I'm named Dempsey for her."

"Ohh," he said again. "So, your daddy's people were Dempseys?"

"On his mother's side."

A slow smile spread over his face. "All right then. Now I gotcha." He stuck his hand out. "Bobby Livesey. Livesey Contracting. You called about needing some work done? How can I help you?"

It took most of an hour to show Bobby Livesey everything that was wrong with Birdsong. We started with the attic, and worked our way all the way down to the cellar. Along the way, Bobby poked and prodded. He tapped the old walls with his knuckles, like a surgeon sizing up the patient's chest. He dug a penknife into the ceiling beams, shone a flashlight into the crawl space. He clucked and made notes with a small silver mechanical pencil in tiny block letters on his clipboard.

Along the way, I gave him an abbreviated explanation of how Mitch had inherited Birdsong from his great-uncle Norbert. I explained that we wanted to fix the house up and flip it.

"Flip?" He frowned.

"You know. Fix it up. Make the repairs so it can be sold for way more than the ninety-eight thousand the county says it's worth. Invest a little money, sell it, and make a nice profit."

He nodded gravely, made a note on his clipboard, and we moved along with the tour.

"Well?" I said when we'd arrived back in the hallway. "What do you think? Can the patient be saved? Or should we just pull the plug and start all over again?"

"What? This old house? This here is a fine old building."

"You're going to tell me they don't make 'em like this anymore?" I kidded.

"No, ma'am," he said soberly, not taking the bait. "They sure don't. This house is a rock. Solid, through and through. Your roof needs work. And yeah, the wiring's about sixty years out of code. But that ain't nothing. You should see some of these sorry new houses I work on around town. Brand-new houses, I'm talking about three hundred, four hundred thousand, they're sellin' for. Ain't a single plumb wall in the place, skinny old wallboard no thicker than a sheet of paper, all of it held together with a caulk gun and a promise."

He thumped the thick molding of the doorway with his knuckles, smiling, as though he'd picked out a perfectly ripe melon. "This house here is a beauty. One of a kind. You just need to shine her up a little, show her some love."

"You can do all that?" I asked. "A new roof, wiring, fix the plaster?"

"Oh yeah," he drawled. "We can do it. That ain't no problem."

"But how much? I'm on a tight budget," I explained. "And I don't need it all to be perfect. It just has to look good enough to sell."

He looked down at his clipboard, and then back up at me. Bobby Livesey was a taciturn man, courtly as only a Southern man of a certain age can be. But his large brown eyes gave him away.

"Just good enough? If that's all you want, you might oughtta get somebody else," he said finally. "I ain't ever studied doing something halfway. Ain't going to now."

I felt a swift pang of regret at disappointing him. "Halfway, no, I don't want you to do it halfway. I just meant, well, money's tight. We'll have to make every dollar count. And I'm willing to do some of the labor. I want to, in fact."

He looked me up and down, took one of my hands and turned it palm side down. The skin was reddened from the cleaners I'd been using, but my French manicure was a dead giveaway.

"What did you say you did, before moving down here?"

"I'm a lawyer by training," I said. "But I worked as a lobbyist. In Washington."

He blinked. "A lawyer, huh? You studying on doing lawyering here in Guthrie?"

I laughed. "No. I'm studying on fixing up this old wreck. And I'm thinking you're the man who can show me how to do that."

The doorbell rang again. *Brrinnnggg. Briinnggg. Briinggg.* Whoever was at the door wasn't nearly as patient as Bobby Livesey had been.

"I better get that," I said. "There's a pot of coffee made out in the kitchen. Maybe you could fix yourself a cup and come up with some kind of ballpark estimate on what the roof will cost? And the wiring?"

"Sure," he said. "That ain't no problem."

his time my visitor was female. She was a fair-skinned young black woman, in her midtwenties, I guessed, with reddish corkscrew curls held back by a tortoiseshell headband, dressed in a black turtleneck sweater and snug-fitting black slacks and high-heeled black boots. She had stepped away from the door, and was looking around the porch with frank curiosity when I opened the door.

"Yes?"

"Hi," she said, smiling widely. "I'm looking for Dempsey Killebrew?" Her right nostril was pierced with a tiny silver ring, and the freckles sprinkled over her nose and cheeks looked like bits of black pepper.

I stepped out onto the porch. "You've found her," I said. "What can I do for you?"

Now I noticed a dark green Ford Focus parked at the curb in front of the house. A casually dressed man with shoulder-length blond hair sat on the hood of the car, holding a long-lensed camera pointed at the house.

The woman nodded at him, and he started shooting, stepping away from the curb and onto the yard.

"Who are you?" I asked, taking a step backward into the house, halfway closing the door to shield myself from the camera. "What do you want? I haven't given anybody permission to take pictures of my house."

She wheeled around. "Greg," she hollered. "Cool it." He lowered the camera to his side, but didn't move off the property.

"Sorry," she said, smiling apologetically. "I'm Shalani Byers. With the *Post*."

"*The Post*?" I said dumbly. "I thought the Guthrie paper was the *Citizen-Advocate*."

"The *Washington Post*," she said, handing me a business card. "I'm a reporter. I was wondering if we could talk?"

My hands went cold, and I could feel my face reddening. "What would the *Washington Post* want to talk to me about, clear down in Guthrie, Georgia?"

"Aren't you the Dempsey Killebrew who works for Hodder and Associates?" she asked.

"Worked. Past tense," I snapped, closing the door another four inches. "I don't have anything to say to the *Post*."

"No comment?" she said, her pen poised above a notepad.

" 'No comment' is for criminals," I said. "I'm not a criminal. I'm just a private citizen. I don't mean to be rude, but I'd appreciate it if you'd leave now. And," I said, peeking out at the photographer, who was snapping away again, "tell your friend to get off my property and stop taking my picture."

"All right," she said, scribbling away. "But if I were you, I'd want to talk to me."

"I sincerely doubt that," I told her.

"Don't you even want to know why my paper sent me all the way down here?"

"No." I closed the door and started to walk away.

"Alex Hodder has been talking to a federal grand jury," she called. "Our sources say he's claiming that an unnamed junior associate, acting completely on her own, hired those two prostitutes on Lyford Cay, to service Representative Licata."

"What?" I yanked the door open. Now the photographer was on the porch, snapping away again. I slammed the door shut.

"Off!" I hollered. "Get the hell off my porch."

"Hodder gave the grand jury the credit card receipts from your company-issued American Express card." The girl's voice was muffled. The door was a solid two inches thick. Like the rest of Birdsong, it was, as Bobby Livesey had said, rock solid.

"Your signature is on the receipts. Did your boss tell you he was doing that?"

"She was a wakeboard instructor," I cried.

"Named Mahogany Foxx. With two *x*'s? Working for a company called the Pleasure Chest?" I heard the photographer snicker.

I pressed my face against the worn paint of the door. It was cool to the touch, and still smelled of the soap I'd scrubbed it down with the day before. It smelled so clean, but suddenly, I felt so, so dirty.

I was a lawyer, for God's sake. I knew better, but I couldn't help myself. "I was given a phone number to call. A woman answered and I told her Mr. Licata wanted to book a session. She never told me her name, or the name of the company she worked for. I never met her. I never laid eyes on her."

"Miss Mahogany Foxx must be riding something else besides wakeboards for four thousand dollars," Shalani Byers said. "Did you know that's how much your credit card was billed?"

I'd had my company-issued AmEx for six months. It was silly, but I'd been nearly giddy the day Alex called me into his office and handed me my own American Express gold card. "Keep it quiet," Alex had said, pressing it into my hand. "The other associates don't have company credit cards. Just you."

I used the AmEx card for business lunches, to book work-related travel, and occasionally, always at Alex's request, to pay for miscellaneous expenses he didn't want billed to his own card. Because of the "bean counters," he'd said. It'd look better for the accountants if certain expenses didn't show up on his card.

"Did you hire a masseuse named Tiki Finesse for Representative Licata?" Shalani asked.

I squeezed my eyes tight and thought back to that night in December, when we were down in Lyford Cay. I was supposed to meet Alex for dinner that night, but he'd canceled the dinner because he said he needed to meet with Licata privately. I'd been bitterly disappointed.

I vividly remembered the conversation.

"Licata doesn't want to go out, because he pulled a muscle in his lower back, working out with the hotel's trainer," Alex told me. "What a fucking baby." Alex's tone was conspiratorial. "Keeps whining about his fucking back. Can you do me a favor? Call that number I gave you earlier, and tell them to send a massage therapist up to the room. Just charge it to your company card."

I'd called the same number, and a different woman had answered the phone. The first woman had sounded faintly British, but the second woman had a harsh, New York–sounding accent. I'd given her Licata's room number, and my credit card number, and she'd assured me all would be taken care of.

Obviously, she'd taken care of the congressman in a way I'd been too dumb to anticipate.

"Licata was complaining of back pain," I told Shalani Byers. "It was supposed to be a therapeutic massage."

"Sixteen hundred dollars, according to my source, who's seen all the records," Shalani Byers retorted. "You ever hear of a sixteen-hundred-dollar massage? I mean, one that doesn't include what the pros call a 'happy ending'?"

"I never see the statements for the AmEx card," I whispered.

"What?" Through the glass sidelights I could see that Shalani Byers was standing with her own face pressed up against the door.

"Go away," I said.

"What's that?" Shalani said. "Come on, Dempsey. Let's sit down and talk. You know. Face-to-face. Like, woman to woman. What do you say?"

"No comment," I said dully, walking away from the door and upstairs.

From the upstairs bedroom window, I watched Shalani Byers and the photographer go back to the Ford Focus. He poked the lens of the camera out the passenger window one more time, and then they drove off.

I waited until I saw the car turn the corner before I took my cell phone out of my purse. Even while I was punching in Alex's cell phone number, I was gripped by paranoia, wondering if, somehow, the girl had managed to plant some kind of listening device on the porch.

"Stop it!" I told myself.

Alex's phone rang once, and went directly to voice mail.

"Alex, it's Dempsey." I was whispering, my paranoia lingering. "A reporter for the *Washington Post* just showed up at my house down here. She's saying awful things." I gulped. "She says you've given my company AmEx receipts to the grand jury. Alex—I really need you to call me and tell me what's going on up there. Okay? Please?"

I sounded desperate and needy and pathetic. I felt exactly the same way. I waited five minutes, hoping the phone would ring immediately, that Alex would hear the panic in my voice and call back to reassure me that Shalani Byers was totally misinformed. But the phone didn't ring. Finally, I tucked it in the pocket of Norbert's overalls and went back downstairs.

I stumbled into the kitchen, where Bobby Livesey was punching numbers into a pocket calculator.

I sank down on the chair opposite his. With shaking hands, I picked up the coffeepot and poured myself a fresh mug, sloshing some on the table. I took a long sip, trying to steady my nerves.

"Everything all right?" he asked, putting the calculator down. "You look like you got some bad news just now."

My hands wouldn't stop shaking. I clasped them in my lap, willing them to be still.

"My past seems to be catching up with me," I said finally.

"Past?" he looked amused. "What kind of past can a young gal like you have? What'd you do—rob a bank or something?"

I bit my lower lip until I tasted blood.

"Hey now," Bobby said, startled. "I was just kiddin'. I didn't mean nothing by it."

"It's all right," I said, struggling to gain control of my racing emotions. I nodded toward the clipboard. "What do you think? Do you have more bad news for me?"

He tapped the paper with his mechanical pencil. "You serious about what you said before? About doing a lot of the work yourself? You ever done any home improvement before?"

"I'm dead serious," I said. "And no, I've never done any manual labor before. You'll have to show me how. But I'm a hard worker, and I've been told I'm a quick study."

"The roof's the big-ticket item," Bobby said, eyeing the figures on the page. "That roof is slate," he added, pointing his finger toward the ceiling. "Some of the tiles are broken, some of 'em are missing. I'm gonna have to peel 'em all off, replace the old tarpaper with one of the new impervious neoprene skins, then put all the slates back. I'll need to see about getting a source to replace the damaged slate tiles. Probably have to be special ordered. I won't lie to you. It's gonna cost."

"Can't we just patch it up—"

"No, ma'am," he said firmly. "No patches. No shortcuts. That roof— you need it done right. Or you sacrifice the integrity of the whole structure. Ain't no use spending money on plaster or wiring or anything else if you don't do the roof just right. You see what I'm saying?"

"I'm beginning to," I told him. I took another long sip of coffee.

"All right then," he said, nodding contentedly. "Now you're talking."

"What else? Besides the roof?" I asked. "You've already told me about the wiring. What about the plumbing? The water pressure in the house is pathetic. Please don't tell me we need all new pipes."

"Naw," Bobby said. He got up and went over to the sink, turning on the faucet. "You got solid-copper commercial-grade pipe in this house. That pipe will be good long after you and me are both dead and in the grave."

He picked up a drinking glass from the drain board and filled it with water. "See that nasty rust in the water, when you first turn on the faucet? The problem is, the old line to the street is cast iron. It's rusting from the inside, you probably only got a half inch clearance inside a two-inch water line. We're gonna have to dig up the front yard. It'll mess up Mr. Norbert's lawn, for sure, but once we replace that cast-iron mess with new pipe, we'll get rid of the rust, and your water pressure will be fine."

"No kidding? It's just the line running to the street? You're sure?" I hadn't had a lot of good news lately, so I was grasping at straws here.

"Oh yeah, the plumbing ain't no problem," Bobby said.

"What about this kitchen?" I asked, gesturing around at the dingy cupboards and outdated appliances. "What's it gonna cost to bring this thing into the twenty-first century?"

Bobby got up and walked over to the sink. He ran his hand over the deep porcelain sink, opened and closed a cupboard door, and said, "Ain't no doubt about it. This kitchen's got some age on it. So, you could just rip everything out. Go over to the Home Depot in Macon, get you some shiny new cabinets, one of them new farmhouse sinks, order up some granite countertops and some stainless-steel appliances."

This was exactly the plan that had been forming in my mind. In my suitcase upstairs, I had a file folder devoted exclusively to pictures of fabulous kitchens, which I'd ripped out of magazines over the years. My favorite one—my dream kitchen—was a Tuscan farmhouse kitchen, with tumbled-marble backsplashes, fumed oak cabinets, an enormous imported blood red Aga cookstove, and a glass-doored Traulsen refrigerator. That kitchen had ancient, exposed hand-hewn ceiling beams, and a separate butler's pantry. According to the magazine, the kitchen belonged to a software entrepreneur who'd sold his company at the age of thirty, and retired to a quail-hunting lodge in Thomasville, Georgia. Of course, that kitchen had probably come in at a neat quarter of a million dollars. At least.

It wouldn't be possible, or even desirable, to reproduce a kitchen like that at Birdsong. But the one thing this kitchen did have in common with that dream kitchen was space.

This dreary old dud was big. It had high—although water-stained—ceilings, and a bank of windows that looked out on Birdsong's weed-infested backyard. It too had a butler's pantry. Of course, its glass-paned cupboard doors were coated in multiple layers of chipped and peeling paint, and somebody had chosen to wallpaper it in imitation redbrick Con-Tact paper, but it was, nevertheless, a butler's pantry.

"New cabinets—let's say just stock cabinets, not custom; stainless-steel appliances; granite; new flooring; the whole shebang. What would that run—ballpark?" I asked Bobby.

His fingers raced over the calculator keys, and he winced when he saw the final tally. "Yeah. That's what I thought. Minimum? If we did all the demo of the old kitchen ourselves—maybe find floor-model appliances—you save a little money that way. We're talking thirty thousand. And that's assuming we don't move any of the water lines or mess with the floor plan."

"Oh." Mentally, I put the kitchen file folder in the far recesses of my mind.

"Yeah," Bobby said. "Kitchens eat up a lot of money. Still, we could make this here kitchen real nice without spending anywhere near that much money."

I was about to ask him what he had in mind when the cell phone in my pocket started ringing.

I grabbed the phone and looked at the display readout.

UNKNOWN CALLER, it said.

"Excuse me, Bobby," I said, jumping up and running out of the room. I took the stairs three at a time, and on the third ring, and the top step, I flipped the phone open.

"Hello?" I said breathlessly.

"Dempsey?" It was Alex. Thank God.

20

"Dempsey?"

"Alex!" I said. "You got my message."

"Where the hell are you?" he asked.

"I'm in Georgia. A little town south of Atlanta, called Guthrie."

"Listen," he said urgently. "I don't have much time. Are you all right?"

"I've been better," I said. "How about you? I've been calling and calling. I even went to your house . . . the night . . . everything happened. Did Trish tell you I came by?"

"No. She never mentioned it. Trish and I . . . well, anyway, that's not why I'm calling. I got your message. What's going on?"

"This reporter from the *Washington Post* showed up here—at the house where I'm staying. Her name was Shalani Byers. And she had a photographer with her."

"When was this?"

"Today, just now."

"You didn't let her in the house, right?"

"No. I kept asking her to leave, but she was pretty insistent. Alex, she claims she has a source on the grand jury—"

"Bullshit!" Alex said angrily. "That's how these shits operate. They come up with a lot of innuendo and speculation, to trick you into saying things you don't mean."

"She said the grand jury has seen the statements for my company-issued AmEx card, Alex. And she claims it shows a four-thousand-dollar charge for that wakeboard instructor I booked for—"

"Never mind that," Alex said quickly. "I can't discuss any of this stuff right now. In fact, Dempsey, it would be a good idea if you didn't call my cell phone again."

"Wait," I said panicking. "Look, this woman says the charges on my card were billed from a company called Pleasure Chest. Alex, she also said there was a sixteen-hundred-dollar charge for the same company, for that massage therapist you asked me to have sent up to Licata's hotel room that night at the—"

"Dempsey! For Christ's sake," Alex barked. "I told you I cannot discuss this. Look, if that reporter comes back, send her away. Don't say anything to her, do you hear?"

"I didn't," I said. "I haven't, but—"

"Take care, Dempsey," he said. "I'll be in touch again. All right?"

He hung up. I flipped the phone closed, then opened it again. I punched the button on the phone's display screen for calls received. UN-KNOWN CALLER it said. No number was listed. Even if I wanted to, I couldn't call Alex Hodder back.

21

Out in the kitchen, Bobby was bent over the kitchen table, rapidly sketching on a sheet of blue-lined notebook paper.

"Everything okay?" he asked, not looking up from his drawing.

"Not so much," I said. I'd been waiting for weeks to hear from Alex, certain he would clear up the matter of my firing, hoping he would assure me that everything was going to be all right. From the moment I'd met him, I'd known that Alex Hodder was a man who was capable of fixing anything that went wrong with my life.

Okay, now I'd heard from Alex. A telephone conversation that lasted a little over a minute had left my future as clear as mud. My stomach churned and my mouth was dry.

I stood beside Bobby and looked down at the sketch. "What's this?"

"Just an idea I had," he said. "For your kitchen."

"Forget it," I said. "After the roof and the wiring and the paint, there won't be enough money left over to do anything to this kitchen." I sank down onto a kitchen chair and stared blankly into my cup of cold coffee, where the creamer made a small milky cloud.

"Sure there is," Bobby said, patting my hand reassuringly. "There's a lot we can do in here, with just a little bit of money."

"And dynamite,' I said bleakly.

"No, now, look here," he said, placing a cabinet door on the table.

"What's this supposed to be?" I asked.

He took the edge of his penknife and scraped at the goopy paint on the door. Underneath the dingy white paint, I could see a rainbow of paint layers, bright yellow, pale pink, even a soft aqua. When he'd scraped a nickel-size patch of paint away, I could see bare wood.

"See that," he said, scratching at the paint with his index finger. "Ain't that pretty?"

"Wood," I said. "I guess so."

"That there's pine," Bobby said. "Good old heart pine. And every single one of these cabinet doors is the same way. Solid pine. None of that pressboard junk or veneer you get these days. The drawers are solid pine too. The boxes and the drawer fronts."

"And?"

Bobby grinned. He reached over and gently squeezed my right forearm. "How do you feel about working up some muscles?"

"What are you proposing?"

"Sweat equity," he said. "We take off every single one of these cabinet doors and pull out the drawers. I'll strip the boxes, you strip the doors. When we're done, you're gonna have cabinets a lot prettier—a lot better—than any of that pricey junk over to the Home Depot."

"Strip how?"

"Could do chemicals, but I'm thinking a heat gun's gonna be cheaper. And quicker," he said.

I looked down at his sketch, which was a simple schematic drawing of the kitchen. "But these doors here"—I tapped the drawing—"look like they have glass panes in them."

"That's right," he said smugly. "I seen it in my wife's magazines she brings home from the beauty parlor. Glass-front cabinets, that's what your high-end kitchens have these days."

"Expensive," I reminded him. "And not in my budget."

"Sure it is," he said, lifting a glass-paned cabinet door from the chair beside him.

"Is that one of the cupboard doors from the butler's pantry?"

"Sure is," he said. "They're the exact same size as the ones in this here kitchen. I'm thinking we swap out some of the glass-pane ones for the solid ones. Don't need all those cupboard doors in the butler's pantry anyway. Shelves are all right in there. We strip these down, they're gonna be pretty as a picture."

He smiled shyly. "What do you think?"

I shrugged. "You've got an island drawn in the middle right where this table is. That's gonna cost."

"That I can build," Bobby said. "Down in your basement? Over by the furnace, somebody left a big ol' pile of lumber, all stacked pretty as you please, up off the floor so it never got wet or warped. Probably left over from building that shed you got out back. Anyway, it's good solid two-by-fours and four-by-fours. I can glue up some of 'em, put 'em on my lathe, and turn you some table legs look just like what I've drawn here."

"I like it," I admitted finally. "What's that hanging from chains above the island?"

"That's a pot rack," Bobby said. "You got an old apple-picking ladder out in that shed. We hang that from some of that chain and put some iron hooks on it, it'll work as good as store bought."

"It all looks great," I said. "But what do we do about countertops? That yellow Formica has got to go."

"No two ways about it," Bobby agreed.

"I guess I could shop around, see if I can come up with something that looks as good as granite, but is cheaper." I looked with distaste at the floor, with its cracked green linoleum tiles. "What do we do about this floor?"

Bobby was in his midsixties, but he dropped easily to his hands and knees and gently pried up one of the tiles just under the table. Again, with the tip of his knife, he scraped at the thick black mastic.

"Huh," he muttered. "This ain't good." He scrambled to his feet, and without another word walked out the door. When he came back a moment later, he had what looked like a heavy-duty black hair dryer in his hands. Snaking the thick black cord over to an outlet by the sink, he plugged it in.

"What's that?" I asked.

"Heat gun I was telling you about," Bobby said. He held up the tip and I could see the glowing red coils. He aimed the gun a few inches from the black mastic, and after a moment, reached into the pocket of his work pants and brought out a sharp-edged scraper. When the black goo began to bubble, he worked the edge of the scraper across it. He grabbed the discarded green tile and wiped the molten mastic on it.

"Look here," he said proudly.

I got down on my own hands and knees to get a look. "It's wood," I said, meeting his grin with one of my own. "Like all the rest of the floors."

"Heart pine," Bobby agreed. "All we gotta do is pull up these old tiles and scrape up that mastic. You can't buy floors this good any-more."

I sat back and looked around the kitchen with new appreciation. "This could be nice," I said finally. "Much better, anyway, than what's here now."

"You bet," Bobby said. He stood up and walked over to the sink. "This old sink, it's pretty grimy." He glanced around, and whispered, "Ella Kate, she's a nice lady, but I don't think housework was ever her strong suit."

"You know Ella Kate?" I don't know why I was surprised. Guthrie was so small it made Mayberry look like a metropolis.

"Oh, sure," Bobby said. "I been knowing Ella Kate, and Mr. Norbert too, for a good long time. Norbert, he was pretty tight with a dollar, but when he got up in years and couldn't get around too much, he'd hire me to do little jobs around the place."

"What can we do about the sink?" I asked.

"Elbow grease," Bobby said. "Get it cleaned up and polished, it'll look as good as those farmhouse sinks in the magazines. Same with these old faucets. They're nickel plated," he continued. "That's the thing about Birdsong. The Dempseys, your people, they had plenty of money back in the day, and they didn't mind spending it. Everything in this house—it may be old, but it's first-rate."

"I guess," I said. "Everything but me."

Bobby gave me a quizzical look.

"Never mind me," I said. "I'm just having a little pity party for my-self."

Bobby picked up his clipboard and handed it to me. His precise block letters covered most of the page, everything itemized. I looked down at the bottom line and smiled. His estimate—for everything, labor and materials—came in right at $78,000.

"When can you start?" I asked.

"How's tomorrow?"

"Fine," I said. I kicked at the loosened floor tile with the toe of my sneaker. "Can you leave that heat gun with me tonight? I've got some aggression I need to work out."

I walked Bobby out to the porch. And when I opened the door, was greeted with the smell of fresh paint.

Jimmy Maynard, my new friend from the hardware store, stood on the porch, brandishing a can of paint in one hand and a brush in the other. The day was sunny, but although temperatures were still only in the high sixties he was again dressed for a day on the golf greens, in blue madras Bermudas and a hot pink golf shirt. He'd painted a three-foot-wide swath of rich green paint on Birdsong's faded pink siding.

"Bobby Livesey!" Jimmy said, putting the paint can down and wiping his hands with a handkerchief he pulled from his back pocket. "You coming to the rescue of Miss Dempsey Killebrew here?"

"Looks like it," Bobby said, pumping Jimmy's hand. "Did Dempsey line you up to do the house painting? I didn't know you'd gotten out of real estate."

"Oh no, I'm still messing with real estate," Jimmy said. "Too old to change my stripes now, you know."

The two men laughed over their shared joke, and Bobby took his leave, promising that he would arrive bright and early in the morning.

Jimmy Maynard nonchalantly opened another can of paint and started brushing a lighter shade of green on the other side of the door.

"What are you doing here?" I asked, crossing my arms across my chest. "Besides defacing my property?"

Jimmy gestured with his brush at his handiwork. "I was over at the hardware store this morning, and I got to thinking about Birdsong. I've driven back and forth past this house at least twice a day for the past twenty years, and every time I pass it, I think about what a beautiful place this could be if it was fixed up. You know I just live up the block, don't you?"

"I didn't know that."

He pointed to his right. "The little brick Colonial Revival. Six houses down. First house I ever bought. I lost it in my first divorce, but then, when Shirlene hooked herself a rich doctor and moved out to the country club, I managed to buy it back. Two marriages and two divorces later, I'm still hanging on to the place."

"You've been married and divorced three times?" I asked incredulously.

"Four, if you count good ol' LaDonna." He was opening another can of paint. This one was an acid green. "Oh hell," he said, putting the lid back on. "That won't work. Looks like baby puke."

"I thought you wanted me to paint the house white," I said.

"Change of plans. White's boring. Dill pickle, this is called," Jimmy said. "Stupid name for a paint, you ask me. I think I'd like it better if we cut it twenty-five percent with white."

"We?"

"Just a figure of speech."

"Back to your marriage record," I said, starting to enjoy myself despite my previous funk. "Why wouldn't I count good ol' LaDonna?"

"That one was a shotgun wedding. Her daddy caught us in the backseat of my Camaro, out at the reservoir. I was seventeen, but ol' La-Donna was eighteen."

"You got married at seventeen? Were you still in high school?"

"Technically," he said. "We moved into a double-wide out at my granny's farm, and I went to summer school so I could graduate early. Her daddy got me a job at the bedspread mill. At the time it was durned good money. For a seventeen-year-old."

I leaned up against one of the porch columns. "Then what happened?"

"I got laid off at the mill, and LaDonna got laid by some dude she met at a dance at the VFW. No hard feelings though. I even let her have the double-wide."

"You're quite a guy, Jimmy Maynard," I said.

He put his hand on my arm, and I shivered involuntarily. "Oh, darlin'," he drawled, with that slow, deadly smile that had obviously affected many a woman in Guthrie, Georgia. "You don't know the half of it."

I gave him a long, searching look. He flashed the grin, full force. I think he thought I'd drop my panties right there.

I shook my head. "You're good. But it won't work on me. You forget, I'm not from here. Anyway, it's a waste of time expending all that charm on me. I'm going to get this old house fixed up, and sold, and then I'm outta here. Two months tops."

He looked hurt. "Why? You don't like me? Let me guess. You think I'm too old for you? Just how old do you think I am, anyway?"

"It's not that," I said quickly. I flashed back to what my roommate had said about my affinity for older men. She was wrong. Dead wrong. Wasn't she?

"What is it then?" he persisted. "Ah, hell. Don't tell me. I bet you came down here to nurse a broken heart."

"That's not it," I said sharply. "I told you already, I'm down here on business, plain and simple. I'm really not in the market for complications."

"Complications?" he hooted. "Anybody who knows me can tell you, I am the least complicated man on this planet. I'll tell you straight up who I am. I like my sippin' whiskey old, my cars fast, and my women young. Oh yeah. Money. I like money. You see, Dempsey Killebrew? With me, what you see is what you get. Ain't that refreshing? No bullshit. No complications. Now, what about it?"

"What about what?"

"You and me. Tonight. Some dinner. Some drinks. Some laughs. I promise, it'll be strictly physical. And I'll still respect you in the morning." He gave me a broad, endearing wink.

"Sorry," I told him. "I already have plans for tonight."

His face fell. "With who? Don't tell me you're seeing little old Tee Berryhill again. What? You got a thing for lawyers?"

My face flushed at the mention of Tee. We'd had one dinner—definitely not a date. His father did the cooking. Did everybody in town know my business already?

"I'm staying in tonight," I told Jimmy. "Just me and the heat gun. It's going to be hot, and it's going to be messy."

I left him standing on the porch, paintbrush in hand.

22

I hadn't lied when I told Jimmy Maynard about my plans for the evening. Still smarting from Alex's phone call, I decided the best way to work out my worries was with a project.

I cleared all the furniture out of the kitchen, stacking the chairs on top of the table, which I'd dragged into the dining room.

For a moment, I stood looking down at the ugly green floor, trying to figure out where to start. The room reminded me of an enormous, scummy pond. The only way to empty it, I decided, was bucket by bucket, or in this case, square by square.

At my request, Bobby had left me a wooden fruit crate full of tools he'd gathered from Birdsong's basement and toolshed. I dug out a measuring tape and measured the room. It was exactly fifteen by twenty. The tiles themselves were eight-inch squares. By my quick computations, there were 630 tiles begging to be demolished.

The old linoleum tiles were worn and brittle and came up relatively easily with the aid of the knife-edged pry bar Bobby had lent me. Each time I whacked the head of the pry bar with the mallet, the sensation filled me with malicious delight. By eight o'clock that night, I'd filled two heavy-duty plastic trash bags with the discarded tiles. I was elated when I dumped the last tile into the last bag. Piece of cake, I decided. At this rate, I might have the entire kitchen rehabbed within a week. And if Bobby could match my pace, I would have Birdsong spiffed up and sold in half the time Mitch and I had allotted. Soon, I thought, I would be seeing Guthrie in my rearview mirror. By April, I would be seeing the cherry blossoms in bloom around the tidal basin.

Cheered by this thought, I made quick work of dragging the bags of discarded tiles outside to the garbage cans. But when I came back inside, it was to find Ella Kate standing in the middle of the kitchen, a look of fury on her face.

"What's all this?" she demanded. "Look at the mess you've made here. What do you think you're doing to my floor?"

Something in me snapped.

"It's not your floor," I said. "I'm sorry, Ella Kate, but that's the truth. Norbert left the house to my father, and he has asked me to get it ready to be sold. That's what I intend to do."

"You Killebrews!" She bit the words out. "Think you know everything. Think you run the world." She stomped out of the room, slamming behind her the door to the hallway.

I vowed once again to get to the bottom of Ella Kate's feud with my father. Later. Right now, I had a floor to demolish.

I plugged in the heat gun and started to work. If the tiles had come up with relative ease, the stubborn black adhesive was a whole different ball game. I had to aim the heat gun inches from the mastic with my left hand, use the heat to soften it, and after precisely two minutes, quickly scrape up the goo with my right hand before it had time to harden again into a seemingly impregnable lump.

In an hour's time, I had barely managed to scrape clean a two-foot square of floor. My wrists were aching, and I'd somehow burned a dime-size spot on my right thumb. Waves of depression and self-pity washed over me. I'd graduated from undergrad school second in my class, been editor of the law review in law school. I'd landed a prestigious job with the most influential lobbying firm in Washington, D.C. But now, from the looks of things, I might well spend the rest of my fleeting youth on my hands and knees on the floor of a decrepit old house in a one-horse town in Mudflap, Georgia.

I flopped down on my back and stared up at the ceiling. The sight of water stains and peeling plaster did little to dispel the cloud of gloom hovering over me.

Stop it! I told myself fiercely. It was just a kitchen floor. Just three hundred square feet. Before tonight, I'd never so much as hammered a nail in place. And now, in just a few short hours, I'd already pried up an entire roomful of linoleum.

Groaning, I rolled myself to my feet. I brewed a strong pot of coffee and went back to work.

After plugging in my iPod, I decided to attack the floor the same way I'd attacked a seemingly impossible workload in law school. I divided the task into manageable chunks. Found a way to do the job more efficiently.

At midnight, when I'd worked my way exactly halfway through the floor, I stood up, did some yoga stretches, and decided to take a short break. I'd gotten hot and sweaty from proximity to the heat gun. I opened the kitchen door, and after a brief hesitation, stepped outside onto the back porch.

Sinking down on the top step, I let the cool night air wash over me, breathing in deep lungsful of some sweet-smelling floral scent. Looking around I noticed for the first time that a thick green vine had wrapped its way around the porch posts, and the waxy, white, star-shaped flowers seemed to be the source of the perfume.

I wondered idly what the name of the flower was. In fact, I wondered what the names of most of the plants in the overgrown yard were. I plucked one of the flowers, sniffed, and tucked it into the pocket of my bib overalls. Maybe, I thought, Tee Berryhill could name the flower for me.

Or maybe it didn't really matter. As I'd already made clear to Jimmy Maynard, my stay in Guthrie was business, not pleasure. And it was time I got back to business.

"Drunk! Eight o'clock in the morning, and she's passed out dead drunk on the floor."

Ella Kate's voice dripped contempt. I lifted my head from my outstretched arms, rolled to my left, and looked up. She and Bobby Livesey stood looking down at me.

"Eight o' clock!" I tried to roll over, but my muscles screamed a protest. I looked around the room. Sunlight made warm butter yellow splashes on the wooden floor around me.

Wood. My kitchen floor was now decidedly wood. I gingerly inched my way up to a sitting position. The better to survey my night's work.

"Dempsey!" Bobby said, giving me a hand and hauling me to my feet. "I don't know how you did it, but you sure did hit this floor a lick last night."

I yawned. "Sure did," I said sleepily.

"Man!" he said admiringly. "I thought it was gonna look good, but I didn't know it was gonna look this good."

"Not bad, huh?" I asked.

The floor was far from perfect. In the light of day I could see numerous specks of mastic still clinging stubbornly to the wood. There were gouge marks in the wood, and singe marks too, where I'd gotten carried away with the chisel or the heat gun, but all in all, I was amazed by what I'd accomplished in one night.

"I liked the linoleum better," Ella Kate said with a sniff. "Olivia picked that tile out herself. Sent all the way to Atlanta to get it. Everybody knows linoleum is what you put on a kitchen floor."

Bobby and I exchanged knowing looks.

"I wasn't able to get everything up," I told Bobby. I held out my mangled fingertips. "As it was, I couldn't get into the tight corners with that pry bar. I must have ruined three or four kitchen knives."

"You done great," Bobby said, walking all around the room.

"What's next?" I asked eagerly.

"Drum sander," Bobby said. "I can rent one over at the Home Depot tomorrow. I got a helper coming over this morning. We're gonna pull up all that slate on the roof and try to get the new underlayment down before another hard rain. Maybe next week, when the roof's done, I can get this floor knocked out."

"No," I said, shaking my head emphatically. "Not next week. I'm on a roll. I'll drive over to Home Depot myself and rent the sander. You'll have to show me how to use it, though."

"Oh no, no, no," Bobby said, laughing. "I know you think you're tough. In fact, you're mighty tough. But you don't want to be messing around with a drum sander. You got to keep working it over the floor, nice and even. And it ain't as easy as it looks. That thing is heavy as a horse, and it's got a kick like a mule. I see where you started stripping the wallpaper in the front room. That'd be a good thing for you to do.

Get that wallpaper off. Or pick out the color you want the outside of the house painted. I like that shade of green Jimmy Maynard painted on the right side of the door. You just leave the drum sander to Bobby."

I looked at him. Raised one eyebrow. He shook his head and held up his hands in a gesture of defeat.

"You're a Dempsey, all right," he said. "Hardheaded. All them Dempseys hardheaded. I don't guess you're any different. Come on, then. A drum sander won't fit in the Catfish. We'll take my truck."

In fact, we rented a drum sander and a corner sander at the Home Depot in Macon.

We stopped at a hot-dog stand that Bobby knew about, the Nu-Way, which he said was famous for its dogs, split open, grilled, and served on griddled hamburger buns with a spicy chili sauce. The day had gotten warm, hot even, so we sat on the flipped-down tailgate of Bobby's truck and had an impromptu picnic, washing the dogs down with icy Styrofoam cups of root beer. We ate in companionable silence, and when I'd eaten every bite of my hot dogs, I embarrassed myself with a tiny, unavoidable belch.

"Whoa!" I said, covering my mouth with a crumpled napkin. "Excuse me."

"Can't be helped," Bobby said. "You ready to get back to work?"

"In a minute," I said, leaning back on my elbows and turning my face up to the sun. It felt so good to be warm, and comfortable, with a belly full of food. Spring came much earlier to this part of Georgia, I decided. The dogwoods that lined the streets of Guthrie were already fully budded out, and waves of pink, white, and coral azaleas made bright splashes of color in nearly every yard I'd seen. This time of year in Washington, I'd still be wearing a winter coat.

I hopped off the tailgate, did a couple of deep yoga stretches, and gathered up the grease-spattered paper sacks from our food. "Now then," I told Bobby. "Back to work."

The drum sander was, as Bobby had informed me, bulky and tricky to maneuver. He fitted me out with a pair of plastic goggles and a dust mask, and when I got a look at my reflection in the kitchen window, I looked like some kind of giant mutant science fiction insect.

"Just keep it moving evenly over the floor," Bobby told me, shouting to be heard above the racket the sander made. "Don't stay too long in one place either, or you'll dig a hole in the floor. Nice, even, sweeping motions. That's what you want with a drum sander."

With Bobby's help, I sealed off the kitchen from the rest of the house with thick plastic sheeting, and then went to work. I spent all day that day, and the next, working on the kitchen floor, becoming totally obsessed with achieving wood-floor perfection, working through three different grades of sandpaper.

At one point Saturday morning, Tee Berryhill dropped by. He took a step backward when I answered the doorbell.

"Lord have mercy, Dempsey," he said. "What have you gotten yourself into?"

I looked down at my Carrharts, which I'd finally broken in with three consecutive washings. My clothing, my shoes, my hair, in fact, every inch of exposed skin on me was covered with a thick film of sawdust. He reached out and gingerly flicked a spot of sawdust from my cheek.

"I'm refinishing the kitchen floor," I reported happily. "No more bile green linoleum."

His eyes strayed from me to the contrasting swatches of green on either side of the front door.

"What's with the paint?" he asked.

"Oh. I'm, uh, trying out colors."

"I like this one, on the left," he said promptly. "Hey, I've been trying to reach you for the past two days. I even dropped by, but you were out. Did Ella Kate tell you I stopped by?"

"No," I said. "But that doesn't surprise me. We've had words, she and I."

"Anyway," Tee went on, "I know it'll seem like last minute, but there's a Middle Georgia Bar Association dinner tonight at the country club. I was hoping you'd go with me. It's not a formal or anything, but it would give you a chance to meet some local folks. I think you'd have a good time."

He smiled winningly, like a schoolboy presenting his teacher with an apple.

"Oh," I said. "That's so sweet, Tee. I'd love to go."

"Good," he said. "Dinner's at eight. Cocktails at seven—"

"But I can't go," I said. "My floor. I'm right in the middle of it."

"Take a break," he urged. "The floor will be there when you get back."

"Sorry," I told him. "Maybe next time."

Ella Kate came and went as I worked, stepping disdainfully over the piles of sawdust I'd swept up, sniffing and muttering dire warnings about how I was ruining what had been a perfectly good kitchen.

I ignored her comments and attacked the sawdust with Bobby's borrowed Shop-Vac. I had a schedule to keep.

Once I'd achieved a satin-smooth floor (or nearly smooth—with the exception of the unavoidable gouged places), I was in a fever to see the project through to completion.

"What's next?" I'd asked as we loaded the sanders in the truck for the return trip to Home Depot late Saturday.

"We put down good thick paper on that pretty floor of yours, and leave it down till we're done with everything else," Bobby said. "Last thing we do, we apply the finish. Guess you need to decide how you want it to look. Do you want a high-gloss finish? Or more of a matte, natural look?"

"Matte," I said promptly. "Why can't I put the finish down now? I'm dying to see how it'll look, now that I'm this close. I could start tonight. I bet it'd be dry by morning."

"Oh, noooo," Bobby said. "Once you put the finish on, you got to let it set and cure for three, four days. Can't nobody walk on it or nothing. You done a good job on that floor, Dempsey. Now, it's Saturday night. I notice you got Tee Berryhill and Jimmy Maynard dropping by here pretty regular. I bet one of them boys would be tickled to death to take a pretty girl like you out on a Saturday night."

"No dates," I said succinctly. "Work. If you won't let me put the finish on the floor, would you do me favor?"

He looked wary. "Depends on what it is."

"Loan me your electric screwdriver. I want to get started on those cupboard doors tonight."

23

When I got out of the shower Sunday morning, I heard my cell phone ringing. Wrapping a towel around me, I hurried down the hall to my bedroom. Fishing the phone out of my pocketbook, I was gratified to see that the caller was Lindsay.

"Linds," I said gleefully. "How are you? How's Stephanie? Do you guys miss me as much as I miss you? Guess what. I've spent the whole weekend stripping the kitchen floor. You should see it, Linds. The most beautiful heart pine. I started on the cabinet doors last night—"

"Who is this?" Lindsay said, her tone flat. "Is this the Dempsey Killebrew I've lived with for the past two years? What have you done with my friend Dempsey?"

"I know," I said, laughing. "How crazy is this? I haven't worn a pair of heels since I moved down here."

"Demps," Lindsay said, pausing. "We need to talk."

"What's wrong?" I said, feeling chilled. "Are you in trouble? Is it Stephanie? Don't tell me she and Greg broke up again—"

"I'm fine. Stephanie and Greg are fine. We're all fine, Dempsey," Lindsay said. "Look. Have you seen this morning's *Post*?"

I sank down onto my bed. I was freezing cold. "No. I don't have any way to see the *Post*. I don't have Internet access at the house. Oh God, Lindsay. Not that reporter. Oh shit. It's bad, isn't it."

"It isn't good," she said, choosing her words carefully. "Especially the photo of you in those overalls. When did you start dressing like Larry the Cable Guy?"

"Oh my God." I said. "I told that guy to get off my porch. I should have smashed the damn camera."

"You should burn those overalls. And lose the plaid flannel shirt. And the bandanna. Immediately. Look. Have you spoken to Alex lately?"

I threw myself backward on the bed. "No. No. No."

"I knew it," Lindsay said. "What a shit he is. I'm sorry, Demps, but that man is a total prick."

"That's not what I meant," I told her. "I have spoken to Alex. But only briefly. After that reporter, Shalani something, showed up here this week."

"Shalani Byers," Lindsay said grimly. "Remember that name, Dempsey. 'Cause I think she's planning on earning herself a Pulitzer by writing about you. And Hoddergate."

"Read me the story," I told her.

"Are you sure you're up for this?" Lindsay said. "It's pretty brutal."

I stood up, gathered the bedspread off the bed, and wrapped it around me, swaddling my still damp, naked body entirely in the bedspread made in a factory I'd been named after.

"Read it," I said. "All of it."

"Even the headline?"

"Every word."

"Okay. The headline says: 'Hoddergate Lobbyist Blames Aide for Hiring Hookers for Congressman.'"

"Oh no," I whispered. "Is this on the front page of the *Post?*"

"Front page, lead story, above the fold," said Lindsay, who'd been a journalism major as an undergrad.

"Go on."

"Here goes: 'Sources close to the government investigation delving into charges that a prominent Washington lobbyist bribed Representative Anthony Licata (R-New Jersey) in return for Licata's support on a crucial energy bill pending before Congress say that the lobbyist has admitted that one of his employees hired prostitutes for Licata.

"'Alexander Hodder, founding partner of Hodder and Associates, whose client roster includes half a dozen oil interests, reportedly supplied the federal grand jury looking into the allegations with credit card receipts showing that his top aide, a woman named Dempsey Killebrew, paid two women a total of $5,600 to provide sexual services to Licata during a November junket to Lyford Cay, the Bahamas. Hodder's name reportedly came to the attention of the FBI during their investigation in to charges of corruption involving Representative Licata.'"

"My name. On the front page of the *Washington Post*," I moaned, pounding the pillows beside me. "Oh God. It can't get any worse than this."

"Oh, but it does," Lindsay assured me.

" 'Licata, sixty-two, married, and the father of four grown children, from Rumford, NJ, has denied any wrongdoing, and has publicly vowed to fight his recent indictment on criminal charges. If convicted of fraud and public corruption, the four-time Republican could face a fifteen-year prison sentence for each incident of bribery.

" 'Hodder, fifty, and married for ten years to Virginia socialite Patricia "Trish" Caldwell, claims he was stunned by his recent discovery of proof that an "inexperienced" associate whom he termed "overzealous in her attempts to impress her superiors" had solicited prostitutes and paid for them with her company-issued American Express credit card.'"

"Inexperienced? Overzealous?" I balled up my fists and chewed on my knuckles. "That's just unreal. Lindsay, Alex Hodder is a complete control freak. He wouldn't even allow me to send a form letter to a client unless he read it, edited it, and initialed it," I cried.

Lindsay just kept reading without comment.

" 'AmEx receipts billed to Ms. Killebrew's card reportedly show that she signed off on a $4,000 charge from a company called Pleasure Chest Ltd., whose employee, a woman calling herself Mahogany Foxx, allegedly provided Licata, who has undergone two knee replacements, with wakeboard lessons. Later, on that same date, November 29, which was the Saturday after Thanksgiving, Ms. Killebrew also authorized another $1,600 charge for a massage therapist named Tiki Finesse to visit Licata in his $1,288-a-night suite at the Lyford Cay Resort.'"

Lindsay snickered. "Mahogany Foxx? Tiki Finesse? Dempsey, where did you find those women? Were those really their names?"

"How do I know their real names?" I shrieked. "Alex told me to call the number and book this girl to give Licata wakeboard lessons. The same thing with the massage therapist. As far as I know, I never talked to either one of them, and I certainly never saw them. I told that to that damned reporter too."

"You should see the picture of Mahogany Foxx in the *Post*," Lindsay said. "I don't see how she walked upright, let alone balanced on a wakeboard, with a set of knockers like that. There's a photo of good ol' Tiki too," she added. "Oh wait. It says here that Tiki's not her real name. Big surprise. Her real name is Thelma Jean Fessenden, and she's from Belle Glade, Florida. I guess this is her police mug shot. It says she has previous arrests for solicitation, rude and lascivious behavior, and assault and battery. Maybe that's how she lost her two front teeth."

"I don't feel so good," I told Lindsay, gripping my belly. "I think I might hurl."

"I can stop reading if you want," Lindsay volunteered. "You could call me back when you feel better."

I swallowed the wave of bile rising in my throat. "I'm never going to feel better. Let's just get this over with."

"All right," Lindsay said, sighing. "Let's see. Oh yeah.

"'Reached Friday at his residence in Georgetown, Hodder said that Ms. Killebrew acted on her own in hiring Ms. Foxx and Ms. Finesse.

"'"I was shocked when I saw the evidence that Dempsey Killebrew had made these completely unauthorized charges for prostitutes," Hodder told the *Post*. "I certainly have never condoned or suggested such an action. Unfortunately, Miss Killebrew's ill-advised and illegal behavior has brought shame and embarrassment to this firm. Naturally, we discharged her as soon as we learned about her involvement in this matter. I have turned over to the grand jury all Miss Killebrew's credit card records, as well as any other paperwork related to her employment here, and I look forward to cooperating fully with the government in an attempt to restore the good name of Alexander Hodder and Hodder and Associates."'"

"How could he?" I wailed. "He's making it look like hiring these women was all my idea. All I did was what he asked me to do. What he ordered me to do. Doesn't it say that I told this Shalani Byers that I was innocent?"

"Lemme see," Lindsay said. "Oh yeah. She says you said, 'No comment.'

Here's some more stuff about you. Ooh. Ouch. Doesn't make you look too good, Demps."

"Read it anyway."

" 'Ms. Killebrew, a 2007 graduate of Georgetown Law School, fled Washington soon after the Hoddergate scandal erupted, and has since gone into self-imposed seclusion in an obscure small town about an hour south of Atlanta, Georgia.' "

"Fled? She's making it sound like I was driven out of town by villagers with pickaxes and torches. I had to move out of Washington because Alex fired me and I couldn't get a job anyplace else. And I am so *not* in seclusion. Lindsay, do people in seclusion shop at the Piggly Wiggly? Do they go to Home Depot?"

"I know, baby," Lindsay soothed. "Do you still want to hear the rest?"

"You mean there's more? How much worse could it get?"

I soon found out just how much deeper Shalani Byers's wounds would go.

" 'Neighbors in Guthrie, Georgia, a down-at-the-heels village with one stoplight and an abandoned bedspread factory, describe Miss Killebrew, twenty-seven, as a shadowy figure who dresses in a dead uncle's work boots and flannel shirts and currently lives in a dilapidated mansion that she shares with an elderly distant relative and an incontinent cocker spaniel.' "

"Liar!" I gritted my teeth. "I never even touched Norbert's work boots. That's a complete fabrication. I borrowed his sneakers, and some overalls and shirts. I bought Carrharts, but it took a while to get them broken in. As for Shorty, Ella Kate walks him three or four times a day. He's irritating, but I don't think he's incontinent."

The other end of the line got very quiet.

"You're starting to scare me, Dempsey," Lindsay said. "We've got to get you out of there before you go completely native. When are you coming home?"

"After this thing in the *Post*? With everybody inside the beltway reading this crap and assuming the worst? Who's going to hire me? What the hell am I going to do now, Lindsay?"

"I don't know," she admitted. "It's not a very flattering story, to say the least."

"Goooooddd," I said, flouncing myself down on my wheezy old mattress. "I'm screwed."

"You need to talk to Alex Hodder," Lindsay said. "The dickhead. This is all his fault."

"I just can't believe Alex is doing any of this," I said. "He knows the truth. He knows I would never have knowingly hired whores for Licata. I never even bought as much as a ham sandwich with that credit card without him okaying it. He would never willingly do this. Not without coercion. The only thing I can figure is, his lawyers are pressuring him to cut some kind of deal with the feds."

"Wake up and look at your back, Dempsey," Lindsay retorted.

I reflexively touched my right hand to my left shoulder blade. "What are you talking about?"

"Don't you see the tread marks?" she asked. "Alex Hodder is throwing you under the bus. And all you can talk about is what a sweet guy he is. Open your eyes, girl."

"He's just protecting himself. And the firm. You can't blame him for that."

"Oh no?" Her voice was mocking. "I was saving the worst for last. Listen to this. And then tell me what you think about good old Alex Hodder."

She cleared her throat and read on.

"'Although the federal prosecutor's office is keeping mum about Dempsey Killebrew's role in the Hoddergate scandal, at least one employee of Hodder and Associates made it clear this week that she believes investigators should take a closer look at Alex Hodder's closest aide.

"'Hodder and Associates executive administrator Ruby Beaubien said the company, at her urging, has hired a forensic accountant to examine "any and all documents and expense records generated by the disgraced junior lobbyist."'"

"Disgraced!" I yelped. "Oh my God, she's calling me a thief and a liar, as well as a pimp. This is unbelievable. I thought Ruby was my friend."

"Wait," Lindsay ordered.

" ' "It was clear to many of us at the firm that Dempsey Killebrew had an unhealthy and inappropriate attraction to Alexander Hodder," Ms. Beaubien said. "Although Mr. Hodder made it quite clear that her attentions were not welcome, and that he did not reciprocate her affection, Miss Killebrew continued, in a grossly inappropriate manner, to pursue a personal relationship with Mr. Hodder, who is a happily married man. Finally, after hounding Mr. Hodder with dozens and dozens of calls to his cell phone, and a drunken midnight visit to his residence, I insisted to Mr. Hodder, that despite his concern for the young woman's welfare, she be terminated." ' "

"Oh. No," I whispered. "No way." I put the phone down and dashed blindly down the hall to the bathroom, where I unceremoniously barfed my brains out.

I have no idea how long I stayed in the bathroom, hanging on to the cold white porcelain commode like a drowning swimmer. I do know that I heard my cell phone ringing several more times. I heard the doorbell ringing, and then Shorty's crazed barking. After a while, Ella Kate started banging on the bathroom door.

"Hey!" she called. "Are you still in there?"

"Go away," I croaked.

"You go away," she countered. "And take that durned phone of yours with you. It's Sunday, the Lord's day, and that phone of yours keeps a-ringin' and a-ringin'. You got men coming and going and wanting to know where you are and what you're a-doin'. It don't look right for a Christian maiden lady like myself to have men hanging around here this way."

"Send them away," I said. "I don't want to see anybody."

"Send them away yourself," Ella Kate said. "I'm going to church. And when I get back here after Sunday school, there better not be any men hanging around. Or I'll set Shorty on them—and you."

I heard her sensible lace-up oxfords clomping down the hallway, and then down the steps and out the front door.

Finally, when my legs were starting to cramp, I stood up shakily and looked at myself in the bathroom mirror.

There were dark circles under my bloodshot eyes, and my face was red and blotchy from crying and retching.

"You look like a deranged person," I told my reflection. "Like a stalker."

I dressed hurriedly—and this time in my own clothes. Even though it was close to seventy outside, I put on the wool pants and sweater I'd worn the day I arrived in Guthrie. I put on makeup—foundation, powder, blush, eye shadow, liner, mascara, the works. I grabbed my pocketbook and the car keys, and hurried out the back door, locking it behind me.

The Catfish coughed twice and the engine cut off once, but when I got it warmed up, I backed down the driveway and onto Poplar Street. I sped down the street and through Guthrie's minuscule business district.

It was Sunday-morning quiet. The shops on Main Street were closed, the streets abandoned. I drove past Guthrie First United Methodist, where I knew Ella Kate was sitting in the front row. I passed Grace Presbyterian Church, with its stately gray granite bell tower, and the sprawling redbrick complex that comprised Guthrie First Baptist. Across the street from the Baptist church, I saw All Saints Episcopal Church, and I spotted Carter Berryhill's sedate Mercedes sedan with the Nature Conservancy bumper sticker parked at the curb out front.

I was careful to stay under the speed limit until I got out to the state highway. Then I floored the accelerator. The Catfish responded sluggishly at first. Norbert and Ella Kate had probably never driven more than thirty-five miles an hour. Now it was time to blow the kinks out of the Crown Vic's powerful engine.

I was doing fifty-five when I hit the I-75 on-ramp, and moments later, was pleased to see how easily the Catfish adapted to seventy and then eighty miles an hour. I didn't slow down until I started hitting Atlanta traffic. I stayed on I-75 until it merged with I-85, and when I saw the exit signs for Lenox Road, I took the off-ramp and followed the road until I started seeing the high-rise towers of Buckhead, and the congestion around Lenox Square Mall.

It wasn't until I pulled into the parking lot of Houlihan's and parked that I had any clear idea of where I was going and what I was going to do. I only knew I had to get away from Birdsong, had to get out of that "down-at-the-heels village with one stoplight" Shalani Byers had described in the *Washington Post*.

I couldn't be the shadowy figure in the scary dead uncle's clothes today. I pulled a mirror from my pocketbook and applied a coat of lipstick. I patted my hair into place, and stepped out of the car.

The Sunday brunch crowd was just starting to stagger into Houlihan's. I told the hostess I didn't need a table, so she gestured toward the bar.

I sat down and ordered a Bloody Mary, and when the salt-crusted tumbler was still half full, I ordered another, along with a cheeseburger, cooked rare, with a side of onion rings. When I looked up and caught sight of myself in the bar-back mirror, I was taken aback. That shadowy figure described by the paper was gone, but so was the Dempsey Killebrew I'd left behind in Washington less than three weeks ago.

picked at my food and sipped my drink, but barely touched the second Bloody Mary I'd ordered. To my surprise, I found I'd lost my taste for liquor—or maybe just my desire for a good strong buzz.

As it grew close to noon, the restaurant began to fill up and the noise level rose. Families dressed in their Sunday best arrived and took the larger tables, and couples and singles drifted in too, dressed in their designer blue jeans and T-shirts with ironic slogans. Finally, I had to move my pocketbook from the vacant bar stool next to mine to make way for another solitary drinker.

After I'd dawdled for nearly two hours, the harried bartender arrived with my check and lingered in front of me, willing me to drink up and get out.

And go where? I wondered, rifling through my pocketbook for cash to pay my check.

I was just pulling out of the parking lot when my cell phone rang. I took it out and answered, "Hi, Dad."

"What the hell have you gotten yourself involved in, Dempsey?" Mitch demanded.

My heart sank. I'd been hoping to call both my parents to warn them about the latest development in the scandal, to give them my side of the story, before things got blown all out of proportion. Obviously, I was too late.

"You saw the *Washington Post?*"

"No, I haven't yet had the pleasure of seeing my daughter's name being written about in connection with hookers and crooked congressmen," Mitch said.

"Then, how . . . ?"

"A reporter called the house at seven a.m., wanting to know if you were my daughter," Mitch broke in. "Pilar is furious. Sunday is our only day to sleep in. The call woke the boys, and now they're bouncing off the walls."

"I'm sorry. I don't even know what to say."

"You could start by telling me that you didn't hire hookers for that man."

"Of course I didn't!" I cried. "Do you even have to ask?"

"But the charges were made to your credit card," he said. "That doesn't look good."

"Alex asked me to book wakeboard lessons, and then a therapeutic massage for Representative Licata. I never knew anything about prostitutes. I never saw the amount charged to the credit card."

"You see!" he cried. "That is total and absolute fiscal irresponsibility. Which is why you're saddled with all this damned loan debt. You're twenty-eight years old—and you don't even own a car. When I was your age, I'd bought my first home and had already established a college fund for you."

I felt my blood start to boil. How many times had I had to listen to my father's rant about fiscal responsibility? It was true that he'd been successful in business at an early age—but it was also true that as the only child of two only children he'd been a trust-fund baby who'd come into his inheritance at the age of eighteen.

"Dad, if you'd just let me explain."

"And this . . . pathetic crush you had on your boss. A married man! It's so . . . disgusting. Good God, Dempsey, what were you thinking? He's what—fifty? Jesus. He's twenty-two years older than you!"

Maybe it was the Bloody Mary. Or maybe it was just that I didn't give a damn anymore. "Oh, right, Dad. I'm twenty-eight. You're sixty. And how old will Pilar be on her next birthday?"

"That's different and you know it," he said.

"Yes. It's different because you say so. Because you're the dad."

"Don't take that tone with me, Dempsey. Remember, it's my name you're dragging through the mud. Mine and Pilar's and the boys."

"Fine," I said, clutching the phone so hard with my right hand that my fingertips were cramping. I felt a stabbing pain between my eyes.

"Look, Dad. This isn't getting us anywhere, so I'm going to hang up now. I don't expect you to understand any of this. But I do think it would be nice if you'd at least give me the benefit of the doubt."

"Wait. Don't you dare—"

I flipped the phone closed and tossed it onto the seat.

25

My cell phone rang again, just as I was hitting the Guthrie city limits, but I didn't want to answer it. The confrontation with my father had left me feeling battered and shaken. But when a minute passed and it started ringing again, I picked it up to see who was calling.

BERRYHILL AND BERRYHILL flashed across the readout screen.

I pressed the connect button. "Tee?"

"Sorry," came the buttery Southern drawl. "You got the old man this time."

"You're not so old," I told Carter Berryhill. "Anyway, after the morning I've had, the sound of your voice is a welcome relief."

"You might not think so when I tell you why I'm calling."

"Uh-oh."

"Where are you, by the way? I know you're not at Birdsong."

"I'm in the car. I took a run up to Atlanta for lunch, but I'm on my way back home right now."

"Maybe you should take a detour," Carter suggested. "Why don't you pick me up at the house and I'll catch you up on some things."

"All right," I agreed. "I'll be there in five minutes."

My heart was pounding and my hands were shaking as I pulled up to the Berryhills' home. Carter met me at the curb. He opened the door and slid into the front seat.

"What's going on?" I asked.

"I want you to pull your car into my garage," he said. "You can park beside my car. Tee's over at the newspaper office."

"Carter, you're starting to scare me," I said, my voice shaky, steering the Catfish into the slot he indicated in the garage beside the house.

"We'll talk inside the house," he said. I followed him in the back door to the kitchen. "Sit down," he said, indicating a wooden ladderback chair at the kitchen table.

He sat down beside me. "I'm sorry to have alarmed you," he said. "But I thought it best to handle things this way. You've had some company looking for you this morning."

"Company?"

"Two FBI agents," he said. "An African-American gentleman and a lady."

I felt the blood drain from my head. "Oh no. How did they, I mean, why?"

"I suppose they went over to Birdsong this morning. And when they found nobody home, they knocked on some doors. I think one of your neighbors told them I might know how to reach you."

"Oh my God," I whispered. "The FBI!"

Carter patted my hand. "I must tell you, I've read the *Washington Post* story. Dempsey, I'm so sorry you've been dragged into this mess. These agents wouldn't tell me why they wanted to speak with you, but I'm sure they're looking into this matter with the congressman."

My face grew hot with embarrassment. I couldn't bear to look my new friend in the eyes. "You must think I'm awful."

He laughed easily. "I think the situation is awful. You, on the other hand, are a delightful, forthright, and honest young woman who seems to have unwittingly gotten mixed up in a very serious situation. If you'll let me, maybe I can be of some assistance."

I looked up. "You don't believe what Alex Hodder is saying?"

"Of course not," Carter said. "I never believe everything I read or hear on the news. This man Hodder is obviously attempting to shift blame to you so that he can extricate himself from this scandal."

"I can't believe he's doing this," I said. "Maybe the newspaper got it all wrong."

"Maybe," Carter said, his voice dubious. "But in the meantime, those FBI agents are camped out in front of your house, waiting for you to get home. I think we'd best do something about that."

"What? Carter, I don't want to talk to the FBI."

"Nobody does," he said, standing up. "But I think, in this case, it's unavoidable. So, let's go on over to Birdsong, and get it over with. I'll let them know I'm your attorney, and that you won't be talking to them without me present."

"I can't afford an attorney," I said. "I'm broke. That's why I moved down here, Carter. Alex Hodder fired me. I'm broke, I've got no place else to live." I bit my lip. "I'm twenty-eight years old and had to go running home to my father for help. I'm a one-woman disaster. You should run the other way."

"Nonsense," he said. "It's agreed then. I'm your attorney. We'll discuss fees later. But for right now, let's go see what these folks have to say."

We drove over to Birdsong in Carter's Mercedes. He asked me questions as he drove, focusing on the Bahamas trip. His responses to my answers were slow and measured. And by the time we pulled up behind the silver sedan parked in front of Birdsong, I felt an unnatural sense of calm settling in.

The agents did not look pleased to see Carter Berryhill. The woman, who introduced herself as Camerin Allgood, seemed to be in charge. She was tall, with a dancer's slender build, and had shoulder-length blond hair and piercing blue eyes. She introduced her partner, Jackson Harrell. He was an inch shorter, which put him just under six feet, with mocha-colored skin and unusual hazel eyes with light flecks. She wore a somber navy pantsuit; he was dressed more casually, in charcoal slacks, a yellow golf shirt, and a blue blazer.

"Shall we go inside to chat?" Carter asked. Harrell looked to Camerin Allgood for guidance.

"We'd prefer to do this interview in the Atlanta field office," she said. "That's procedure."

"Miss Killebrew has some appointments this afternoon," Carter said smoothly. "It would be more convenient for her to speak to you here. Or at my office, which is only five minutes away, whichever suits you better."

"Here is fine," Agent Allgood said. They trooped up the front walkway after me. As I struggled with the front-door key, I was thankful for having cleared away the worst of the clutter at the front of the house.

"You'll have to excuse the way the place looks," I said, swinging the door open. "My father just recently inherited this house, and I've only started working on the restoration this past week."

"Nice place," Jackson Harrell said, running his hand over the leaded glass sidelights. "How old is this house?"

But before I could answer, Camerin Allgood interrupted.

"Miss Killebrew, let's get this started, shall we?" Her voice was icy.

"All in good time," Carter said. He looked around the hallway. "Very nice, my dear. You've done wonders with the place already."

I flashed him a grateful smile. "There's not a lot of furniture in these front rooms, so I guess we'll have to talk in the kitchen."

"Fine, kitchen, basement, whatever," Agent Allgood snapped.

I opened the kitchen's swinging door and gestured for them to sit around the wooden kitchen table.

No sooner were we seated than Agent Allgood unsnapped her briefcase. She brought out a small silver tape recorder, and flipped open a file folder. "Sign here, please," she said, indicating a line on a sheet of paper. "This will indicate that you've agreed to having our discussion tape-recorded."

"Maybe you could tell us what it is you're going to be discussing," Carter said evenly.

"Let's start with public corruption," Agent Harrell said. "Bribing a United States congressman in general, specifically Representative Anthony Licata. Is any of this sounding familiar to you?"

My mouth was dry as dust. I swallowed. "I never—"

"Miss Killebrew," Agent Allgood broke in, "let's put our cards on the table here. I'm sure you're aware that we executed a search warrant on Representative Licata's office some weeks ago. I'm sure you're also aware that we have the hard drives from the offices of Hodder and Associates. That would include the hard drive from your computer. Containing documents and communications among you, Mr. Hodder, and Representative Licata. In addition, we are in possession of certain other documents that were voluntarily surrendered by your employer Mr. Hodder. That would include the records of purchases charged to an American Express credit card, issued to you by Mr. Hodder."

"Alex told me that woman was a wakeboard instructor," I cried. "I never met her. Or the masseuse."

Agent Harrell snickered. "You tellin' us a woman named Mahogany Foxx sounds legit? And her working for a company called Pleasure Chest? We're talking about surfing lessons for a man in his sixties, with two bum knees? You tellin' us you weren't curious about charges to a credit card—your credit card—amounting to nearly six thousand dollars? And you're a lawyer? Georgetown Law School?"

"I'm a lobbyist, for God's sake," I cried. "Part of my job was to entertain clients. Business dinners. Tickets to ball games, concerts at Wolftrap, those kinds of things were legitimate business expenses for our clients. Alex instructed me to use my company credit card to pay for the wakeboard lessons," I said. "He never told me the woman's name. He just gave me a phone number to call. He said, 'Set it up.' And I did. I didn't know that's how much they charged to my AmEx card. The bills were sent directly to the office manager. I never saw them."

"Riiiight," Agent Harrell said. "Listen—"

"Enough," Agent Allgood said, slapping her palm on the top of the kitchen table.

She leaned forward, so that her face was only a few inches from mine. "Miss Killebrew, do you know who you're dealing with here? Do you understand what's at stake here?"

"She understands," Carter said dryly. "We both do. But I don't appreciate your trying to intimidate my client."

"Trying to intimidate?" Harrell said. He laughed softly.

"I don't think Miss Killebrew understands at all," Agent Allgood said. She sat back in her chair, and crossed her legs. She was wearing gorgeous navy blue crocodile pumps with three-inch stacked heels. I never knew feds had good shoes.

"Fifteen years in a federal prison," Agent Allgood said. "That's for every count of bribery she's convicted of. Plus a hefty fine. Disbarment, of course. And that's just for starters."

"Fifteen years!" All the blood drained out of my head. I felt faint.

Carter squeezed my hand under the table.

"What is it you want from her?" Carter asked. "She's told you what she knows. She was instructed to call a phone number, to make arrangements for surfing lessons and a therapeutic massage. You obviously have the AmEx records. You have Mr. Hodder's version of what happened, and Representative Licata's version. And now you have my client's."

"Cooperation's the name of the game," Agent Harrell said, giving me an understanding smile.

"I have cooperated," I said. "I'm telling the truth."

Agent Allgood stood up and walked over to the back door. She opened it and looked out into the yard, at the bright green buds leafing out from the trees crowded up against the back door. "This is a nice place down here," she said when she turned around. "But it's gotta be pretty boring after leading the party life up there in D.C."

"I didn't party that much," I said. "I had a life. An apartment. Friends. A job. Up until recently."

"Yes," she said. "But Alex Hodder took care of all that. Didn't he? As soon as things started to heat up, he fired you. Didn't he? Or, should I say, his office manager fired you?"

I shrugged. I didn't know what she wanted from me.

"He's playing you, Dempsey," she said, giving me a pitying smile. "You know that, right? He probably set everything up from the very start, so that if anything went wrong with the payoffs to Licata, you'd be the one to go down. Not him."

Carter squeezed my hand again. This time it felt like a warning.

"Dempsey, Dempsey," she said, sighing softly. "You were in love with Alex Hodder, weren't you?"

"No." It came out with a squeak.

"Dude's good lookin'," Agent Harrell said. "Got that whole silver-fox thing going on. Takes good care of himself. Dresses nice. You believe he's fifty? I would have said more like forty, but that's what the driver's license says. I was a young girl, I might get a crush on him too."

Camerin Allgood shot him an annoyed look. "Jackson?"

"I'm just sayin'."

"We took a look at your cell phone bills, Dempsey," Agent Allgood said. "The day Licata was indicted? The day you and your boss were all over the news? You called Alex Hodder's cell phone nineteen times."

"I was trying to find out what was going on," I said. "The FBI came in, they took our computers, shut the office down. CNN was saying Alex was mixed up in this vote-buying thing. I was concerned."

"I'll bet," Harrell said. "Especially after they fired your butt."

Carter was squeezing my hand again. So I shut up.

"What is it you want from my client?" Carter repeated.

"Assistance," Harrell said. "A little help. So we can nail Alex Hodder's ass to the wall. Nail him up good, right beside that slimeball Licata. Yeah. We want us a congressman, and a big old lobbyist."

"Spell it out, would you please?" Carter said.

Camerin Allgood opened her briefcase again. She picked up the little tape recorder and stowed it inside the case. Then she brought out a small black plastic box, about the size of a pack of chewing gum.

"What's that?" I asked.

"That's your get-out-of-jail-free card," Agent Harrell said jovially.

26

"No," I said flatly. "That's a bug, right? You want me to wear a bug and talk to Alex and get him to admit he bribed Licata? So you can send him to jail? Forget it. I won't do it."

"Dempsey," Carter said. "I think perhaps you should let the agents explain what they want before you turn them down."

He crossed his arms over his chest and turned to the woman. "It is a recording device, is it not?"

"It's a bug," Camerin Allgood said. "We'd like Miss Killebrew to contact her former boss, set up a meeting, see if she can get him to talk about that trip down to the islands with Representative Licata."

"No," I said. "No way."

"Dempsey." Carter put a warning hand on my arm.

"Talk to her, Mr. Berryhill," Harrell suggested. "Explain how these things work."

"You'd give her immunity from prosecution, I'm assuming?" Carter asked, looking at Agent Allgood.

"That's not up to me," she said, flipping her hair over her shoulders. "You'd have to talk to the U.S. attorney about that. I'm just authorized to suggest that the government would look very favorably on working out an arrangement with your client, should she be of assistance to us in our investigation."

"Alex isn't stupid," I said, pushing the black plastic case away. "Even if I did agree to wear this thing, why would he be dumb enough to meet me, and if he did meet with me, which he won't, he'd never talk about Licata, or about what went on down in Lyford Cay. So you guys are just wasting your time."

Camerin Allgood gave a tight smile. "We never waste the government's time, Dempsey. Because we don't have a lot of it. I'll tell you what. You think about our conversation here. Think about what's at stake. As in your future. You may be naive when it comes to men, but I don't think you're dumb. I think you're a smart cookie. And I'll bet a smart cookie like you can come up with a way to keep from going to jail."

She uncrossed her legs and stood up. "You've got my card. Call me. Sooner would be better than later."

Jackson Harrell stood too, and shook Carter's hand. I didn't offer him mine. I let them out of the house, and stood on the porch watching as they drove away down the street.

"Shiiiiiit," I said, letting the word out in a long, deep exhale.

"My sentiments exactly," Carter said.

I leaned against one of the porch columns and closed my eyes. "This is all such a mess. How in the hell do I get myself out of it?"

"Keep doing what you're doing. Telling these people the truth."

"I did. They don't believe me."

"I think they do. Otherwise you wouldn't be standing here right this minute."

"You think I should do what they want."

He nodded. "I don't see any other way out."

"I don't even have Alex's phone number," I said, my face reddening. "I called him, after that reporter showed up here. I left a message on his voice mail, and he called me back."

"What did he say?" Carter asked.

"Nothing, really. He told me not to talk to any reporters, and not to call his cell phone number again. And when he hung up, I saw that he was calling from 'unknown caller.'"

Carter sighed. "Well, I'm sure the FBI can get a phone number for Alexander Hodder. That's one of their specialties."

"And then what?" I asked. "Do you really think I can just trick him into meeting me? Oh hi, Alex, how's tricks? Did you really bribe Representative Licata to vote our way on that energy bill? And could you just talk into this phony red flower on my lapel?"

Carter laughed. "I'm sure you could be much subtler than that."

I felt better. But only a tiny bit.

Tee drove up in the Mini Cooper. He hopped out and crossed the yard, coming toward us.

"Hey you," he said when he got to the porch. "I've been trying to call you all morning. And then I got home and spotted your car in my slot in the garage." He looked from me to his father. "What's going on? You two planning an armed insurrection?"

"Sorry," Carter told his son. "I've got to cite attorney-client privilege."

"Oh," Tee said. "For real?"

"My past caught up with me today," I said finally. "Your dad is trying to help me out of this fix I got myself into."

"You didn't get yourself into it, you were dragged in," Carter corrected me. "If you don't mind, I'm going to go over to the office and start doing a little research. Call me if you need me, or if those agents get back in contact."

He clamped a hand on his son's shoulder. "Dinner tonight?"

Tee glanced at me. "I was hoping to take Dempsey to dinner."

"Of course," Carter said quickly. "Great idea. Get her mind off her troubles. I'll talk to you later then."

We watched him drive off. I felt a wave of despair wash over me.

Tee saw the expression on my face change. "Dad showed me the story in the *Post*. You feel like talking about it?"

"No. I don't know. Maybe. God, I'm an idiot."

"Then let's talk about something else," he said. "How's the house coming along?"

I shot him a grateful smile. "Not too bad, actually. You want to see?"

Tee was suitably impressed with the kitchen floor, once he raised the paper Bobby had taped down over it. "Amazing," he said. "You did all this yourself? Pulled up the linoleum and stripped and sanded it? All in one weekend?"

"I got a little crazy," I admitted. "That's how I get when I start a project. I can't stop once I get started. Stupid, huh?"

"Not at all." He gestured toward the pile of cabinet doors stacked in the corner. "What's going on with those? You getting new cabinets in here?"

"Nope. Can't afford new," I said. "Bobby says they're good, solid heart pine. Like the floors. He's going to take down the cabinet boxes and strip them. My job is to strip the doors. Or, that was my plan."

I sat down at the kitchen table, suddenly overwhelmed by everything that had taken place that day.

Tee sat down beside me. He picked up my right hand and examined it. "You've got calluses, did you know that? Blisters too. I'd say your manicure is shot."

He lifted my hand to his lips and gently kissed the palm. He took my left hand, examined it gravely. "This one's shot too," he announced, giving it the same treatment. "And you've got a splinter."

I raised an eyebrow.

"You can tell me to stop," Tee offered, holding both my hands in his. "Send me packing."

"Or?"

He leaned forward and kissed my forehead. "Or you could let me hang around for a while." He grinned. "Let me finish what I've started. I'm crazy that way."

"Tee." I'd begun to say something, but he was pulling me closer. A moment later, I was in his lap, with my arms around his neck. Tee was kissing me, so sweetly, so tenderly, I felt all my troubles fall away—if only for a little while.

Then I heard the front door open, and heavy orthopedic shoes clomping down the hallway, followed by the skittering of Shorty's toenails. I jumped up, red faced and embarrassed, like a teenager caught raiding her parent's liquor cabinet.

Tee looked just as startled, but then he started to chuckle. "Dad's right," he said under his breath. "We really do have to do something about that old lady."

Ella Kate burst into the kitchen. "FBI!" she cried. "You got the law down here after you, girl. And the whole town knows about it."

Shorty sat down on his haunches and gave a short, angry bark, echoing his mistress's tone.

"It's a misunderstanding," I said.

"It's a good thing your grandmama isn't alive to hear about this," Ella Kate said, her face shriveled with anger. "Dragging the family name through the mud. She's turning over in her grave, is what she is. And your uncle Norbert too. None of them ever got so much as a parking ticket in their whole lives. Killebrews!" she snorted. "Trash. That's what your daddy's people are. Nothin' but trash."

"Now wait just a minute," Tee said. "Miss Ella Kate, you've really got no call to talk to Dempsey this way. Especially since you are living under her roof, essentially without any right of your own to be here."

She wheeled around and looked Tee up and down. "Young Berryhill," she snapped. "Think 'cause you're a lawyer you can talk to an old lady any way you please. I'll bet your daddy would take a switch to your behind if he knew you were sassing me like this."

Tee just laughed. Ella Kate turned and stomped off down the hall and up the stairs. Shorty followed in her wake.

We heard her door open, and then close with a slam, and the loud click of the lock echoing in the high-ceilinged hallway.

"Oh, God," I wailed. "Everybody in Guthrie knows about this mess."

"Well, they think they do," Tee agreed. "It's a small town. There's not a lot going on, now that the school superintendent's in jail for downloading kiddie porn on his county computer."

"You made that up," I said.

"If I'm lyin', I'm dyin'," Tee said, crossing his heart. "We got nearly two hundred new subscriptions to the paper out of dear old Dr. Winship's troubles. Scandal's a real circulation builder, you know."

I looked at him. "So, you're saying next week I'll be on the front page of the *Guthrie Citizen-Advocate*?"

He had the good grace to blush. "No," he said. "You haven't been arrested, haven't been charged with anything. You had a visit from law enforcement. That's all. No news there."

"Yet," I reminded him.

He sighed. "I just came over here to see if I could take a pretty lady to dinner. I had no idea I'd end up having a face-off with a crazy old woman."

"You asked me if I wanted you to go away," I said.

"I did," he agreed. "And if I remember correctly, I seemed to be making some headway in convincing you to let me stay, until we were so rudely interrupted."

"You really want to hear all about my troubles?" I asked. "It's a big, nasty, dirty mess, Tee. As your father pointed out, the FBI isn't kidding around. They basically threatened to throw me in jail if I don't help them."

"Seriously?"

"Seriously," I said. "They cited me chapter and verse. Public corruption. I could get fifteen years in prison for each count. Plus disbarment."

"So do what they want you to do," Tee said. "That's what Dad advised, right?"

"It's not that easy," I said. "They want me to wear a wire, to set up a meeting with Alex Hodder and get him to admit, with the FBI listening in, that he bribed a congressman. It's ludicrous. Alex won't return my phone calls. He'd never do it. Anyway, I don't have the nerve. My stomach hurts just thinking about it. I'm screwed, Tee. I told you before, run away."

"Naw," Tee drawled. He slipped his hands around my waist. "It's too late. I'm already in too deep. I'm not going anywhere. We'll figure it out, Dempsey. Together."

27

I took a deep breath and looked around the kitchen. I had no idea how to save myself from the disaster that threatened to ruin my career as well as my reputation, but it turned out I had accidentally stumbled upon something I was actually good at: fixing up this broken-down old house.

Tee cocked his head and observed me. "About that dinner?"

"I just . . . can't," I said. "I'm a coward, I know, but with the FBI sniffing around town I just don't feel like facing everybody in Guthrie."

"Not everybody knows," Tee said.

"Name one person who doesn't."

He gave it some thought. "I'm almost positive Oliveann Dismukes hasn't heard about your troubles."

"Who's she?"

"Oliveann is head cashier at the Family Dollar store out on the bypass," Tee said. "I happen to know that she's down in Flovilla this week because her daughter just had twins. So Oliveann definitely does not know or care about your troubles."

"I'm still not going out to dinner," I said. "For one thing, I've got absolutely no appetite. And for another, I really want to get started on stripping these cabinet doors."

He gave a deep, martyred sigh. "Very well. If I can't tempt you to dine with me, can I at least talk you into letting me help with the stripping?"

I handed him a pair of rubber gloves. "Be my guest. But don't blame me if you get hooked on the smell of chemical stripper."

He gestured toward the pile of tools in the corner. "I thought I'd use the heat gun."

"Uh-uh," I said. "I've only got the one gun. So it's stripper and gloves for you, buddy boy."

He looked wounded. "But . . . guns aren't for girls. Guns are for boys. This is the South. Ask anybody."

"My house. My rules."

We unrolled a heavy rubberized canvas tarp over the paper-covered floors, and then Tee dragged in two sets of sawhorses Bobby had dropped by earlier. We divided the stack of cupboard doors in half. I picked up my iPod and was about to plug in the earbuds.

"Hey!" Tee said sharply. "You get tunes and not me? No fair!"

"Are you always this whiny and demanding?" I asked.

"Yes," he said. "Are you always this bossy and territorial?"

"Always," I told him.

"Okay then," he said, pulling me toward him. "At least we know where we stand with each other."

I returned his kiss with a laugh and then pushed him away. "Work first, play later. If you go upstairs to my bedroom, you'll find the docking station for my iPod. But I warn you: I don't want to hear any complaints about my playlist. You don't like Michael Jackson or Sheryl Crow, you're outta luck."

When he came back downstairs with the iPod station, he looked bemused.

"What?" I asked, setting the speaker system up on the kitchen table.

"I love what you've done with your bedroom."

I blushed. Earlier in the week, I'd gone back up to the attic to rummage around some more. I'd come across what looked like an old army foot locker. Instead of the pile of moth-eaten military uniforms I expected, the locker turned out to hold unexpected treasures.

Folded across the top was a beautiful hand-stitched quilt in soft pastels, pale pinks, peaches, aquas, yellows, and greens. I didn't know very much about quilts, but I thought the pattern, of interlocking circles, was probably double wedding ring. From the look and feel of the still-crisp fabrics, the quilt had never been used. Right beneath the quilt was a stack of yellowing bed linens, two sheets and four pillowcases, all with delicate lace tatting on the hems, the pillowcases bearing an elaborate flowing monogram, its letters so intertwined I couldn't quite make out any letter. The stack was tied with a wide, faded pink satin ribbon.

At the bottom of the trunk, I'd found a large cardboard box. The flowing script on the pink-and-white-striped top said "Beedle Bros. Department Store," and the lid literally fell apart in my hands when I lifted it off. Inside the box, nestled in tissue-paper wrapping, was a set of delicately detailed pen-and-ink sketches and watercolor drawings of wildflowers, trees, and birds. I'd been so utterly charmed by the drawings, I'd lifted them out of the box, one by one, spreading them across my bed. There were a dozen drawings in all, none of them signed, each more enchanting than the next.

I knew the watercolors deserved to be matted and framed and protected under glass, but there was no money in my budget for such extravagance. Instead, I'd carefully pinned them to the wall opposite my bed, with sewing pins I'd discovered in a pin cushion in the bottom of the same trunk.

Thrilled with all my discoveries, I'd carefully soaked the sheets and pillowcases in a bathtub full of hot soapy water and bleach before running them through the clunky washing machine in the basement. Then I'd hung them out on the clothesline stretched from the back mud porch to the trunk of a pine tree, hoping that the sun would whiten them further. I'd hung the quilt out on the line too, to dispel the last traces of mustiness from all those years in the footlocker.

I'd even borrowed the flowered rag rug I'd found in Uncle Norbert's bedroom. It too had gotten a soaking and some time on the clothesline, and now, every morning when I swung my feet onto that hard wooden floor, I was happy to have the rug's welcoming warmth.

My bedroom was my one refuge in this house—the one place I'd been able to clean up and fix up enough to take pride in. It was my happy place.

"Thanks," I told Tee. "I still want to paint the walls, and get rid of those nasty old ruffled nylon curtains, but I had to buy a new mattress first, and that cut into my budget. Bobby, God bless him, picked up the mattress for me and dragged it up the stairs. And, of course, eventually I want to frame those watercolors. Aren't they lovely?"

"Very pretty," Tee said, plugging in the docking station. "And well done. Where did you get them?"

"They were in a box in a footlocker I found up in the attic," I said. "Along with the quilt, and the bed linens, and some damask dinner napkins. They're all monogrammed, like the sheets, but the design is so intricate, I can't make it out."

"Hmm," Tee said, not really listening. "That's nice."

"None of the stuff in that trunk has ever been used," I added. "It's like somebody was anticipating needing them, packed them away, and never came back. I'd love to know who did the tatting, and the water-colors, of course."

"One of your Dempsey relatives, no doubt," Tee said. "Nobody else has ever lived here but Dempseys."

I gestured toward the doorway. "Do you think that stuff belongs to Ella Kate?"

"No way," Tee said quickly. "I don't think Ella Kate has a domestic bone in her body. Anyway, if it was hers, why would it be up in your attic? Ella Kate didn't move in over here until the last year or so your uncle Norbert was alive."

I turned on the iPod and plugged in my heat gun. Tee laid a cabinet door across his sawhorses, and made a show of snapping on the rubber gloves. When he uncapped the can of chemical solvent, I opened the back door to ventilate the room. The night air was surprisingly mild. Maybe spring really was on its way to Guthrie.

"I guess the trunk and its contents will just be another of Birdsong's unsolved mysteries."

"You could ask your dad, couldn't you?" Tee suggested.

"I could, but he knows even less about his mother's family than I do."

Tee shook his head. "I just find that so hard to believe. Doesn't he have any curiosity about his family? Don't you?"

"Mitch is an 'of the moment' kind of guy," I said matter-of-factly, aiming the heat gun at my first cabinet door. I watched with fascination as the old layers of paint began to loosen, then bubble up. "He's not the least bit sentimental about family stuff—unless, that is, it involves him and Pilar and the boys."

Tee winced. "Does that hurt your feelings?"

I placed the scraper's blade at the edge of the cabinet and applied even pressure, pushing away a long, thick ribbon of softened paint, scraping all the way to the opposite end of the door. Then, I wiped the gummy paint from my scraper and applied the heat gun to the next edge.

"Dempsey?"

"I know my dad loves me," I said finally. "He's just not very demonstrative with me. Not the way he is with the twins. And I'm okay with that. I think he regrets that he didn't have a closer relationship with me, and maybe, with Gavin and Garrett, he thinks he's getting a second chance at being a better parent. Or a different one, anyway."

"That's a remarkably mature attitude to take," Tee said.

I laughed ruefully. "Well, maybe I just talk a good game. Things aren't all that rosy between my dad and me right now."

"Why's that?"

"We had a fight," I admitted. "He called me up this morning, after that reporter called him about the story in the *Post*. He was absolutely livid that I'd dragged his good name through the mud."

"Did you tell him your side of the story?" Tee asked.

"I tried. He didn't really want to hear."

"I'm sorry," Tee said. He stared down at the cupboard door. He'd only managed to scrape away a few inches of the paint.

"Do you realize what a great dad you have?" I asked. "I really envy the relationship you guys have."

"We weren't always this tight," Tee said. "I was your typical pain-in-the-ass teenager. Dad rode me really hard—he didn't like my friends, my grades, or most of my choices. When I went away to college, I swore I'd never be anything like my old man. I was never going to be a lawyer like him, and I definitely was never coming back to live in a backwater like Guthrie."

"You'd never know that now. Anybody can see that he adores you, and is insanely proud that you're his son. What changed things?"

"My mom got sick," he said. "And when it was clear that she wasn't going to get any better, I guess Dad and I both decided our differences were pretty petty. Going into practice with him was sort of a last gift to Mom."

"That's so sweet," I said, blinking away sudden tears.

"Well, don't go getting all sloppy on me," Tee said. "I think you have a pretty idyllic notion of us. We're not perfect. We fight and fuss and cuss just like any other family. And he's still pissed that I want to spend more time running the paper and less time practicing law."

"But he won't stand in the way of your running the paper."

"No," Tee said. "He just likes to give me a bunch of grief about it, every chance he gets."

Tee put his scraper down and walked over to where I was working. "You're almost done with this door," he said accusingly. "And I've been hacking away over there with that smelly stuff, and I'm not even halfway finished."

"I'm quick on the trigger," I said smugly. "So sue me."

He held out his hand. "It's my turn now. Gimme the gun."

"No way."

He stood behind me and nuzzled my ear. "Please?"

"If I give you the gun, what do you give me?"

He switched to my left ear. He needed a shave and his stubble tickled my neck.

"Go away," I said, swatting the air ineffectively. "I'm very busy here. I have no time for your tomfoolery."

He wrestled the heat gun away from me with very little effort, then turned me around to face him. He carefully placed the gun on the sawhorse. "Seriously now. No tomfoolery, as you so quaintly put it. I have an important question to ask you."

I put my arms around his neck. "Okay. Ask away. But I am not giving you my heat gun. You'll have to get your own if you want one that badly."

"I will," Tee said. He kissed me.

"What's the question then?" I asked.

He kissed my forehead. He kissed the tip of my nose. He kissed the hollow of my neck in an exquisitely leisurely way, while his hands closed around my butt, pressing us together.

The next thing I knew, something sharp and prickly was slashing at my shoulders and my head.

"Stop that!" Ella Kate hollered, smacking me on the back with a broom. I broke away from Tee, and he ducked, just barely missing Ella Kate's next swing.

Instead, she landed a blow on my right cheek. "Trash!" she screeched. "I won't have such trashy behavior under my own roof. You hear? I won't have it." She swung again and smacked me on the right arm.

"Ow," I protested, rubbing my arm. "That hurts."

"Ella Kate!" Tee cried, grabbing for the broom. "Cut it out!"

"You cut it out, you little pissant," Ella Kate replied, clutching the broom to her chest. "Get out of my house, right this minute, or I'll call the police. I'll call your father too, Tee Berryhill. Don't think I won't tell him about your behavior."

"What behavior?" Tee asked, his face reddening. "I was kissing a girl. She was kissing me back. We're not teenagers, Ella Kate. Anyway, this really is not your house. It belongs to Dempsey and her father."

"This is a respectable house," Ella Kate whispered. "Respectable! If you two want to cat around, you can just go to a motel. I won't have the two of you he-ing and she-ing under this roof. If Norbert knew this was going on here, he would be spinning in his grave. Killebrews!"

She took the broom and hit me squarely on the top of the head with it. She turned to Tee and gave him a vicious slap in the crotch, and then she calmly strolled out of the kitchen, broom in hand.

28

"Are you all right?" I asked Tee.

"I'm fine," he said. "Just grateful she didn't hit me with the broom handle. Now, that would have been painful."

"Sorry about that," I said, raking my fingers through my hair just to make sure Ella Kate's weapon of choice hadn't left me with a headful of cobwebs or worse. "I've been trying to get her to warm up to me. I drive her to the drugstore, and to run errands, I even buy treats for her dog, but I don't think it's working. She still detests me."

"Don't take it personally," Tee advised. "According to my father, she's always been what he calls 'eccentric.'"

I picked up my heat gun and switched it on again. "Eccentric. That's one of those colorful Southern euphemisms, right?"

"Exactly," Tee said. He wrapped his arms around my waist again. "Now, about that question."

"Better make it quick," I said, glancing over his shoulder. "Don't forget, she does have a shotgun."

"Which makes my question all the more relevant," Tee said. "Look. You've been under a lot of pressure here lately. I can't even get you to let me take you out on a proper date. And we sure as hell can't get any privacy, what with Ella Kate lurking around here, and me living with Dad. One of my law school classmates has a little cottage down on the coast, on Saint Simon's Island. Let's take a run down there next weekend. We'll have a nice dinner, ride bikes, take a walk on the beach. Just relax. What do you say?"

"I don't know," I said.

His face fell.

"It's just not good timing . . . with this Hoddergate thing hanging over my head, and the damned FBI agents skulking around town, and this newspaper reporter calling my family and friends."

"All the more reason to go away," Tee said.

I put both my hands on his chest. "I can't. Not right now. Give me some time, please, Tee?"

He sighed. "All right. No pressure. The offer stands. There's just one thing I need for you to do."

"Anything."

"Hand over the gun."

29

I t was pitch black when I woke up the next morning. I groped in the darkness for my cell phone, and saw that it was only 6:30 A.M. I lay back in the bed and groaned. Tee and I had worked on the kitchen cabinets until my hands and arms ached from all the scraping and sanding. We'd managed to finish stripping all the cabinets, but I still had plenty of sanding left—not to mention priming and painting.

I willed myself to go back to sleep, but it was no good. After five minutes of staring at the ceiling, I got up, shoved my feet into some slippers, and struggled into my bathrobe. Coffee. I needed coffee. Stat.

Soft, heartbreaking whimpers echoed through the high-ceilinged hallway. I hurried into the kitchen, where I found Ella Kate, sitting on the floor, cradling a writhing Shorty in her arms. She was dressed in faded red flannel pajamas, hair lank, wild eyed.

"Ella Kate?" I asked, crouching down beside her. "What's wrong? Is Shorty sick?"

"What do you think?" she snapped. "He ain't right, that's all I know. He wouldn't eat no supper, and Shorty never misses a meal. I took him outside to do his business last night, but he wouldn't go. Now he's bad sick."

"Poor baby," I said, looking down at the sad-eyed cocker. "Is there anything I can do for him?"

"Get that bottle of castor oil," she said, jerking her head in the direction of a bottle sitting on the kitchen counter. "I been trying to get some down him, but he keeps jerking away from me. I'll hold him, and you dose him."

"Castor oil?" I wrinkled my nose.

"Just get it," she ordered. "That's what my mama gave all us young'uns when we had a bellyache."

"Is it safe for a dog?"

"Get it!"

I did as I was told.

She clamped her arms around the wriggling dog. "Hold your hand over his nose so he'll open up his mouth, then, when he does, you pour that stuff down his throat."

I uncapped the bottle of castor oil, and clapped my left hand over Shorty's snout. I held the open bottle over his jaws, but just as I tipped the bottle forward, he flailed wildly with his front paws, and the bottle went flying, an evil-smelling arc of viscous oil spreading over the stack of freshly stripped cabinets.

"Oh no!"

"Now look what you done," Ella Kate cried. "You done spilt every last drop of the castor oil."

"I'm sorry," I said, hurrying to mop up the mess with a wad of paper towels. I stopped short when Shorty let out another high-pitched moan.

"He's bad sick," Ella Kate said quietly.

I bent over to stroke the dog's head, but Ella Kate pushed my hand away. "Leave him be," she said gruffly. "He don't trust strangers."

I didn't bother to point out that I was hardly a stranger. Shorty's listless brown eyes told volumes about his obvious suffering.

"Maybe we should call a vet."

"I done that," she said. "Think I'm an old fool? They got an answering machine, says to call back at nine. Unless it's an emergency. Then they say to go to some hospital I never heard of, clear down in Macon."

"I think it's an emergency," I said. "Where's the hospital?"

She shrugged, holding the dog closely against her chest. "Shorty don't like doctors. I know he ain't gonna like a hospital."

I sat down on the floor beside her. Gingerly, I touched the dog's pale pink belly. It was hard to the touch, and Shorty yelped and jerked away from me.

"It's definitely his stomach," I said. "Look, I really think we better get him to that animal hospital. I'll run upstairs and get dressed. Can you call the vet back and get an address for the clinic?"

She nodded absentmindedly, then bent over Shorty, stroking his head and crooning some tuneless song.

When I got downstairs, Ella Kate had somehow managed to change into a shapeless cotton housedress and worn blue cardigan sweater. But her wiry white hair was uncombed, and she still wore her battered brown bedroom slippers, a fact I dared not point out to her.

The first pale peach fingers of daylight were dawning as Ella Kate seated herself in the front seat of the Catfish, Shorty clutched tightly in her arms.

"Don't you have a crate or something he could ride in?" I asked, glancing nervously over at Shorty, whose head hung droopily over Ella Kate's arms.

"No, ma'am," she said firmly. "I'll hold on to Shorty. You just drive where I tell you. Now, let's get a move on!"

My hands clutched the steering wheel tightly as I sped through the quiet streets of Guthrie.

"Turn left up here, and that'll take you to the bypass," Ella Kate directed. The only other words she spoke to me on the forty-five-minute ride to the Middle Georgia Animal Clinic were tersely worded directions. I drove, Shorty whimpered, and Ella Kate sat stone still, her jaw clenched in concentration.

When we got to the animal clinic and reported Shorty's symptoms to the young receptionist, she nodded calmly, charting the dog's vital statistics on a clipboard. "He's hurtin' bad," Ella Kate said pointedly.

"I'll take you back right now," the girl said, showing us to an examining room. A minute later, another fresh-faced young woman, her brown hair swept back in a ponytail, came into the room.

"Oh, fella," she said softly, when she saw Shorty writhing in Ella Kate's arms. "You are feeling lousy, aren't you?" She held out her arms to take the cocker spaniel, but Ella Kate jerked away.

"He don't like strangers," she said. "We'll just wait for the vet."

"No wait at all," the girl said calmly. "I'm Chrissy Shoemaker. Dr. Shoemaker. We're sort of short staffed today."

Ella Kate stared. "Are you sure you're old enough to be doctorin' people's pets?"

"I'm thirty," Dr. Shoemaker said. "And I've been in practice here for three years."

"Hmmph," Ella Kate said, clearly unconvinced.

"I'll take good care of him, I promise," Dr. Shoemaker added, holding out her arms again.

Shorty whimpered, but finally, Ella Kate handed him over.

Dr. Shoemaker placed Shorty on a stainless-steel examining table. She stroked his head and caressed his floppy ears. "Okay, fella," she said. "Let's see what's going on with you."

She checked the dog's eyes and ears, looked down his throat, and took his temperature. "Nothing here," she said.

"It's his belly," Ella Kate said. "He's got a bad bellyache."

Dr. Shoemaker gently rolled Shorty over and examined his abdomen. She looked up at Ella Kate. "His tummy is pretty rigid. Is there a chance he's eaten something he shouldn't? Like a remote control or a lipstick or something like that?"

"I don't wear lipstick, and I don't own a remote control," Ella Kate said stiffly. "Shorty hadn't ever eaten nothing like that before."

"Well," Dr. Shoemaker said, "I have a feeling he's got a foreign object in that belly of his. If you'll step into the waiting room, we'll take some blood and do an X-ray to see if we can spot what's hurting the poor little guy."

"X-ray?" Ella Kate's head jerked up.

"Don't worry. He won't feel anything," Dr. Shoemaker said, opening the door to allow us to leave the examining room.

Ella Kate and I sat on a couple of molded-plastic chairs in the empty waiting room. The only reading materials were pamphlets dealing with spaying and neutering animals. I read one of the pamphlets. Very educational. Ella Kate sat and stared out the windows.

After ten minutes, Dr. Shoemaker rejoined us. "He's definitely got something in his stomach," she said. "We won't be able to tell exactly what it is until we operate."

"Operate!" Ella Kate exclaimed. "Can't you give him something to make him throw up whatever it is? You saying you're gonna cut on Shorty?"

"If he could have passed it normally, he probably would have by now. I'm afraid surgery really is the only option," Dr. Shoemaker said. "But it's a very common procedure. Dogs and cats are constantly eating things they shouldn't. I did three of these surgeries last week. You should see the assortment of stuff I've found in pets' tummies. Don't worry. We'll take very good care of Shorty."

Ella Kate's lips compressed into a thin colorless line. "I reckon if you gotta, you gotta."

"We gotta," Dr. Shoemaker said. "We'll put him to sleep and it shouldn't take too long. Would you like to go on home, and I can call you to let you know what we found?"

"No, ma'am!" Ella Kate said, looking directly at me. "I'm a-stayin' right here."

The minutes dragged by. The phone rang, and people came and went with their pets. Ella Kate stared out the window. I stared at everything else.

For lack of anything better to do, I tried to strike up a conversation with Ella Kate.

"Just how old is Shorty?" I asked.

She shrugged. "He was just a pup when I found him. That musta been eight or nine years ago."

"He was a stray?"

"Yes, ma'am. He was eating out of a trash can behind the Piggly Wiggly. Poor little thing was about half starved. Had sores all over his paws. Nobody else wanted him. Just like me. I took him on home and doctored him up myself. Pretty good, since I never even had no pet growing up."

"Never? Not even a goldfish?" I'd had a fairly fractured childhood myself, moving from Lynda's house to Mitch's house, and then all around the country, whenever Mitch's job required it, but I'd always managed to have a cat or a dog—or even a hamster, for one short summer.

"My mama and daddy had eight head of children," Ella Kate said. "Mama said she didn't need another mouth to feed. And then, when I got grown, I was working and didn't have no time for a dog. Anyway, Livvy liked cats."

"Livvy?"

"Olivia," Ella Kate said, looking away. "She'd be your grandmother. Livvy always had cats. Up until she married, she was always real partial to Siamese cats, but she did have a calico kitten one time that somebody left on her doorstep, after she busted up with Mister Killebrew and he went off and took the baby with him."

"Baby? You mean my father? Mitch?"

"That's right," Ella Kate said. "Mister Killebrew wouldn't let Livvy have a pet of any kind. He didn't allow animals in his house. Never mind that it was really Livvy's house that her mama and daddy gave her. He said cats were nasty dirty, and she especially couldn't have a cat after the baby, which was your daddy. He said he'd heard a cat would suck the breath right out of a little baby. Nothing Livvy said could change his mind."

"That's terrible," I said.

"He was a terrible man," Ella Kate said, tossing her head. "Rotten old bastard, and I don't care if he was your granddaddy. He broke Livvy's heart when he took that little boy away. She never was right after that."

"Ella Kate," I said, leaning forward. "Why did he take my father away from Guthrie? Wasn't that pretty unusual back then, for a man to get custody of a child instead of the mother?"

"I wouldn't know. Look here," she said, changing the subject abruptly. "You and young Berryhill. What's his daddy think about him romancing you, and you being a client and all?"

I laughed despite myself. "I don't know that Tee is 'romancing' me. And I don't know if Carter has an opinion either way. Tee and I are just friends. He was helping me strip the kitchen cupboards last night. He's a nice man."

"Looks to me like the two of you were getting good and friendly last night," she observed, arching one woolly gray eyebrow.

I blushed and hoped there would be another subject change. But her next topic didn't make me any more comfortable.

"Say. What happened to them government agents that come around the house this weekend?" she demanded. "What all did they want with you?"

I paused. How much did Ella Kate already know? And how much should I tell her?

"It's confidential," I said finally. "The FBI is investigating an elected official in Washington, D.C., and they wanted to ask me a lot of questions about him."

"I heard that much at church," Ella Kate said. "Way I heard it, you're mixed up with some Yankee congressman, and you and your boss, a married man, were in cahoots to try and bribe him."

"They were talking about me at your church?" I was mystified. And mortified. "Nobody in this town knows me."

"Huh. People know you better than you think they do. Anyway, they think they do. It's a little-bitty town. Everybody knows everything, even if they don't."

"What you heard is a lot of lies," I said hotly. "I did not bribe a congressman. And I certainly did not hire prostitutes for anybody. Those FBI agents, they told me yesterday that if I don't help them, they'll charge me with bribery. I could get fifteen years in prison. And be disbarred."

"If you're innocent, why don't you just do what them FBI people want you to do?"

I knotted and unknotted my hands. My back was stiff from sitting in the hard plastic chairs. I stood up, stretched, and walked around the waiting room, which smelled of disinfectant and dog hair.

"It's not that easy," I told Ella Kate. "The FBI wants me to call my old boss and get him to agree to meet me, and then trick him into admitting what he did. I'd have to wear a bug so the FBI could record everything he says."

"What's so hard about that?" she asked.

"Everything," I cried. "It's so sneaky. So dishonest."

"Ain't he the one who really did bribe a congressman?"

I sighed. Maybe it was time to face facts. Alex Hodder was a liar and a cheat, not to mention a man who had no compunction about letting me take the blame for his crimes.

"Alex took Congressman Licata on expensive trips, which were paid for by our client, an oil company. They were supposed to be fact-finding missions, but as far as I know, the only fact Licata was interested in was what time was tee time, and at what five-star restaurant he was getting a free meal. My boss knew Licata was on the take, so he just kept offering him free stuff, like the trip to the Bahamas. Alex knew that if Licata had a good time, he would vote to support the energy bill the oil companies wanted passed."

"Hmmph. Sounds to me like your boss and that congressman were crooked as a dog's hind leg."

"Maybe so," I admitted.

"And the FBI wants you to help put them in jail," she said.

"Yes."

"And if you don't do what they want, they'll put *you* in jail," she continued.

"That's about the size of it," I said glumly.

"What's Carter Berryhill got to say about all this?"

"He's trying to stall them. But eventually he thinks I'll have to do what they want, if I'm going to get out of this mess."

The door to the waiting room opened, and Dr. Shoemaker walked out. She wore blue paper booties over her shoes, and a blue cap over her hair.

"Miss Timmons?"

"Yeah?" Ella Kate sat still. Her face was fierce, but her voice was quavery, and when I looked down, I saw that her time-worn hands were shaking. I put my hand over hers. She didn't push it away.

"Is he dead?" she asked, ducking her head.

"Not at all," the vet said with a laugh. "Shorty's a tough little customer." She held up a plastic bag, through which we could see a bit of bright pink fabric. "But he really shouldn't be eating women's panties."

I stared. There could be no doubt. Shorty had apparently dined on my thong.

Ella Kate's narrowed eyes went from the plastic bag to me. "Hmmph," she said. She stood up. "Can I take him home now?"

"Not just yet," Dr. Shoemaker said. "We'll want to let the anesthesia wear off, and then observe how he does. He can't have any food for a couple of days, so we'll be giving him IV fluids. If he does as well as I expect, he should be ready to go home by midweek."

Ella Kate reached into the pocket of her sweater and brought out a worn black leather billfold. "How much?" she asked.

The vet studied Ella Kate for a moment. "Do you mind if I ask your age?"

Ella Kate bristled. "I don't see why that's any of your business. I'm old enough to take care of a pet by myself, and old enough to pay his doctor bill too."

"I see," Dr. Shoemaker said. "I don't mean to be rude, but the reason I asked is that we have a special rate for senior citizens."

"I'm eighty in September," Ella Kate shot back.

"Then it's a hundred dollars," the vet said. "Would you like us to set up a payment schedule for you?"

"No, ma'am," Ella Kate said. She took a wad of worn-looking bills out of the billfold, and counted out five tens. "You can put that on the bill now, and when we come fetch him later on, I'll give you the rest."

"Fine," Dr. Shoemaker said.

Ella Kate held out her hand. "I'll need a receipt."

t was nearly noon when we left the animal clinic and headed home. Ella Kate buckled herself into the passenger seat of the Catfish, and stared resolutely out the window at the passing countryside.

"Going to be a beautiful day," I said, trying to make conversation. The narrow two-lane road wound through lush green countryside. Pale pink wildflowers bloomed in shallow ditches along the roadside, and when I rolled down the windows, the smell of wet dirt and new grass washed over me. We passed fields full of horses, and cattle, and once, a grassy pasture that was full of goats. The sun was warm on my face, and despite everything else that was going on in my life, I was suddenly glad to be experiencing a spring day in Georgia.

"Mighty hot for this early," Ella Kate said ominously. "It's that global warming they been talking about on the television. Probably looking at another year of drought too."

"But it's rained several times since I've been in Guthrie," I pointed out.

"That don't mean nothin'," Ella Kate said. She pointed a knobby finger at a field we were passing. Stunted-looking trees were planted in rows, their outspread branches spiked with pale green leaves. "Them peach trees there, you see how sorry they look? Greening up early now, but if we get hit with a frost, that'll be the end. Last year's drought hit 'em bad. Worst peach crop in years. Lots of folks done give up farming altogether after last year."

"That's a shame," I said. "I've never seen peaches growing on a tree before. I don't think I knew they grew peaches in this part of the state."

"Used to be," she said gloomily. "Round here was big for peaches.

When I was a little girl, peaches was a big money crop in these parts. Your daddy's people, the Killebrews, I believe they were in the peach business. Not no more. No money in farming nowadays. Not in peaches, nor cotton, nor peanuts."

I heard my cell phone ring. I reached for it in my pocketbook, but it wasn't in the outside pocket where I usually keep it. It rang again, and a third time, before I realized it must have fallen out of my purse and onto the floor of the car. I groped around on the floor and grabbed the phone, answering on the fourth ring. "Hello?"

"Dempsey?" It was Carter Berryhill. "Where on earth are you? I've been trying to reach you all morning."

"Sorry," I said. "Shorty had a medical emergency. We had to take him down to the hospital in Macon. I didn't realize my phone had fallen out of my purse."

"Shorty? Do I know a Shorty? More to the point, how do you know somebody named Shorty? And why didn't you just take him over to the hospital right here in Guthrie?"

"Shorty is a dog, Carter," I said. "Ella Kate's cocker spaniel. He was really sick, and the vet's office in Guthrie didn't open until nine, so we had to take him down to the hospital in Macon."

"Ohhh, Shorty," Carter said. "Right. Is he okay? I know Ella Kate dotes on that critter."

"He swallowed, uh, something he shouldn't have," I said, blushing again at the thought of the vet holding the pair of panties she'd retrieved from Shorty's belly. "They did surgery, and he's fine now. He'll be coming home in a few days."

"Well, that's good," Carter said. "When do you expect to be back here?"

"Maybe forty-five minutes or so?" I said. "Is something wrong?"

"Our friends from Washington have been by to see me this morning," Carter said. "I imagine they've been by to see you too. They really are an annoyingly insistent presence. I think we should put our heads together and come up with a strategy, if you're up for it."

"Of course," I said, my pulse racing. "I'll come over as soon as I get back home."

"Well, no big rush," Carter drawled. "There is one thing you might could do that would be helpful in dealing with these people."

"What's that?"

"See if you can come up with some kind of timetable that reconstructs all of your dealings with Alex Hodder and the honorable Representative Licata. Anything at all will help us—notes, or files, or memos, anything like that."

"I'll try," I said, "but I don't have anything on paper. The feds took the hard drive from my computer, and they seized literally all my files at work."

"They took everything?"

"As far as I know," I said. "But I wasn't at the office when the FBI agents showed up, and the next thing I knew, our office manager called to say that I'd been let go. She told me not to bother coming in again. They boxed up all the personal effects from my desk, and had them messengered over to my apartment."

"Here's your hat, what's your hurry," Carter said.

"Exactly." The memory of it still stung, all these weeks later.

He sighed. "Well, in that case, we'll have to rely on your memory."

"I've got my laptop back at the house," I told him. "When I get home, I'll try and make some notes about all my dealings with Licata."

"Good," Carter said. "Don't worry about form or structure. Just get it down on paper, stream-of-consciousness style, if that works for you. Give me details. What Licata was like, how Alex Hodder interacted with him, all those kinds of things. Think carefully about that weekend in the Bahamas, if you would. And your dealings with those women."

"I'll try," I promised.

I closed my phone and glanced over at Ella Kate to see her reaction to my phone call. But I needn't have worried. Her eyes were closed and her head drooped forward. She snored softly.

I felt a sudden pang of pity for the old woman. Dr. Shoemaker had assured us that Shorty would heal quickly, but I knew Ella Kate had endured a night of terror, watching helplessly while her beloved pet suffered. He was all she had.

When we got back to Birdsong, she was still sleeping. I tapped her shoulder gently. "Ella Kate?"

Her eyes opened slowly. She blinked rapidly. "What time is it?"

"It's one," I told her. "We're home."

"Good."

I got out of the Catfish and went around to open the passenger door for her, but she hopped out on her own. She thrust a fistful of dollar bills into my hand.

"There," she said.

I looked down at the crumpled bills. "You don't have to do that."

"I'm obliged to you," she said stiffly. "Shorty coulda died."

"I was glad to be able to help," I told her.

She nodded curtly. "Good. You'll carry me back down yonder to fetch him when they say he's ready to come home?"

"Of course." I bit my lip. "Look, Ella Kate. About those panties Shorty ate. They were mine, of course. I really am so, so sorry. I don't know how he got hold of them."

Her eyes crinkled at the corners. For a second there, I thought I glimpsed something like a mischievous twinkle.

"You mean you wear them things as drawers?"

I blushed. "Well, yes."

"I ain't ever! That thing ain't no bigger 'n a rubber band. No wonder all you gals walk around like you got a hitch in your gitalong."

⌐

As I set up my laptop on the kitchen table at Birdsong, I realized that it had been nearly a month since I'd used it. The last time, in fact, had probably been the week after I'd been fired. After Alex refused to return my phone calls, I'd e-mailed him countless times, and obsessively checked my e-mail in-box, both on my BlackBerry, and on my laptop, over and over again, to check for any replies. There'd been none, of course, only a slew of messages that first week, from friends and colleagues on the hill, wondering how I was faring in the aftermath of Hoddergate.

I hadn't bothered to check my e-mail since arriving in Guthrie.

Ruby had asked me to turn in my company-issued BlackBerry. And Birdsong, with its antiquated wiring, certainly didn't have Internet access, and besides, with the exception of my roommates, and the FBI, nobody else in Washington seemed to realize I was still alive.

Just out of curiosity, I clicked on the wireless button on the laptop, to see if there were any networks in range. There were two, one called BeeBop and the other SpaceCadet, but both were secured networks requiring a password I didn't have and couldn't guess.

Just as well. There was no time to wade through the month's worth of spam I surely would have amassed by now. I opened a blank document and paused. Carter wanted me to write down everything I could remember about all my dealings with Licata, especially my memories of that weekend down at Lyford Cay. Stream of consciousness, Carter had said. Fine. I started typing.

I'd been working at Hodder and Associates for four or five months, in a capacity Alex liked to call "utility girl." That meant I helped out other staffers when they needed somebody to help draft a policy statement, or work on a speech for one of our corporate clients. Then, last November, one night when I was working late, Alex came out of his office and walked over to my cubicle. "Well, Dempsey Killebrew," he said, perching on the edge of my desk. "You're burning the midnight oil. I hope we're paying you well for all your dedication."

The next week, Alex e-mailed to tell me how pleased the client was with my speech. That Friday morning, he called me into his office to tell me he was assigning me to work on the Peninsula Petroleum account. I was excited and flattered by the attention.

Most of my work was pretty cut and dried. I drafted position papers, did research on energy policy, and once or twice accompanied Alex to meetings with Peninsula executives when they came into town, or to subcommittee hearings on the hill.

Sometime last spring, our company arranged for Peninsula to be a "major patron" for a fund-raising dinner to benefit a children's hospital in the district. I was given tickets to the dinner, and during the cocktail hour, Alex introduced me to Representative Anthony Licata. Alex was on a first-name basis with "Tony," as he called him. At one point, before we were seated, Alex pulled me aside and told me I'd be seated at Tony's table, as would Peninsula's president, Mel Patterson, and his wife.

"Tony loves pretty young things," Alex told me, giving me a big wink. "Now, I'm not asking you to flirt, or do anything improper, I'm just telling you he likes to be seen with pretty girls. Makes him feel like a big stud. At dinner, make sure you get him seated right next to Mel. Ask him how his golf game is coming along. Mel's a member over at Burning Tree, and I happen to know Tony's dying to play that course."

I did as Alex had asked. Representative Licata hit it off right away with Mel Patterson, and I overheard Mr. Patterson invite him to be his guest the next weekend at Burning Tree.

My impression of Representative Licata? He is, as Alex said, a man who likes to think he is a ladies' man. He never really made a pass at me, but I did catch him staring at my cleavage on more than one occasion at that first dinner, and then later, when we were in the Bahamas. He likes expensive Scotch; we always had to make sure we had a couple bottles of Laphroaig for meetings with him. I know he cheats at golf too, because Alex told me Mel Patterson complained about all the "gimmes" he took during their games at Burning Tree.

The Monday after the charity dinner, Alex wanted to know how the evening had gone. He told me it was important for "Tony" to understand how important his vote would be on upcoming energy legislation.

At Alex's request, I wrote several papers outlining our client's position on off-shore drilling and other energy-related policy matters. The FBI seized my Day Runner, so I don't have exact dates or times, but I know we had at least half a dozen more lunch and dinner meetings with Licata in the months before the energy bill was scheduled for hearings.

The first week of December Alex called me into his office and asked me if I had any plans for the upcoming weekend.

At first, I thought maybe he was asking me to go away with him. He never really hit on me, but all those lunches and dinners and late nights working at the office, I thought there was something between us. But he was married, and I tried to tell myself I was not interested in a married man.

I paused in my typing here. Just how honest should I be with Carter Berryhill? He was courtly and honorable and for some inexplicable reason, he seemed to think that I was somebody worthy of his respect. Did he really need to know about my pathetic crush on my boss? Should I admit that if Alex had asked me to go away, I probably would have gone?—God help me. If it came up, I decided, I would tell Carter about my feelings. I prayed it would not.

Alex told me that Peninsula Petroleum was sponsoring a "fact-finding" retreat down in the Bahamas for the upcoming weekend. I was to prepare a paper about alternate energy solutions being used in the Bahamas. He stressed that I should not tell any of my coworkers about the trip, because he didn't want to be bothered with petty office jealousies. I should, Alex said, tell my friends that I was visiting my father down in Miami. When I protested that I didn't like to lie, Alex told me it wouldn't really be a lie, since we'd have a layover in Miami, and there would be plenty of time for me to "visit" with my father over the phone.

Alex assured me the position paper was no big deal. "Just hit the high points. You know, maybe three pages, bullet points, like that." He said he didn't want Ruby, our office manager, gossiping about our going away together, so he asked me to make all the travel arrangements, including a suite of rooms at the Lyford Cay Resort for him, Tony Licata, me, and one of Peninsula Petroleum's junior executives, first-class plane tickets, dinner reservations for Friday and Saturday nights, and a tennis lesson for Alex, on Saturday morning. He also told me that if I needed to buy myself some "resort wear" for the Bahamas, I should do that, and charge it on my company credit card since it was a business expense. "Get yourself something foxy," he told me. "Something that'll show off those legs of yours." The way he said it made me uncomfortable then, and it makes me uncomfortable now.

About the American Express card. In October, I think, Alex gave me a platinum American Express card. It was a company card, to be used when I was paying for dinners, or corporate travel, he said. But the other associates didn't have one, Alex explained, so I should keep it quiet, because we didn't want to stir up any interoffice drama. Everything would be direct-billed to Hodder and Associates. To be honest, I was ecstatic about being given such a perk. I did buy new clothes for the trip, but I ended up putting all of it on my own Visa card.

I couldn't bring myself to tell Carter about the cocktail dress I bought for the trip to Lyford Cay. The memory was just too painful. I'd spent hours looking for just the right dress, something so fabulous Alex couldn't help but see me as more than just an office flunkie. It was a coral-colored silk chiffon slip dress, with a deep V-neck and a flirty little ruffle at the hem, which was, as Alex requested, several inches north of my knees. I had high-heeled metallic gold sandals to wear with the dress. The saleswoman at Saks told me the dress must have been made for me. "With your coloring, you should never wear anything except coral," she'd said.

I had everything all planned out. I'd wear the coral dress for dinner Friday night. Licata would be there, and the Peninsula guy too, of course, but once Alex saw me in that dress, he would forget all about business. What an idiotic fantasy! And thank God nothing had gone as I'd planned.

was hungry. I hadn't had any breakfast, or more important, any coffee. I ground some of my precious French roast beans, and while the coffee was brewing, I fixed myself some cheese and crackers. I sat back down at the table with a sigh and reread what I'd written. I dreaded writing about the trip to the Bahamas. I would have liked to have forgotten the trip ever happened. But it had, and Carter Berryhill was right. I needed to remember it—and every little detail of what had gone on down there. I nibbled on a saltine and started typing again.

Alex was emphatic that I should tell nobody about the trip to the Bahamas. I met Alex at Reagan National that Friday morning, and Representative Licata showed up at the gate just as we were getting ready to board. I asked Alex about the Peninsula exec whose trip I'd also booked, but he just said the exec had to cancel at the last minute.

When I greeted Representative Licata, he eyed me up and down and told me how much he liked my outfit—and he insisted I was to call him Tony for the rest of the trip, which I had no intention of doing.

Our flight left D.C. at nine thirty A.M, and as soon as we were seated, Licata ordered Bloody Marys for all three of us. I barely tasted mine, but by the time we got to Miami, I could tell Licata was already buzzed.

When we got to the hotel, Alex announced that he and Licata were going to head over to the golf course to see if they could get a "walk on" tee time. I'd thought we were going to have lunch together so I could present Licata with the paper I'd prepared. I guess Alex could tell how disappointed I was, because he had me give him the paper, and he promised he and Licata would discuss it while they played.

Instead, I changed into my bathing suit and sat by the pool all afternoon, reading. Sometime after four, Alex walked up and sat on the lounge chair next to mine. Alex said he and Tony had only played nine holes, and he seemed annoyed by that. He ordered a mojito from one of the waitresses at the pool bar, and we chatted for a few minutes, until his cell phone rang. Alex answered, and I could tell he was talking to Licata. When he hung up, he rolled his eyes and said Tony was bored, and wanted to try something different.

Alex got up, walked over to the bar, and chatted with the bartender there. When he came back, he handed me a slip of paper with a phone number on it. "Call this gal and set up a wakeboard session for Tony," he told me. "Tell her the client's name is Terry. Licata doesn't want anybody down here to know his real name. He'll be ready in fifteen minutes. Just have her charge it to your AmEx card." I agreed, and Alex said he had to go up to his room and return some e-mails and make some phone calls. He said he'd see me at dinner.

I didn't have my cell phone in my beach bag, so I used one of the resort's house phones and called the number Alex had given me. A woman answered. She didn't tell me her name, and I didn't ask. I just set up the session, as Alex had directed me to. She asked me how long a session "Terry" wanted. I knew nothing about wakeboarding, but I was pretty sure that after all the drinking and golfing Licata had been doing, he wouldn't be up for anything too strenuous. I told her an hour would probably be enough time, and she laughed and said she bet he couldn't go even fifteen minutes. After I hung up, I threw the slip of paper in the trash.

God, how dumb could I have been? It never, ever occurred to me that I was talking to a madam. It didn't occur to me to wonder why Alex didn't set up a wakeboard session for himself, or to wonder why Alex didn't put it on his own credit card, or why it was okay to make hotel, restaurant, and golf arrangements under Licata's real name, but not "wakeboard" lessons. In hindsight, all I can say is, Alex was my boss, and I was used to doing as he asked. Dumb. Dumb. Dumb.

Our dinner reservation was for seven PM, so I'd spent a leisurely hour getting ready for my big night. I'd pulled my hair up in a French twist, and even broke open the bottle of Hermès perfume I'd treated myself to in the duty-free shop at the airport. The coral dress, I thought, made me look totally hot. I allowed myself to fantasize about what Alex would say when he saw me in it, and how we would plot to slip away from Licata—maybe for a moonlight stroll on the beach?

Alex and Licata were sitting in the lobby bar when I went downstairs to dinner. I could tell Licata was nearly wasted. He practically drooled down the front of my dress, and I had to sidestep to keep him from kissing me. We went in to dinner, and Tony proceeded to order another round of drinks. I asked him how his wakeboard session had gone, and he gave Alex a huge wink—"Just what the doctor ordered," I think he said. Alex brought up the subject of the upcoming energy legislation, but Tony just told him he didn't want to mix business with pleasure at dinner. There was some talk about golf—Licata was disgusted with his short game, and Alex suggested he take a lesson the next morning with the resort's golf pro—adding that it would be Peninsula Petroleum's treat. Tony thought a lesson was a great idea. At some point, a combo started playing. Tony insisted that I dance with him. At first, I tried to get out of it, but Alex gave me a quiet nod, signaling that if Tony wanted to dance, I should dance. It was a slow song, and I was dreading it—Tony had been drinking steadily through dinner, but he turned out to be amazingly light on his feet. After that, I danced once with Alex.

It pained me to write about the dance with Alex Hodder. The band was playing "Unforgettable" by Nat King Cole. Alex was a perfect gentleman. He complimented me on my dress and told me I was the most beautiful woman in the room. He said he'd read the policy paper, and I'd done an outstanding job with it. I don't think it was my imagination that he held me a little tighter as we danced, or that his hand lingered on my bare arm, and once, lightly touched my breast. When the song ended, he kissed me on the cheek and told me *I* was unforgettable. The prick.

> Tony had ordered a bottle of champagne—Veuve Cliquot, the most expensive bottle the hotel offered—and after drinking half a glass, I started getting headachy. When I excused myself, Tony and Alex announced they were going to go out to the pool bar and smoke cigars and have a brandy.

I did have a little bit of a headache from the champagne, it was true, but I was also secretly hoping that Alex would take the hint and get rid of Tony so that we could have some time alone together after dinner. I went back to my room and waited up—for the call that never came. I wound up falling asleep in my hot little cocktail dress. When I woke up in the morning, the dress was a wrinkled disaster, and I had a nasty little hangover.

> At breakfast the next morning, Licata was none the worse for wear. The men left for their golf match, and I spent the rest of the day at the pool, reading and sunning. I'd gone up to my room to shower and get ready for dinner when I heard a knock at the door. It was Alex. He told me that Tony hadn't been able to play the full eighteen holes. "He's whining about pulling some muscle in his back during the wakeboard lesson," Alex said. "Tony thinks a massage might help." He handed me a piece of paper; he'd written "massage" on the back of it, and another phone number. "Give them a call and have them send somebody up to his room," Alex told me.

"Use the same name, Terry, and charge it to your AmEx."
Alex left, and I called the number, and a woman answered. I
think she just said Relaxation Therapy, or something like
that. I know she didn't tell me a name, and I didn't ask. I
gave her Tony's room number at the hotel. She did ask me if
there was anything special he liked. I thought she meant
massage technique. So I told her he'd hurt his back. I gave
her the AmEx number, the same as I'd done with the wakeboard instructor, and I hung up. Alex eventually told me that
he and Tony had decided to order room service and discuss
the upcoming bill. He apologized and told me to enjoy my
dinner. I ordered room service, and didn't see either of them
again until the next morning, at checkout.

My cheeks were flaming as I recounted the last night of the trip to
Lyford Cay. Alex Hodder had set me up. He'd used me as a pimp for
Tony Licata. I'd been so hurt that night, it hadn't occurred to me to
wonder why Alex couldn't come down for dinner. With what I knew
now, I was sure he and Tony Licata had enjoyed some kind of kinky
three way with a hooker named Tiki Finesse, which I had booked and
paid for with my company-issued AmEx card. Tiki hadn't been the only
girl getting screwed on that trip, but she was the only one who got
paid.

My cell phone rang. It was Carter. "Dempsey?"

"Oh, Carter, hey," I said. "I was just finishing up my notes about the
weekend down in the Bahamas. You were right. I did remember a lot
more than I had before. I'll just save everything I wrote, and I'll be
right over."

32

C arter Berryhill was sitting at the desk in the reception area of his office, frowning down with distaste at the computer there. His white hair was neatly combed, but his bow tie was slightly askew, and he was coatless, with the sleeves of his heavily starched dress shirt rolled up to the elbows. His glasses were perched on the very tip of his long, elegant nose.

"Oh, Dempsey," he said, when I walked in the door. "Thank heavens." He stood up and ushered me into his office.

He took his jacket from a wooden hanger on the back of the door and shrugged into it. "You'll have to excuse me, my dear," he said. "Scott, our receptionist, is late coming back from lunch, and the phone's been ringing off the hook, and my printer is out of ink, and I thought I'd just use his printer because I can't seem to replace my ink cartridge, but Scott uses some word-processing program that I cannot fathom."

He sat down behind his desk and straightened his tie. "Don't ever grow old, my dear," he said. "That's my advice."

"You're not old." And he wasn't, I decided. He was debonair and charming, well dressed, well read. And if I hadn't already developed a crush on his son, I probably would have fallen madly in love with Carter Berryhill Senior.

"Well," he said, "so you've finished the assignment I gave you?"

"I have," I said. "If you'll show me where to set up my laptop, you can take a look at what I've written."

"Right over there," he said, pointing to a conference table in front of a picture window that looked out on the square. I plugged the laptop in and pulled up the document I'd ruefully labeled HODDERGATE.

"Why don't you let me take a crack at replacing your ink cartridge while you read," I asked.

"You're an angel of mercy," Carter replied. He handed me the ink cartridge, and we switched places.

It took me less than a minute to get Carter's printer working again. I sat back in his desk chair and watched while he read what I'd written.

"Hmm," he said once. And then, a few minutes later, he shook his head. "The swine!" he said. I couldn't tell if he was referring to Licata or Alex Hodder. Carter had a yellow legal pad, and occasionally he'd stop and scrawl something on the pad. It took him fifteen minutes to read everything, and when he was finished, he read it again, and took more notes.

"Interesting," he said finally.

"I guess you're wondering how a person with any brains at all could have been so stupid," I said, staring out the window to avoid meeting his eyes. Carter, I was sure, was smart enough to read between the lines—and to extrapolate all the stuff I'd left out of my tale of woe.

"No," he said slowly, tapping his pen on the legal pad, "I'm just wondering about that piece of paper Alex Hodder gave you with the massage therapist's phone number. Tell me about that. What did the paper look like?"

I closed my eyes. "It was like, sort of a square, maybe lightweight cardboard?"

"Yes. Not really a slip, as you described the paper he brought back from the bar, when he had you set up Licata with the wakeboard instructor."

"No. Bigger than that."

"Good. Anything else?"

I squeezed my eyes shut tight again, and tried to put myself back in my hotel room.

"Alex had just come from the golf course," I said, picturing him in the bright green Lyford Cay golf shirt he'd worn that day. He'd had a matching green golf visor, and I could see the golf gloves sticking out of the back pocket of his pants.

"Did he write the phone number on something you had in the room?" Carter asked.

I had to think about that.

"No. He pulled the paper out of his back pocket," I said. "He'd already written on it."

I opened my eyes. Suddenly, I could see the paper quite plainly.

"It was his scorecard!" I told Carter. "From the golf course. It had his name, and Tony's, on the front, and I remember noticing that they'd quit playing after the twelfth hole."

"Tony's back was allegedly bothering him, you said in your notes," Carter observed. "Do you remember what you did with the scorecard? After you called to set up the 'massage' for Tony?"

"My bathrobe!" I stood up and put both hands on Carter's desktop. "I think I shoved the card in the pocket of my bathrobe!"

Carter stood up too. "My dear," he said slowly. "Is there any chance it's still there? All these months later?"

Carter drove me back to Birdsong and waited in the driveway with the motor running. I burst in the front door and ran to my room, taking the stairs two at a time. I threw the closet door open and rummaged wildly through the garments hanging there. I grabbed my worn blue terry-cloth bathrobe from the clothes hanger and shoved my hand in the pocket.

Nothing. Unless you count a crumpled-up tissue and a tube of lip balm.

I could have cried. I threw myself down on the bed and stared up at the ceiling. I'd worn that bathrobe almost every night since Christmas. Wouldn't I have noticed a folded-up golf scorecard? I squeezed my eyes closed again, and put myself back in that hotel room at the Lyford Cay Resort.

I remembered taking a long shower in the luxurious marble-tile bathroom, enjoying the hotel's grapefruit-scented soap. Afterward, I'd swaddled myself in the thick velvety bath sheet, and slathered myself with tangerine-scented moisturizer. And I remembered thinking I probably smelled like a fruit basket. I'd touched up the polish on my toenails—the color was called Tahiti Sweetie—and I was blowing my hair dry when I heard the room's doorbell ringing. It was that kind of hotel. Each room had a doorbell.

Then what? I'd grabbed the bathrobe on the back of the bathroom door, and belted it around me before going to see who was at the door.

Wait! I hadn't used my own shabby blue bathrobe, which was still hanging in the closet in the bedroom. I'd grabbed the complimentary hotel bathrobe. It was white and silky, and monogrammed with the hotel's logo.

I sat up on my bed and smiled. I got down on my knees and pulled my suitcase out from where I'd stashed it that first night at Birdsong.

My father wasn't a particularly religious man. Mitch Killebrew's religion was patriotism. He believed in the flag, he believed in the work ethic. He didn't believe in stealing. I was raised to believe in what Mitch believed in. I was honest, to a fault. It had gotten in the way several times in my career as a lobbyist.

But that weekend at Lyford Cay, when I'd been treated as a glorified gofer, I'd been so disgusted, so disappointed, I'd decided I was due a souvenir. I hadn't charged my resort wardrobe to Hodder and Associates, as Alex had suggested. But I had decided, in a last-minute fit of pique, while I was packing, that I would treat myself to a remembrance of that weekend. And that white, silky, monogrammed bathrobe would be just the thing.

I flipped the top of the suitcase up and began rifling through the clothing. I tossed aside all the suit jackets and business attire I'd packed away on my arrival in Guthrie. No need to dress for success if you were already a gold-plated failure. The heels and boots were tossed aside too—including those strappy gold sandals that I hadn't worn since that ill-fated night at Lyford Cay. On the bottom of the suitcase, I found the white bathrobe. I snatched it up, and I could feel something stiff through the silky fabric.

I pulled the paper out. It was still folded in half. The ink had run a little, so that you could hardly see that Alex had birdied the fourth hole, or that Tony had double-bogeyed the tenth, eleventh, and twelfth holes. But on the back of the card, in the same handwriting as on the front, was the word "massage" and a hastily scrawled phone number.

I touched the card to my lips and kissed it, tenderly, reverently, thankfully. Surely, this truly was my get-out-of-jail-free card.

33

Camerin Allgood and Jackson Harrell walked into Carter's office unannounced. Carter glanced over and gave me a surreptitious wink.

Agent Allgood dropped into one of the wingback chairs facing the desk, leaving Harrell to drag a chair over from the conference table.

The FBI agent was dressed in form-fitting blue spandex running tights and a baggy gray UVA sweatshirt. Her hair was tied up in a pony-tail. Harrell wore running clothes too, although his consisted of loose gray sweatpants and a long-sleeved Falcons jersey.

Agent Allgood opened her briefcase and brought out the silver tape recorder again. She held it up and spoke into it. "This is Special Agent Camerin Allgood. Our location is Guthrie, Georgia. The date is March twenty-eighth, and Special Agent Jackson Harrell is with me in the law offices of . . ."

Carter handed her a business card.

"Carter Berryhill Senior," she said. "We are here to take a statement from Dempsey Killebrew, and her attorney is present for these proceedings."

"Turn off the tape recorder, please, Agent Allgood," Carter said pleasantly.

Her eyes narrowed. "That's not agency policy."

Carter folded his hands on his desktop. "Nonetheless, we won't be proceeding until you've turned off the tape recorder."

She looked at Harrell, who shrugged.

"Fine," she said. She punched the stop button and tossed it into her open briefcase.

"You called us," she said finally, sitting back in her chair. "I'm assuming your client has decided to assist us in our investigation."

Carter opened a manila folder and pushed it across the desk toward Allgood. "My client has come up with a piece of evidence you might find interesting."

Agent Allgood picked up the folder gingerly, using only her fingertips.

"Don't worry," Carter told her. "This is a copy. The original is in my office safe. Feel free to examine it."

Agent Allgood picked up the paper and read it without comment. She handed it over to Agent Harrell.

"A golf scorecard, from Lyford Cay Resort," Harrell said finally. "Alex is a decent golfer. Tony, not so much. In fact, it looks like Tony stunk the place up, especially the last three or four holes they played. What, they didn't finish the round because they were too busy hooking up with whores?"

"Check the back of the scorecard, why don't you," Carter suggested.

Harrell turned it over and nodded thoughtfully. He handed it across to Agent Allgood, who read the back, then turned the paper over to look at the golf score again.

"A scorecard, for Alex and Tony—which Alex and Tony, we're not sure about," she said finally. "And on the back, a phone number. Pretty convenient for Miss Killebrew."

"It's Alex Hodder's handwriting," I sputtered. "You can check it out yourself. Check with the pro shop at the resort. Alex and Licata played twelve holes of golf that Saturday morning. I arranged the tee time myself. Alex Hodder came up to my room. He told me Tony's back was bothering him, and he asked me to call that number and book him a massage."

"And you kept the piece of paper with the phone number," Harrell said. "Which you failed to mention until it started to look like you might do some serious jail time for bribing a public official."

"I'd forgotten all about the scorecard," I said hotly. "Until today. I just assumed I'd thrown it out, because I did remember throwing away the piece of paper with the phone number for the wakeboard instructor. But Carter asked me to write down everything I could remember about my dealings with Licata. I did that. I wrote it all down, and brought it over here earlier today."

"And I read what she'd written," Carter said, holding up the pages he'd printed out. "She was able to come up with more details about the trip to the Bahamas with Hodder and Licata. I asked her some questions about the evening Hodder came to her hotel room—"

Harrell sniggered. Allgood shot him a dirty look.

"Nothing happened!" I insisted. "He gave me the phone number and asked me to book the massage session for Licata, in his room. We were supposed to have dinner together, but Alex said there'd been a change of plans. He left. I ordered room service. You can check with the hotel. Check the AmEx receipts, since you seem to have all of them. I ordered dinner for one. Caesar salad, mahimahi with mango salsa, half a bottle of white wine. And a piece of cherry cheesecake," I said, blushing. "It was my last night in the Bahamas. I decided to treat myself."

"Riiight," Harrell said.

Carter, bless him, cleared his throat. He looked from me, to Agent Allgood, to Agent Harrell.

"If you-all don't mind," he said slowly. "I'd like to talk deal." He handed both the agents a sheaf of paper, which I knew was the printout of my Hoddergate document.

"Miss Killebrew has gone into detail about her recollections of her dealings with Representative Licata and Mr. Hodder," Carter said. "You already have the AmEx receipts. And now you have her statement and more important, you have proof that Alex Hodder instructed her to call what she believed was a legitimate massage therapist, to authorize what she believed was a legitimate therapeutic massage for Representative Licata."

Camerin Allgood smiled, but not in a good way. Her small, perfect teeth reminded me of a carnivorous rodent.

"It's a start," she said.

"What more do you want?" I asked desperately, leaning forward until I was only inches from Camerin Allgood's sweat-beaded face. "I'm not Mata Hari, okay? I'm a lobbyist, not a secret agent. My boss gave me an assignment. I did what he asked. I had no *friggin'* idea my boss, and his client, were bribing a United States congressman. I didn't think I was doing anything illegal, so I didn't get any notarized dossiers, and I didn't happen to have a video camera on me down there in the Bahamas. You can believe me, or not believe me, but that's the truth." I crossed my arms over my chest, just willing Camerin Allgood to push me one inch closer to a nervous breakdown.

She leaned back in her chair, and a moment later, I leaned back in mine.

"The scorecard is helpful," she said finally. "We already have samples of Alex Hodder's handwriting, so we should be able to authenticate the card."

"Thank you!" I blurted out.

She stood up. Harrell looked surprised. He stayed seated.

"Jackson?"

He stood, like an obedient sidekick. Or lapdog.

Agent Allgood threw the sheaf of papers in her briefcase and snapped it shut. "We'll need the original scorecard to give to the forensics unit," she said.

Carter nodded. "Fine. But before we surrender the original, we'll want a written agreement from the U.S. attorney's office stipulating that my client fully cooperated with this investigation, and that his office will drop any pending charges against Miss Killebrew."

"That's not how it works, Mr. Berryhill," Agent Allgood said, staring down at Carter. "We'll get a subpoena if we have to. Anyway, if your client wants to prove her innocence, she needs to stop obstructing this investigation."

"My client is obstructing nothing," Carter said, his tone still pleasant. "She wants this investigation ended, and more important, she wants her name cleared in connection with these odious charges."

Odious! I'd never heard anybody use the word before. Coming from Carter Berryhill, the word dripped filth. Odious was exactly how I felt about the whole stinking mess Alex Hodder had gotten me into. "Odious" could be my word for the day. The week, even.

"Before this incident erupted," Carter went on, "my client was a respected member of the bar. She had a promising career in public relations. All of that ended when your people raided Representative Licata's office. Somebody started leaking information to the press. All of a sudden, my client loses her job and her standing in the community. Her reputation is smeared. Stories appear in the *Washington Post* accusing her of bribery and solicitation. My client's father and mother read those stories, Agent Allgood. How do you think they felt, seeing their daughter's name dragged through the mud like that?"

"Leaks!" Harrell said. "We got nothin' to do with leaks. Don't try to put that crap on us. We got no control over what some hack writes in the *Post*."

"Somebody talked," Carter snapped. "Somebody who had access to the evidence you people seized from Licata's office and from Hodder and Associates. That's why a reporter from the *Post* showed up on Miss Killebrew's doorstep down here last week."

He glared up at Camerin Allgood, who took a half step backward.

I wanted to cheer. I wanted to jump up and high-five Carter Berryhill Senior, who'd just forced the baddest badass fed to back down.

Instead, I kept my cool. I stayed seated, with my hands folded in my lap.

"I'd appreciate it if you'd get back to us by the end of the week with that written agreement," Carter said. "My client wants to get on with her life."

Allgood nodded curtly. She left as quickly as she'd entered, with Jackson Harrell jogging to keep up with her quickstep.

34

When I saw the feds drive away in their government-issue navy sedan, I jumped up and gave Carter both the high five and a hug.

"Carter! You were brilliant! Did you see the way that bitch Camerin Allgood backed down? She practically tucked her tail between her legs when she ran out of here."

He grinned. "I have to admit, our little confrontation today was the most fun I've had in a very long time. We country lawyers don't often get a chance to back-sass government agents."

"You were awesome," I said. "I want to be you when I grow up."

"That's very flattering coming from a young lady of such high achievements as yourself," Carter said. "But don't delude yourself, Dempsey. We might have bested them in this skirmish, but those two are the FBI. They'll be back, and they won't back down until you give them everything they want."

"I don't care," I said. "I can prove everything I told them now. So Alex Hodder and Tony Licata can just . . . kiss my ass."

"Let me pose a theoretical question, if I may," Carter said. "Suppose those FBI agents do go away. Suppose they decide not to prosecute you. What's the next chapter in the Dempsey Killebrew story?"

I blinked. "I get on with my life, just like you said."

"Which life is that? Your life as a lobbyist in Washington? Or your life here, in Guthrie, fixing up Birdsong?"

My stomach lurched. Carter Berryhill could be a real buzz killer when he wanted to be.

"Dempsey?" He touched my arm gently. "I'm sorry. Your personal life is none of my affair. Please forget I asked."

"No . . . it's okay," I said haltingly. "It's a good question. I don't really know what happens next. Since I've been down here, things have been such a mess. I mean, Birdsong was so *not* what I was expecting. I thought I'd just, you know, slap a coat of paint on it, maybe change some light fixtures. But it's so overwhelming! Every time I start working on one thing, I discover something else that needs to be fixed. Or stripped, or sanded, or rewired, or replumbed, or replaced. It's, like, there's no end in sight. So I've just been, sort of, taking things one day at a time."

"Something tells me that's not your usual approach to life," he said with a smile.

"No," I said ruefully. "I'm used to approaching a project, analyzing it, breaking it down into compartments, and then checking off each compartment as it's completed. You wouldn't know it by the situation I'm in right now, Carter, but in my real-life world, I'm actually a very efficient, goal-oriented person."

"This is your real life, Dempsey," he said. "And contrary to your own, rather harsh assessment, I think you're doing an exemplary job with Birdsong. And not just the house either."

His kindness brought me to sudden tears.

"Stop being so nice to me!" I said fiercely. "You're making me cry, and I don't feel like crying. I feel like celebrating." I looked over at the handsome grandfather clock standing in the corner of his office. "God, it's nearly six. I've barely eaten today. I'm hungry! Where's Tee? I am totally sick of canned soup and cheese and crackers and Hot Pockets. Tee's been pestering me to go to dinner with him at that country club of yours. So let's go already. Let's go out to dinner, all three of us, to celebrate."

"Oh," Carter said. "Tonight? Well, I don't think Tee will be able to make it. He's got to cover the county commission meeting for that damned paper of his."

"Fine," I said. "It'll be just the two of us then." I tucked my arm in his, and did a serviceable job of fluttering my eyelashes. "Of course, you'll have to give me time to go home and shower and get gussied up."

"Oh, my dear," Carter said. "I'd like nothing better. But I'm afraid

I have a previous engagement. You'll have to give the Berryhills a rain check."

"Of course," I said, laughing awkwardly. "Actually, I've got so much to do back at the house, I have no business going anywhere, except to work. Bobby Livesey is coming over tomorrow, and he wants to get started hanging the cupboard doors, and I haven't even begun sanding them yet. Never mind me, Carter. I guess I was just giddy from the relief of being out from under this Hoddergate mess."

"I'd love to take you out to dinner any other night, Dempsey," Carter said. "With or without my son."

"I'll hold you to that promise," I said, backing out of the office with as much dignity as I could muster.

I started up the Catfish's engine with no clear idea of where I was going or what I was going to do. Aimless, that's what I was. My first thought was that I'd take myself out to dinner. Who needed a date? This was the twenty-first century, right? I drove past Guthrie's two restaurants, and was surprised to see that they were both closed. Oh, right. It was Monday. Lots of restaurants were closed on Mondays. Out of desperation, I drove over to the Canton Buffet out on the bypass. Its gravel parking lot was full, and a line of people stretched out the door. I'd apparently found Guthrie's idea of a weeknight hot spot.

Suddenly, Chinese food didn't seem so appetizing. I drove over to Boulevard and pulled into the Bi-Lo shopping center, which was just outside the Guthrie city limits. FROZEN FOOD FESTIVAL! proclaimed a hot orange banner draped across the front of the supermarket. Ah yes, these were my people.

I loaded up my grocery cart with all the makings for a multiethnic food fest: frozen burritos, frozen egg rolls, frozen pizza. In an impromptu fit of international goodwill, I even dropped a box of frozen piroshkis into my buggy, wondering, as I did so, if anybody in the entire history of Guthrie, Georgia, had ever sampled a frozen piroshki. To wash down the entrées, I picked up a bottle of inexpensive chardonnay, selected purely because I loved the whimsy of its name, Dimmlylit

Cellars. Out of guilt, I even made a run down the produce aisle, to pick up a bag of prewashed salad greens and an anemic-looking cucumber.

The store was mostly empty. As the checkout-line cashier rang up my purchases, I tried not to look too obvious as I scanned the tabloid headlines. The *Star* claimed it had witnesses who could prove that Princess Diana was living in a Mormon conclave under an assumed name. Since I was planning an evening of gourmet excess, I decided to add a helping of empty literary calories to the agenda. The cashier, a rail-thin middle-aged woman with a frizzy red perm laughed when she saw me add the tabloid to the conveyor belt.

"Yeah, I had to buy that one too," she said. "Where you reckon these magazines come up with this shit they print?"

"Dunno," I admitted. "But I guess it's a safe bet Prince Charles isn't going to sue them for libel, right?"

"That's the truth," she said. She cocked her head and gave me a closer look now that I'd established myself as a confidante. "Hey, excuse my manners, but aren't you the Dempsey girl who's fixing up that old house downtown?"

"That's me," I said lightly. I held out my hand, and we shook. "I'm Dempsey Killebrew," I said. "Mr. Norbert was my great-great-uncle, although I'm sorry to say I never met him."

She gestured at her name badge. "I'm Janette. Janette Hoover. Head cashier, like that counts for anything when there's just the three of us anyway, and Beatle, he don't count because he's only half days."

"Nice to meet you, Janette."

"You're the one from Washington, right?"

"Yes." I was hoping we were going to leave it at that. I took out my billfold to pay for my groceries.

"Listen," she said, her voice lowered in a conspiratorial whisper. "There's something I want to tell you, if you don't mind me saying so."

"All right."

"I just wanna tell you that I've seen them federal agents running around town the past few days, asking a lot of questions about you."

"Oh." I felt my face reddening. I had a sudden desire to join Princess Diana in that Mormon conclave.

"Makes me so mad I could just spit!" Janette fumed. "We got to get the government out of our private lives. From what I hear around town, they're trying to say you bribed a congressman, and I don't know what all. I think that's just a bunch of shit, ya know?"

"Well . . . thanks," I stammered. "I appreciate your vote of confidence."

"Every single one of those jokers up in Washington is a crook, as far as I'm concerned," Janette said. "And I know you've got Mr. Carter Berryhill working for you, so you must be good people. Mr. Carter, he handled my divorce, and my mama's divorce, and my sister's divorce too. Next time you see him, you tell him Janette says hey, will you?"

"I certainly will," I said, handing over my money.

She bagged up my groceries and then, glancing around to make sure no government types were spying on us, she casually flipped in copies of the *National Enquirer* and the *Weekly World News*. "On the house," she whispered. "Check out the article in the *Enquirer* about John F. Kennedy's love child with Marilyn Monroe!"

By the time I got back to Birdsong, I'd mapped out a plan for the evening. I would uncork my bottle of Dimmlylit wine, drop in a couple of ice cubes, and enjoy a leisurely dinner while perusing the literature I'd just gotten. Eventually, I promised myself, I would get around to sanding those cabinet doors. But first, I was determined to celebrate my small victory over the FBI.

It had gotten dark out, but I noticed, with appreciation, that Ella Kate had thoughtfully turned on the porch light for me. Maybe, I thought, her attitude toward me was thawing. Maybe we'd even share a piroshki or an egg roll tonight.

I heard cheery whistling as I picked my way up the broken concrete sidewalk toward the house. Did I say cheery? Definitely not Ella Kate.

"Hello?" I called out. As I got closer to the front porch, I smelled fresh paint fumes.

"Well, hey there, lady," Jimmy Maynard called. I stepped up onto the porch. He'd been painting, all right. In fact, the whole wall had been transformed with a soft green shade of paint that looked suspiciously like dill pickle cut with 25 percent white.

I set my grocery bags down on the porch and gaped.

"You're speechless with gratitude, right?" He wiped his hands with a rag. He was dressed the way I'd seen him dressed every other time we'd met—in golf clothes. Tonight he wore a pale yellow polo shirt topped with a blue-and-green-striped sweater vest, worn over khaki shorts. He wore Top-Siders and no socks. Despite all the painting he'd done, there was not a drop of paint on him that I could see, and the porch floor was similarly tidy.

"I don't know what to say," I said finally. "You're amazing, to say the least."

He'd rigged up a work light on a tripod, and it was aimed at the wall he'd painted.

"Amazing." He grinned, and his even white teeth shone in his deeply tanned face. "The lady says I'm amazing and she hasn't even seen my best work yet." He dropped a kiss on my cheek. "But you will, darlin', you will."

"Should I ask what you're doing?"

He shrugged. "I was at the Benjamin Moore store this morning, buying some decorator white for one of my rental properties, and I started looking at paint chips, and I said, dammit, Jimmy, if you don't put a coat of dill pickle on Dempsey's house, nobody will. I came over here, knocked on the door, and nobody was around. I went on and ran some errands, and when I came back by, Ella Kate came to the door and said you'd gone out—she didn't know where, or when you'd be back. She tried givin' me the old Ella Kate skunk eye, but I flung it right back at her."

"You've painted the whole front of the house," I said, walking back and forth. "I can't believe it. In one afternoon."

"Well, not the whole front," Jimmy said. "Just the first floor. I thought you might think I was pushy if you came home and found my extension ladders set up and everything. Fortunately for you, Birdsong hadn't been painted in so long, most of that old pink paint had flaked right off. I ran a palm sander over the front here, cleaned it up with my Shop-Vac, got her primed, and just did manage to get a base coat down before it got too dark to see."

"I don't know what to say."

"Say you like it. Say you love it. Say you'll have dinner with me and stay over for breakfast too."

I laughed despite myself. "You're something else, Jimmy Maynard."

"I'll take that as a yes then," he said.

"Yes, I like the paint. Yes, I'll have dinner with you. But that's as far as it goes," I warned.

"We'll see," he said, and then he began to whistle again.

35

Jimmy promised to put away my groceries while I ran upstairs to shower and change. I paused in front of Ella Kate's door on my way to the bathroom. I hesitated, then knocked. "Ella Kate?"

She opened the door a crack and looked out at me.

"Did the vet call? Any news about Shorty?"

"He's doin' good," she said. "They told me we can carry him home tomorrow night, probably. Unless he has a setback or something."

"Great," I said. "I'm so glad he's all right."

She closed her door without any more idle chitchat.

I had no idea where Jimmy Maynard planned for us to have dinner, but as I stood in front of my closet, I decided any place, even the Canton Buffet, would be a treat, because it was a change. I didn't want to get too dressy, because I didn't want Jimmy thinking that I thought this was a real date. But on the other hand, he *had* just painted half of my house. The least I could do was put on something other than Uncle Norbert's flannel shirt and overalls. In the end, I put on a gauzy white embroidered peasant blouse with a drawstring neck, and a turquoise-and-yellow cotton skirt that fell loosely to my ankles. I felt funny about the blouse's low neckline, so I fished around in my jewelry box until I came up with one of my mother's necklaces. You'd have sworn it was some expensive Navajo turquoise and silver antique at first glance, but Lynda had proudly told me that the green "gems" were in reality bits of smashed Heineken bottles she'd found on the side of the road, set into aluminum strips made from flattened-out soda cans. I had dangly drop earrings to match, and when I twirled in front of the cloudy old mirror on the back of the closet door, I felt strangely lighthearted and carefree.

It was the first time since I'd moved to Georgia that I'd worn makeup—
and earrings.

Jimmy gave an appreciative wolf whistle when I walked into the
parlor. He put down the paper he'd been reading—the *National
Enquirer*—and stood up. "Well, Miss Dempsey Killebrew," he said. "You
do clean up nice. Now I guess I'll have to go home and change into
something that won't make you embarrassed to be seen with me."

"Not at all," I said. "You look fine. I just felt like dressing up tonight.
It's sort of a celebration, actually."

"I'll want to hear all about it," he said. "Right after I slip into something a little more comfortable."

We pulled into the driveway of his house, which was, as he'd promised, only a few houses down from Birdsong. "I'll wait in the car," I told
him. I was secretly feeling a little uneasy about being alone in a house
with a man who'd cheerfully told me—from the first moment we'd
met—that he planned to seduce me.

"Awww," he said. He put one finger under my chin. "I swear, I'll be
a perfect gentleman. Come on inside, I'm a real estate agent, I got to
show off my place, you know."

I don't know what I'd been expecting, but I can honestly say I wasn't
expecting what I saw when I walked through the door of Jimmy Maynard's tidy brick Colonial Revival cottage.

"Wow."

The inside of the house was light years away from the outside. It had
been totally gutted, leaving exposed whitewashed roof beams and rafters, and exposed air-conditioning ductwork. The wooden floors were
stained ebony, and finished with a high gloss. I was standing in one
large, multipurpose room. A kitchen—all high-tech and industrial-
chic stainless steel—was situated at one end of the room, at the other, a
wall of glass blocks sectioned off what I supposed was the only private
space in the house, the bathroom and bedroom. Each wall was painted
a different, bold color—tomato red, cadet blue, school bus yellow, acid
green. The furniture was contemporary—and surprisingly good. I
walked over to a scooped-out white leather lounge chair.

"Is this?"

"Yup," he said with a smirk. "Eames. Walnut base. Signed and numbered, original leather upholstery. I bought it for ten bucks from a guy who sets up at a flea market at the drive-in in Atlanta. Told me he got it out of a dentist's office."

I walked over to the sofa, a low-slung chrome and black leather creation with characteristic strapping. A white tulip Saarinen table stood to the side of the sofa. "And this?" I asked, patting the sofa.

"Florence Knoll," he said. "Now this, I did buy off eBay. I got it for two hundred bucks, but of course, the seller hit me up for another two hundred bucks in shipping."

"And it's worth?"

He showed me the teeth again. "Last time I checked? A couple thousand."

"You're really into contemporary furniture," I said. "I'm impressed."

"I'm impressed that you're impressed. You sure you're a lobbyist?"

"I read a lot of shelter magazines. You sure you're not gay?"

He laughed. "Touché."

He pointed toward the kitchen. "There's a bottle of wine in the fridge. Pour a glass for both of us, and make yourself comfortable. I won't be but a minute."

I wandered over to the kitchen. The refrigerator was the one I'd lusted after, a glass-doored Traulsen. I saw the wine, and took two glasses from a rack that hung over the sink. I poured two glasses—and took my own glass over to the sofa.

The cell phone he'd left on a console table near the door rang.

"Just ignore the phone," Jimmy called from the other room. "The damned thing never stops ringing. One of the hazards of being in real estate."

I sat down and sipped my wine and leafed through a magazine on the coffee table. I glanced toward the wall of glass blocks, and nearly died. The blocks didn't just separate the bedroom from the main room, they also housed a walk-in shower. There, outlined in all his wavy glory, was a very naked Jimmy Maynard, lathering up and whistling up a storm. I took a gulp of my wine and tried hard to concentrate on the April issue of *Elle Decor.*

Ten minutes later, Jimmy strolled out, dressed in a starched button-down blue oxford-cloth shirt, knee-length black shorts, and black loafers buffed to a high sheen. He smelled like soap and aftershave and his damp hair still bore comb marks.

"Hey," he said, picking up the glass of wine I'd poured him.

"Hey yourself," I said. "Do you ever wear long pants?"

"Nope," he said. "And I'll tell you why. In the nineties, when I was in between marriages, I told myself, Jimmy, it's time to grow up and work in the adult world. I got myself a job as a financial analyst. Worked in a high-rise tower in Buckhead. Drove a Jaguar, had an hour and a half commute every day. Made in the high six figures. And I hated every damned minute of it.

"One day, I just up and left. Took my parking pass and my security pass, and just left 'em on my desk. On my way back down here to Guthrie, I threw my necktie out the window, doing eighty on I-75. I came home, sold the Jag, bought myself a four-wheel drive, and threw out every goddarned pair of custom-tailored long pants I owned." He preened a little and stuck out an ankle to admire himself. "Many women have told me my legs are my best feature."

"You do have nice muscular calves," I observed.

He sat down beside me and threw an arm over my shoulder. "You ain't seen nothin' yet, darlin'."

I scooted away and put down my empty wineglass. "I hate to be obvious—but didn't you promise me dinner?"

"I did," he said. "And I never break a promise to a beautiful lady."

⟶

Jimmy had the top down on his Jeep. He handed me a new yellow baseball cap with MAYNARD REALTY embroidered across the bill. I tucked my hair up under it, and off we went. The moon was nearly full and the sky was a deep velvet blue. He drove with one hand draped across the steering wheel, and the other across the back of my seat. His cell rang twice; both times he looked at the caller ID, shrugged, and let it go to voice mail.

"You like prime rib?" he asked.

"Sure."

"Good," he said. "It's prime rib night at the country club."

He turned on the radio, and punched buttons until he came to the station he wanted. "'The Sixties on Six,'" he said. "God, I love satellite radio."

I recognized the song that was playing, "Under the Boardwalk," by the Drifters, because it was one of Mitch's favorites.

Jimmy glanced over at me. "How 'bout beach music? You like beach music?"

"Sure."

Another grin. "You're battin' a thousand."

"I grew up listening to the Drifters, the Tams, and the Platters," I told him. "My dad's a beach music nut."

"Ouch. Now I really do feel like an old fart."

"You'll get over it."

We pulled up in front of a sprawling one-story white stucco building nestled in ribbons of blooming azaleas. A discreet stucco sign told me we'd arrived at PINE BLOSSOM COUNTRY CLUB.

Jimmy zoomed up beneath a portico, and a valet-parking kid trotted out to take the keys.

We strolled through the foyer, a tasteful affair with overstuffed sofas and glass display cases bristling with silver trophies, and into the dining room, a large, glass-walled room that looked out on the up-lit golf course.

"Mr. Maynard," cooed the hostess, a middle-aged blonde with a short skirt and long legs. "We've got your regular table ready."

The room was crowded with well-dressed people, the men in sports coats, the women in spiffy pants outfits or dresses. It made me glad I'd forsaken my overalls for the night. But nobody seemed to be looking askance at Jimmy in his shorts.

"Don't they have a dress code here?" I whispered as we made our way through the room.

"Sure," he said, steering me with his hand on the small of my back. "There's rules, and there's exceptions to rules. I try to be the exception whenever I can."

Every other diner, it seemed, turned from their table to say hello, or got up to pump Jimmy's hand.

"Do you know every single person here?" I asked as he pulled out my chair for me.

He scanned the room. "Hmm. Nope. There's a couple of people I don't recognize. Yankees, probably."

The waiter brought over a large tumbler of ice and a beaker of what looked like bourbon. "Here's your Knob Creek, Mr. Maynard." He looked at me. "And for the lady?"

I shrugged. "I'll have what he's having."

Jimmy laughed and patted my hand. "You're a fast learner, Dempsey Killebrew."

The waiter brought a basket of warm bread, and salads, and I dove into mine without any prompting.

"I love a lady who appreciates good food," Jimmy said, leaning back in his chair to watch me eat, and ignoring his own salad.

"I'm starved," I admitted. "I've been living off what my mom calls 'bird food' for days now."

By the time the huge platters of prime rib and baked potatoes arrived at the table, I'd polished off all of my salad and half the basket of rolls. Jimmy, on the other hand, merely picked at his salad, while downing two beakers of bourbon. There hadn't been time for him to eat, because every minute or two, his cell phone rang, or an old friend wandered up to the table to say hi and trade golf jokes.

"This is Dempsey," he'd say, by way of introduction. "Oh yes," came the invariable response. "Can't wait to see what you'll do with Birdsong." And after an awkward pause, "Hope the thing in Washington works out."

After the third variation of the Birdsong theme, I sighed. "Everybody in this whole damned town knows all about me."

Jimmy stabbed a piece of beef and chewed thoughtfully. "You're a hero, Dempsey. From what all we hear, the FBI tried to push you around, and you told 'em to stick it up their W-two. This is still the heart of Dixie, darlin'. We may make noises about the New South and all that mess, but what we really mean is, 'Fergit, hell.' So you're kind of a celebrity. Don't sweat it. Sit back and enjoy the ride."

I was about to tell him how little I was enjoying this particular ride when I saw a familiar figure get up from a table in the far corner of the room. I'd have known that mane of silver hair and erect posture anywhere. As I watched, he pulled out the chair for his dining companion, a striking brunette of about fifty, dressed in a low-cut black sweater, pearls, and well-cut black slacks. The woman stood, gave him a warm kiss on the cheek, and they strolled through the room, hand in hand, stopping at one table to chat.

"That's Carter Berryhill!" I said in surprise.

Jimmy turned and strained his neck to see. "Yup."

I felt a stab of something—jealousy?—in the pit of my stomach. "Who's that woman with him? I've never seen her before."

"That's because she hasn't been around for the past year or two," Jimmy said calmly. He took another bite of beef. "Damn, they do a mean prime rib here."

"Jimmy!" I rapped my knife on my water glass. "Pay attention here. Who is that woman who was kissing Carter Berryhill?"

He put down his fork. "Why, that's just ol' Veronica Lanier. Or maybe she goes by her maiden name now, which I never did know, since she gave poor ol' Hammond Lanier the heave-ho. Your buddy Carter was Veronica's divorce attorney, which was good news for her, because between Carter and Tee, they made sure that Veronica got the gold mine, also known as all the Coca-Cola stock, the house in Highlands, and the newspaper, and Hammond got the shaft. Poor dumb bastard."

"Wait. That's the woman who owned the paper—and she didn't want to pay the Berryhills' legal fees, so they ended up taking over the *Citizen-Advocate*?"

"Same one," Jimmy agreed. "Well, not the exact same. I think ol' Veronica's had some work done. I know she's been livin' down in Florida, but those grapefruits she's sportin' tonight were just oranges before she took Hammond to the cleaners."

I gave him an annoyed look. "You're a pig, Jimmy Maynard."

He chuckled and took a sip of bourbon. "So I've been told."

"Tee told me they had to take that woman to arbitration after she disputed their legal fees. You'd think the Berryhills would have a grudge against her. But here's Carter, playing kissy face with her in dark corners at the country club. I totally don't get it."

"You don't have to get it," Jimmy drawled. "But from the looks of things, ol' Carter's gonna be getting a little sumthin' from Veronica. Hell, maybe she's working off those legal fees you're so worried about. I say good for Carter. There might be snow on that roof of his, but there's still some fire in the furnace." He grinned that bad-boy grin of his, drained his drink, and signaled the waiter to bring another.

Jimmy leaned across the table, took my hand, and kissed the palm. "See? Us old farts, we've still got a lot to offer a woman. What do you say we skip dessert and go back to my place for some fun?"

I snatched my hand away. When had he turned from endearing charmer to slobbering drunk? Maybe right after his third Knob Creek?

"Jimmy," I said sweetly, "I do think we should skip dessert. But I've had a really long day today, starting with an early morning trip to Macon. So, if you don't mind, I'd really like to go home now."

"After I finish my drink, okay?" he said, craning his neck toward the bar to check on the waiter's progress.

I turned around, hoping that the waiter would not be on his way back to our table, just in time to see another member of the Berryhill law firm walk into the dining room with another gorgeous brunette in tow.

Jimmy saw him at the same time I did. "Hey, Tee!" he called, a little too loudly.

Tee looked around the room to see who was greeting him. When he saw Jimmy, waving madly, he gave a perfunctory smile. Then he saw me, sitting right beside Jimmy, and the smile froze.

36

"Awwww, sheee-uut," Jimmy drawled. "I didn't see he was with her."

"Quick, who is that woman?" I demanded. "They're coming over here!"

"You don' wanna know," Jimmy said.

Tee and the brunette approached the table.

"Hey, Jimmy," the brunette said. She wore a cream-colored business suit, had sapphire-colored eyes, a pointy chin, and full, pouty lips, and in her four-inch spike heels, she towered over Tee by at least an inch. "Who's your friend?"

"Hey, Shirlene," Jimmy mumbled, looking away. "This is . . . uh, Dempsey."

"Hi, Jimmy, hi, Dempsey," Tee said. There were two bright pink spots on his cheeks. He shoved his hands in the pockets of his slacks. "So . . . this is awkward."

"Ain't it just," Jimmy said, jiggling the ice in his empty glass. "Good thing we were just about to leave."

The brunette grabbed the glass out of his hand and gave it a sniff. "Jimmy Maynard! Have you been drinking bourbon?"

Jimmy slumped backward in his chair and gave her a lazy smile. "Why, yes, ma'am, as a matter of fact I have."

Shirlene rolled her eyes and gave a huff of exasperation. "Dempsey? Is that your name?"

"Dempsey Killebrew," I said, holding out my hand.

She took mine and gave it a brief shake. "Shirlene Peppers. Look, Dempsey, did Jimmy drive you over here tonight?"

"Unfortunately, yes."

"Lorrrrd," she said. She had both hands on her hips and she looked down at the two of us as though she'd caught us skipping school.

"If you're gonna sleep with the man, there's something you need to know. You never give Jimmy Maynard bourbon. He just can't handle brown liquor. Everybody in town knows that. He can drink wine and beer till the cows come home, and a little vodka at parties, even, but you *do not* give this man whiskey. Understood?"

"Whoa! Time-out. Who said I was sleeping with him? And besides that, I didn't give him anything," I protested. "The waiter brought him over a drink before we even sat down."

The aforesaid waiter had the misfortune to arrive back at the table at that exact moment, with another beaker of poison water for Jimmy Maynard.

"Manny!" Shirlene said, whirling around to face him. "Is this true? Did you serve Mr. Maynard bourbon, even after what happened the last time?"

Manny stared down at his lace-up black shoes. "Yes'm."

"Lorrrrd," Shirlene said again, shaking her head with disgust. She looked from me to Jimmy to Tee. "Well? What are you planning to do about this mess?"

Why did I feel like I was the one facing detention—or worse, expulsion? "I was hoping to get out of here without causing a scene," I said in a low voice. "But I think that's probably a lost cause now." When I looked up, a dozen people sitting at the tables around us glanced quickly away—down at their plates, or off into the distance.

Shirlene waved away my concern. "Oh, don't mind these people. They know how Jimmy gets when he drinks whiskey. So—can you drive home? Because I promise you, he cannot."

"Uh, no. I never learned to drive a manual transmission."

She gave another exasperated huff. "I forgot about that damned Jeep of his. Idiotic car for a grown man to drive. Tee? Would you mind? I'll get Manny to pack us up a couple of to-go boxes. We really can't let Jimmy loose on the highway."

"Hey!" Jimmy said. "I resent that remark. I can drive just fine."

"Shut up!" Tee and Shirlene said in unison. Jimmy put his head down on the table and closed his eyes.

"I'll drive the Jeep back to my house and he can walk over and get it in the morning, after he sobers up," Shirlene said. "Tee, can you guys load him into your car and take him home? I really can't deal with him after he's been drinking."

Tee shrugged. It didn't appear that you gave Shirlene Peppers any guff once she started issuing orders. He put an arm under Jimmy's shoulder. "Come on, Jimbo. Time to go home."

It was no easy trick folding a six-foot-two drunk into the front seat of that Mini Cooper, but somehow, between us, we managed to wedge him into the passenger seat. I had to go around to the driver's side to squeeze into the tiny backseat.

Tee drove, the silence broken only by Jimmy's occasional snore. I could tell from the ramrod set of Tee's shoulders that he was pissed. Well, I was pissed too, if you wanted to get right down to it.

But I was more worried than pissed, worried that Tee would think Shirlene Peppers was right about my relationship with Jimmy Maynard.

I cleared my throat. "Not that it's any of your business," I said finally. "But I am definitely *not* sleeping with Jimmy Maynard."

"Fine," he said curtly. "You're right. It is none of my business. Sleep with whomever you please. But you were having a cozy dinner with him, weren't you? Funny—every time I ask you out, you're too tired, or too busy, or too worried about what people think about you."

"That's bullshit!" I cried. "I would have gone to dinner with you tonight. Hell, I even asked your *dad* if the two of you could go to dinner to celebrate tonight. He made up some pathetic excuse about you having to cover the county commission, and said *he* had a previous engagement. I guess he did! I saw him earlier with that Veronica Lanier woman. She was all over him, like cheap perfume. And then you march in with your own little cutie-pie. You really should have checked with your dad, Tee, before showing up in a public place with another woman."

Tee's head whipped around to look at me. "Dad? You saw him with Veronica? Where was this?"

"Right there at the country club, they left no more than ten minutes before you and *Shirlene* came in," I said, fuming. "I guess the country club is where the Berryhill men have all their affairs, right?"

"I'll be damned," Tee muttered. "I didn't know Veronica was back in town. He never breathed a word to me, the sly old dog."

"It's none of my business," I went on. "But it seems to me that Shirlene Peppers is just a little bit long in the tooth for you. What is she, fifty or something?"

"She's the same age as your boyfriend Jimmy here," Tee shot back.

"He is not my boyfriend!"

"Well, Shirlene's not my girlfriend. Come on, Dempsey, give me a little credit here. Dad told you the truth. I did have to cover the county commission meeting. That's where I met up with Shirlene. She's the county attorney, for God's sake. I was trying to pump her for details on the search for a new county manager. Shirlene and I went to law school together."

"Sure you did," I said coldly. "Only it must have taken Shirlene a good ten years longer than you to get out of law school."

"You're impossible," he said. "It took Shirlene six years to get out of undergraduate school, going nights and working days. It wasn't until after she divorced Jimmy that she could afford to go to law school."

"What did you just say? Did you just say Jimmy and Shirlene used to be married?"

"He didn't mention that?"

"He told me the first or second time we met that he'd been married and divorced several times. I remember he talked about a wife named LaDonna, and yeah, I guess, now that you mention it, he did mention being married to somebody named Shirlene."

"Yeah, she left him for Wayne Peppers, a gastroenterologist here in town. I think she regretted marrying Wayne about two seconds after they got back from the honeymoon. Unfortunately, Shirlene hired some hack from Griffin to handle the divorce. She got hosed, even though Wayne was the one doing the running around."

I closed my eyes. How did these people in Guthrie keep all these exes straight? "Wait." A sudden thought occurred to me. "You're telling me Shirlene was married to a Dr. Pepper?" I started to giggle. "That's hilarious." Once I got started, I couldn't stop. "Dr Pepper!" I yelped. "I'm a Pepper, she's a Pepper. Get it?"

"Peppers plural," Tee said, his voice cold. "Wayne Peppers. Not Pepper. Get it?"

"Dr. Peppers," I said, my voice strangled with laughter. I couldn't stop giggling. I giggled so hard I snorted, and then I giggled some more.

"You have a weird sense of humor," Tee said, shaking his head.

"I know, but I haven't had a lot to laugh about lately," I said, wiping the tears from my eyes. "That's why I wanted to go to dinner with you tonight, to celebrate."

"What were we going to celebrate?" he asked cautiously.

Suddenly, Jimmy sat up straight in his seat. "She told the FBI to go fly a kite!" he said, slurring the words. "Old Dempsey here's a badass." He belched loudly, then slumped back down in his seat again.

With great effort, the two of us managed to pour Jimmy Maynard out of the Mini Cooper and into his own bed in his own house. "I'm fine," he kept saying. "Lemme finish my prime rib." Tee dragged him into the glass-walled bedroom and pushed him over onto the bed. He pulled Jimmy's loafers from his feet and looked over at me. "I draw the line at some things," he said. "He can just sleep with his clothes on tonight. It won't be the first time."

We locked up the house and walked back to the Mini Cooper. I got in the front seat and handed Tee the Styrofoam to-go box from the country club. "Here's your dinner," I said lamely. "I'm sorry you didn't get to eat it in peace." I took a deep breath. "And I'm sorry I jumped to conclusions about you and Shirlene."

"You should be sorry," Tee said. But he reached across the gearbox and took my hand in his. He glanced over at me. "You doin' anything tonight?"

"I was hoping to have a celebratory dinner with my gentleman friend."

"Your place or mine? Wait. I'm thinking my place. Unless you confiscated that broom from Ella Kate."

"What about your dad?" I asked. "It's kind of late. Won't we disturb him?"

Tee chuckled. "Oh, I'm pretty sure with Veronica Lanier in town, the silver fox is spending the night out tonight."

ee unlocked his front door and pulled me inside. As soon as the door was closed, he had me pinned against it. He ran his hands down my arms and locked them around my waist, pulling me to him. "Where have you been keeping this outfit?" he asked, nudging the blouse neckline over my shoulder with his chin, kissing my skin as he bared it.

"In the closet," I managed, but I soon realized his question was largely rhetorical. In very little time he'd pulled my blouse free of the skirt waistband, and with his thumbs, he pushed my breasts out of the bra cups. He lowered his head and kissed them until I was dizzy and breathless.

"Hey," I said, catching his chin in my hands. I kissed him on the mouth, he kissed me back, and we stood there like that, melted into the paint for what seemed like a long time.

"What about your dinner?" I asked, when I managed to pull away for a breath.

"I hate prime rib," he told me. "Come on." He tugged me by the hand into the silent, darkened house.

We stopped in the living room. He shrugged out of his blue blazer and tossed it over the back of a nearby chair. He pulled me down onto the brocade sofa, and flung the heap of needlepoint pillows onto the floor with one sweep of his arm. "Come here," he said. We sank into the cushions. His kisses were sweet and urgent, and his hands were busy. In what seemed like seconds, he'd worked the zipper of my skirt down, and my arms free of my blouse. I managed to loosen his striped rep tie and unfasten the top button on his heavily starched dress shirt. But my fingernails, broken off short by all my labors at the house, fumbled ineffectively with the next one.

"Why do they make the buttons on men's shirts so tiny?" I asked, tugging his shirt loose of his slacks and running my hands up his bare chest.

"Don't know," he mumbled, kicking off his loafers. "We'll have to look into that. Later."

I heard the slow, reassuring tick of the clock on the mantel as I worked at unbuckling his belt. My blouse came fully off. His shirt buttons finally came free of the buttonholes.

"Wait!" I said urgently, as headlights shone in the front windows. I sat up and reached desperately for my clothing.

A moment later, the lights were gone.

"False alarm," Tee said, pulling me back down onto the sofa. "I told you, Dad's out for the evening. Now, will you relax?"

"I'm sorry."

"Show me how sorry you are," he suggested.

I stood up again and let the skirt fall to the floor.

"That's a good start," he said, his arms crossed behind his head. "What else ya got?"

I stepped out of the skirt and kicked off my ballet flats. Dressed only in my bra and panties I took a step toward him. Headlights swept the room and I dove onto the sofa, right on top of him.

"I'm sorry," I said again. "I just feel so exposed here."

He kissed my bare shoulder, groaned, and stood up. "Come on then," he said, tugging me by the hand. I barely had time to grab up my clothes.

"Maybe this isn't such a good idea," I said as he pulled me out of the living room and into the kitchen. The only light there was the LED display on the range. "I just . . . feel like I'm back in high school, getting felt up by my boyfriend out in the driveway, while my dad's inside, peering out the window."

He stopped in his tracks with a look of mock outrage on his face. "You let your boyfriend feel you up? In high school? What kind of nice girl does something like that?"

"I was a senior," I explained. "And he swore he wouldn't try anything below the waist."

"I would hope not," Tee said, backing me up against the refrigerator. He cupped one hand under my butt, and with the other hand, tugged at the waistband of my panties, rolling them down with agonizing slowness.

"You didn't let the guy do anything like this, right?" he said, nuzzling my neck, and exploring between my legs.

I gasped. "Never. Swear to God."

"Good," Tee said.

I let my fingertips trail down his chest, and bent and kissed his nipples. My fingers found his zipper. I tugged it down an inch and stopped, hooking one finger inside the fly of his briefs.

"Will you still respect me?" I asked.

He clamped his hand over my own. "You won't believe how much I'll respect you."

I pressed my hips into his and locked my arms around his neck. He reached around my back and with a single swift motion unhooked my bra.

"I don't know," I said, nipping his earlobe and letting my bra fall to the floor. "You've got some pretty expert moves. You weren't one of those fast guys my mother warned me about, were you?"

He cupped one of my breasts in his hand and put his lips to the nipple. A moment later, he looked up at me. "Me? Fast? Nah. Slow and steady, that's my motto."

He was true to his word too. He explored my body in exquisite detail, touching and kissing me until I forgot who I was and where I was.

"Tee," I finally managed. "Isn't there someplace else we could do this?"

Before he could answer, there was a loud clatter behind me. I jumped, and Tee took a step backward, nearly stumbling in the process. He righted himself, and hitched up his slacks with one hand. I giggled nervously despite myself.

"It's just the damned ice maker," he said through gritted teeth.

"Sorry."

"Come on," he said. "We're through in here."

I grabbed up my bundle of clothes and followed him into a small utility room that smelled of bleach and detergent. A wooden rod held a row of freshly laundered hanging clothes, and beside it was a shelf unit of cleaning supplies.

"Here?" I asked, looking with alarm at the gleaming white washer and dryer.

"Not here," Tee said. He took me in his arms again. "Although, come to think of it, if we waited till the spin cycle . . ."

"Forget it," I said, shivering in the unheated room. He pulled me closer, and his hands roamed down my bare spine. "You never fantasized about doing dirty things in the laundry room?"

"Honestly? No."

He sighed. "We're going to have to work on your imagination, Dempsey Killebrew." He took a flannel shirt off a hanger and draped it over my shoulders, pulling my arms into the sleeves, but leaving it unbuttoned, his hands deliberately grazing my breasts.

"Shoes?" he asked, glancing down at my bare feet.

"Where are you taking me?" I asked. "Tee, I'm nearly naked. I can't."

He put his fingers to my lips. "Shh." He kissed me lightly.

There was a peg rack of coats and jackets by the back door, and on the floor, a row of boots and shoes neatly lined up. He knelt at my feet and lifted my right foot. He kissed the instep, and then slipped my foot into a bleached-out sneaker three sizes too big. He lifted my left foot and did the same thing. He ran his hands up the back of my calves, and I shivered in expectation. He kissed one of my knees, and then the other, running his hands up the front of my thighs. He clasped my butt in both hands, and kissed the bare skin below my navel, and then below that, his beard scratching at my tender skin.

"Oh my God, Tee," I begged.

He stood up without another word, and slid his feet into a pair of loafers. He opened the back door. I gasped as the cold air hit my naked skin. He grabbed my hand and pulled me out the door.

"Come on," he urged.

The full moon spilled pale yellow light onto a small, brick-walled garden. A tall tree's budded-out limbs stretched toward the sky, and hedges of knee-high boxwood outlined beds of bare-limbed rosebushes.

Pea gravel crunched beneath our feet as Tee steered me down the garden path.

As my eyes grew accustomed to the half-light, I could make out a small outbuilding at the end of the path. It was white clapboard, with a steeply pitched roof and a pocket-size screened porch.

Tee pushed the screen door open, and it slapped shut behind us. The porch was only big enough for two painted wooden rocking chairs. Ignoring them, Tee wrenched the wooden door open, its hinges screeching in protest.

Moonlight streamed into the room through a window high in the pitched roof. We were standing in one large room, open to exposed rafters. Everything was unpainted wood—floors, walls, and ceilings. It smelled like the inside of a forest. There was a desk, piled high with papers, and a computer, against one wall, and a chair shoved up to it. I could see a small closet through a half-open door, and on the far wall, facing me, another half-open door revealed what looked like a bathroom.

A highly polished mahogany four-poster bed took up most of the room, its covers rumpled, pillows piled high. A shirt and a pair of jeans were slung over one of the posters.

"What is this place?" I asked, running my hand over the plank walls.

"It's my place," Tee said, closing the door behind us and making a show of locking it. "Sorry about the mess. I wasn't expecting company tonight."

"Your place? You don't live in the big house?"

"Nope." He took me by the hand until we were standing at the foot of the bed. "It used to be a potting shed. Dad and I built it for Mom one summer."

"This was a potting shed?" I stepped out of the sneakers. The pine boards were cool and smooth underfoot. "Pretty fancy."

"She liked to come out here and sit and read her gardening books and seed catalogs," Tee said. "Dad had it plumbed, and put in heat and air too. He thought she needed her own space, since he had a den, and, of course, the law office. She loved it out here. I was living in my own place, in town, but after she died, Dad seemed pretty lonely. I sure as hell wasn't ready to move back in here after being out on my own all that time, but then, I got to thinking about the shed, and it seemed like it might be a good compromise."

"It's wonderful," I said, clasping my arms around his waist. "Like a little playhouse."

"Guys don't play house," Tee said. He kissed me for a long time.

I shrugged out of my flannel shirt. "You don't know what you've been missing."

We both dozed off, and when I awoke, I was on my side, with Tee spooned up behind me, one bare arm slung over my side, his hand cupped around my breast. His breath was warm and sweet on my neck. I wriggled out from under him. He rolled to the other side of the bed.

I got up and went into the bathroom. I looked at myself in the mirror. My hair was wild, my cheeks and neck and chest scraped pink from beard burn. I tiptoed back out into the main room and groped around on the floor until I found my panties and the flannel shirt. I had no idea where the rest of my clothes were. I sat down at Tee's desk and moved the mouse on his computer until the screen came glowingly to light. It was nearly 4 A.M.

I went over and sat on the side of the bed. I kissed Tee's lips lightly. He smiled, but didn't open his eyes. I kissed him again, parting his lips with the tip of my tongue.

"Mmm. Nice," he said, pulling me down onto the bed beside him. "Are we gonna play house again?" He nuzzled my neck and pushed the sheet down to show me how ready he was to resume play.

"No," I laughed regretfully. "Listen, Tee. I've got to get home."

"Noooo," he said, moaning and rolling over with his back to me.

"Seriously," I said. "Home. Please?"

He rolled back over. "Stay. Please?" He grabbed a handful of the flannel shirt and gently tugged. He frowned. "You're dressed. I like undressed better."

"Me too," I admitted. He was adorable, with his hair mussed and his eyes heavy lidded with sleep and desire. The most adorable man I'd ever seen, naked or not. I bent to kiss him, and that was a mistake. He ran his hands up under the flannel shirt, and I felt my resolve begin to melt.

"See?" he said, yawning, his fingers lazily circling my nipple. "You know you want to stay."

"Can't," I said, maneuvering out of his reach. I had to avoid temptation.

"It's the middle of the night, baby," Tee protested, propping himself up on one elbow. "Come back to bed. I'll take you home first thing in the morning. I'll even fix you breakfast. Biscuits. Did you know I can make biscuits?"

"Another time," I promised. "It's almost four. I'll stay next time. But right now I've really, really got to get home. Bobby's coming today, and he always shows up right at daylight. I've still got to get those cupboard doors sanded—"

Tee swung his legs over the side of the bed. "And you don't want Bobby Livesey to catch you sneaking up the front walk with your panties in your pocketbook and a smile on your face."

I blushed.

"I knew it," Tee said, yawning again. "Still worried about your reputation." He stood up and padded, naked, toward the bathroom. I watched him go, savoring the sight of his slim hips tapering down to pale, muscular buns. He looked over his shoulder and caught me watching. I blushed again.

"Some renegade you are."

38

While we'd been steaming up the windows in Tee's shed, the temperature outside seemed to have dropped a good twenty degrees. I ran through the boxwood garden and stood expectantly by the back door. "Hurry," I urged, as he fumbled with the door to the utility room. "I'm freezing."

"Keep your pants on," he muttered, jiggling the door handle. He glanced back at me and laughed, as I hopped up and down, wearing nothing more than panties, a flannel shirt, and a pair of his old shoes.

"It's not funny," I said, my teeth chattering. "I think my fanny's getting frostbite."

"The damned thing's stuck," he announced.

"Let me try," I said, nearly shoving him aside. I jiggled and pulled, but the door wouldn't budge. "What about the front door?"

He grimaced. "Don't you remember? I locked the dead bolt."

"What?"

"As I recall, you were worried about Dad dropping in on us."

"And now I'm worried I'll freeze to death out here," I said. "Don't you have another door into the house? How will your dad get in if the dead bolt's set?"

"There's a door from the garage into the kitchen," Tee said.

"Fine. Show me the way.'

"Can't. The only way into the garage is with the automatic clicker thingy."

"In your pants pocket, right?"

"My jacket pocket," he said sadly. "Which I think is in the living room."

"Shit!" I cried through lips that were rapidly turning blue. "You did this on purpose."

He crossed his hands over his T-shirt-covered chest. "Swear to God. It never occurred to me. Baby, I was in such a hurry to get into the house and your pants, it didn't dawn on me that you'd need to make a fast getaway."

"Now what?" I wailed. "How am I going to get my clothes?"

He wrapped his arms around me and pulled me close. "We go back to bed, where it's nice and warm. Dad'll be home in a couple of hours. He'll let us in."

"Oh no," I cried. "I can't face your father like this. What'll he think?"

Tee gazed down at my bare legs. "He'll think I'm one lucky sumbitch."

I thumped his chest. "Not funny." I turned around and headed back toward the potting shed, walking as fast as the oversize shoes would let me.

"Now you're talking," Tee said, hurrying to catch up with me.

Inside the shed, I pulled aside the covers on the bed. I searched the chair beside the bed, then got down on my hands and knees to look under the bed.

Tee stood in the doorway, watching the spectacle with obvious enjoyment. "Whatya lookin' for?" he asked.

"The clicker thingy," I said. "I'll bet it was in your pants pocket, along with your car keys. I definitely remember those keys jingling when—"

"You were peeling me out of my britches at the height of your animal lust?"

I shot him a dirty look.

"I'm just sayin'."

I finally found the khaki slacks on the back of the chair by the computer.

"Aha!" I said, triumphantly holding up the car keys. "Now will you take me home?"

"Sure," he said, taking the keys from me. "But you're gonna have to give me back my shirt and my shoes first."

"There's not a key to the house on this key ring?"

He shook his head sadly. "Sure. But there's that dead bolt thing . . ."

"Dammit, Tee," I fumed. "This really isn't funny. You're just gonna have to give me some pants or something to put on for the ride home."

"Okay," he said. He went into the closet and came out with a pair of drawstring flannel pajama bottoms. They were hot pink, decorated with red cartoon cupids. He tossed them to me.

I raised an eyebrow.

"Christmas present from an aunt in Florida," he said. "She might be senile."

I stepped into the pants and snugged the drawstring as tight as I could, but the bottoms were still so big they looked like clown pants. "All right, funny guy," I said. "Take me home."

Tee hummed happily as he drove through the predawn darkness. I shot him another dirty look, which he pretended not to notice.

"Do you really think your dad spent the night out with that woman?" I asked, trying in vain to finger-comb my hair.

Tee yawned widely. "Who knows? Dad's not one to kiss and tell." He picked up my hand and kissed the back of it. "And neither am I."

"That's sweet," I said, softening. "But before I spend another night with you, I want my own set of keys, and my own clicker thingy for the garage door."

He grinned. "So . . . there's gonna be a next time?"

"Do you want there to be?"

He looked surprised. "Dempsey, what did you think was happening back at my place tonight?"

I blushed and looked away.

"Hey." He pulled the Mini Cooper over to the side of the road, but left the motor running.

"Hey," he said it softly, putting his hand under my chin and turning my head toward him so that I had no place else to look. His dark eyes glittered. "I'm falling for you, Dempsey. Do you not know that?"

I felt a lump in my throat. I swallowed hard. "Do you really know what you're getting into here, Tee? We had fun tonight. But maybe we should just leave things like that. Just fun."

"Uh-uh," he said, shaking his head vigorously. "I wasn't kidding earlier when I told you I'm the slow and steady type. Fun's good. Fun's great. But I want more than that. I'm not some oversexed frat-boy type like Jimmy Maynard, Dempsey. I want you. And I think you want me too."

"You don't know me," I said, tears springing up unexpectedly. "You can't know what I want. I don't even know that."

He sighed deeply. "Have it your way then." He put the Mini Cooper into gear and pulled back onto the road. His shoulders had that tensed, squared-off look again.

Five minutes later, he pulled into the driveway at Birdsong. The house was dark. A light blinked on in the upstairs bedroom, and then off again, just as quickly.

"Oh God. Ella Kate's spying on me," I fretted. "She saw me leave earlier with Jimmy. What's she gonna think when she sees me coming home with you? Looking like this?" I pulled at the fabric of the pink flannel pajama bottoms.

Tee shook his head. "She damned sure ain't gonna think any worse of you than you already think of yourself." He got out of the car and came around to my side and opened my door.

I climbed out of the Mini Cooper and reached for his hand, but he held it stiffly by his side. He left me at the bottom porch step. "I'll get your clothes back to you today," he said. He walked rapidly away, and in a second was swallowed up in the predawn darkness.

I fell into my bed dressed in the clothes I'd come home wearing, and went right to sleep. I didn't dream of Tee, or Jimmy Maynard, or even Alex Hodder. I dreamed about the house. I dreamed I answered the doorbell, and Mitch and Pilar were standing on the doorstep with the twins and a mile-high stack of luggage.

In my dream, I was showing Mitch all the work I'd done on Birdsong, but everything was changed. We walked into rooms I'd never seen before. They were ugly, crowded with trash and ruined furniture, windows streaked with dirt. Mitch was speechless with anger and Pilar was screaming because she couldn't find the boys, and all the doors had suddenly disappeared.

I awoke suddenly, my heart pounding, the flannel shirt drenched in sweat. I looked at the clock on the nightstand. It was only 6 A.M. I knew I wouldn't sleep anymore.

I showered and dressed in my work clothes. Down in the kitchen, the harsh yellow light from the bare overhead bulb seemed somehow reassuring. Here was the floor I'd refinished. There were the cabinets I'd stripped. It was all there, even the strong chemical odor of stripper. I could see and touch and smell the concrete results of my hard work. I brewed a pot of coffee and poured myself a huge mug. I gulped down the coffee and went back to work.

With the iPod buds lodged firmly in my ears, and the protective plastic goggles strapped on my head, I set the first cupboard door across the sawhorses and fired up the palm sander.

I'd finished the first three doors and was about to tackle the fourth when my sander suddenly went dead on me. I picked it up and flicked the switch off and then on again. When I turned around, I saw Ella Kate standing by the counter, holding the unplugged orange extension cord in her hand.

She was dressed in Uncle Norbert's bathrobe and wore an expression that said she was mad enough to spit nickels.

I flipped the goggles off and unplugged the earbuds. "Oh, hi," I said weakly.

"What in h-e-double-ell do you think you're doing here?" she sputtered. "Do you know that it's not even daylight outside? People are tryin' to sleep." She waved toward the back door. "People can hear that goddarned contraption of yours clear over next door."

I put the sander down. "Oh. I'm sorry. I guess, I just thought, well, you're usually up way earlier than me every morning. It didn't occur to me that you'd still be in bed."

"In bed?" She flung the orange cord to the floor in disgust. "Of course I'm in bed. I was up all night the night before last with a sick dog. Then, I seen you go out the door with one man last night, dressed to kill, and I wake up to see you come sneakin' in like a thief in the night—dressed in another man's nightclothes! What kind of a trollop are you? It ain't decent!"

I blushed down to the roots of my hair. "Ella Kate," I stammered. "I'm sorry. It won't happen again. I swear."

But she didn't hear me. "Of all the inconsiderate, selfish girls in the world, you beat 'em all. You hear me? After yesterday, when you acted all sorry about Shorty, I thought maybe I was wrong about you. I thought maybe you had some Dempsey goodness in you. Well, I was wrong all right. You're Killebrew, through and through." She stormed out of the kitchen, slamming the door behind her.

Stung, I sat down at the kitchen table and stared into my mug of coffee. It was coated with a fine layer of sawdust. I felt my head start to pound. I got up and found the aspirin bottle. I popped three aspirin and washed them down with cold coffee and an even colder sense of guilt.

I was still sitting at the table like that when Bobby came bustling in the back door.

"Hey there, Dempsey," he said cheerily. He picked up one of the cupboard doors and ran a calloused hand over the wooden surface. "Well now, this looks nice. Looks real nice. You're turning into a fine woodworker. Couldn't have done a better job myself."

"Sure you could have," I said dully. "A trained monkey could have done all this."

"Ohhh," he said. "You having a bad morning?"

"I'm having a bad year," I said. "Don't mind me, Bobby."

He clucked his tongue. "I got something out in the truck that's gonna change your whole outlook on life. Hang on a minute, and I'll show you. I got a helper with me today, just for this very thing."

Bobby picked up a scrap of wood and wedged the kitchen door open with it. He went out like he had come in, whistling.

A moment later, he was back, trying to wedge a huge chunk of furniture through the back door. "Hold it steady now," he called to the unseen helper. "Turn it to the left a little, and I'm gonna back in here. That's good. Keep turning."

In a minute, the helper appeared in the doorway, a younger version of

Bobby, with a ballcap turned backward, and a smooth, serious dark face. He wore baggy blue jeans that sagged at the waist, showing three inches of boxer shorts, and sparkling white Air Jordans.

"Easy, son," Bobby said quietly. "Let's put it down right over there, in the center of the room. See where I got the pot rack hanging from the ceiling? Right under there."

"Can I help?" I asked, moving out of the way.

"We're good," the younger man grunted.

"There now," Bobby said as he pushed the piece an inch this way, and then the other way. He stepped back and crossed his arms over his chest. "What you think of that, Miss Dempsey?"

The morning's gloom lifted away as I looked at the piece Bobby had built for me. It was the island he'd promised, of clear, golden heart pine boards. Somehow, he'd seen the picture of my dream kitchen, even though I'd never shared it with him. The island had a butcher block top at least two inches thick. There were deep drawers under the top, on the sides of it, and a shelf that ran along the bottom. The legs were shapely and turned to look like a piece of fine antique cabinetry.

"Oh, Bobby," I cried. "I can't believe you built this. It looks like something out of a museum. It's perfect. Better than I ever dreamed."

"Oh yeah," he said quietly, pulling out a breadboard from one end of the island, and then showing me the knife slots he'd added at the other end. "It worked out kinda good, I think." He pulled out a drawer to show me the dovetailing.

"It's magnificent," I said, throwing my arms around his shoulders.

"It ain't no problem," he said, ducking his head shyly.

I realized I was embarrassing him and let go. "Sorry," I said. "I got carried away."

"This here's my youngest, Trey," Bobby said, gesturing toward his helper. "Trey, this is Miss Dempsey. She's fixing up this big old house all by herself. Ain't that something?"

"Not by myself," I corrected him, reaching out to shake the hand Trey extended. "Not by a long shot. Your dad does all the heavy lifting. He's a true master craftsman. I just try to stay out of his way and learn a little bit."

Trey nodded and looked around the kitchen with interest. "Hey, this is kinda cool," he said. "Old school, right?"

"Old school, definitely," I said.

Bobby ran a hand over the island again. "All right then. Me and Trey are gonna get up on your roof this morning, and see if we can't get started fixing it up. I see you're coming good on those cupboard doors."

I made a face. "Not that good. I got up early and started sanding 'em down, and woke up Ella Kate and half the neighborhood. You might want to stay out of her way today. She's on the warpath for sure."

"Aw," Bobby said. "She don't mean nothin' by it."

"She hates me," I said. "Pure and simple. I know I made her mad this morning, but I still can't figure out why she's hated me since the minute she laid eyes on me. She keeps saying I'm Killebrew—like that's some kind of poison."

Bobby glanced over at Trey, and then away. "Son, you want to start getting the ladder and tools off the truck?"

Trey nodded agreeably and went out the kitchen door.

"He looks just like you, Bobby," I said. "I hope he's as good a man as his father."

"I think he favors his mama a little bit," Bobby said. "Lucky for him."

"How about a cup of coffee before you get up on that roof?" I asked. "I made a big pot first thing this morning, and it's got me so jittery I might jump out of my skin."

"Coffee'd be good," he allowed. I poured him a mug and he took a sip.

"Man," he said, looking up in surprise. "That's some good stuff."

"French roast beans. I grind them fresh myself," I said. "I'll get you a bag next time I go to Macon."

"I'd be glad to pay you for 'em," Bobby said.

I waved away his offer.

He put his cup down and shifted uncomfortably from one foot to the other. "About Ella Kate," he said, his voice lowered.

I leaned in closer.

He clucked his tongue. "I ain't got no business tellin' you about this, but I mentioned to the wife the other day how Ella Kate's giving you such a rough time, and she says you got a right to know some things."

"What kind of things?"

He hesitated. "My wife's auntie worked for the Dempseys way back in the day. Right here at Birdsong. She's an old, old lady now. Oldest member at her church, she'll be a hundred in July, if the Lord keeps her well."

He squirmed again, and grimaced.

"Bobby," I urged. "It's not gossip if it's true, if that's what's worrying you. And I swear, I won't tell a soul what you tell me here today."

The kitchen door popped open, and Trey stuck his head inside. "Excuse me? Dad? I got the ladder set up, and the ropes and tools rigged the way you asked me to."

Bobby set his cup down and stood up. "That's good, son. I'm coming right now."

I grabbed hold of Bobby's shirt. "Wait! Bobby—"

He just shook his head. "Not in front of the boy. It ain't right."

39

F uelled by caffeine and angst, I finished sanding all the cabinet doors and drawer fronts by noon. Bobby and Trey were in and out of the kitchen half a dozen times that morning, but I could never corner Bobby alone to make him spit out whatever it was that he really didn't want to tell me about the bad blood between Ella Kate and the Killebrews.

The unseasonable warm spell we'd been having was over, and temperatures had dipped back down into the fifties, so Bobby and Trey seemed glad to take their lunch break in the kitchen, after I went outside and insisted they come in.

When he'd finished with the ham sandwich and slice of pecan pie "the wife" had packed for his lunch, Bobby admired my cabinet-sanding prowess again, and proclaimed the doors ready for the next step.

"Got to clean up every bit of sawdust out of this room," he cautioned, bringing in his Shop-Vac. "You got to get up under the cabinets, in the corners, every inch of this room got to be clean as a whistle. Can't be a speck of dust or grit in here, once you get started putting a stain and finish on them doors, or it'll ruin all your pretty work."

"It'll be as clean as an operating room," I pledged. "What comes after that?"

He gave me a gummy-feeling piece of fabric he called a tack cloth, and instructed me to wipe down all the newly sanded wood. He gave me a can of Minwax stain, and showed me how to brush it on the doors and drawers, all of which he'd had me line up neatly on the old yellow linoleum countertops.

"What about these countertops?" I asked. "I looked at some granite the other day, but I just don't think it's in my budget, much as I hate to give it up."

Bobby nodded sympathetically. "Yeah, granite ain't cheap. But I got me another idea that might work, if you don't mind."

"Anything."

He opened the door to the basement and disappeared down the stairs. When he came back up, he was carrying a heavy, water-stained cardboard box. He set it on the table with a thud, and lifted out a plain four-inch white tile. "What do you think about that?"

I took the tile and turned it this way and that. "Not very inspiring," I said.

He scratched his head for a moment, and took four more tiles out of the box. He laid them out on the tabletop, so that the squares became interlocking diamonds. "What you think about that?" he asked. "Maybe with some gray grout? Thing is, Dempsey, Mr. Norbert and them, they never threw nothin' away around this place. I think this here tile is left over from when they put in that bathroom upstairs, for Mr. Norbert. And there's two more boxes of it down in that basement. More than enough to do your kitchen countertops. All for free. All we got to do is buy us a bag of grout."

I smiled. "You said the magic word, Bobby. Free."

"All right then," he said. "Let me get back up on that roof."

I spent the rest of the day sucking all the sawdust and grit out of the kitchen, and then wiping down and staining the cabinets and drawers. At one point late in the afternoon, I heard Ella Kate come clomping down the hallway. I ran out and caught her by the front door.

"Ella Kate? I know you're mad at me, and I'm sorry about that. You're right. I was insensitive and selfish. Have you heard anything about Shorty? Is he ready to come home from the hospital yet?"

"Goin' to get him right this minute," she said, brushing aside the hand I'd laid on her arm.

"I'd be happy to drive you down there," I told her. "Just let me get cleaned up a little bit, and we'll go."

"No need," she said. "I got me a ride." She turned and went out the door.

So much for détente, I thought.

I was about to head back to the kitchen when I saw a car, a black Lexus, pull into the driveway. At first I assumed it was Ella Kate's ride, but then I saw a woman—a tall brunette dressed in a dark brown pants suit—climb out of the car. As she drew closer on the front walk, I realized my visitor was Shirlene Peppers. I also realized that her pants suit was Armani, her shoes were Manolo, and the calfskin hobo bag slung over her shoulder was Gucci. I could have resurfaced my whole kitchen in imported Italian marble, not to mention replumbed all of Birdsong, with just the money Shirlene had spent on what she was wearing that day.

I looked down at my own attire—my faded Redskins football jersey, and Uncle Norbert's overalls. I had a blue bandanna tied over my hair, and sawdust leaking from every corner of my body. I sighed and opened the front door.

Shirlene Peppers was looking around the front porch with obvious curiosity. Or maybe it was just distaste.

"Hi there," I told her.

"Well, hello," she said, eyeing me up and down.

"Excuse the mess," I said. "It's a work in progress. And by that, I mean me and the house."

"Love the new color," she said, gesturing toward the front porch.

"That's all Jimmy's doing," I said with a laugh. "He picked out the color, and then before I knew it, he was painting it too."

"That's Jimmy," she said. "Which is why I stopped by. Do you have a minute?"

"Sure," I said, opening the door wide. "Let's go into the parlor. There's not much furniture in there, but it'll keep us away from the chemical fumes in the kitchen. I've been staining my cabinets." I pointed to a splotch on the sleeve of my jersey. "Here's the color."

"Nice," she murmured.

I dragged two dining room chairs into the parlor. Shirlene took one and I sat in the other. I tried to sit up and not feel as intimidated and inadequate as I actually did. Close up and in person, Shirlene was the real deal. Her skin was deeply tanned and flawless, her makeup was minimal, but expertly applied. Her dark hair was gleaming, and today, worn in a simple twist held with a tortoiseshell comb. Her long fingers wore pale pink polish, and on her left ring finger, she wore a humongous diamond solitaire. Everything about her was high gloss and high class.

She took a deep breath. "About last night. I want to apologize."

"No need," I told her. "Jimmy's harmless, I know. And I should have realized he was drinking too much. But it all happened so fast. One minute he was sober and charming, and the next minute—"

"He was a big ol' drunk," Shirlene put in. "But, honey, that's his fault, not yours. Anyway, that's not what I want to apologize for. Look. I jumped to a conclusion as soon as I saw you last night, and I feel awful about that."

"Why?" I asked.

She crossed her legs and jiggled her right foot so hard that the stiletto heel she was wearing nearly flew off.

"Why? Because you're young and cute and Jimmy was eyeing you like a cat eyes a big ol' bowl of cream. So I just assumed you were sleeping with him. But I still can't believe that's the first thing that came out of my mouth after we were introduced." She smiled sadly and twisted the ring around until the stone faced her palm.

"And I can't even blame it on the liquor talking, because I hadn't even had a drink at that point. I raised a big ol' stink, for sure. When I got home last night, I had three messages on my answering machine from girlfriends wanting to know if it was true I'd gotten into a catfight at the club with Jimmy's new girlfriend."

I laughed. "One thing I've learned about Guthrie—news travels fast in a town this small."

"Honey, you don't even know the half of it," she said. She uncrossed and then recrossed her legs. "I called Tee this morning, to apologize to him too."

I tried to look uninterested.

She raised an eyebrow. "I hope he told you that we are *not* an item.

Lorrrrd, he is young enough to be my son. Not that I wouldn't grab hold of Tee Berryhill in a New York second if I thought he was interested in an old cougar like me."

I hooted. "Shirlene, you are totally too young to be a cougar. And as long as we're having true confessions here, when I saw you and Tee walk into the club together last night, I jumped to conclusions too. So I think we're even. No apologies necessary."

"You mind my asking what Tee told you about me?"

"He explained that you were a classmate from law school, and that he was taking you to dinner to try to pump you for details about something to do with the county commission."

She sighed. "I knew Tee had an agenda, when he asked me out, but it hurts just the teensiest bit to hear it in black and white like that. I was trying to delude myself into thinking he was fascinated with me because of the Botox and all the Pilates I've been doing."

"Botox?" I leaned in to get a closer look. "Really? Wow. I never would have guessed. You really do look amazing."

"Thanks," she said airily. "That's one of the few perks from having an ex-husband who's a doctor. Wayne's buddies at the hospital still extend me professional courtesy. I get the Botox free, and I assume Wayne's still getting Viagra for free, because the last girlfriend of his I laid eyes on looked like she'd just lettered in cheerleading over at the vo-tech."

We shared a laugh over that remark. And then Shirlene twisted her ring again, and recrossed her legs. "Did Tee tell you anything else about me?"

"He mentioned that you and Jimmy were married, before you married Wayne," I said, half apologetically.

"You didn't know that already? Jimmy didn't tell you?"

"Actually, Jimmy did tell me that he'd been married and divorced three times, and that he had an ex-wife named Shirlene. But I didn't really connect the dots, not even when you came up to the table last night. As soon as Jimmy spotted you with Tee, he started slamming back the bourbon, even heavier. I think it upset him, seeing you with Tee."

She cocked her head. "You think?"

"I'm new in town," I said. "So I'm not really up on all the local intrigue, but yeah, I just figured there was some sort of history there."

"History? Yeah, I guess you could say Jimmy and I have a history. Don't know if you'd call it Romeo and Juliet or Antony and Cleopatra. But there's definitely drama, and definitely comedy. Cheap laughs and cheap thrills."

I really didn't know what to say next. The silence got a little awkward.

"Well," Shirlene said finally, standing up and smoothing out a non-existent wrinkle in her suit jacket. "I was dreading coming over here and facing you today, but this has actually been kinda fun, in a sick way, once we got the messy part over with."

"Thank you for coming by," I said. "It was really sweet of you to set me straight on some stuff."

I walked her out to the door and onto the porch. She was halfway down the front walk, but then she turned around and walked rapidly back.

"Say, Dempsey," she said. "It seems like I spend most of my time these days hanging out with lawyers and politicians. And all my old girlfriends are busy with their jobs, or their kids and husbands. It was great hearing a little girl talk for once. I was wondering—maybe you'd want to do lunch, or maybe dinner, sometime soon? If you don't mind doing chick stuff with an old cougar?"

"I'd love it," I told her. "Seriously."

"One more thing," she said. "From one girlfriend to another. Tee Berryhill is a great guy. One in a million. And he's totally stuck on you. So, girlfriend? Take it from somebody who's been around the block and made all the mistakes there are to make, relationship wise. Don't screw this up. This is for real."

40

I t was just getting dark when I heard the clatter of ladders and tools being loaded outside the kitchen.

The back door opened and Bobby stuck his head inside. "Okay, Dempsey, me and Trey are quittin' for the day."

"Come on in, Bobby, and let me fix you a cup of coffee to warm you up," I urged. The temperature had been dropping all afternoon, and the wind had started to kick up too. I'd actually been a little nervous about the thought of the two of them up on that steep roof.

"No, ma'am," Bobby said. "I got tar all over my boots. I'm not tracking that all over these floors you worked so hard on. Listen, the radio says we're fixing to have some ugly weather—they're even talking we might get some ice and hail. We got the underlayment down, and then me and Trey tacked down some tarps, just in case we do get ice. But, now, if it does storm, we'll lay off the roof tomorrow, and that'll be a good time for me to go ahead and tile these countertops if you want."

I walked outside to take a look at the sky. Just as he'd said, charcoal-colored clouds were stacked low on the horizon, and the wind was whipping dried leaves and branches. A light rain had started to fall. "Wow, this looks like the kind of snow clouds we got in D.C.," I said, hugging my arms to ward off the chill. "Could we get snow this late, and this far south?"

"Might could," Bobby said. "This time of year, ain't no tellin' what the weather could do."

"Thanks for letting me know about the storm warnings," I told him. "I never turn on a television or radio here, so I would have been totally in the dark. And don't worry about coming tomorrow if the weather gets too bad."

"Ain't no weather too bad to keep me from working," Bobby assured me. "I'll see you tomorrow then." He got in the truck with Trey and was ready to drive off.

"Hey, Bobby," I called, running up to the truck. He rolled down the window. "You think you could teach me how to lay tile? Now that I'm done with the cabinets, I'm kind of enjoying working with my hands."

"Oh yeah," Bobby said enthusiastically. "I'll bring an extra trowel when I come tomorrow. You can learn tiling easy as pie. That ain't no problem at all."

The skies opened up just as I made it back inside the house. The rain slashed down, and the wind rattled the windows so hard, I wondered if it was actually a tornado we were about to experience.

It occurred to me that I should probably keep an eye on the weather. But the only television in the house was the one in Ella Kate's room. I'd noticed an old plastic-cased clock radio downstairs in the basement laundry area though.

Since I'd moved to Birdsong, I'd avoided the basement as much as possible. It was dark and smelled like mildew and spiders, so my trips down there were limited to putting laundry in the washer and taking it out of the dryer.

I sprinted down the stairs to the laundry room. The clock radio was sitting on the shelf where we kept the bleach and detergent. It wasn't plugged in, and the cord was frayed, so I had no idea if it worked or not, but with the wind howling outside, I decided now would be a good time to find out.

Back in the kitchen, I set the radio on the kitchen table and plugged it in. The clock dial lit up immediately, lifting my spirits, and when I turned the tuning dial, I was rewarded with the soothing sounds of an announcer from WSB. I'd lived in Atlanta as a teenager in the mid-nineties, and I didn't remember all that much about those times, but I did remember that my father listened to the news on WSB when we were in the car, which was always a source of contention because I always listened to 96 Rock, which he referred to as "96 Crap."

As I listened to the radio, I set about fixing myself dinner, popping a frozen Stouffer's lasagna into the oven. I opened the bag of precut greens and made myself a tossed salad with the lettuce and sliced cucumber. I poured myself a glass of the Dimmlylit Cellars wine, and sat down at the table to eat my salad and wait for the lasagna.

The traffic report in Atlanta was the same as it was every time I heard it on the radio in the Catfish. Interstate 285 was backed up in all directions, traffic was bumper to bumper for a ten-mile stretch of Georgia 400, starting at Holcomb Bridge Road, and the downtown connector was impassible. I supposed traffic was the same in D.C. Maybe they were getting late-season snow too.

For the first time since coming to Guthrie, I felt really isolated. I'd been so busy working on the house, and dealing with my legal problems, that I hadn't had time to make friends. I hoped Shirlene Peppers was sincere in her offer for some chick time, because I was ready.

The weather report came on as I was lifting the lasagna out of the oven, and the news wasn't good. A rapidly moving cold front, ice and high winds moving east from Birmingham. The National Weather Service had posted storm warnings for Bibb, Butts, Clayton, Henry, and Jackson counties, effective until nine P.M.

I looked at the kitchen clock. It was 6:30. I wondered where Ella Kate was. She'd left in midafternoon. She would have had plenty of time to get to Macon and back with Shorty by now. Was she caught in the storm? I had no idea who'd given her a ride to Macon. Would they have stopped on the road if the weather was ugly?

Stop it, I told myself. Ella Kate would not have spent a minute worrying about me if our roles were reversed. The only reason she ever checked up on me was to reconfirm her opinion about my decidedly loose morals.

Morals. I plopped a slab of lasagna on a plate, and sprinkled it with canned parmesan cheese. All day long, I'd deliberately kept myself too busy to think about Tee Berryhill. Now, a long evening stretched ahead of me, and thinking about my short-lived romance seemed inescapable.

Me and Tee. Tee and I. What was the matter with me? I'd had what I now knew was a schoolgirl crush on Alex Hodder—a married, totally inappropriate, and totally dishonest scoundrel—for nearly two years, and all it had gotten me was woe and sorrow.

Suddenly, a wonderful, adorable, intelligent, sexy, available man had inexplicably decided he was falling for me. Why had I deliberately pushed him away the second we'd become intimate?

It wasn't as if this was my usual pattern. I'd had boyfriends since my teen years. Those romances had died natural deaths. I wasn't commitment phobic. I didn't fear intimacy. So—what the hell was wrong with me? How had I managed to mess things up with Tee so fast?

My cell phone was sitting on the kitchen counter. I had Tee's number. What was to keep me from calling him and apologizing for being such an idiot? I picked up the phone and studied it. There were no missed calls. What was to keep Tee from calling me? From trying to persuade me that we really could have something together?

I checked the phone again. I had four bars. Full reception. Nothing was keeping us apart. Technically speaking. Nothing except that lump in the pit of my stomach. I took a bite of lasagna. It sat there, on top of that lump, and gave me instantaneous heartburn. Or maybe it was just the heartache talking. I dumped the plate in the trash and poured myself another glass of wine.

Inactivity, I decided, was not a good thing for me. I rambled around the house looking for something to do. I'd read all the magazines I'd brought with me from D.C., and the moldering old books I'd found scattered around the house—crumbling hymnals, *Reader's Digest* condensed books, and Ella Kate's stack of lusty-busty romances—had no appeal.

I walked around the kitchen and admired my handiwork. When I got to the cabinet doors, I came up with a plan of action. Bobby had diligently removed all the old paint-clogged hinges and hardware from the cabinets and drawers before I'd refinished them. They were in an empty margarine tub downstairs on Norbert's workbench, where Bobby had promised to clean them up with paint thinner—"good as new."

Why shouldn't I clean them up myself tonight? I went back downstairs and fetched the hardware, the can of paint thinner, a wad of steel wool, and an empty one-gallon Folger's coffee can.

Upstairs, I donned a pair of heavy-duty rubber gloves and poured about an inch of thinner into the coffee can, nearly swooning from the strong fumes. I dumped in half a dozen sets of hinges, just to see what would happen. The thinner started to cloud up with old paint, which I took as a good sign.

I sat down to wait, and it occurred to me that the rain had stopped. I opened the kitchen door and stuck my head outside, and a needlelike sliver of ice impaled itself in my scalp. In fact, it was now raining ice. I went out to the front porch to check conditions there, and found that the front walkway was already slicked with a thin layer of deadly looking black ice, and tiny stalactites—or were they stalagmites? I could never keep them straight—were dripping from the tree limbs.

Where the hell was Ella Kate? I considered calling the Berryhills, ostensibly to consult Carter about Ella Kate's possible whereabouts, but down deep I knew I really just wanted to hear Tee's voice. And I was not ready to give in to that temptation. Yet.

I paced around the house. WSB was already announcing school closings for tomorrow and widespread power outages in metro Atlanta. But we were a good sixty miles south of Atlanta—and the storm—weren't we? The announcer suggested that listeners trace the storm's progress on WSB.com, or tune into WSB-TV. Which would have been helpful if I'd had Internet access, or a television.

My thoughts turned again to Ella Kate. Or rather, Ella Kate's television set. She had the only one in the house. I was genuinely worried about her welfare. What would be the harm in going into her room, just to turn on the television to see what the StormTracker radar systems were showing?

As I ran upstairs, I promised myself that I would enter her room, check the storm's progress, and leave immediately. She would never have to know. Anyway, I rationalized, this was Mitch's house—and mine, by default. I had every right to be in any room of the house that I pleased. What if the storm caused the wiring in the television to short out, or go haywire, and start a fire? My going into Ella Kate's room was strictly a matter of household safety. The life I saved could be my own. And if the theoretical fire spread—to the neighbors, or the rest of the block—wouldn't I actually be performing a heroic deed?

That's what I told myself. But when I tried to turn the doorknob and it wouldn't budge, I just plain got pissed off. Who was this angry old lady anyway? She was a squatter here, a freeloader. What right did she have to lock doors and declare parts of my house strictly off-limits?

I knelt down on the floor and tried to look through the keyhole, but the room inside was dark. Damn you, Ella Kate, I muttered to myself.

I went to my own room and got a slim penknife that I'd found in the top dresser drawer. I tried jamming it into the lock, but the blade was slightly too wide.

Back downstairs to the dreaded basement. From Norbert's workbench I gathered up three sizes of screwdrivers, a rusty ice pick, and a long implement with a mother-of-pearl handle and a hooked end that I guessed might have been a buttonhook. I went into the laundry room to see if there were any other potential lock-picking tools lying around. And then I spotted it, hanging from a rusty nail beside a worn-out rag mop. A huge metal key ring, bristling with old-fashioned skeleton keys.

I dropped the tools and took both flights of stairs two at a time. In the detective novels I'd devoured as a teenager, the last key on the ring would have opened the door. Or broken off and jammed the lock. But tonight, the first key I chose, totally at random, worked like a charm.

The doorknob turned easily. I swallowed hard and pushed the door open. The room was pitch black and musty smelling. I felt around on the wall for the light switch, and immediately knocked something to the floor. I heard the crash of shattering glass just as I flipped the switch.

A torrent of sensations washed over me—dread, guilt, apprehension. No matter what I told myself, this was breaking and entering. It was intrusion. It was irresistible. I shivered in anticipation.

In my mind's eye, I'd imagined many times what Ella Kate's inner sanctum looked like. One version had it decorated like a wild west bordello, with red-velvet-flocked wallpaper, chandeliers dripping with cut crystal, and a gilt-edged canopy bed with a mirrored ceiling. On the opposite end of the spectrum, I'd imagined her in a nun's cloister, with plain white walls; a hard, narrow cot; and only a wooden kneeler and a Bible rack illuminated by a single guttering candle.

None of those scenarios matched what actually met my eyes when the light came on. The room was crowded, wall to wall, floor to ceiling, with furniture and knickknacks, so that it looked like an antiques warehouse. Pushed up against the wall with the light switch was a walnut highboy dresser. Its top was littered with cat figurines—glass ones, porcelain ones, clay ones. Dozens of cat doodads. I looked down. Lying on the floor in about a hundred pieces were the remains of one of those kitschy kitties, the one that I'd knocked over.

"Shit." I'd have to get a broom and dustpan to hide the evidence of my crime. Later.

I wedged myself into the room through a narrow opening that Ella Kate had fashioned as a path. It was a tight squeeze. Ella Kate weighed maybe ninety pounds. I did not. Next to the walnut highboy was a matching dressing table, its top covered in old perfume bottles; talcum powder cans; and a highly polished sterling silver mirror, comb, and brush set. Stacked on top of each other, next to the dressing table, were the rest of the missing chairs from the dining room.

I guessed that the only reason the table was still sitting in the dining room was because my ninety-pound freeloader hadn't been physically able to haul it up the stairs and shove it into this room.

Here were more of the missing furnishings: an ugly maroon plush-covered sofa; a mahogany piecrust occasional table, stacked upside down atop a walnut drop-front secretary; and a pair of dusty armchairs. There were more dressers—plain oak ones, a tall cherry bachelor's chest, even a fancifully painted pine dresser. I saw at least three more bed frames, including a pair of carved pineapple four-poster beds and a high-backed carved Victorian full-size bed. Mattresses were upended against the walls, wedged in by tables and bookcases. Paintings and glass-fronted prints were stacked on every flat surface.

I picked up one of the largest framed prints, and rubbed at a thick patina of dust on its glass surface. The subject was a hand-tinted exotic bird, maybe a toucan or a mynah. I squinted at the tiny writing on the bottom of the print—was this an Audubon folio? There were five more framed prints the same size, all of different birds, in the stack.

I had to suck in my stomach to thread my way deeper into the room. The sheer volume of stuff was overwhelming. Chairs and lamps and even packing crates filled with shredded newspapers—and china and crystal—were everywhere. I could only guess that the few family items that remained downstairs were only there because they wouldn't fit up here.

Finally, I worked my way into a tiny bare space in the room. I had been right about one thing. Ella Kate apparently slept in a narrow single bed with a plain, rounded-off metal headboard that reminded me of a hospital bed. It was made up with white cotton sheets and an old green army blanket. Neatly folded at the foot of the bed was a pastel patchwork blue-and-white quilt.

It looked so unlike anything Ella Kate would own that I had to take a closer look. I unfolded the quilt. The fabrics—pale blue ginghams, purple calicoes, and green stripes—were worn to a tissuelike softness. The pattern was an appliqué design of straw-hatted boys in overalls. The quilt was too small to fit even a twin bed. Was it a crib quilt?

On the bedside table was a framed black-and-white photograph. It was a studio portrait of a young woman. She was in profile, chin up, eyes sparkling, lips slightly parted, as though anticipating something wonderful. Her sweater and pearls, not to mention the smooth combed bangs and ponytail, told me the photograph had been taken sometime in the 1950s, when the sitter would have been in her late teens. I recognized the subject immediately, Olivia Dempsey Killebrew. My grandmother.

There was a Victorian walnut-mirrored chifforobe on the wall beside the bed. I opened the door. Packed inside were decades' worth of clothing—a time-traveled wardrobe of poodle skirts, cotton shirtwaist dresses, tulle-skirted prom dresses with sequin-dusted bodices, cotton blouses with prim Peter Pan collars, and stretchy side-zipped Capri pants. I let my fingertips trail across the hem of a black velvet cocktail dress with a red satin flounce at the hem.

None of these clothes could have belonged to Ella Kate, even before age and osteoporosis had started to shrink her to her present size. Ella

Kate was a wren who dressed in shades of dun. These brightly colored garments had belonged to a more exotic creature. Like my grandmother.

I sat down on the bed to try and take it all in. Ella Kate had been hoarding Birdsong's furnishings and she'd created a kind of shrine to Olivia.

Sitting on a chest only a couple of feet from the bed was a pine blanket chest that held Ella Kate's television—a fourteen-inch Zenith with a set of makeshift coat-hanger and aluminum-foil rabbit ears duct-taped to its top.

I sank down on the bed, and remembering my original quest, turned on the TV. It was already turned to WSB. The weatherman stood in front of a map of Georgia, droning on about power outages—twenty thousand customers in DeKalb, seventy thousand in Fulton. Trees and power lines down. The Georgia State Patrol had closed off Interstate 75 south of the airport, all the way to Macon, because of icy overpasses and numerous wrecks. The state department of transportation had dispatched dozens of sand trucks, but a spokesman was urging people to stay off the roads.

The next shot was of a miserable-looking blond reporter, huddled into a hooded coat, standing on an overpass at I-75 and the Lakewood Freeway. An unseen hand held an umbrella over her as she described an eight-car pileup on the roadway below.

"Shit." The storm was worse than I'd thought. And if I-75—one of the heaviest-traveled roadways in the state—was closed all the way to Macon, then the secondary roads would be in even worse shape.

Where was Ella Kate? I could only hope that whoever had given her a ride to the animal hospital had had the good sense to pull off the road and wait out the storm.

I made my way to Ella Kate's window—that same window from which she'd peeked out at me the night before—to check on conditions on the street outside Birdsong. The streetlight at the curb shone down on the icy, abandoned street. The trees in the front were bent double from the weight of the ice. Nobody was foolhardy enough to be out in this weather.

Maybe, I thought, if trees and power lines were coming down, I should think about moving the Catfish into the garage. I dreaded going out in the ice, but I dreaded even more being stuck at Birdsong without transportation.

That's when it struck me. The driveway was empty. The Catfish was gone. And so was Ella Kate.

41

I pressed my forehead against the cold window glass and shut my eyes. Ella Kate had gotten herself a ride, all right. She'd been so furious after our fight that she'd decided to drive to Macon by herself—a final show of defiance.

There was no time to sweep up the broken cat figurine or to try to hide the fact that I'd trespassed on the elderly woman's privacy. I didn't bother to shut off the television or the light, or even close the door.

I ran downstairs and got my cell phone.

He answered on the first ring.

"Dempsey? Are you all right? Is your power out? We just had a huge oak tree come down in the backyard here. It hit the shed, and most of my mom's roses are flattened."

"I'm fine," I said breathlessly. "It's Ella Kate. We had a fight this morning, and I was supposed to take her to Macon to get Shorty, but she was still so mad at me, she told me she'd get her own ride, and I just thought, well, she got a friend to take her—"

"Hang on," Tee said. "Slow down. Where is Ella Kate?"

"That's just it," I babbled. "I only just now realized it. Tee, she took the Catfish! She left this afternoon, before it started storming. She wasn't even wearing a sweater, and it's freezing out, and she's so shriveled up, I bet she can't even see over the steering wheel. She hasn't come back, and I just saw on WSB that there are trees down everywhere, and all kinds of wrecks, and the highway patrol has closed off I-75. And she's out there! I don't even know where to begin to look, and I don't have a car—"

I was sobbing, but I didn't care.

"We'll take Dad's Mercedes," Tee said. "Dress warm. I'll be there in five minutes. And don't worry. Ella Kate's old and skinny—but she's too damned mean to die in an ice storm. Not yet anyway."

After I hung up, I ran upstairs and put on a pair of Norbert's long johns, and over that my heaviest pair of wool pants. I put on a pair of cotton socks, and over that a pair of hunting socks, and over that my only low-heeled boots.

Getting dressed calmed me down some. I called the animal hospital where we'd taken Shorty, but all I got was a recorded message telling me that it was after hours, and in case of an emergency I should dial the on-call vet.

I repeated the number to myself while I stabbed it into my cell phone.

"Hello? Is this the vet from Mid-Georgia Animal Hospital?"

"Actually, this is Verna, Dr. Shoemaker's assistant," the woman said. "Do you have an emergency?"

"I do. My, er, cousin brought her cocker spaniel, Shorty, into the hospital yesterday. He ate my panties. Ella Kate was supposed to pick him up this afternoon, and she left, but she hasn't come back, and I'm terrified she's caught in the storm—"

"Your pet's name is Shorty?"

"My cousin's pet," I corrected her. "Did she pick up Shorty today? Her name is Ella Kate Timmons. She's kind of elderly and she's not supposed to be driving—"

"Ma'am?" The woman's voice was slow and annoyingly syrupy. "Could you slow down? You're breaking up and I'm not sure what it is you want me to tell you."

"Ella. Kate. Timmons." I enunciated each word slowly and loudly. "She's eighty. Did she pick up her dog today? The dog is named Shorty."

"Ma'am? I'm not at the hospital, so I'm not sure which pets got picked up. I can tell you that we closed early, because of the storm."

"You closed?" I was on the verge of tears again. "How can an animal hospital close? I thought you were like an emergency room. Emergency rooms don't close."

"Ma'am? Dr. Shoemaker had to go out on a call to a barn fire in Jackson. We've got six burned horses we're treating, and the vet techs are both with her. We called as many clients as we could to tell them about the closing, but with the storm and all, we're doing the best we can. All the pets at the hospital are fine, and we should be open in the morning, if the roads are all right and Dr. Shoemaker can get back."

A horn honked outside. "Never mind!" I shouted, and I disconnected.

I grabbed my ski parka from the hall closet, and at the last minute stuffed a heavy, metal, army-surplus-looking flashlight in the pocket. I ran out the front door and was only two feet from the edge of the porch when I slipped on a patch of ice and fell flat on my butt.

The floor was so slick I couldn't gain any footing to stand back up. Instead I butt-walked forward until I was able to pull myself up on the wooden stair-rail. The front walkway looked just as dangerous, so I cut through the lawn, planting each boot firmly in the ice-crusted grass.

It was a relief to haul my frozen wet ass onto the red leather upholstery of Carter Berryhill's Mercedes.

"You okay?" Tee asked sympathetically. "That was a nasty fall you took."

I grimaced and tucked a strand of hair behind my ear. "Mostly just my ego is bruised."

He caught my hand. "You're cut," he said evenly.

The palm of my right hand had a nasty red gash that was seeping blood. "I'm okay," I repeated. "I can't even feel it, I'm so cold."

Tee reached across me and opened the glove box. "Dig around in there," he instructed. "Dad usually has Band-Aids or at least a fast-food napkin."

I found a yellow paper napkin and blotted my hand with it.

"Where to?" Tee asked.

"Toward Macon," I said. "I called the animal hospital where Shorty's being treated, but they closed early today because of the storm, so they couldn't even tell me if Ella Kate made it in to get him."

I directed Tee to follow the route Ella Kate and I had taken two days earlier. He drove as fast as he could, dodging downed trees, and in a couple of places, power lines. The Mercedes's radio was tuned to an all-news station, reporting the path of destruction the ice storm had taken.

"I-75 is closed down all the way to the Florida border," Tee told me.

"I can't ever remember an ice storm as bad as this one—and as late as it is."

"She's out here somewhere," I muttered, swinging my head from one side of the road to the other. "She's gotta be."

"Maybe not," Tee offered. "Maybe she picked up Shorty and decided to go off on a junket or something. You said the weather was still all right when she left the house."

"But she would have had plenty of time to get there and back, unless something happened," I said. "And anyway, she wouldn't just go off and take Shorty on some kind of pleasure trip. He had surgery yesterday. She's been worried sick about him."

He glanced over at me. "Why did Shorty need surgery?"

I looked out the window, not daring to meet his eyes. "He . . . ate a pair of my panties."

I heard the strangled sound of laughter.

"Not funny," I said dully. "He could have died. He almost did. Because of me."

"Sorry," Tee said sheepishly. We'd come to a fork in the road. "To the left?"

"Yes," I told him. "To the left, and then a quick right."

"How far is the hospital?" he asked.

"Maybe . . . forty miles from Guthrie?"

The trip that had taken forty-five minutes one day ago now took an hour and a half. Three times we had to stop, get out of the car, and drag tree limbs from the roadway. Finally, we got to the veterinary clinic. The parking lot was empty, the neon sign turned off.

"Now what?" Tee said, turning in the seat to face me.

"I don't know," I said, biting back another onslaught of tears. It was nearly ten o'clock. Ella Kate had been gone for more than six hours. She could be anywhere—or nowhere.

"Hang in there, kid," Tee said, giving me a crooked smile.

I fished my cell phone out of my jacket pocket. "I'm going to start calling hospitals," I told him.

"Check the jails too," Tee advised. "If somebody got between that old lady and her dog, no telling what she might have done. Let's just backtrack. Maybe we overlooked something. A motel or something, where she might have pulled in to wait out the storm."

I called all the Macon-area hospitals Tee suggested, but none of them had any record of admitting a mean old lady named Ella Kate Timmons—or her equally testy cocker spaniel. And I called three different sheriff's departments to see if any of them had worked a wreck involving a bulldog-red Crown Victoria driven by a feisty old lady. Nobody had seen Ella Kate Timmons.

The icy rain had finally subsided, but the roads were so treacherous that we literally inched along at slightly over five miles an hour. Fortunately, most of the citizenry of middle Georgia had decided to take the weatherman's advice and stay off the roads.

When we got to the fork in the road where we'd turned from Guthrie, I had an idea. "Turn the other way," I told Tee.

"But that's the wrong way," he protested. "That'll take you to Pecan Springs."

"Ella Kate hasn't driven in nearly a year. It was rainy and windy, and she'd only been to the vet clinic once before, and that was with me driving," I said. "She was probably scared and confused. Maybe she just took a wrong turn."

He nodded agreement. "No harm in checking it out."

We'd gone only a couple of miles when I spotted a darkened roadside restaurant, surrounded by a large asphalt parking lot. The place had once been called the Cozy Cabin, but a large FOR SALE sign was tacked to the parking-lot billboard.

"Turn in!" I told Tee, pointing to the far edge of the lot. There, half hidden under the splayed-out branches of a fallen pine tree, was the Catfish.

I was out of the car before Tee could turn off the ignition. The Mercedes's headlights illuminated the damage in sickening detail. The tree trunk rested squarely on top of the hood of the red Crown Vic. I could see the sparkle of glass from the shattered windshield scattered on the asphalt. The Catfish's roof was caved in, and the pine branches obstructed my view into the car's interior. My gut twisted. If Ella Kate was in the car . . .

I ran over to the driver's-side door, and tried to push the branches aside. "Ella Kate," I screamed. "Are you there? Ella Kate?"

Tee was beside me now, yanking at the tree limb. "Can you see anything? Is she in there?"

I pulled the flashlight out of my pocket and aimed it at the door. A long smear of red trailed down the driver's-side window.

"Oh my God," I said breathlessly, my hands shaking so badly I dropped the light.

Tee picked up the light and held it aloft. When I looked again, I could see a woman's head, gray hair covered with a faded blue scarf, slumped against the door. And suddenly, a small brown-and-white head, bobbing up and down inside the car, barking furiously, pawing at the blood-streaked window.

"Shorty!" I cried. "We're here, buddy. We're right here."

42

"We've got to get her out of there," I said, trying to shove the branches out of the way to get to the door handle. But it was no use. A thick limb rested on the side of the door. Tee grasped the limb and yanked, but it barely moved. I ran around to the passenger side of the door, but another limb had it wedged shut.

I ran back to the Mercedes for my cell phone. "I'm calling 911," I told Tee. "We'll never be able to move that tree with just the two of us."

"Ask them to bring a chain saw," Tee called.

"Nine-one-one. Do you have an emergency?"

"It's my cousin," I said breathlessly. "A tree fell on her car, and we can't get her out."

"Is she conscious?"

"No. I mean, I don't know. We can see her inside the car, but she's not moving. And there's blood. And she's elderly. Please hurry!"

"Do you know how long she's been unconscious?"

"No! She left Guthrie around four P.M., and we just found her. She's probably been here for hours. Can you get somebody out here with a saw or something? We've got to get her out of that car."

"Ma'am? What's your location?"

I looked around for a mile marker or street sign, but in the darkness, all I could see were Tee's headlights, trained on the wrecked Catfish. There were no street signs and no mile markers.

"We're in the parking lot at an old restaurant called the Cozy Cabin, on the road to Pecan Springs."

I could hear the tapping of a computer keyboard, and the 911 operator's soft breathing.

"Got it," she said a moment later. "Georgia 501, at Bobolink Crossing, does that sound right?"

"Don't know," I said. "Wait. Yeah. Georgia 501. I remember the road sign. How long? We can't even tell if she's breathing."

"Hang on, hon," the dispatcher said softly. "We've got units scattered all over the county. I'll get somebody there as soon as I can."

I flipped the phone shut and ran back over to Tee, who was now using what looked like a steak knife, hacking ineffectively at the branch wedged against the Catfish's driver-side door. "I got 911, but they've got wrecks all over the place tonight," I told him. "No telling how long it'll be till they get here."

"This was all I could find in Dad's trunk," he said apologetically, his breath forming little white puffs in the chilled air. "If we had some rope or something, we could tie it to the tree and try to drag it off the car, but the only other things in the trunk are a set of jumper cables and this."

He held up an old-fashioned-looking white metal box with a large red cross emblazoned on the side. "I think this is left over from Dad's Boy Scout days," he said apologetically.

I peered through the branches, trying to catch a better view of Ella Kate. "It'll be good to have anyway if we can get her out."

"Is she breathing?" Tee asked, pushing at the branches.

"Can't tell," I said. "But one way or another, we've got to get her out of this damned car. She could freeze to death in this weather."

"I'm open to suggestions," Tee said, looking around the parking lot. My eyes went to the glass shards scattered on the asphalt.

"The back window," I said, running around to the rear of the Catfish. "We can't get in the front because the tree trunk's blocking it, but if we could break out the back window—"

"The jack!" Tee cried. He pulled it out of the Mercedes's trunk. "I completely overlooked it."

Several smaller tree limbs partially obscured the rear window of the Crown Vic. He clambered onto the trunk. "Back away a little," Tee said, lifting the jack over his head.

He swung the jack with a loud grunt, and landed a blow squarely in the middle of the window. I heard the soft crunch of the safety glass. He lifted the jack and took another swing, and then another. I climbed up onto the trunk to get a better look. The glass was shattered, but clumps of it still clung to the window frame.

Tee took the end of the jack and punched in the remaining glass.

From inside the car, Shorty started barking.

Tee started to climb into the backseat. "No, let me do it," I begged. "If I can let the driver's seat down, maybe I can pull her backward into the backseat, and then you can pull her out."

He nodded agreement, and held aside the tree branches so I could climb inside the Catfish.

As soon as I was inside the car, Shorty started to whine. "I'm coming, buddy," I said softly. I reached over the headrest and felt for Ella Kate. Her hair was damp with blood, but when I touched the side of her face, and felt that it was clammy, but not completely cold, I could have wept with relief.

"I think maybe she's in shock," I called to Tee. I swung a leg over the seat and awkwardly climbed into the front.

Ella Kate's face was ashen and streaked with blood. I touched a patch of withered skin under her jaw, and could feel her thready pulse. I grabbed one of her arms, stick thin beneath the thin cotton of her housedress, and rubbed vigorously.

Shorty whined again. I picked him up and cradled him in my arms. "Okay, guy," I crooned. "We got ya. You're okay. You're goin' home." Tee reached through the open back window, and I handed the quivering dog over to him.

"I'm gonna put him in the Mercedes, and start the engine to try to keep him warm," Tee called. "Be right back."

As gently as I could, I laid Ella Kate down across the front seat, and then, straddling her, began working the lever to lower her seat back. When the driver's-seat back was nearly prone, I put her back into position in the seat, and climbed into the backseat.

"Got her?" I asked, as Tee, kneeling outside the open window, reached in with both arms.

"Yup," he said. I pushed, and Tee pulled, and within seconds, we'd worked Ella Kate out through the back window of the Crown Victoria.

He picked her up like a rag doll, and carried her to the Mercedes, laying her across the backseat. As I jumped down from the trunk of the Catfish, I had an idea. I crawled back inside the car and grabbed the keys from the ignition.

Once I was outside again, I managed to pry the trunk lid open a few inches, and feel around inside, grabbing a rough hunk of fabric.

"Here," I said, running over to Tee's side. "One of Uncle Norbert's army blankets."

We tucked it around Ella Kate's unmoving body. "What now?" he asked. "Do you want to wait for the EMTs, or go ahead and get her to a hospital?"

"Hospital," I said grimly. "The dispatcher couldn't tell me how soon an ambulance could get here."

While Tee drove, I opened the first-aid kit and found some yellowed cotton balls and a bottle of rubbing alcohol. I dabbed the alcohol-soaked cotton on a nasty scrape on Ella Kate's cheek. She moaned softly.

"Ella Kate," I said, rubbing her hands between mine. "It's Dempsey. We found you. We're on the way to the hospital. Shorty's here. He's okay. You're gonna be okay too."

She was very cold and very still. But she was alive.

I called the 911 dispatcher while Tee drove, and she gave us directions to the nearest emergency room at the Medical Center of Central Georgia.

"How's she doing?" Tee called over his shoulder.

"She's breathing," I reported. "And maybe I'm imagining things, but I think I'm seeing a little color coming back to her face."

"Can you see any injuries?" he asked.

"Just the cut to her face," I said, "but God knows, I'm no doctor. How's Shorty doing?"

Tee reached out and patted the dog's head. "I think he's flat worn out," he said. "But he's breathing too, so I'm just gonna think positive thoughts and assume everybody is okay."

Fifteen minutes later, we saw the lights of the hospital's emergency room entrance. Tee pulled up to the ambulance ramp, a pair of wide double doors opened, and two orderlies rushed out with a gurney. Shorty gave a half-hearted warning bark when he saw his mistress being unloaded by strangers, but Tee quickly picked him up and held him close to his chest.

"Can you stay with Shorty while I go back with Ella Kate?" I asked.

He nodded agreement. "I saw a McDonald's as we were driving up. Maybe I'll go get us a couple of cheeseburgers."

Shorty whimpered softly. "I wouldn't give him much," I warned. "He has just had stomach surgery. Maybe just a piece of bun or something."

"Can I bring you something? It's been a hell of a long night."

I shook my head no.

"Call me on my cell as soon as they give you a report on her, will you?" Tee asked. "I've got to give Dad an update. He's kinda fond of the old buzzard."

I promised I would, and he leaned in and gave me a quick kiss that seemed as natural as the hug that followed.

The next couple of hours were a blur. I gave the admissions clerk what little vital statistics I had on Ella Kate, along with the Medicare card I'd found in her pocketbook. I found a seat in a waiting room crowded with patients and families whose lives had been impacted by the storm. There was a cartoon show on the television, and lukewarm coffee from a machine. At some point, a young Pakistani woman in surgical scrubs came out to the emergency room waiting area to fill me in on Ella Kate's condition.

"Ms. Timmons—is she your mother?" Dr. Bhiwandi asked, sitting down in the empty chair next to mine.

"God forbid," I said with a laugh. "She's sort of a cousin, I've been told."

"But you are her next of kin, correct?"

It took a moment for me to absorb the idea, but I nodded, in a half-hearted way.

"Well, whatever relation you are to her, she is very fortunate that you went looking for her," Dr. Bhiwandi said briskly. "I think she's slightly concussed. She fell on the ice. She has contusions on her arms and backside, and she has a hairline fracture to her right hip."

"It's not broken?" I said anxiously.

"No," Dr. Bhiwandi said. "She's in some pain, and we've given her medicine for that. And she's somewhat dehydrated, so we're giving her IV fluids, as well as antibiotics because of the cuts and scrapes. Other than that, your cousin seems surprisingly intact, and lucid, given her age and the circumstances of her rescue."

"Rescue? I wouldn't say it was really a rescue. She was missing, and my friend and I went looking for her, that's all. She's not really supposed to be driving. The sheriff took away her driver's license earlier this year."

"Ms. Timmons is seventy-nine," Dr. Bhiwandi said. "Or so she told me before she drifted off to sleep again. Believe me, at her age, and with her illness, she would not have survived for long in this cold if you and your friend had not found her. So I would call it a rescue, definitely. And what about her husband? How did he fare in this accident? She seemed quite concerned about him. Was he brought in here tonight too?"

"Oh, Ella Kate's not married," I said.

She frowned. "Shorty? That's who she was worried about. A friend, perhaps?"

"Cocker spaniel," I said. "I guess you'd say Shorty is her best friend. He was in the car with her. I think he's all right. If Ella Kate wakes up again, you can tell her Shorty's just fine."

"You can tell her yourself," Dr. Bhiwandi responded. She stood up and yawned. "Forgive me. It's been a very long night. We're waiting for a room to open up, and as soon as that happens, and she's had some sleep, you can have a nice visit with your cousin. I know she'll be anxious to see you."

"Well, maybe," I said, biting my lip at the memory of our last, angry exchange.

A high-pitched beep came from the pager on Dr. Bhiwandi's hip. She unclipped the pager, looked at its screen, and sighed. "I'm sorry. I seem to have a small crisis with another patient." She shook my hand, and turned and walked quickly back toward the treatment area. I was about to call Tee, to give him an update, but something the doctor had said struck me.

"Dr. Bhiwandi?" I called, rushing toward the treatment room door. She stopped and turned around.

"Yes?"

"You said something about Ella Kate's illness? What illness is that?"

She raised an eyebrow, and her smooth, placid face was suddenly full of furrows.

"The breast cancer, of course."

The door opened, and a nurse popped her head out. "Dr. Bhiwandi?"

"Sorry," the doctor told the nurse. "Sorry," she told me. And then she was gone.

43

I walked slowly back to the chair where I'd been sitting. A sullen-looking teenage girl was sitting there, holding a bloody towel to her right cheek. An infant slept in a baby carrier at her feet. The girl glowered up at me and I beat a hasty retreat.

Every seat in the emergency room waiting area was taken. Toddlers were whining, babies were crying, adults moaned and coughed and stared blankly at the droning television.

I found a vacant piece of wall and collapsed against it. My cell phone rang. It was Tee.

"Hey," he said. "I thought you were going to give me an update on Ella Kate."

"Sorry," I said. "Where are you?"

The outer door opened and Tee walked in. "Right here," he said.

I closed the phone and put it back in my pocket.

"She's all right," I said. "The doctor just now came out to talk to me. She's got a slight concussion, a hairline fracture to her right hip, and some bruises on her arms and butt. She apparently fell on the ice. They're giving her IV fluids, pain meds, and antibiotics, and they'll admit her as soon as a bed is freed up."

"Thank God," Tee said, leaning up against the wall beside me. His hand glanced mine, and I pulled away.

"Tee. Ella Kate has breast cancer."

"What? Since when?"

"I don't know. The doctor just sort of casually mentioned it. I guess she assumed I already knew about it."

"You didn't."

"She never said a word about cancer to me. I mean, I took her to the drugstore, to pick up some prescriptions, but I just assumed they were for high blood pressure or something. I had no idea—"

Suddenly, my legs felt rubbery and my head was fuzzy. I sank down to the floor, pulling my knees up to my chest and resting my forehead on my knees.

Tee dropped down beside me. "Hey," he said, touching my shoulder. "Are you okay? Do I need to get a nurse or somebody?"

"I'm okay," I said. "Just . . . numb. It's a lot to take in." I looked up at him. "How about you? Did you eat something? Where's Shorty?"

"We split a Big Mac," Tee said. "I ate most of it though. I walked him in the parking lot for a little bit. He's obviously pooped. I left him sleeping on the backseat of Dad's car."

"Did you talk to your dad?"

Tee nodded. "He was relieved to hear from me. I told him I'd call again in the morning, once we know more. He's gonna call a tow truck to pick up what's left of the Catfish."

I groaned. "It's probably totaled, huh?"

"DOA," he said cheerfully. "How about you? Want to get out of here? I got us a room for the night. There's a Comfort Inn right down the street. We can sneak Shorty in."

"Tee—" I started.

He cut me off at the pass. "There's no sense in trying to drive back to Guthrie tonight. The roads are still all messed up, and I figured you'd want to check on Ella Kate in the morning. No arguments, okay? The room's a double. You can have your own bed, and Shorty can bunk with me. Just us boys."

"All right." I struggled to my feet. He gave me a hand up. He was like that. Solid. "How come you're so nice to a bitch like me?" I asked.

He gave me a lopsided grin. "I'm a sucker for a pretty face."

I stripped down to my long johns and crawled into the bed. When I woke up in the morning, Tee was just coming into the room, with a wriggling bundle wrapped in Uncle Norbert's army blanket under his arm, a Styrofoam coffee cup in hand.

He put Shorty down on the floor, and the dog sat down on his haunches and solemnly surveyed the room. After a moment, he trotted over to my bed and put his paws on the edge of the mattress. I reached down and hauled him up and onto the bed. I reached over and scratched his ears. He sniffed my hand tentatively, then lay down on top of the covers.

"I guess this means we're friends," I told Tee. "I think this is the first time he's ever given me the time of day."

"Who, Shorty? He's not such a bad little mutt," Tee said, handing me the coffee. "At least he's housebroken. He got up at the dot of seven and started scratching at the door. We went outside, he did his thing, and then we went for coffee. We decided to let you sleep while you could."

I sat up in bed and pried the lid off the coffee. "Thank God," I said, taking a sip of the steaming brew. I looked up at him in surprise. "Not bad."

"We're in Macon, Dempsey," he said, sitting down on the bed opposite mine. "They've got Starbucks and running water and everything."

"That's not what I meant," I said, taking another sip. "How's the weather?"

"Not a cloud in the sky," Tee said. "The sun's shining, most of the ice is gone. It's as if the storm didn't even happen."

"It happened," I said, making a face and holding up my hand, which had started to throb. Angry red streaks emanated from the jagged cut on the palm.

"You might need stitches," Tee said. "Maybe you should let the ER docs look at it when we check on Ella Kate."

I yawned and stretched and swung my feet out of the bed. "I just want a shower," I said, heading for the bathroom.

I noticed with gratitude that Tee was an exceptional bathroom sharer. The toilet seat was down. The sink had been wiped clean. His damp towel was folded and hung on the rod on the back of the door, and he'd left me clean towels, and more important, a toothbrush, on the bathroom counter.

Tee was lounging on his bed, watching SportsCenter on the television, when I came out of the bathroom, reasonably clean, although dressed in the previous day's clothes.

I sat down on the edge of his bed. "How come you're so perfect?" I asked, eyeing him suspiciously. "I treat you like crap. And then you help rescue my extremely unpleasant cousin, take care of her dog, rent us a room for the night, bring me coffee in the morning, and even get me a toothbrush and toothpaste? All of this without trying to jump my bones? Are you for real?"

His eyes never left the television. An announcer in a bad plaid jacket was doing an in-depth analysis of the Atlanta Braves pitching staff.

"What?" he said absentmindedly.

I picked up the remote and clicked the television off. "Okay, so you're not perfect. You keep on watching television when somebody's talking to you. Did you even hear anything I just said?"

He took the remote away from me and switched the television on again. "Damn," he said. "Smoltzie's gone. We got no relievers, and nobody who can go the distance. And don't even get me started on the infield. We're toast. I don't know what the front office is thinking. We never should have let Andruw Jones go. He had a slump, but lots of guys have slumps."

"Tee?" I said, waving my hand in front of his eyes. "Anybody home? I'm trying to have a serious conversation here?"

He gave a deep, martyred sigh, and turned down the volume, although he did not turn the television off.

"I am a far from perfect man," he said finally, his eyes meeting mine. "My faults are legion. According to some women in my past, I have an unfortunate tendency to hog the covers. I'm absentminded. I might not remember your birthday until the day before, if I'm in the middle of a big case or work gets crazy, and I lose things, I mean, things like keys, cell phones, and sunglasses. I lost a car once, in the parking lot at Lenox Square Mall, at Christmas. I don't like big loud parties, because I suck at small talk and I can't remember people's names. I crack my knuckles when I'm bored. I fall asleep in movie theaters, unless it's a James Bond movie. I won't eat raw oysters. They are an abomination against man, so don't even try to get me to try them. I feel the same way about lima beans and sushi. But I'm loyal to a fault. And I really, really care about you, Dempsey. I keep thinking you're gonna wake up one morning, and realize that you care about me too, and you'll quit treating me like crap."

I bit my lip.

He rolled his eyes and turned up the volume again. "Don't start crying on me again, okay?" Tee said. "I'm no good with criers."

I laid my forehead on his shoulder. He'd somehow managed to find himself a clean shirt. "I'll try not to be a crier," I said, in a tiny voice. "And Tee? I hate sushi too. And I really, really do care about you. Really."

"Good." He gave my shoulder an awkward pat. "Anyway," he said. "I kinda like the dog."

Ella Kate was sitting up in the hospital bed, spooning red Jell-O into her mouth at an alarming rate. Her iron gray hair was matted to her head, and she had a piece of gauze adhesive-taped to the cut on the side of her face, and an IV needle attached to her arm, which was blooming with ugly purplish-black bruises. Her other arm had a matching set of bruises.

I stood in the open doorway and knocked tentatively. "Ella Kate? Do you feel like company?"

She pursed her colorless lips. "I feel like going home is what I feel like. Where's Shorty? They told me Shorty was with you."

I could tell she was feeling like herself, all right.

"Shorty's fine," I told her. "He's out in the car, with Tee. They won't let dogs in the hospital or I would have brought him to see you."

"Huh," she grunted, dropping her spoon into the empty plastic dish and pushing it to the back of her tray. "I reckon you come to get me then. If you'd a come an hour ago, I could have saved payin' another day for this room. Now they're gonna charge me who knows what, and I don't even get to eat a free dinner." She fumbled around among the bedcovers. "Where's the buzzer? Let's get that nurse lady in here and get this durned IV contraption unhooked so I can get on home."

I took a deep breath. "Actually, I spoke with the doctor before I came in. They want to keep you here for another day or so. Did they explain that you have a hairline fracture in your hip?"

"Somebody said something about a fracture," Ella Kate said. "But I say, if it ain't broke, ain't no sense in me staying around here layin' in the bed. I can do that at home, just fine, for free."

"It's not just the fracture," I said. "You're dehydrated, and that's why they're giving you fluids. They're also giving you antibiotics because of the cut on your face, and they just want to keep you under observation for a little while longer."

"Observation!" she said, slapping the sheets disgustedly. "That's a fancy way of sayin' they want to get their hand in my pocketbook and keep it there till I'm bled broke."

"I think Medicare probably covers your hospitalization," I said gently.

"Like fun," she said, staring up at the ceiling. "What else did that doctor tell you? What's her name again? Some funny kinda foreign name I never heard of before."

"Her name is Dr. Bhiwandi," I said. "She's very nice. Smart too. One of the nurses told me she has degrees from Duke and Emory Medical School."

Ella Kate snorted. "Emory! What's wrong with the University of Georgia? Does she think she's too good to be a bulldog? I wouldn't give you a dime for a doctor didn't go to the University of Georgia."

"Well, no. I mean, I don't know," I stammered. I'd been with Ella Kate for less than five minutes and she'd already worn me down to a frazzle.

Ella Kate crossed her arms over her chest. "I need to get me an American doctor."

"Ella Kate!" I said. "That's not fair. I'm sure Dr. Bhiwandi is an American citizen. She speaks perfect English. Much better than mine."

"Norbert had a doctor that was a foreigner," Ella Kate said darkly. "And you know what happened to him."

"What?"

"He died, didn't he?" She nodded her head, satisfied that she'd uncovered a grand medical conspiracy.

"But . . . I thought Norbert was almost a hundred years old when he died," I protested. "And didn't he have a heart attack?"

"He was only ninety-seven!" Ella Kate said fiercely. "Had a mind as sharp as a tack."

But not as sharp as your tongue, I thought to myself.

I sat down, uninvited, in the chair beside her hospital bed. "Listen, Ella Kate," I said. "There's something I need to talk to you about."

She clasped and unclasped her hands. "I'm sorry about the car," she mumbled. "I know'd better, but I took it anyway, got myself lost like the old fool I am, and nearly killed Shorty." She laid her head back on the pillow, and swallowed several times. "I reckon the car's wrecked pretty bad, ain't it?"

"I'm not worried about the Catfish," I told her. "We can get another car. It's you I'm worried about."

"I thought that foreigner doctor told you I was gonna be fine."

"She did. She also told me you have breast cancer."

Ella Kate stared up at the ceiling. "That ain't no concern of yours. And it wadn't any of her bidness tellin' you my bidness." With obvious effort, she grunted and turned on her side, leaving me facing her back.

"I don't think you're supposed to be moving around like that," I offered.

"Go away," she said, her voice muffled.

Lord knows, I wanted to go. I wanted to run down the hall and get far, far away from this hateful old hag. But I stayed anyway.

"How long have you known about the cancer?" I asked.

"Awhile."

"What are you doing about it?"

"Prayin'."

"Is it . . . I mean, have you had surgery? Or anything?"

There was a long silence in the room. I thought I heard her sniff. Her back shuddered a little.

"They done give me a mastectomy already," she said, her voice quavery. "That was a long time ago. Last year, the cancer come back, on my left side. I seen a doctor in Atlanta about it. Wadn't no need to spread the news around town."

She rolled herself back so that she was facing me now. The IV tube was tangled around her shoulders. I stood and carefully lifted the tubing free of her body. Her bones beneath my fingertips felt as fine and as brittle as twigs.

"I seen me a good, American doctor who went to the University of Georgia. This boy's neighbor's nephew is the vet that takes care of UGA. You know UGA? He's the bulldog mascot. Lives down in Savannah. Those bulldogs, they're all pure white English bulldogs. Same family's been raising them all these years. Norbert cried like a baby when UGA number six died. You know they bury all them dogs right up there at the stadium in Athens."

"I didn't know that," I said truthfully.

"I seen all about it on WSB," Ella Kate said. "This doctor in Atlanta, he was all set to cut on me, but then I told him no. I beat cancer one time. I was younger then. But I'm seventy-nine years old now. If the Lord wants to take me, I reckon I'm ready to go."

Ella Kate narrowed her eyes, steeling herself for a fight.

"Has the cancer spread anywhere else?" I asked.

"They tell me it ain't got any worse," Ella Kate said.

"I'm glad," I told her. And surprisingly, I was glad.

"You ain't gonna fuss at me? Try to make me change my mind?"

"Nope. It wouldn't do any good."

"Durn tootin'," Ella Kate said. Her thin lips crinkled up a little on one side, in what might have been a smile.

44

W hen I climbed into the front seat of the Mercedes, Tee handed me a paper sack. I pulled out a still-warm cheese Danish and another cup of coffee. He started the engine and pulled out of the hospital parking lot.

"Now you're just showing off," I said, biting into the Danish.

"How's Ella Kate?"

"Meaner than ever," I told him. "She's pissed off because she has to stay for at least another day, which she's sure is just a diabolical plan by the hospital to steal all her money. She's also unhappy that her doctor didn't go to med school at the University of Georgia, and that she's a 'foreigner.'"

"That Ella Kate," Tee said. "She's just a big ol' ray of sunshine, ain't she?"

"I asked her about the cancer," I said, sipping the coffee.

He winced. "How'd that go?"

"About like you'd expect. She told me it was none of the doctor's 'bidness' and none of mine neither. She had a mastectomy years ago, but she said the cancer recurred on the other side last year. Her doctor in Atlanta wanted to remove the cancerous breast, but Ella Kate told him no deal. She says she's too old to go through surgery again, and if it's her time, so be it."

"So . . . what's she doing about the cancer?"

"Praying."

"And what are you going to do?"

"Me?" I broke off a tiny piece of the Danish and turned around and offered it to Shorty, who eagerly lapped it up. "What can I do? She's a grown woman. I can't force her to accept treatment she doesn't want. Maybe she'll change her mind, but I doubt it."

"I don't disagree," he said. "I guess what I meant to say is, have you thought about your future? At Birdsong? In Guthrie? Does this change things?"

"Why should it? Ella Kate will be discharged tomorrow, probably. I'll have to fix her up a place to sleep downstairs, I guess, until her hip gets better. But the work on the house is going better than I expected. Bobby is supposed to come today to start tiling in the kitchen. He says he'll teach me how to tile too. Big fun, huh?"

Tee steered the Mercedes out of Macon traffic and back onto the state highway to Guthrie. The only signs that an ice storm had blown through the night before were some stray tree limbs and roofing shingles scattered on the roadside. The morning sunlight had already dried up most of the rain. My hand throbbed, reminding me of everything that had happened.

"Ella Kate is not going to get better without treatment, Dempsey," he said after a while. "My mother died of breast cancer, you know. I don't know the type of cancer Ella Kate has, but I can tell you, things are probably going to get really awful by the end. And here's the thing— you're going to be the one to take care of her. You're it, you know? The only family she's got."

"Yeah. Next of kin. Bummer."

"I told Dad about the cancer," he said. "You know, he's Ella Kate's lawyer too. The old man's a stickler for client confidentiality, but he did tell me that she can afford whatever health care she needs. Doctors, hospitals, round-the-clock nursing care. Whatever. She's not hurting for money."

"Yippee," I said dully. "Maybe we'll both check into the Ritz-Carlton and order room-service chemo. Except Ella Kate would probably refuse chemo."

"Something to think about," Tee said, glancing over at me.

I didn't tell him that I'd been thinking about little else, ever since Dr. Bhiwandi told me about Ella Kate's cancer.

When we got back to Birdsong, Bobby's pickup truck was parked in the driveway. The bright blue tarp tacked to the roof fluttered in the breeze, and Bobby and Trey were struggling to lift an enormous white object out of the truck bed.

Tee pulled the Mercedes to the curb and hopped out. "Let me give you a hand," he called to the men. Even with Tee holding up one end of the thing, the men staggered under the weight of it.

I got out of the car and offered to help, but they bravely declined my assistance. "We got it," Bobby grunted, his knees wobbling crazily. Eventually, they wrestled the thing into the open kitchen door, and onto a set of waiting sawhorses.

"Look here, Dempsey," Bobby said proudly, mopping his brow. "Look what I brung you from the dump."

The thing was a kitchen sink of *Titanic* proportions. Porcelain over cast iron, it had double basins, and ridged drainboards jutting out from each side, along with a rounded humpback backsplash. The faucet was nickel and the handles were cross-hatched, with porcelain buttons in the center, *C* for cold and *H* for hot. The basins were filthy and matted with dried leaves and unspeakable detritus. The sink was absolutely gorgeous.

"Oh, Bobby," I said, running my hand over the cool porcelain. "From the dump? For real?"

"For true," he said, grinning with pleasure. "What do you think?"

"It's spectacular," I said. "Better than a double-glass-door Traulsen."

"Better than an eight-burner double-oven stainless-steel Viking with the griddle in the middle?" he teased.

"Better than a Fisher and Paykel warming drawer or a Miele dishwasher. Better than a brushed-nickel Waterworks bridge faucet, better than custom Ann Sacks tile, better than . . ." I struggled to come up with another superlative dredged from my extensive knowledge of shelter magazines.

"Huh?" Trey said.

"Got me," Tee told him. "I think they're talking about kitchen stuff."

I went over to the old sink, the old, stinking, battered, stained, chipped pink porcelain sink, and picked up a bottle of Windex from the counter beside it. I tore off about a yard of paper towels, and set to work on the *Titanic* sink, spritzing and rubbing while the men looked on, bemused.

"This here," I said, patting the new sink, "this is the shit."

Trey nodded his understanding. "Gotcha."

"Was it really at the dump?" I asked Bobby. "Who would get rid of something like this?"

"You'd be surprised," he said. "I get lots of good stuff out there."

"He calls it the Mall of Guthrie," Trey volunteered. "Half the stuff in our house came from there. Mama hollers at him about it, but he just keeps on bringing stuff home."

"Did you mind getting a new bumper for your car when I drug it home from the mall?" Bobby asked.

"No, sir," Trey admitted.

"See, there's lotsa folks round here don't like nothin' old," Bobby explained. "They want shiny and new. Even if ain't nothin' beneath the shine except cardboard and sawdust."

"I saw a sink just like this in the December issue of *Elle Decor*," I told him. "I think it was in Meg Ryan's house on Nantucket."

Tee looked down at the sink with obvious distaste. "It's kinda gunky, isn't it?"

"You wait," I told him. "It will be awesome. It will be the centerpiece of this kitchen."

"If you say so."

Bobby preened for just a moment. "You right about that, Dempsey. We get this thing cleaned up, this sink gonna be just the thing."

"Speaking of cleaning up," Tee said, glancing down at his watch. "I better get home and get to work on that downed oak tree in our backyard before Dad decides to try to cut it up by himself."

"Oh yeah," Bobby said. "I rode by your house this morning, Tee. That's some kinda mess you got over there. And what about Ella Kate? Did you-all track her down last night?"

"Eventually," I said. "It's a long story. The short version is that she took the Catfish to go pick up Shorty at the animal hospital in Macon, got caught in the middle of the ice storm, and pulled off the road to wait it out. A tree fell on the car, trapping her and Shorty inside."

"Sweet Jesus!" Bobby said. "I didn't have no idea."

"She's all right," I said hastily. "She's got some bumps and bruises, and a hairline fracture of her hip, so they kept her in the hospital last night."

"And the Catfish?" Bobby asked, looking from me to Tee.

"The Catfish might be totaled," Tee said. "But the good news is, they'll probably let Ella Kate come home from the hospital tomorrow."

I walked Tee outside to the Mercedes. "Thanks," I told him. "For everything."

"You're welcome," he said.

W e spent the rest of the morning prying the old Formica countertops off and the sink out of its cabinet, and hauling them
out to Bobby's truck for a return trip to the dump. Then,
Bobby and Trey nailed down a new plywood top, and on top of that, a
layer of green backer board that he explained would be the platform for
the new tile.

After two days of emotional highs and lows, it was a relief to lose
myself in working on the house again.

Right before noon, my cell phone rang. My caller was Dr. Bhiwandi.

"Good news, Ms. Killebrew," she said, in her crisp British-influenced
accent. "Your cousin is feeling much, much better. If she continues like
this, we will send her home to you in the morning. Do you have any
questions for me?"

I had more questions than she could answer in a lifetime. I started
with the most obvious. "Will she be able to walk?"

"Yessss," Dr. Bhiwandi said. "She needs to stay ambulatory so that
we don't get any nasty complications like pneumonia or blood clots.
However, we may send her home with a walker. And, of course, no
stairs or anything taxing. We'll also want to schedule her for some
physical therapy when she gets stronger."

No stairs. Walker. Physical therapy. Oh, Ella Kate was going to love
this set of doctor's orders. I could hear her complaints already.

"Dr. Bhiwandi," I said. "About Ella Kate's cancer. I want you to know
I wasn't aware that she had cancer until you let me in on her secret."

"Oh. Oh dear."

I laughed. "My cousin is uh, pretty cantankerous, as I guess you've
noticed."

"She's very high spirited," Dr. Bhiwandi agreed.

"That's one way of putting it. Anyway, I did ask her about the cancer this morning. And she's absolutely dead set against any further surgery."

Dr. Bhiwandi sighed. "I see. Well, we hear that sometimes in patients your cousin's age. There is a quality of life issue. Your cousin's mental state is quite good for her age. When I saw her a little while ago she was alert and focused on going home. It seems she knows what she wants. And probably, you will have to respect her wishes in that regard."

"I don't have much choice in the matter," I said ruefully. "Is there anything . . . I should know? About her prognosis? Or a timeline, or anything else like that?"

"Without any more information about the nature of her cancer, or her bloodwork, I really can't tell you very much," Dr. Bhiwandi said. "I'm afraid you'll need to talk to her surgeon and her oncologist."

"And I'm afraid she won't share that with me," I said. "She's pretty secretive about a lot of stuff. So . . . you can't tell me what to do? If she's in pain, or something like that?"

"I'll speak to her about following up with the oncologist. If the cancer advances and she starts experiencing pain or other symptoms, you should urge her to let you take her to a doctor. We have very good methods of pain management that will allow her to stay comfortable at home, without being admitted to a hospital, if that's what you're worried about."

Dr. Bhiwandi gave me more instructions about Ella Kate's prescriptions and the details of bringing her home from the hospital.

I hung up and looked over at Bobby, who'd been trying different arrangements of tile on the new plywood countertops. He had a tool he called a nipper, and was cutting the corners of the tiles to fit around the new junkyard sink.

"Ella Kate's coming home from the hospital tomorrow," I told him.

He looked up. "That's good, right?"

"I guess. The thing is, she won't be able to climb stairs."

He nodded. "We gonna fix her up a room downstairs?"

"Can you give me a hand? I thought maybe we'd clear out Norbert's study, and move her bed down here. It's close to the bathroom, so I think it would work."

"Oh yeah," he said, putting down the nippers. "Me and Trey can handle it. That ain't no problem."

I opened the door to Norbert's study and looked around. The yellow covers of the *National Geographic*s gave the room a weird golden glow. I looked at Bobby. "You know anybody who'd like to have fifty years of *National Geographic?*"

"Not me," Bobby said.

"Me either," I said. "Do they have a recycling center at that dump of yours?"

"Sure do. That's where I get some of the wife's favorite magazines," he said.

We brought in a wheelbarrow from the toolshed and loaded it up with shelf after shelf of old magazines. It was nasty work. Clouds of dust and paper particles rose up every time we touched the magazines, and what seemed like millions of tiny cigar-shaped bugs came swarming out of the pages.

I barely managed to stifle a scream at the sight of that first bug when it scuttled across my wrist.

"What the hell?" I asked, madly stomping bugs as fast as they emerged from the rotting paper. "This is what I hate about living in Georgia. Bugs! Roaches and spiders, and now these—"

"Silverfish," Bobby said, flicking a couple to the floor. "They're nasty, but they won't hurt you none."

Without another word, he went out to the kitchen and brought me a pair of work gloves that extended nearly to my elbows. I tied a bandanna over my hair and plugged the iPod into the docking station, and gritted my teeth and got back to work. As I cleared out magazines and stomped bugs with my dead uncle's old work boots to the tune of "Billie Jean" I wondered what my old roomies in Washington would say if they could see me now. Dempsey Killebrew, former fashionista, was a bona fide construction worker. All I lacked were some tattoos and a pickup truck to call my own.

When the shelves were finally cleared and the magazines on their way to the dump, Bobby carried Norbert's old desk and chair down to the basement. I swept and dusted and mopped and scrubbed the room with my new favorite cleaning solution—Fabuloso, which smelled like the chemical version of an apple orchard, and which I'd found in the Mexican foods section at the Bi-Lo.

Bobby got a ladder and swiped down several decades' worth of cobwebs along the ceilings and window casings. He even washed the windows inside and out. By the time we were done cleaning, weak afternoon sunlight sparkled through the old wavy glass windows.

"What now?" Bobby asked.

"Furniture," I said. "Let's bring Ella Kate's bed, dresser, nightstand, and easy chair downstairs."

"We might oughtta wait till Trey gets back from the dump," he said. "You don't wanna be carrying no dresser down them stairs."

"I can do it," I assured him. "Anyway, I feel kind of funny about letting anybody else besides you see Ella Kate's room."

Bobby raised an eyebrow.

"She's a total nut about her privacy," I said. "She always keeps her door locked. Day in and day out. And I wouldn't have gone in there, except yesterday, when the weather was getting so scary looking, I needed to find out what the storm was doing. And she has the only television in the house."

He nodded his understanding, but it didn't make me feel any less guilty.

"You'll have to see it to believe it," I told him finally when we were upstairs.

Bobby stood wordlessly in the open doorway.

"Oh my," he said, taking it all in. "Oh my my."

"It's all the furniture from the rest of the house," I said.

He inched his way through the narrow path to Ella Kate's bed, and stopped when he reached the faded chintz-draped dressing table with the silver-topped mirror, combs, brushes, and cold cream jars.

"This here was Miss Olivia's," he said quietly, nodding at the silver-framed photograph on Ella Kate's nightstand.

"It's all my grandmother's furniture and stuff, isn't it?"

"And then some," Bobby agreed.

"What's it doing here?" I asked.

He stood with his hands on his hips, looking around the room. "Well," he started. "I know she was tore up pretty bad when Mr. Norbert finally died. He was sick a good long time, and you know, she wouldn't let nobody else in the house to take care of him. Had to do it all her ownself. Maybe she started moving this stuff up here after she found out that Mr. Norbert left the house to your daddy. She mighta thought you-all would come down here and cart all this stuff outta here."

"We wouldn't have," I said quietly.

"Ella Kate didn't know that. She only knew it was Mitch Killebrew got the house, and you know she and the Killebrews had bad blood between 'em."

I sat down on Ella Kate's bed. The bedsprings creaked and the mattress sagged badly.

"Bobby, will you tell me now?"

He put his hands in the pockets of his overalls and looked around the room.

"The wife's aunt told me there was talk around town. Back when your granddaddy got the divorce and up and took the baby—that's your daddy—with him. And Miss Olivia was left back here in Guthrie."

"What kind of talk?"

He squirmed uncomfortably. "Which one of these dressers you want to take downstairs for Ella Kate?"

"This one," I said, nodding at a heavy walnut chest of drawers standing near the door. I'd seen Ella Kate's simple white cotton underpants, shirts, and slacks folded in it the day before.

"Bobby," I said patiently. "I know you don't like to repeat gossip. And I respect you for that. But this is my family we're talking about here. If you have an idea about why Ella Kate acts the way she does, it would help me to understand her better."

"Yeahhh," he said reluctantly.

"So. Will you tell me what you know?"

He started pulling the drawers out of the dresser, and stacking them outside in the hallway.

"Bobby?"

He sighed. "Reckon you got a right to hear it. You know that when your grandmother, Miss Olivia, up and got married to Mr. Killebrew, it was a big surprise around Guthrie."

"I'd heard that."

"He was from away, and Miss Olivia, she'd gone off to college in Atlanta, was gonna be a schoolteacher or something like that. And Ella Kate, she was your grandmama's best friend since they were little-bitty kids. And cousin too, although I don't rightly know exactly how the family connection goes on that."

"Nobody seems to know," I agreed. "Except maybe Ella Kate."

"What we heard was that they got married up in Atlanta, right before Christmas, that first year Miss Olivia went off to college. And then, of course, they moved on down here, to Birdsong, right afterward. And Ella Kate, she was Miss Olivia's roommate at Agnes Scott, and she was kinda shy and a little backward, you know? Her people had all these children, and they didn't have no kind of money. Everybody always figured one of the Dempseys give the Timmonses the money to send Ella Kate off to college."

"Interesting," I said.

"So, with Miss Olivia dropping out of college, I guess Ella Kate didn't have no reason to stay up there at Agnes Scott College. So she come on home to Guthrie too."

"And she went to work at the bedspread mill."

"Sure," Bobby said. "Got a good job in the office. She wadn't no lint head, working out on the floor like everybody else."

"So Olivia had a shotgun wedding?"

He squirmed and jingled some change in his pockets. "Back then, it wadn't like it is now, with the young folks talkin' 'bout hookin' up, and having babies and never gettin' married and all like that. It caused some talk—them two getting married all the way up in Atlanta instead of back here at Guthrie First United Methodist, where the Dempseys paid for the stained-glass windows, and the church steeple, and even the pipe organ, over the years."

"So, maybe they just sort of told all the home folks a little white lie about when they actually got married," I mused. "Maybe they moved the date up by a few weeks."

"They did say your daddy was born premature," Bobby admitted. "And he was a sickly baby. The wife's aunt said Miss Olivia had a real hard delivery. She weren't right for a long time after your daddy was born."

"Why'd they get divorced?" I asked.

"Nobody knows," Bobby said. "Miss Olivia's daddy was an important man in this town. Owned the mill, went to church with the doctors and lawyers. And the judge. All anybody knew was, one day, they were married, living here at Birdsong, and the next, they were divorced. And your granddaddy left town and took little Mitch with him."

"How on earth did he get a judge to award him custody instead of Olivia?" I wondered. "Especially if Olivia's father was friends with the judge. You would think they would have run him out of town on a rail."

"Seems like your granddaddy had some dirt on your grandmama," Bobby said. "And it wadn't nice. Not nice at all." He looked meaningfully at Ella Kate's bedside table, with its shrine to her old friend.

"No!" I said. "Really? My grandmother and Ella Kate?"

"Don't know if it was true. Thing is, he mighta tol' the judge it was true. And that woulda been a big old scandal. Guthrie, it's a small town. It ain't like up there in Atlanta where you got your gay pride parades and all like that. Maybe Miss Olivia's daddy made a deal with Mr. Killebrew to keep it quiet. Nobody knows."

"What does your wife's aunt think?" I asked.

Bobby made a face. "She didn't like your granddaddy Killebrew no way! She called him a lying, two-faced Yankee. What she says is—that man got Miss Olivia pregnant, and then, when he seen how rich her family was, he decided to get him some of that money for his own self. He just made up any old kind of lie he could get away with. And then he took the money, and that baby, and got as far away from Guthrie, Georgia, as he could get."

"Mitch can only remember coming back here a few times after the divorce," I told Bobby. "And then, of course, Olivia died when he was still pretty young."

"Yeah, that was awful sad," Bobby said. "Auntie says Miss Olivia pined for that boy. She never was right again after he took that baby away from her."

"What did she die of?" I asked.

"Uh, heart disease, or something like that," Bobby said.

"But she was so young!" I protested. "Barely in her twenties."

"Your uncle Norbert, he had a bad heart," Bobby pointed out.

"And he lived well into his nineties," I countered. "What else aren't you telling me? Come on, Bobby, I know there's something else."

Bobby came over to the bed and took the drawer out of the nightstand. He set it outside in the hallway. He stacked the framed photographs on another dresser, and leaned down and unplugged the lamp.

When he stood up again, his face was solemn.

"I told you Miss Olivia had a hard time in delivery, right? The doctor gave her some pills to help her sleep. And when she was so depressed, after your granddaddy took the baby away, he give her some pills to help calm her down. The wife's aunt, she did the washing and ironing over here, and some housecleaning too. One morning, when she come to work, she went upstairs to ask Miss Olivia something. Only Miss Olivia wouldn't wake up. Auntie, she shook her and shook her, but it was too late. She was dead."

"Oh my God," I breathed. "She killed herself. With an overdose."

"The doctor told the family it was heart disease," Bobby said staunchly. "But they give Auntie a train ticket to Mobile to visit her cousin the very next day."

He picked up the nightstand and took it out to the hallway. I took the hand-knotted quilt off the foot of Ella Kate's bed, and then, carefully, stripped the bed of the thick white chenille bedspread, the same spread my grandmother's family had been making for decades. I folded it into quarters, and then carried it and the rest of Ella Kate's bedding downstairs, to her new room.

46

Trey drove the last truckload of papers and magazines and kitchen debris to the dump just as the sun began to dip down below the horizon.

I saw the truck pull away from the house from the window in what had been Uncle Norbert's study, and what would now be Ella Kate's bedroom.

Bobby unrolled the worn pastel hooked rug with its faded pattern of pink roses on the freshly mopped floor. Then we placed the bed facing the window so she could watch the comings and goings on the street outside. I'd washed the curtains from her old bedroom, and hung them now in her new room. Her bed linens were freshly laundered too, and I'd dusted and polished the furnishings so that they gleamed and the whole room smelled like lemons and beeswax.

I re-created Ella Kate's old room as best as I could, minus the warehouse full of furniture.

She'd still have Olivia's dressing table with the sterling-silver brushes and combs and jars, and she'd have the dressers too, the ones with her things and the one that held Olivia's clothing. I brought down all the framed photographs and arranged them around the room, along with a representative collection of the porcelain cats. I prayed Ella Kate wouldn't notice the absence of the cat I'd broken the night of the storm.

When we'd finished, we stood in the doorway surveying the day's work.

"This looks real nice, Dempsey," Bobby said. "Real homeylike. Ella Kate is gonna love it."

I snorted. "She's going to hate it. And she'll hate me for doing this.

She'll be furious that I trespassed in her old room, even angrier if she figures out I roped you into helping me out."

"Had to be done," Bobby said. "She might get her bowels in an uproar at first, but she'll get over it pretty quick. Long as Shorty's here, she'll be all right."

As if on cue, Shorty ran through my legs and into the room. He was still sore from his surgery, so I had to lift him up and onto the bed, where he immediately curled up on Ella Kate's pillow as though he owned the place.

"See? Shorty likes it just fine," Bobby pointed out. "And soon as Ella Kate gets used to the idea, me and Trey will move them sofas and chairs back downstairs where they belong."

After he'd gone, I wandered into the kitchen to check out our progress there. We'd had to put the tiling project on the back burner while we moved Ella Kate's things, but before we'd started on the bedroom, Bobby and Trey had slotted the junkyard sink into its place on the cabinet base, and hooked up the faucet.

Without thinking, I went to my bucket of cleaning supplies, found a can of scouring powder, and began working on the stained porcelain.

It took me a good half hour, but I managed to scrub away most of the old stains and caked-on debris. There were some minute chips in the porcelain in a couple of places near the top of the sink backsplash, but to my mind they were hardly noticeable. I was working on polishing the nickel faucet and handles when my cell phone rang.

The caller ID screen told the tale. Mitch. I felt my gut clench. We hadn't talked since that angry exchange over the *Washington Post* story.

I let it ring three times before answering, wondering how I would handle him.

"Hi, Dad," I said. Wow, way to put him in his place, Demps, I thought.

"Now listen, Dempsey," he started.

Uh-oh.

"I just had a visit from a woman named Camerin Allgood. Does that name ring a bell with you, young lady?"

I winced. He hadn't called me "young lady" since discovering I'd blown all my freshman year meal money on a spring break road trip to Key West.

"The FBI agent. Yes, we've met."

"She showed up at my office and announced she was with the FBI. My secretary nearly had a coronary!"

"I hope your secretary is all right, Dad," I said.

Especially since if she did have a heart attack, he would blame it on me.

"She'll live," he said. "The point is, this Agent Allgood woman says you are refusing to cooperate with the FBI. I told her in no uncertain terms that I thought she was mistaken. I told her I was sure you wanted to clear up this whole shameful episode and get it behind you, and that of course you would want to do anything in your power to help the government bring this slimeball congressman to justice. That's right, isn't it?"

"Uh, Dad," I said. "I do want to get it cleared up. And I have been cooperating. The thing is, I've given them concrete proof that I hired those women at the direction of Alex Hodder. They have this crazy idea that I should wear a wire and get Alex to incriminate himself, which is ludicrous. He'd never do that. I told them that, Dad. I gave them the evidence. They have everything they need already."

"That's not what Agent Allgood told me this morning," Mitch huffed. "This woman is a veteran at these kinds of investigations. And if she says she needs you to wear a wire, I say you damned well better do as they ask."

"Dad—" I started.

"This whole thing has gotten completely out of control," Mitch went on. "I think you need some solid legal advice."

"I have a lawyer, Dad," I interrupted. "Carter Berryhill and I have met with these agents twice. And he told them that I'm not going to do anything until they bring me a signed agreement from the U.S. attorney's office, stating that they won't pursue charges against me."

"Carter Berryhill?" Mitch bellowed. "You mean that country-bumpkin lawyer handling my great-uncle's estate? For God's sake, Dempsey, use some common sense, for once. Now look. I've talked to somebody in our Atlanta office, and they've recommended an ace criminal attorney. He used to be a federal prosecutor, and he's handled dozens of cases like this. I'm calling him tomorrow."

I felt the blood pounding in my ears. My gut clenched and unclenched. I held my breath, let it out.

"What, Dad?" I said. "I can't hear you. I think my cell phone battery is dying."

I punched the disconnect button. If the phone hadn't been my only link to the outside world, I think I would have stomped on it with the same disgust I'd used earlier on the silverfish.

And now the doorbell was ringing. My day was complete.

I glanced down at my attire, hoping that my visitor wasn't Tee. My overalls were caked with grime and dead silverfish, and my hands were rubbed raw from all the cleaning compounds I'd tortured them with.

When I opened the front door, I immediately wished I hadn't.

Jackson Harrell leaned up against the door frame, gazing around the porch with frank curiosity. He was dressed in starched and pressed blue jeans, a starched yellow dress shirt, shiny white Nikes, and a dark blue baseball cap with FBI emblazoned across the bill. He was the face of the new FBI. I wanted to slam the door in that face, but I restrained myself.

"How ya' doin'?" he asked.

"What do you want?" I said stonily.

He looked taken aback. "Hey now. You call that Southern hospitality?"

"I don't feel particularly hospitable right now, to tell you the truth."

"Bad day?" he asked, starting to step inside.

"I've had better." I stepped in front of him to keep him from going any farther. "No offense, Agent Harrell, but I'm kind of busy right now. So, if this is a social call, I'm going to have to ask you to give me a rain check."

His easygoing smile vanished. "Oh, it's not social," he said. "This is business. All business."

I felt the blood drain from my face. "In that case, I'll ask you to wait out here on the porch until I can get my attorney over here."

"You do that," he said, folding his arms across his chest. "I can wait."

I slammed the door and went for my cell phone.

"Tee? Is Carter there?"

"No," Tee said. "I'm down at the newspaper. He's at home, as far as I know. What's up?"

"The damned FBI is here again," I said. "It's that Agent Harrell. And he says he means business. I wouldn't let him in. I'm not talking to him until your father gets here."

"Good thinking," Tee said. "I'll get hold of Dad and send him over there right away. Did the guy give you any idea of what he wants?"

"I didn't give him a chance. But I do know that that woman, Agent Allgood, showed up down in Miami at my father's office today. They're pressuring him to pressure me to wear the damned wire."

"Jesus!" Tee said. "These guys don't give up."

"Neither do I," I said grimly.

After I hung up the phone, I ran upstairs and jumped in the shower, fuming. I had no intention of meeting with Harrell while looking like a fugitive from a pest-control convention.

Did he think he could just drop in and scare the crap out of me with his big, bad FBI self? Uh-uh. No more. I was done being intimidated, patronized, pushed around. I nearly scrubbed the skin off my body while I plotted my revenge on all those who'd done me wrong. Leading the list were Alex Hodder and Congressman Anthony Licata, with Agents Harrell and Allgood right behind. And my father. I wouldn't mind showing him up while I was at it. As I scrubbed, a plan began to form. It was evil, vindictive, and manipulative. It was a thing of real beauty.

I washed my hair and blew it dry, then pulled it back in a semisevere French twist. I put on makeup, including enough black eyeliner to give me the feeling of a warrior queen. I dressed in my best pants suit, the black wool Dolce & Gabbana one with the tight-fitting jacket—what Lindsay always referred to as my "Power Ranger" suit. I put on pearl earrings and the gold Piaget watch Mitch had given me when I graduated from law school. For the first time since I'd arrived in Guthrie, I found the need for heels, my black Jimmy Choo boots.

When I'd dressed, I stood in front of the wavy mirror on the back of the closet door and assessed the look. Hair: professional, not too dykey, not too girlie. Clothes: excellent. The pants suit, which had cost an ungodly sum, gave me a tall, slim, stripped-down silhouette. Jewelry: also excellent. The pearl Tiffany earrings had been my mother's graduation gift. They were precious to me because I knew she'd chosen something she thought I'd like, rather than the funky, ethnic jewelry Lynda herself favored. As for the watch, I knew Mitch had bought it in a deliberate attempt to outspend Lynda, which he'd managed, in spades. He'd given me a piece more suitable for a Wall Street hedge funder than a junior lobbyist, because that's what he secretly hoped I would someday become—the gift was aspirational rather than inspirational, but no matter. I'd noticed that Agent Harrell wore a Rolex. My Piaget would trump his in any contest. Shoes: double check. The wicked two-inch boot heel, along with my hairdo, would give me what I estimated was a one inch advantage over Agent Harrell.

The doorbell was ringing again. I marched carefully down the stairs, clinging to the banister with both hands to avoid tripping and falling in the now-unaccustomed high heels. When I got downstairs, I could see three men through the front-door sidelights: Carter, Agent Harrell, and yes, Tee Berryhill. I took a deep breath and squared my shoulders. Showtime.

47

Jackson Harrell did a double take when I opened the door. I like to think he was astonished by my thirty-minute transformation.

"Agent Harrell," I said coolly, motioning him inside. "I can't say it's a pleasure to see you again."

"My dear," Carter said, kissing my cheek and giving me a malicious wink. "You look lovely tonight."

Tee trailed in the door last, giving me a long, searching look. When Harrell and Carter were out of earshot and eyesight, he kissed me too—only with a little more passion and a lot more tongue. "Love the outfit," he whispered in my ear.

I dragged the dining room chairs into the parlor, choreographing the seating so that Harrell was seated closest to the drafty windows.

"Well now," Harrell said, looking from me to the Berryhills. "Now that the whole choir is assembled, I guess we should just get down to brass tacks."

"Oh. Isn't Agent Allgood joining us tonight?" I asked.

Harrell shifted in his seat. "She's out of town on business."

"Yes," I said. "I understand she's been down in Miami. I spoke to my father just now. He mentioned that Agent Allgood paid him a call. Unannounced. At his place of business."

Carter's fluffy white eyebrows shot up. "What?"

"Yep," I said, making a show of crossing my legs. "I guess it's a new tactic. Maybe something you guys learned from the Department of Homeland Security? Pressuring family members to get a witness to cooperate? Or maybe just trying to embarrass them by showing up and announcing to everybody within shouting distance that a federal agent wants to speak to them about 'government' business? Personally, I think it's pretty tacky."

"Tacky? It's unconscionable," Carter said, his face coloring. He turned to Harrell. "You people have no business involving her parents. Miss Killebrew has told you she'll cooperate. We gave you proof that Alex Hodder instructed my client to hire what she reliably believed was a massage therapist and a surfing instructor."

"Wakeboard instructor," I told Carter. "Apparently there's a difference."

"I don't care if she was a mambo teacher," Carter said. He was really getting himself worked up on my behalf. It was wonderful to behold. He leaned toward Harrell. His ears got quite pink when he was angry. "These efforts to intimidate Miss Killebrew must stop. Immediately. After our last discussion with you, we were assured that you would take the evidence we gave you—Alex Hodder's golf scorecard, with his handwriting on it—and in return, we'd receive a written agreement from the U.S. attorney's office that no charges against my client would be pursued."

"Hey!" Harrell said, holding up both hands as though to fend off a physical attack from Carter Berryhill. "Don't get your boxers all bunched up at me, Mr. Lawyer. I'm the good guy here. I made the case for leaving Miss Killebrew out of this thing. My partner and I went to the wall for your client. We even took it to the SAC."

"SAC?" Tee said, looking puzzled.

"Special agent in charge," Carter explained.

"Right," Harrell went on. "The thing is, the U.S. attorney is another story. You can't quote me on this, but the thing is: Congressman Licata is a Republican. And he happens to be on some key subcommittee that's been jerking the Justice Department around on the matter of appropriations for nickel-and-dime stuff like travel and continuing education. You believe that? This motherfu . . . excuse me, allegedly corrupt public official, is telling us we can't buy a coach ticket to Sheboygan to interview a suspect, and in the meantime, he's taking under-the-table blow jobs in exchange for a vote on an oil bill."

Carter's pink ears officially turned red. "Really, Agent Harrell, what's that got to do with Miss Killebrew?"

"My boss, and his boss, they want this case watertight. They want it signed, sealed, and delivered to a jury with a pretty pink bow on top. So, while the scorecard is good, excellent even, we're gonna need just a little bit more."

He picked up the briefcase at his feet and laid it across his knees. He unsnapped the latches and brought out the plastic case he'd shown me on his last visit. It was the box with the bug.

"Miss Killebrew," he said, turning his back on Carter, "my instructions are to tell you that we will need you to get Alex Hodder, on tape, and on camera, discussing how he—using you as a dupe—hired prostitutes to service Representative Anthony Licata during your trip to Lyford Cay, Bahamas, last year. We're gonna also need for you to get him to tie that into the fact that Hodder's oil industry clients paid for that trip, with the intention of bribing Licata in exchange for his favorable vote on an energy bill that stood to make them billions in profits. And in exchange for that, of course, we will not be looking at prosecuting you for public corruption."

"Would you like anything else?" Tee asked. "Maybe while she's at it she should get Hodder to confess to how he cheated on his taxes and provided a hideout for Osama bin Laden? That way she could score a hat trick—working for the FBI, the IRS, and the CIA all at the same time."

"Tee?" Carter said quietly.

"Fine," I said.

"Absolutely not," Carter said heatedly. "We had an agreement with you folks that Miss Killebrew would not be expected to try to entrap her former boss."

"You people are unbelievable," Tee went on. "It's an abuse of power, is what it is. You bully, you threaten, you intimidate, all in the name of ferreting out crime. Dempsey's a private citizen. She's committed no crime."

"Well, now," Harrell started. "The crime thing, that's still under investigation. We do have her American Express receipts, and we have statements from the prostitutes that she was the one who procured their services."

"Fine," I repeated, a little louder this time. "I'll do it. Okay? I'll wear the friggin' bug. I'll call up Alex Hodder, and I'll lure him down here, and somehow, I'll get him to admit what he did. All of it. Okay?"

"Say what?" Harrell said.

"Now, Dempsey," Carter said. "You absolutely do not have to do this."

"Yes," I said. "I'm afraid I do have to do it. I want this thing done. Over with. I'm sick of having these charges hanging over my head. I'm sick of wondering if I'll ever get another decent job, of wondering how I'll support myself . . . I'm sick of that feeling of dread I get when my phone rings or there's a knock at the door, of wondering if it'll be Agent Harrell here, or his sidekick, or God knows who else."

Carter was shaking his head in sorrow. Tee was rolling his eyes. Harrell was practically jumping up and down for joy.

"I'll do it," I told Harrell. "But in my own way, and in my own time."

"See," Harrell said slowly, "we got a deadline on this thing—"

"I said I'd do it," I repeated. "But I do have a pressing family commitment that has to take precedence. Once that's taken care of, I'll set it up. Myself," I emphasized. "I'll get Alex to agree to meet me, and then it's up to your people to make sure you get it all on tape or video or whatever. Because I am only doing this one time."

"Great!" Harrell said. He stood up, beaming. "The SAC is gonna be very pleased. And of course, Agent Allgood, I'll call her tonight and give her the good news."

"You do that," I said sourly, standing up and straightening the crease in my trousers.

He looked around the room with interest. "Say, how's that kitchen project of yours coming along? I'd love to see it. I watch all those home handyman shows on television, you know. Always got a little project of my own goin'. Kinda my hobby, you know? Maybe we could exchange restoration tips, like that."

I drew myself up to my full height and rested my fingertips ever so lightly on the sleeve of his starched shirt. "I don't think so, Agent Harrell," I said. "My kitchen is closed for the night."

Tee laughed out loud. "Come on, Jackson, old buddy," he said. "I think the lady has had enough of you. I'll show you to the door."

48

The three of us were sitting around the kitchen table. I brought out the dust-covered bottle of Jack Daniel's I'd found at the back of the top shelf in the closet in Uncle Norbert's study and held it up for the men's inspection. "The seal's never been broken," I pointed out.

"Your uncle was not a teetotaler," Carter said, "but he was a decidedly frugal man. This bottle was probably a Christmas gift from me, now that I think about it."

I took three tumblers off the kitchen shelf, cracked open a tray of ice cubes, and apportioned four small cubes to each glass before pouring three fingers' worth of whiskey into each glass and handing them to my guests.

As for myself, I topped the liquor off with a lot of water before rejoining Tee and Carter.

Carter took a sip of the whiskey and nodded approvingly. "Well, Dempsey," he said finally. "That was quite a performance you gave tonight."

"You were really, really scary looking, with the heels and the hair and all," Tee agreed. "And that suit! I think I felt my balls shrink a little when you opened that front door."

"Son!" Carter said, trying to look shocked.

"It's all right, Carter," I said, sipping my own whiskey. "I don't know if I would have put it quite that way, but I definitely was trying to assert myself with Jackson Harrell tonight."

"Because?" Tee said, looking at me quizzically over his glass.

"No offense, gentlemen," I said, "but I am sick and damned tired of being pushed around by men."

"Your father?" Carter asked sympathetically.

"Camerin Allgood showing up at his office put him over the edge," I said. "He was so angry he was foaming at the mouth when he called tonight. He can't fathom why I haven't been cooperating with the FBI."

"But you have," Carter said. "They're being completely unreasonable."

"As is Mitch," I said. "He's even looked into hiring a new 'top-notch' criminal attorney to represent me."

Carter shrugged and tried not to look hurt. "He's your father. He's concerned about your well-being. It's perfectly understandable. I'd be happy to catch your new attorney up to speed on things, if you'd like."

"I don't want a new attorney," I said quickly. "My father is not concerned with my well-being. He's mainly concerned with his own reputation."

"Surely not," Carter said.

"Don't get me wrong," I said. "My father cares about me. He just doesn't respect me, or my judgment. And let's face it, this mess I've gotten myself into hasn't given him much reason to have confidence in me."

"Your father is an idiot if he thinks you brought this on yourself," Tee said hotly. "Does he know anything about this Alex Hodder character?"

"Tee," Carter said slowly. "I'm not sure it's your place to call Mitch Killebrew an idiot."

"I've called him much worse," I told father and son.

"The thing is," I said, turning to Carter, "I really shouldn't even have asked you to come over here tonight. But I was just so . . . shaken . . . when Mitch called to tell me the FBI had come to see him. And then, when Harrell showed up on my doorstep . . . I just, I don't know, I was terrified."

"You had every right to call me," Carter said reassuringly. "I'm your attorney."

"But your retainer," I started. "The Catfish. Tee said it was totaled. And I don't have any money of my own. Not even any collateral." I looked around the kitchen. "The house is Mitch's. He's paying for all of this."

"The Catfish is far from totaled," Carter said. "Those old Crown Victorias were built to take a beating. I spoke to Shawn at the body shop this afternoon. He's ordered new glass for the windshields, and he thinks he can find some other body parts at an auto-salvage yard he knows about down in Jackson. Shawn assures me he can have the Catfish back to you by the end of the week."

"For real? But how much is that going to cost?"

"Not a thing," Carter said. "Shawn's girlfriend had an unfortunate shoplifting incident a few months ago. I worked things out with the judge and the merchant, and Shawn was truly grateful."

I took a long sip of whiskey, and appreciated the slow burn as I let it trickle down my throat.

I took a deep breath. "There are some things I need to tell you. Both of you. Alexander Hodder is a lot like Mitch Killebrew. I think that's probably what attracted me to him in the first place." I could feel the heat rising in my cheeks. I didn't dare look at Tee.

"My father is successful and demanding, and my whole life, no matter what I did, I could never quite figure out how to win his approval. When I decided to go to Georgetown, and take out loans to pay for it myself, because he refused to, I really thought I was striking a blow for my own independence. And when I did well in law school, and graduated with honors, I do think Mitch really was proud of me, in his own way.

"Of course," I added, "he was fit to be tied when I told him I was going to become a lobbyist instead of actually practicing law. Stephanie, one of my roommates in D.C.? She said I only became a lobbyist out of a perverse need to piss off my father."

I took another sip of Tennessee courage, and plunged ahead with my shameful confession.

"I had job offers from other firms. But as soon as Alex Hodder interviewed me, I knew I'd take the job, if it was offered. It was, and I took it."

The Piaget's watchstrap was starting to chafe. I slipped it off my wrist and set it on the tabletop, well away from our glasses.

"Alex knew I had a silly schoolgirl crush on him. He deliberately played me along, flirting and flattering me. I knew he was married. I'd met his wife at social functions and at Alex's birthday party. Of course, I convinced myself that their marriage was a sham. In my twisted little fantasy world, I figured one day, she would even give us her blessing and step out of the picture, since Alex and I were so obviously perfect for each other."

I rubbed at the irritated skin on my wrist and glanced up at Carter, and then at Tee.

"Sick, huh?"

"The son of a bitch exploited you," Tee said. He reached into his glass and pulled out an ice cube. He wrapped it in the paper napkin I'd given him, and taking my hand in his, gently pressed the cold, wet napkin to the reddened skin on my wrist.

I realized that I'd let my story get off track. And it was important that I get back on topic.

"Steph always said I had daddy issues. And she was right. Alex still thinks I have daddy issues. As far as he knows, I'm still the stupid, naive girl who called his cell phone nineteen times the night he fired me. As far as he knows, I'm still desperate for his attention and his approval. Alex underestimates me. And that, hopefully, is going to be his undoing."

Carter raised one of those fluffy white caterpillar eyebrows of his. "Dempsey?"

"Don't worry, Carter," I said. "I've had my wake-up call. In a major way. It's been painful, but totally worth it. I'm stronger and wiser. And just pissed off enough to do something about it. I have a plan."

"I have no doubt," Carter drawled. "Of course, I've only known you for a short time, but I can assure you that I have nothing but admiration for your intelligence, and your tenacity. The thing that brings me pause, however, is what I see as your alarming and emerging capacity as a schemer." He glanced over at Tee, who was still holding my hand in his.

"Son? I would advise you to proceed with all due caution in your relationship with this young woman." He nodded his head in my direction. "I have known her father's maternal family for many years. And I can now tell you, without reservation, that she is a Dempsey, through and through."

Tee nodded gravely. He raised my hand to his lips, and kissed first the back of my hand, and then the palm.

"I'll keep my eye on her," he promised.

49

E lla Kate was dressed and sitting in a wheelchair when I walked into her hospital room the next morning.

"You took your own sweet time gettin' here," she said, jerking her head meaningfully at the clock that hung on the wall next to the television.

"It's only nine o'clock," I told her, refusing to be badgered. "I had to fill out a lot of paperwork, and the nurse wanted to go over the doctor's discharge orders with me."

Her pale eyes narrowed. "What kinda orders? I'll tell you one thing right now, missy. They ain't puttin' no more tubes up me or in me. No, ma'am. Not no way."

"Relax, Ella Kate," I said. "It's nothing like that." I held up two slips of paper. "Just a couple of prescriptions. One for pain medication, and then something to make your bones stronger. The doctor says you have osteoporosis."

"What I have is bones that are seventy-nine years old," she said tartly. "Unless you've got a ticket for a time machine there, I doubt there's anything anybody can do about that."

"You got me there," I admitted. "I see you're all packed up."

Her bony hands clutched a wrinkled brown paper sack tight in her lap. "I got what I come with, so let's get this show on the road."

For the first time I noticed her apparel. Instead of her usual cotton slacks or housedress, or even a bathrobe, today Ella Kate was dressed in what appeared to be a set of green surgical scrubs so large that they fairly swallowed her.

"Uh, Ella Kate," I said. "Where'd you get the scrubs?"

"You mean these pajamas?" She plucked at the fabric of the collarless top and looked pleased. "Those fools in the emergency room cut my good dress all to pieces. I let 'em know what I thought about that. Raised such a ruckus I made 'em gimme something new to wear home. They're nice and roomy, I'll say that. The britches even have a drawstring."

"Wow," I said. "Comfort and style."

"And free," she said, nodding approvingly. "Now, let's go before somebody decides to stick me with a needle or add something to my bill."

"We're just waiting for an orderly," I said. "They won't let me wheel you out to the car myself."

"Probably afraid I'll sue 'em if something goes wrong," she said darkly. "Which I would. In a heartbeat."

The door to the room opened then, and a tall, thin black woman in white scrubs looked down at her clipboard, and then at Ella Kate.

"Mrs. Timmons? Are you all ready to go home?"

"It's Miss Timmons. And yes, I'm raring to get out of this place."

"I know that's right." The woman smiled widely, showing a gold incisor. "You been settin' in that wheelchair since I give you your bath this morning."

"Let's go already," Ella Kate said, refusing to be jollied.

I followed behind the wheelchair, and when we got outside the hospital, Tee was parked at the curb in the Mercedes. He hopped out and ran around to help transfer Ella Kate out of the chair and into the car.

"Hold on to this for me," she said, shoving the brown paper sack at him. He put it on the seat of the car and then put a hand under her arm, to lift her out of the wheelchair.

"I ain't crippled," Ella Kate snapped, starting to push herself out of the chair. But her face turned white, and she sank back down into the chair with a little gasp of pain.

"We'll give it a minute," Tee said kindly. And after a moment or two, Ella Kate clamped her lips tight and allowed herself to be slowly lifted and settled into the backseat of the car, surrounded by a bank of pillows we'd brought.

She closed her eyes and laid her head back against the leather seat and breathed heavily from the exertion of the move.

"I'm sorry," I said, turning around from the front seat. "I know you're in pain. We'll get you home and into bed just as quickly as we can. Shorty's waiting for you. He wandered around the house for an hour last night before settling in on your bed. I think he's been missing you."

"Fine," she muttered, keeping her eyes closed. And a moment later, I heard her snoring softly, her mouth slightly ajar.

She was still sleeping when we got to Guthrie, so Tee took me by the drugstore, to get her prescriptions filled, and to pick up the walker I'd arranged to buy.

When we finally got to Birdsong, Ella Kate was still sleeping. I sent Tee ahead to unlock the door, and to give me a moment alone with the old lady.

"Ella Kate?" I touched her shoulder, and she shuddered awake. "We're home," I told her.

"Good thing," she said, yawning widely. "I never could get no sleep in that durned hospital. Them nurses wake you up every hour on the hour to stick you or take your temperature or just ask you how you're sleeping."

I took a deep breath. I'd been dreading this moment. "Ella Kate," I started. "The doctor says that with your hip injury, you can't be going up and down stairs."

"I can walk!" Ella Kate protested. "She done told me I can walk fine."

"Yes, I know you can walk. But the stairs would be dangerous. So . . . I moved your bedroom downstairs."

"Moved?"

"Yes, ma'am. We cleaned out Norbert's old study. I scrubbed it, and got rid of all the magazines and bugs. And we put your furniture in there. Not all of it, of course, but the things that would fit. You'll need to have room to maneuver around with your walker. You and Shorty."

Ella Kate fixed me with a death stare. "You went into my room. You touched my things."

I nodded. "Yes."

"You got no right," she said bitterly. "Birdsong might be your daddy's house, but them things are mine. Norbert give 'em to me. They ain't a thing in that room that a Killebrew can lay claim to. Livvy's things, those are Dempsey family property. Not yours. Not your daddy's."

"You're right," I said gently. "They're your things. And I've put as many of them as would fit into your new room."

Tee opened the back door of the Mercedes. "Ella Kate? Ready to come home?"

"I ain't got no home," Ella Kate said, turning her back to me. "Reckon you can just tote me inside and drop me down any old place like a sack of taters."

We got Ella Kate into the house and her new bedroom. She bore the move—and the obvious pain—in stony silence. Her stoic expression softened only slightly when Shorty jumped up onto the bed and covered his mistress's face with passionate licks. I put her pill bottles on her bedside table, along with a glass of water, and set her walker beside her bed.

"Can I get you anything?" I asked. "Did they feed you breakfast at the hospital?"

"Get out," she said.

I closed the door behind me and went out to the kitchen to join Tee.

"I think you're growing on the old bat," he said jokingly, offering me a cup from the pot of coffee I'd made earlier in the morning.

"It's a good thing she can't really get around yet," I told him. "Or climb the stairs to my room. Otherwise I feel sure I'd wake up in the middle of the night and find her standing over me with a dagger or a loaded pistol."

"You're exaggerating," he said. "I'm sure she's grateful that you saved her life. Hers and Shorty's."

"I'm beginning to have second thoughts about that whole episode."

"She does seem a tad more hostile toward you than usual," he admitted. "Any idea what that's about?"

I set my cup down on the table and stood up. "Follow me," I told him.

Tee stood in the doorway to Ella Kate's room and gaped. He stepped inside and made his way between the crowded banks of furniture and knickknacks. He pointed at the stacks of photographs of Olivia Dempsey Killebrew.

"Does this creep you out the way it creeps me out?"

"It did at first," I admitted. "And then, after I finally pestered Bobby into telling me what he knew about this whole family-feud thing, it all started to make sense. I get why she hates my father and anybody named Killebrew. And I get why she's so permanently pissed off at the world."

Tee picked up an old black-and-white snapshot. It was of two young girls, and from the looks of their hairstyles, had probably been taken in the late forties or early fifties. The girls were dressed in oversize white men's shirts and dungarees with rolled-up cuffs. They were barefoot, seated on a porch swing, with their arms wrapped around each other, grinning goofily into the camera lens.

"Do we know these people?"

I nodded. "That's my grandmother Olivia on the right, and Ella Kate on the left."

"Hey," he said, looking from the picture to me. "Dad told me your grandmother was the hottest ticket in town back in the day. He was right. Olivia was a stone fox. And you look just like her."

"Thanks," I said, doing a little curtsy.

"And Ella Kate was a brunette!" he said. "Nowhere near as cute as your granny, but definitely a long way from the dried-up old prune she is today."

I sighed. "Well, she hasn't had an easy life, that's for sure."

"That's what Dad always says," Tee agreed. "Although he's never supplied me with any of the specifics. I guess I've known Ella Kate my whole life, but I can't remember a time when she wasn't the meanest old lady in town. She's only maybe ten years older than Dad, but I've never thought of him as old. Not like Ella Kate."

"Your dad is the youngest sixty-something I've ever met," I said. "I know his life hasn't always been easy, especially after losing your mom to cancer. But compared to Ella Kate, he's had a happy, fulfilled life. He had your mom, and you, and a home, and work that was meaningful, and friends."

Tee looked down at the snapshot of the two young girls. "And Ella Kate had a girl crush. On your grandmother."

"Or something like it," I said. I gave him the shortened version of what Bobby had divulged to me about Olivia's rushed marriage to my grandfather.

"Oh." Tee raised an eyebrow, and the way he did it reminded me exactly of the way Carter raised his eyebrows to express amusement or puzzlement. In the midst of all this discussion about family dynamics, it gave me great hope, for Tee, and for whatever future we might have together.

"Yeah," I said. "Exactly. The town must have been abuzz with gossip. The newlyweds and the baby moved in here at Birdsong, with Olivia's parents. I guess they gave my grandfather a job in management at the mill. And Ella Kate came back home to Guthrie and got a job at the mill too. Although Bobby made a point of telling me she 'wadn't a lint-head.' I think she did something in accounting. She didn't have a whole lot of other options open."

"But the happy couple didn't stay happy for long," Tee commented.

"Nope."

"How old was your father when they split up?"

"Maybe two? He's never talked that much about his childhood, or his parents. According to Bobby, everybody in town assumed Big Mitch basically blackmailed Olivia's father into keeping quiet and letting him take the baby."

"And Olivia stayed behind in Guthrie," Tee said.

"Right here in Birdsong," I said. "Bobby says his wife's auntie reported that after that Olivia was never the same again. She died when my dad was nine."

"I think I see where this is going," Tee said. He put the snapshot on the pile with the others. But I picked it back up and slipped it into the pocket of my slacks. Tee was right, I could definitely see something of myself in this picture of Olivia.

"The auntie came in to Birdsong, to help out with the washing and ironing," I told Tee. "One morning, she came upstairs, to this bedroom, I suppose, to ask Miss Olivia a question about something. Only Miss Olivia wouldn't wake up."

"Suicide?"

"The official story was 'heart trouble.' But she couldn't have been more than twenty-five or so when she died."

"Ooh," Tee said in a mock whisper. "The journalist in me smells a cover-up."

"And the romantic in me smells heartbreak," I said. "Come on." I tugged him by the hand. "Let's go back downstairs. This is all making me very sad. And it's too early in the day to be sad."

Tee pulled me close to his chest. "Don't be sad," he said, turning my chin up for a kiss. "Just because your grandfather was a prick, and your father is kinda, sorta a prick, that doesn't mean all the men in your life are destined to be monsters. For instance . . . me. I'm not a monster."

I put my arms around his neck and kissed him soundly. "No. You're definitely not a monster, T. Carter Berryhill. You are definitely one of the good guys."

He smiled. "Keep that in mind, young lady."

I winced. "Do me a favor, will you? Don't call me young lady?"

His cell phone rang then. He pulled it out of his pocket and glanced at the readout screen. "Oops. Gotta run. It's deadline day at the paper, and then I've gotta get over to the courthouse and file a will for probate. How about you? Are you playing nursemaid to Ella Kate all day?"

"Not all day," I said. "I'll hang around this morning, in case she needs anything, but after that, I've got a trap to set."

"And a rat to catch?"

"Hopefully."

Tee put his cell phone back in his pocket. "You really don't have to do this, you know. I think these FBI agents are full of crap. They don't have enough to make a case against you, so they're using you to do their job."

I stepped out into the hallway and closed the door to Ella Kate's room. "I really do have to do this, Tee. Alex Hodder used me. Now it's my turn to use him. And after this is all behind me, I can start thinking about what comes next."

"Us," Tee said firmly. "That's what comes next. You and me."

I patted the pocket of my slacks and felt the snapshot of my grandmother in happier days. "We'll see."

50

I sat at the kitchen table and stared down at my cell phone. I'd spent the past hour rehearsing what I'd say to Alex, and how I'd say it. You can do this, I told myself. You have to do it. His cell number was still programmed into my phone. All I had to do was touch the line with his number, and it would dial. All I had to do was work up the nerve.

The Jack Daniel's bottle was sitting on the countertop, right where I'd left it the night before. I opened the freezer and took out one of the aluminum ice cube trays. I took one of the tumblers from the dish drainer and filled it with ice cubes, and then I poured three fingers of courage over the ice.

It wasn't five o'clock. It wasn't even noon. I tipped the glass to my lips and took a swallow. It burned going down. I took another swallow, and this one didn't burn nearly as much.

When I'd downed the whiskey, I picked up my cell phone and tapped the icon for Alex Hodder's cell phone number. It rang once, and I got a recording telling me the number had been changed. I should have figured as much after the last time Alex had called me from a blocked number.

I tried calling the Hodder and Associates number, and got a recording saying the number had been changed to an unlisted one "at the request of the recipient." "Who ever heard of a lobbying firm with an unlisted number?" I muttered.

Damn. Reluctantly, I dug out the business card Jackson Harrell had given me on his first visit. I got the Atlanta field office, and asked for Harrell. The receptionist told me he was away from the phone, but invited me to leave a voice message.

"Agent Harrell, this is Dempsey Killebrew. I've been trying to reach Alex Hodder, but all the numbers I have for him have been changed or disconnected. So I may need your help with that."

I hung up and fumed. The kitchen counter was still waiting to be tiled, but I didn't want to start a new project until I could complete the job in one sitting. I walked out into the parlor and took another look at the peeling wallpaper there. I'd been itching to strip it from the walls, but it was nowhere near the top of my to-do list.

No matter. I was in the mood to tear down or rip up. Wallpaper seemed like a fine medium with which to work out aggression. I dragged a ladder into the parlor, then I ran upstairs and donned my work clothes—Norbert's overalls, a T-shirt, and the Chuck Taylors. I slipped the cell phone into the bib pocket of the overalls.

Back in the kitchen, I poured a cup of Spic and Span into the bottom of a bucket, and filled it halfway up with the hottest water I could stand. Then, taking a big sponge and a pair of rubber gloves and a plastic drop cloth, I went out to the parlor. I climbed up the ladder and with the sponge slopped soapy water at the top corner of the first strip of wallpaper, trying to make sure the liquid saturated the old paper. I wet the whole strip, from ceiling to floor. I waited five minutes, then, removing the rubber gloves, I picked at the edge of the wallpaper with my fingernail, worrying it away from the wall little by little. I slathered on some more soapy water, and was rewarded with the sight of the paper bubbling up as the chemicals dissolved the old glue. Finally, I grasped the upper edge of the first strip of paper and slowly pulled it away from the wall. I managed to pull off a two-foot strip of paper before it tore.

I was starting to soak down the bottom half of the wall again when I heard clattering noises from the front porch. I climbed down and went to the door.

Jimmy Maynard stood on the porch. He'd laid out a canvas drop cloth over the whole length of the porch floor, and was now leaning a tall aluminum extension ladder against the front wall. The day was sunny, but the temperatures were in the low sixties, and Jimmy was dressed, as always, in a pair of khaki Bermuda shorts, a paint-spattered Margaritaville T-shirt, and immaculate Top-Siders.

"Well, hey, Dempsey," he said. "How's it goin'?"

"Jimmy," I said, looking around the porch. "What on earth are you doing?"

"Finishin' what I started," he said.

"Jimmy, I can't have you painting my house," I protested. "I can't pay you for this. It's just not in the budget. I've got a new roof to pay for, and we've still got bathrooms to do."

His face colored deep red, and he stubbed at the floor with the toe of his shoe. "Uh, look, Dempsey. See, this is my way of apologizin' to you for the way I cut up at the country club the other night."

"Now wait," I said.

He shook his head obstinately. "Naw. I made an ass of myself and embarrassed you in front of half the population of Guthrie. Shirlene was right. It was inexcusable. And I want you to know, I've been on the wagon ever since. Well, not from beer, but whiskey. Definitely whiskey."

My lips twitched with suppressed laughter, and I hoped he wouldn't smell the Tennessee sour mash on my own breath. "You weren't that bad, Jimmy," I said. "Let's forget it—deal?"

He put out his hand and we shook. "Deal," he said. "But, uh, hey. You mind if I ask you something?"

"I guess not. Doesn't seem like it's possible to keep a lot of secrets in this town."

"Ain't that the truth?" he said. "What about you and the Berryhill kid? The other night. After I got myself shit-faced, the two of you dropped me at my place. You even put me to bed, right?"

I looked away, sensing what was coming. "That's right. Shirlene took your car back to her place."

"And what happened after that? Between you and Tee Berryhill? I mean, it's a damned fact that he's got the hots for you in a major way."

"What makes you think anything happened?" I asked, trying to sound casual.

Jimmy howled like a lovesick bassett hound. "I knew it. I'm passed out drunk in the bed and he snakes my girl right out from under me."

I gave Jimmy a playful punch on the arm. "Jimmy Maynard, you and I know that I am not your girl. You don't even really want me to be. I don't want to be mean about it, but you said it yourself. You're too old for me."

He laughed good-naturedly. "Well, hell, since you put it that way, I guess you're right. I reckon I'm just like the dog that chases cars because he can. He don't stop to consider what'd happen if he ever caught one."

"Well, maybe you need to consider chasing a car that's more vintage appropriate," I told him. "And speaking of which, Shirlene stopped by to see me the day after your, uh, accidental alcohol overdose," I said.

"Awww, hell," he said. "I bet she gave you chapter and verse about what a bad boy Jimmy Maynard is."

"Not at all. Of course, I didn't realize when we met at the club that you two had once been married."

He sighed. "Ancient history."

"Not that ancient. You know, I think she mostly came over here to check me out—to see just how involved I was with you."

"Oh yeah?" He looked at me sideways. "What'd you tell her?"

"The truth. That we were just pals. And that I intended to keep it that way."

"Gotcha," Jimmy said, trying to look sad. I was not convinced. "I bet she told you you were smart to steer clear of me."

"Not exactly. What she did say was that marrying Wayne Peppers was the biggest mistake of her life."

"She told you that?"

I crossed my heart with my forefinger, and just as I did, the bib of my overalls started to ring. I dug out the cell phone and looked at the readout screen. GOVERNMENT CALLER, it said.

"Excuse me, Jimmy," I said, and I turned and went back inside the house.

"Miss Killebrew?" The caller was Camerin Allgood. Now they were tag-teaming me.

"Hello, Agent Allgood," I said coolly, walking rapidly back to the kitchen. "I understand you met my father."

"He told you that, did he?"

"Bringing my father into this was totally unnecessary," I said. "And I don't appreciate it. At all."

"Understood."

She was a cool customer, I'd give her that. Unflappable. I wished I could be unflappable.

"You're looking for a phone number for Alex Hodder?"

"Yes. Neither of the numbers I have is working. I thought you people could probably get me a number for him."

Silence. Nothing. I could hear the wheels turning under that blond hair of hers.

"We might be able to do that," she said finally. "What did you have in mind?"

"I have in mind to call Alex and set up a meeting so we can get the proof you people need to put him in jail and my life back together again. That's what I had in mind."

So much for unflappable. I was more like unglued. I walked over to the counter and poured another three fingers of Jack Daniel's over the half-melted ice cubes in my tumbler. I knocked back half of it in one big swig.

"Miss Killebrew? This is what we were afraid of. You seem like a very emotional young woman. The SAC and I would like to sit down with you before you contact Mr. Hodder. We can coach you, give you some scenarios that might work."

"Emotional?" I said. "You think? This is my life we're talking about here, Agent Allgood. In case Agent Harrell didn't fill you in on the conversation we had yesterday, I'll repeat the gist of it for you. I'm going to do what you want. I'm going to set up a meeting with Alex Hodder. At that point, you can feel free to coach me, or give me scenarios or a printed script."

I downed the rest of the icy whiskey. And down deep in my gut, I felt a warm calm wash upward and spill over into my frontal lobe. I was aware that it was only a temporary, alcohol-induced state, but I didn't care. I was suddenly, magically, in control.

"And, Agent Allgood?" I said sweetly. "You can get us on video or film or satellite dish for all I care. But this is a one-shot deal, as far as I'm concerned. My lawyer is going to draw up an agreement, and you people and the rest of your gang at the Justice Department had better get on board. I want an agreement that in return for my full coopera-tion, no charges will be pursued against me."

"That's not how it works," she sputtered. "The U.S. attorney may agree to draft something, but—"

"All or nothing," I said. "But I'm going to need that phone number so I can get the ball rolling on my end."

She sighed, and then she gave me the number.

"We'll want to set up the meeting in D.C.," she said urgently. "Some-place public, where we can get clear access with our equipment. We'll fly you up a few days early, go through some possible scenarios. You'll have to get Hodder to be very explicit in admitting his role in the public-corruption charges. We wouldn't expect you to get him to admit to the bribes, but we would like to tie in Licata's vote on the oil bills. And speaking of which, it would be good to get Congressman Li-cata—"

"Good-bye, Agent Allgood," I said. "I'll be in touch as soon as I know something. And one more thing. Stay the hell away from my family."

I clicked the phone shut. I picked up the Jack Daniel's bottle and kissed the black label with an exaggerated smack. "My hero."

Even though my buddy Jack Daniel had my back, I was still uneasy about making the phone call and setting my plan in action. So I stalled. I boiled some eggs, diced them, and mixed them up with some mayon-naise and sweet-pickle relish. Egg salad. This was about the extent of my culinary repertoire. I'd had a roommate in college who swore she couldn't study without an egg salad sandwich, so I'd learned to make them by default. I slathered more mayonnaise on two slices of mushy white bread, slapped the sandwich together, and then cut it into four neat squares, which I placed on a plate. I fished a can of Coke out of the fridge, and poured it over a glass of ice.

I put the meal on an aluminum tray painted with garish white and green magnolia blossoms, and added a paper napkin and the salt shaker. I was just about to head down the hall to Ella Kate's room when I heard a slow, deliberate thump coming from that direction.

Thump. Slide. Thump. Slide. I held my breath, waiting for her to make her way to the kitchen.

I busied myself with making a sandwich for myself, augmented with slices of bread-and-butter pickle. I popped a Diet Coke and sipped a little. I hoped I wouldn't lose my buzz.

She thumped and slid her walker into the kitchen. Her face was pale, with a thin sheen of perspiration. She was still wearing the green hospital scrubs, now accessorized with a pair of slip-on disposable surgical booties.

"I made you some lunch," I said, pointing to the tray. "I was going to bring it to your room."

"Never mind," Ella Kate said. She held on to the walker with one hand, and tried to lift the tray with the other, but it wobbled precariously, slopping Coke over onto the tray.

"Let me help," I said, picking up the tray. "Do you feel like eating here in the kitchen, or shall I take the tray back to your room?"

I could tell she hated taking anything from me, especially assistance. But she was nearly helpless, and we both knew it.

"I'll eat here," she said finally, bumping the walker over toward the table. She grasped the back of the high-backed oak chair and gritted her teeth in concentration while trying to slide it back and away from the table without losing her balance.

I wanted to help, but knew it was the last thing she wanted from me. She swayed a little, then managed to lower herself onto the seat of the chair. Wordlessly, I slid the tray in front of her.

"I'll come back when you're done," I said, and I fled upstairs, to my own room, and my own impossible task. I sat on the edge of my bed and willed myself to get on with it.

I'd written Alex's number on the back of my hand. I punched in the number and held my breath. He picked up after two rings.

"Christ!" he said. "Dempsey? How the hell did you get this number?"

I'd imagined all kinds of opening lines to and from him, but this was one I hadn't thought about. I decided to go with the truth.

"Alex? Are you all right? Look, I'm sorry, but I got your number from the FBI, because the last number you called me from was blocked."

"The FBI! Christ."

"I know. It's unbelievable. Look, Alex. We really need to talk."

"I can't go into that right now," he said, his voice lowered. "I'll have to call you back. I'm in a meeting here."

"That's what I need to talk to you about," I said, deliberately letting a note of panic creep into my voice. "We need to meet, Alex. It's really, really important. These FBI agents keep showing up down here. They won't leave me alone. They even went to see my dad, at his office in Miami."

"What do they want with you?"

"What do you think they want?" I said coyly.

"I can't go into it right now," he repeated. I could tell he probably really was in some kind of meeting, but I wasn't about to let him off the hook that easily.

"Okay. I'll call you back. Will ten minutes give you enough time?"

"No!" he said sharply. "Let me have my secretary call you, and we'll slot a time to have that discussion."

His secretary? How damn dumb did he think I was? Oh. Yeah. That's right. In Alex Hodder's book I was the intellectual equal of a potted geranium. It made me so mad I could feel my toes curling in their slightly oversize Chuck Taylors. I gripped the cell phone so tightly my fingertips went white.

I wanted to tell him to have his alleged secretary slot him a time to go directly to hell.

From downstairs I heard the slow, methodical plunk, slide, of Ella Kate, making her agonizingly slow journey back to her room. I wanted to throw the phone down and run to her aid. Because she was helpless, right? But not so helpless she didn't have me twisted around her little finger again. Helpless was good. Helpless was effective.

I breathed in and then breathed out, and the Jack Daniel's fumes reminded me of my mission here. I uncurled my toes, and then I relaxed my hold on the cell phone.

"Dempsey? I'll have my secretary give you a call, all right?"

"No!" I cried. "Alex, I don't know what to do. My lawyer says I should just hand it over to the feds and be done with it, but I'm afraid. I don't trust them. But they're saying I could get fifteen years in prison. Prison! And I'd be disbarred. I wish I'd never shown that stupid golf scorecard to anybody. I should have just thrown it away."

"Dempsey," he said sternly. "What the hell are you talking about? What scorecard?"

"Alex, it's your golf scorecard. Remember, when we were down in the Bahamas, with Congressman Licata? You wanted me to arrange to have a massage for Tony, so you wrote the woman's phone number down on the back of your scorecard. And you gave it to me. Remember? I'd forgotten all about it, but then I found it again. That's what my lawyer wants me to hand over to the FBI."

"The scorecard . . . ?" Alex's voice, always so strong and confident, cracked a little. It was starting to dawn on him.

"From Lyford Cay," I added. "You and Tony only played twelve holes because Tony said his back was hurting him. Let's see. You birdied the third and fifth holes. But, oh, wow, I don't know a lot about golf, but it looks to me like Tony sucks pretty bad. He shot a seven three holes in a row! Okay, Alex," I said. "I know you're super busy. Just ask your secretary to call me as soon as possible, please?"

I punched the disconnect button. I threw myself backward on my bed and kicked my legs and thrashed my arms up and down to get the blood flowing again. I was back in the game.

51

According to my Piaget, exactly eleven minutes had passed when my cell phone rang again. I checked the caller ID and saw that Alex was calling me from a blocked number again. He was rattled, all right.

"Hello?" I said it tenuously. "Is that you, Alex?"

"Dempsey? I'm sorry to have been short with you before. I've been in meetings all morning with a new client, and I just really couldn't afford to blow them off at the drop of a hat."

"A new client? How nice," I said.

"My only client, at the moment," he said. "As you can imagine, this whole damned Hoddergate deal has had a disastrous effect on my business."

It hadn't exactly been great for my own life, I thought. At least Alex had a business. And a house, and a car, and a rich wife . . .

"I can only imagine," I said, struggling to sound sympathetic. "Reporters are pigs. That woman from the *Washington Post,* I could just wring her neck."

"That bitch," he ranted. "Shalani something. You can't tell me this isn't a race thing. In fact, this whole thing is just a liberal-media witch hunt. It's no accident that Tony Licata is a Republican, and the most senior member of the New Jersey delegation. If the Democrats can get him thrown out of office—"

"Alex?" I said meekly. "I'm really worried."

"Yeah," he said abruptly. "Look, Dempsey, that scorecard you mentioned. I don't know what you think it means, but I can assure you, you've got things all mixed up. Why would your lawyer want you to give it to the FBI?"

"That's what I want to talk to you about, Alex," I said. "I just don't really know where to turn. He's telling me one thing, and the FBI is telling me something else, and I can't sleep at night, worrying about it. And then I found the scorecard from Lyford Cay. It was in the pocket of my bathrobe, Alex. Remember, that night, you came up to my hotel room, and we were supposed to go to dinner together, but then you said Tony wanted a massage. I was really looking forward to that dinner," I said sadly. "I had a new dress and everything, you know? I still have it. It's hanging in the closet here in this dump where I'm living, and the price tag is still on it and everything."

"Dempsey!" Alex said. "I have no memory of any of this nonsense you're talking about at Lyford Cay. It's unfortunate that you took it upon yourself to hire those women, but it has nothing to do with me, and we both know it."

I sighed deeply. Dramatically even. "All right, Alex. I guess the weekend didn't mean as much to you as it did to me. But I was sure that golf game meant a lot to you. I mean, you even signed the scorecard! I guess you were pretty excited about the first nine holes, shooting a thirty-two and everything. The second half didn't go as well, but if I were you, I'd still want to save that scorecard. Especially because of that phone number you wrote on the back. You won't believe this, Alex, but after I found the scorecard, I called the number. Guess what? Tiki Finesse still has the same number and everything. I guess she's sort of a local celebrity down there now. Her hourly rates have gone way up."

I could hear shallow breathing from the other end of the line. "Alex? Are you still there?"

"I'm here," he said sourly. "What do you want?"

"I'm not even sure," I wailed. "I'm just really confused. I'm broke, and my father isn't even speaking to me because of this whole mess. I'm stuck down here in this hellhole of a town. I can't work—I mean, who'd hire me?"

"I'm not sure I'm the best one to ask about any of this," Alex said. "Hell, I'm not even sure I should be talking to you, period."

"I know," I said, letting a little tremor work its way into my voice. "It's awful. And the thing is . . . I miss you, Alex. I'm afraid of what could happen to you." I let out a tiny little sob of despair. "If the FBI saw that scorecard, with Tiki's phone number on it, in your hand-writing—"

"I can take care of myself," Alex said. "Look, Dempsey, maybe you should come up here for a weekend. It's hard to talk on the phone. Maybe if I saw that scorecard you're talking about, I'd have a better understanding of things."

"Oh God," I said breathlessly. "I would love to come to D.C. for a weekend. To get away from here? That would be awesome. I could see Stephanie and Lindsay and maybe get my nails done."

"I could probably clear my calendar for this weekend," Alex said. "Move some meetings around."

"Oh," I wailed. "Oh no. I can't come to D.C. I'm broke. Ruby made me give back my company AmEx card, and all my credit cards are maxed out. Alex, it wouldn't be safe for you to be seen with me up there, after all those hateful stories and photos they've run of you in the *Post*. Everybody in town knows what you look like."

"We wouldn't meet out in the open, for God's sake, Dempsey," Alex said impatiently. "I could just come up to your hotel room."

"Which the FBI would probably have bugged or something," I prompted. "Anyway, I just told you. I'm broke. I can't afford a plane ticket or a hotel room. I can't even afford a cab ride to the airport in Atlanta."

There was another pause, more shallow breathing. I was pretty sure the mention of the FBI bugging hotel rooms had given his blood pressure a little goose.

"This is ridiculous," he said finally. "I can't talk about this right now."

He hung up.

I stared down at the phone. Just when I'd thought I almost had him ready to swallow the bait, the slimy bastard had somehow managed to wriggle off the hook. What now? Should I call him back, beg him to meet with me?

I stood up and belly-flopped down onto the bed. I lay there, face-down, spread-eagled, waiting for inspiration to strike.

In the end, it wasn't inspiration at all. It was an ill-tempered seventy-nine-year-old with a bum hip and a dog with a tiny bladder.

"Dempsey!" Ella Kate's shrill voice echoed in the high-ceilinged downstairs hall. "Dempsey! You hear me, girl?"

I put the cell phone back in the bib of my overalls and got up and walked downstairs. The door to her new room was ajar, so I poked my head inside.

"I'm right here, Ella Kate," I said patiently. "Is there something I can get for you?"

She'd somehow managed to move the armchair I'd put at her bedside into position in front of the picture window, and she'd pulled aside the curtains to give herself a better view of the outside world. "Shorty needs to go out," she said, leaning back in the chair. The cocker spaniel pawed urgently at the door. "And that Jimmy Maynard fella is outside paintin' this here house green. I'd like to know who give him the right to paint a house bilious green without any say-so from folks who've been livin' all along in a perfectly fine pink house. Who's payin' for that foolishness, is what I want to know."

"I'll let Shorty out," I said. "And as for Jimmy, I—"

She pointed out the window with a knobby finger. "And another thing. There's a silver car settin' right out in front of this house with them two FBI agents sittin' in the front seat. Been out there for the past half hour. What do you reckon they're up to?"

52

I crouched down in the shrubbery at the end of Birdsong's driveway and peered out around the edge of an overgrown camellia bush. For once, I was glad of a to-do that I hadn't had the time or energy to actually do. I could see the tail end of the government-issue sedan, and sure enough, the heads of agents Harrell and Allgood. For a moment, I flashed on an eighties movie I'd seen, where the good guy realizes he's being followed by the cops—and he sneaks up behind the cop car and sticks a banana in the tailpipe. I was fresh out of fruit, and anyway, I wasn't really sure what a banana in the tailpipe would accomplish, except give me a fit of the giggles, which I was already on the verge of.

Instead, I crept along the curb, keeping low, trying not to snigger, until I was right behind the sedan. I could hear them talking; they were discussing whether to get Chinese or Mexican for lunch. If they'd asked, I would have suggested they try the Corner Café, but they hadn't asked my opinion. And they hadn't asked my permission to snoop around outside my house either.

I couldn't keep up the creeping routine for long, my thigh muscles were screaming from the unfamiliar exertion. So I duckwalked up along the passenger side of the car, and when I was even with the front door, I popped up.

"Hey!" I said, pressing my face against the window.

"Jesus!" Agent Harrell exclaimed. He dropped the black plastic doo-hickey he'd been aiming at the house, and in the excitement, he knocked over a cup of coffee that had been sitting in the console cup holder.

"Christ!" Agent Allgood cried, mopping at the hot coffee stain spreading over her ivory wool slacks.

"Oh, sorry," I said, opening the sedan's back door and sliding onto the seat. "Did I surprise you guys?"

"Not at all," Agent Allgood said, tossing a coffee-soaked paper napkin to the floor. "Do we look surprised?"

"You kinda do," I said. "Whatya doin' out here? You should have rung the doorbell. I made egg salad sandwiches for lunch. It's my specialty, and if you don't mind my saying so, it's a lot better than that crappy chop suey over at the Canton Buffet."

"You were eavesdropping on us?" Harrell asked, his voice incredulous.

"Sure. You were eavesdropping on me, weren't you?"

"Cute," Camerin Allgood said. She opened the door and got out of the car. "Come on, Jack, these slacks are wool. I need to get this coffee stain out before it sets."

"Yeah, coffee's a bitch to get out of wool," I agreed, getting out of the backseat. "Come on inside, and I'll see if I can find some Spray 'n Wash or something."

Half an hour later, Camerin Allgood was sitting at the kitchen table, wrapped in my bathrobe, cutting the crusts off her egg salad sandwich. Jackson Harrell polished off two sandwiches, then got up to admire the island counter Bobby had made me.

"This is gorgeous," he said, running his hand over the satiny wood. "Your guy made this himself? Right here in Guthrie? You know what something like this would run up in Dunwoody, where I live? You couldn't touch this for under ten thousand. This is some craftsmanship right here."

"Jack," Agent Allgood said wearily. "Can we swap household tips a little later? I really think we need to brief Ms. Killebrew on her next move, in case Hodder calls her back."

"You don't think he'll call?" I asked nervously. The Jack Daniel's buzz had worn off, and I was growing increasingly anxious, staring at my phone, willing it to ring.

"He'll call," Harrell said, opening one of the cabinet doors to examine how it was made. "Dempsey, is it all right if I call you that? Is this an oil-based stain, or did you go acrylic?"

"Oil," I said. "And you can call me Dempsey if I can call you Jack."

Agent Allgood rolled her big blue eyes heavenward. "If you'd just let us brief you before you called him, I would have explained why it would be better to have the meet in D.C. than down here."

"I'm not going to Washington to meet Alex Hodder," I said. "He knows too many people up there. Anything could happen. If he wants to bribe me, he can just come down here and do it on my turf."

"And that's another thing," Agent Allgood said. "We never discussed blackmail. That was never on the agenda."

"Maybe not yours," I said calmly. "But I think blackmail is the only way to get Alex to play ball. He'd never agree to talk to me otherwise. You were listening in. He thinks I'm a dumb little twit. He actually thought at first that he could bullshit me into believing that golf scorecard was a figment of my imagination. Blackmail is what Alex Hodder understands. Low-life, double-dealing scumball that he is."

"What if he doesn't call back?" she asked. "What's your play then?"

"I don't have one," I admitted. "So he's gotta call."

"Just for the sake of conversation," Harrell asked. "How much were you planning on sticking him for?"

"Jack!" She got up and paced around the room, and the bathrobe, ankle length on me, hit just below her knees. She did have good legs. "This isn't good," she fretted. "Not kosher at all."

"I've been thinking I don't want to seem greedy," I told Harrell, nibbling on a potato chip. "Nothing like a million dollars."

"That's good," Allgood said, "since according to him, his business is sucking wind."

"I doubt he's in any danger of starving," I said. "Have you seen their house? In Georgetown? They've got a place on Martha's Vineyard too. He invites big clients up there in the summer, to go out on their sailboat."

"Her sailboat," Allgood said. "Everything's in the wife's name. We checked."

"And that's another reason to stay reasonable," I said. "I'm thinking two hundred thousand. If I asked for a hundred thousand, Alex wouldn't take me seriously. But two hundred thousand, he should be able to raise that, no problem. If I really were the type of person to blackmail somebody like Alex Hodder, that's what I'd ask for."

"Chump change," Harrell said dismissively. He swooped in on the potato chips and scooped up a handful. He had really big hands. "How you gonna live on a couple hundred K in D.C.? The price of gas, rent, food, another year or so, you'd be living on ramen noodles and generic peanut butter."

"I could live pretty well down here on that kind of money," I said. "Once we get the house finished, in another month or so, I could maybe hang out a shingle and practice law. I'd have to take a crash study course to pass the Georgia bar exam though, and I'll probably need a new car. They say the Catfish can be fixed, but it's such a gas hog—"

"People?" Camerin Allgood looked disgusted. "What the hell are you two talking about? We can't let her blackmail Alex Hodder. Even if he is a lowlife scumdog, it's against the law. And anyway," she said, "it's not going to happen. He hasn't called. He's not going to call." She sighed deeply. "This thing is a major career fucker. I should have listened to my dad and stuck with ballet."

My cell phone rang, vibrating merrily on the wooden kitchen tabletop.

I reached for it, but Harrell planted his big paw on top of mine. "Give it another ring. You know, play hard to get. And hey, don't undersell yourself. As long as it's all rhetorical, anyway, go for three hundred thousand. Think of it as the difference between a Honda Accord and a BMW."

The phone rang for a third time. Agent Allgood swatted Harrell's hand. "Would you please let her answer the friggin' phone?"

My hands were trembling as I flipped the phone open. My throat felt like it was closing shut. "Hello?" I croaked.

"Dempsey?"

"Alex?"

"Are you alone?" His voice was barely above a whisper.

"No," I croaked. "I've got two FBI agents sitting right here in my house, listening in on every word you say. Hang on, I'll put you on speakerphone."

Jackson Harrell's eyes nearly bugged right out of his genial face as I did just that. Agent Allgood scrambled around in her pocketbook before bringing out what looked like a miniaturized tape recorder.

"Not funny, Dempsey," Alex said. "Not the least goddamned bit funny. And not your style at all."

"I'm sorry, Alex," I said mournfully. "I'll try to be serious from now on. Okay? Are you ready to take me seriously now?"

"What do you want?"

"I want world peace, a planet in perfect harmony. I want the FBI to leave me the hell alone. I want a Porsche 911 Carrera convertible and I want to stay out of jail and not get disbarred," I said promptly. "I don't think it would be fair to ask you to foot the bill for the peace and global harmony thing, but on the other hand, I figure it'll cost me a minimum of three hundred thousand for the rest of my wish list, and since you got me into this stinking mess in the first place, I don't feel bad about asking you to pay to get me out of it."

I was shocked to see Camerin Allgood pump her arms over her head and mouth something that looked like You Go Girl!

"That's a lot of money," Alex said. "You may think I'm rich, but you are seriously deluded, Dempsey. My professional life is in the toilet, thanks to you. I've got lawyers on round-the-clock retainer, and my doctor says I have bleeding ulcers."

"I do think you're rich, Alex," I said. "As for a professional life, mine is gone. Toast. So excuse me if I seem a little, well, callous toward your well-being. I've got lawyers to pay too, you know. Although I can't afford the kind you've hired."

"This is getting us nowhere," Alex said finally.

"I agree totally," I said. "But, Alex, I want you to know that I never, ever thought I would be in a position like this." I gave a little sniff, to let him know how bad I felt about what I was going to say. "I'm backed into a corner here, Alex, and I don't know where to turn, or what else to do. The absolute only thing I have going for me is this little-bitty square of cardboard. The scorecard, from the Lyford Cay Resort golf course. With your signature on the back, along with the phone number of a known prostitute."

I heard a sharp intake of breath on the other end of the phone.

"This isn't like you, Dempsey," he said sadly. "I am stunned. Stunned and feeling deeply, deeply betrayed."

Harrell balled up his fists and rubbed them under his eyes, as though he were shedding real tears for Alex Hodder's sense of personal betrayal.

"Well, Alex," I said. "That's just something I'm going to have to learn to live with."

"Let's say I can meet the figure you just mentioned," Alex said. "What would I get in return?"

"The scorecard," I said promptly.

"Forgive me for asking, but why would you be willing to sell me the only thing that proves your alleged innocence in this matter?"

"It's all I've got," I said truthfully. "My lawyer down here isn't the sharpest knife in the drawer, but he seems to think the feds aren't really interested in me, per se. Right now, if you take that scorecard out of the picture, it's a matter of he said, she said. They want to put Tony Licata in jail. My lawyer says I'm young, and fairly innocent looking."

"Innocent my ass," Alex exclaimed. "Blackmail? This just isn't like the Dempsey Killebrew I know. Is there somebody down there—some boyfriend, maybe—who's putting you up to this?"

"A boyfriend? Is that what you think? That I'm too dumb to come up with a way to squeeze money out of you all by my own stupid, bimbo self?"

"No, no," he said hastily. "That's not—"

"The price just went up, asshole," I said, steel in my voice. "Four hundred thousand. You can come down here to Guthrie to pick up your merchandise. How about I pencil you in for Monday, noon? I'll get my secretary to move some meetings around."

"Wait," Alex said. "Monday? I can't raise that kind of money by then."

"Call me from the Atlanta airport, when you get in, and I'll give you directions to the meeting place," I said. "And, Alex?"

"What else?" he said bitterly.

"Better bring cash. Your check's no good with me."

"Four hundred thousand?" Camerin Allgood said. "Are you insane?"

"A Porsche 911 Carrera convertible," Jackson said, nodding his head up and down. "Girl, I like your style."

The back door opened, and Jimmy Maynard came in, whistling. He stepped carefully out of his Top-Siders, which were still spotless, and padded over to the sink, where he soaped and washed his hands. Drying them on a paper towel, he turned and gave Camerin Allgood, still dressed in the bathrobe, a long, appraising look.

He flashed her a brilliant smile and extended his hand. "Hi there, gorgeous. I don't believe we've been introduced before. I'm Jimmy Maynard. What brings a tall drink of water like you to our fair village?"

Agent Allgood went over to her briefcase and brought out her leather badge holder, which she held up for Jimmy's inspection. "I'm Special Agent Camerin Allgood," she replied. "And I'm here on official government business."

His smile faded and he took a step backward. He gave me a reproachful look. "You coulda warned me she was a G-man."

"G-woman," I corrected, laughing. "And anyway, what was that you were telling me about going on the wagon and not chasing cars you couldn't catch?"

He sighed. "What can I tell you? Old habits die hard." He nodded respectfully at Agent Allgood. "Excuse my rudeness, ma'am. I hope it won't reflect poorly on my friend Dempsey here, who is a law-abiding citizen."

He turned to me. "I've got the porch about finished, Dempsey. I'm gonna knock off for lunch, and come back later on this afternoon to cut in around the windows."

"Jimmy," I said. "You really, really don't have to paint my house."

"I always finish what I start," he said stubbornly. He gave me a wink and left.

Agent Allgood walked over to the back door and watched him walk down the driveway. "He doesn't look like any housepainter I've ever known before."

"Oh, Jimmy's not really a housepainter," I told her. "He's actually quite successful in real estate and insurance. He just paints other people's houses as a hobby, sort of."

"Cam?" Agent Harrell said. "Can the two of you quit ogling men long enough for us to discuss the business at hand?"

"Right," she said crisply. "Alex Hodder. It's going to be a pleasure to put that guy behind bars."

amerin Allgood stood over the ironing board in my kitchen and stared down at her spot-cleaned slacks. "Hey," she said. "It worked. The coffee's gone. Thanks."

"No problem, Agent Allgood," I said. "I got to be pretty good at stain removal while I was living in D.C. What with the cost of dry cleaning and all."

"Next thing, you girls will be going out together for cosmos and pedicures," Jackson Harrell said. "Could we please discuss some logistics here?"

"Bite me, Jack, okay?" Allgood said, smoothing the iron over her slacks.

"We need a place for the meet," Harrell said. "Someplace a little out of the way, but where our equipment can get decent reception."

"Normally, we'd have you meet him in a hotel room," she told me.

"Sorry. I'm not checking into the Econo Lodge," I said. "How about the café, on the square?"

"No good," Harrell said. "I've eaten there. Always a big crowd, so there'd be too much ambient noise. And that's a shame, because the food there is pretty decent. Man, that chicken and dumplings they do on Thursdays? And the fried okra? Makes me wanna slap my granny."

"Jack!" Allgood said. "Focus. Meeting."

"Right," Harrell said. "We're gonna need someplace quiet. Someplace we can install the cameras, like that. What about right here at the house?"

"No way," I said quickly. "My, uh, cousin, is just home from the hospital. She's old, and crotchety, and no telling what she'd do if Alex Hodder showed up here."

"Probably wouldn't work anyway," Allgood said. "Hodder's pretty cagey. He wouldn't trust you not to have your house bugged. Look, Jack. Why don't we take a drive around town, scope things out a little bit. We'll find a place, get things set up, and we'll call her as soon as we're ready."

Harrell nodded and stood up. "Sounds like a plan. You gonna put on your pants before we go?"

"Bite me," she said succinctly. She walked into the hallway with her slacks draped over her arm, and a minute later, she was back, fully clothed, with my bathrobe over her arm.

"Here you go," she said. "Thanks for the loan. And the lunch."

"You're welcome," I said. I sensed a bonding between us. We probably wouldn't be going out for drinks anytime soon, but at least she wasn't still trying to put me in jail for the rest of my adult life.

I walked the two FBI agents to the front porch. "What should I do if Alex calls back?" I asked. "You know, like, what if he tries to back out, or whatever?"

"Just keep strong," Allgood told me. "Remember, you're in control now. Not him. In fact, if he does call back, just don't answer. Keep him guessing."

"Like all you women do," Agent Harrell said. "Torture the bastard."

Camerin Allgood shot him a look. "So. We'll let you know about the meet place as soon as we've got it set up."

I nodded.

She bit her lip, and fussed with the strap of the briefcase slung over her shoulder.

"Hey, uh, Dempsey," she said awkwardly. "I feel kinda bad about something."

"What's a little intimidation and harassment between pals?" I said lightly.

"Well," she said. "It wasn't like it was something I enjoyed or anything. It's my job, you know? Definitely not my favorite part of the job though."

"What are you talking about, Agent Allgood?" I asked.

She shot Harrell a look. He frowned and shook his head, as if to warn her off. But she plunged ahead.

"Your mom, okay?" she said. "It wasn't just your dad I went to see. I went out to California too. To talk to your mom. She seemed like a pretty cool lady. Way too cool to have ever been married to your dad."

I felt my breath catch. "You did what?"

"She flew out to California and showed up at your mother's house," Harrell said helpfully. "To talk her into talking you into helping us out."

I took a step backward, into the house. "I don't believe you people." I slammed the door in their faces.

54

I didn't have long to ponder the implications of a meeting between the FBI and my mother. In fact, I hadn't even had time to find my cell phone to call Lynda before I heard a car come roaring up to the curb outside and slam on the brakes.

"Dempsey?" Ella Kate called from down the hallway. "Dempsey! Girl, what is going on around here?"

I went back to the front door and peeked through the sidelights. The car was a gleaming black Cadillac Escalade. As I watched, a petite woman got out of the driver's side. Her long, honey blond hair fell in soft waves to her shoulders, accented by braided dreadlocks on either side of her deeply tanned, heart-shaped face. She wore a form-fitting chrome yellow long-sleeved top, and an orange-and-yellow-flowered chiffon skirt that fluttered around her knees. Her shapely tanned legs ended in orange platform espadrilles. She wore huge white-rimmed sunglasses, so I couldn't see the expression on her face, and she had so many chains and strings of beads and baubles around her neck and wrists, that I could hear, from inside the house, the chink of glass and gold as she walked, haltingly, up the front walkway of Birdsong.

She stopped, halfway up the walk, and lifted the sunglasses up and into her tangled mass of curls, staring up at the house through kohl-rimmed eyes, and shaking her head slowly, as though she couldn't believe what she was seeing. Her coral-tinted lips moved, and I could read what she was saying, even from where I stood, staring out at her.

"Oh. My. God."

I opened the door and stepped onto the porch. "Lynda?"

She dropped the bulky Louis Vuitton carryall to the ground and flew up the front steps.

"Sweetheart!" she cried, flinging her arms around me and hugging me tightly—so tightly that I could feel the jagged chunks of automotive glass on her necklace biting into my sternum.

"Lynda!" I gasped, struggling to extricate myself from her embrace. "Mom, what are you doing here?"

She let me go, but cradled my face between her long, bejewelled fingers. "Angel," she crooned. "How could I stay away? Knowing what my little girl is facing?" With a fingertip, she traced a line under my eyes.

"Such dark circles," she tsk-tsked. "You haven't been sleeping. Or moisturizing properly."

"I'm fine, Mom," I said. "Really. I'm glad to see you, but really, there was no need."

"Of course there was a need," she said briskly. "Now, let's get my things out of the car, and then we can figure out this situation of yours."

I followed her to the Cadillac. "Is this yours?"

"Oh Lord, no," Lynda said, holding out the key fob and giving it a click so that the trunk popped open. "It's a rental. You know I never drive a domestic car. But on such short notice, there wasn't time to try to find a Jag or a Benz. Leonard swears this was the best he could do."

The trunk held two more Louis Vuitton bags, one a small twenty-one inch, the other an elephant-size affair that could have held all of my own belongings, with room to spare. Lynda reached in and grabbed the smaller suitcase. I heard the distinct sound of glass bottles clinking together.

"The Stoli," she said, catching my look. "I mean, Guthrie's still dry, right? I just wasn't taking any chances. Not in this kind of an emergency."

I wrestled the larger suitcase out of the trunk. It weighed as much as an elephant too.

"Um, Lynda, this suitcase is pretty big. Just how long were you planning on staying?"

She was already heading up the front walk. "As long as it takes to save your life," she called back.

When I caught up with her, she'd dropped her bags in the foyer, and was walking around the parlor, taking it all in with a practiced eye.

"Well," she said, her voice trailing off. "This is . . . challenging."

"You should have seen it when I got here," I told her. "Not exactly what I was expecting."

She pursed her lips. "I'm sure your father described it as Cinderella's castle. Am I right?"

"Not a castle," I said. "But he did tell me it was a showplace. And in all fairness to him, the photo he had made it look pretty fabulous."

"And that photo was taken when? During the Nixon administration?"

"I guess he thought, because his mother's family was such a big deal down here, owning the bedspread mill and all, it was still okay."

"Ah, yes," Lynda said mockingly. "The storied home place of the storied Dempsey family. Look away, look away, look away, Dixieland."

"It's not that bad," I said quietly.

She saw the hurt on my face. "Of course it's not," she said quickly. "Listen to me! I'm here five minutes and already your father's negative energy is seeping into my aura. It's a lovely house, Dempsey, and I can tell you've done amazing things with it. Now, let's open up my suitcase, and fix ourselves a little 'freshie,' and you can show me everything."

True to her motto of Be Prepared, Lynda had left nothing to chance. The smaller of the two vintage Louis Vuitton suitcases had originally been manufactured to hold eight pairs of shoes. But my mother had modified the suitcase to her own needs, slipping bottles of Stoli, tonic water, Perrier, and almond-stuffed olives, not to mention two bags of limes, into the elastic-ruched satin pouches of the suitcase.

While I fixed the "freshies" according to her detailed instructions, Lynda walked about the kitchen, exclaiming over the new island, the stripped pine floors, even my beloved junkyard sink.

"It's like a movie set," she declared, seating herself at the kitchen table. "I love it. So real. So organic. Only my brilliant daughter could have conceived of such a transformation."

"You like it?" I asked, taking a cautious sip of my drink. Mindful of my earlier intake of Jack Daniel's, I'd deliberately added only a drop or two of vodka to my tonic and lime. "I've still got a lot to do in here. Bobby just taught me how to lay tile for the counters. I mean, marble would have been great, or even granite, but that was so not in my budget."

"Budget!" Lynda said, taking a long sip of her own drink. "Listen to you. Making budgets, stripping floors and cabinets, laying tile. And all the time these horrible federal agents are hounding you."

"Well, maybe not hounding me," I admitted. "Listen, Lynda. I am so, so sorry they dragged you into this. I love seeing you, but it was totally unnecessary for them to get you involved. I'm absolutely fine. We've got things worked out, and in a few days, this whole nightmare will be over."

I picked the slice of lime out of my drink and sucked the rind. "See? We can have a nice visit this weekend, and then you can fly back to California and Leonard. He's probably already going crazy without you."

She frowned. "Hmmm. Not so much. Anyway, I have no intention of abandoning you again. I am here. Come what may, for the duration."

"But where will you stay?" I blurted out. "You do realize, we don't have a Ritz-Carlton in Guthrie. We don't even have a Motel Six."

Now it was my mother's turn to look hurt. "I thought I'd stay here with you, of course. It's such a huge old place. And your mother is a girl of very simple needs, Dempsey, I can assure you. Just give me a little cot up in the attic someplace, and I'll be fine. Unless, you'd rather I leave . . ."

She was doing it. Making me feel guilty. "No, no," I protested. "It's not that I want you to leave. I love having you here. But the house looks bigger than it really is. It's a work in progress. But that's all right. You can have my room, and I'll sleep in Ella Kate's old room. No. I'll sleep in Norbert's. The mattress is awful, but that's okay."

"Ella Kate?" Lynda frowned. "You mean that batty old aunt of your father's? I didn't even know she was still alive, let alone living here at Birdsong."

I sighed and started to reconsider my stand against vodka. "It's a long story," I said finally. "But basically, Ella Kate moved in here when Great-uncle Norbert got sick. She took care of him, and after he died, she just sorta . . . stayed. And anyway, she's not Dad's aunt. She's a distant cousin. Of sorts."

"She looked ancient when I met her, back before you were even born," Lynda said. "And that was nearly thirty years ago. I still don't understand why she's living here, with you. Shouldn't she be in a nursing home or something?"

"Ella Kate is seventy-nine," I said. "And except for the fact that she just totaled a car and fractured her hip, and the fact that she has breast cancer, she's actually in pretty decent shape, for her age."

Lynda set her drink down on the tabletop. "Breast cancer. Well, that settles it. I wasn't going to say anything, but since you brought it up, I think I have to let you know that I've been feeling . . . assaulted with wave after wave of negative ions since I walked in the door of this house. It's very unsettling."

"Negative ions?" I said blankly. "Here? At Birdsong?"

"Don't worry, precious," Lynda said. "I'll take care of everything." She walked out to the hallway, and I could hear her unsnapping the lock on one of her suitcases. A moment later, she was back with what looked like a home-made broom. The handle of the broom had been made from a slender tree limb, stripped of all its leaves. Tied to the head of the broom, with an inch-wide wrapping of raffia, was a large bundle of dried-out-looking weeds.

"Now then," Lynda said. She closed her eyes and took a deep breath. She exhaled slowly, then inhaled and exhaled.

She marched out to the foyer. I followed in her wake. She opened the front door wide. Then, standing in front of the door, she began making sweeping motions in the air, as though sweeping imaginary particles of fairy dust outside. After a minute or so of that, she began walking slowly through the downstairs rooms of the house, moving clockwise, sweeping the air. She swept up high, and she swept low, down at baseboard level. And while she swept, she hummed a high-pitched wordless tune.

I followed along behind. She swept the parlor and the dining room. She swept the downstairs bath, and the kitchen and the hallway. When we got to Ella Kate's closed bedroom door, I held my fingers to my lips, to gesture that we should be quiet. Lynda nodded knowingly, and swept vigorously around the entire door frame.

She started for the stairway. I paused, and then decided not to stop her. After all, maybe the house did have some negative ions. It wouldn't hurt to let my mother chase them away.

Lynda did a repeat of her downstairs ritual, spending extra time in Ella Kate's old bedroom. Her eyes widened when she saw the stacks of furniture and knickknacks, but she said nothing. Apparently silence was an important part of the ceremony. She swept my own room too, even going so far as to open the closet door and all the windows, giving them a vigorous going-over.

She swept back down the upstairs hallway, and then down the stairs. Finally, she swept her way into the kitchen. She stopped only to open the kitchen door wide, at which point she made one last, huge, grand sweep out the door.

Satisfied, she closed the door and smiled. "There now."

She glanced over at me. "Match please."

I found the box of wooden kitchen matches in a drawer by the back door and handed her the box.

"Light it please," she said. I did.

"Now, light the herbs," she instructed. Again, I did as she asked, holding the match to the end of the leafy sticks. It took a moment, but soon a thread of white smoke wafted off the herbs, and the room filled with an earthy, tangy scent.

"What, exactly, are we doing?" I asked, staying well away from the burning weeds.

She didn't answer. Lynda walked out into the hallway, and I followed. She waved the smoking sticks in a triangular pattern around the front door, humming tunelessly. She waved the herbs in front of the windows, and around the doorway to the parlor. She stooped down low and left a trail of white smoke along the baseboards, and she stood on her tiptoes and let the smoke rise ceilingward. She walked and hummed and waved the burning herbs in every room of the house, and I followed her, eventually managing to echo, in some fashion, the melody of her tuneless tune.

When she'd smoked the house out to her complete satisfaction, she went back into the parlor. She knelt down, and tenderly placed the smouldering broom on the grate in the fireplace.

She took another deep breath of the herbal smoke. I did the same. She gave me a blissful smile. "Much better, don't you think?"

"I guess. Anyway, what did we just do here?"

"Dempsey? You've never done a purification before? Followed by a smudge?"

"Afraid not," I said. "You know how Dad is. What were those herbs you were burning?"

"Just the usual," she said. "Sage, of course. You don't do a smudge without sage. Plus cedar, lavender, mint, rosemary, dill, parsley. Ordinarily I use fennel too, but the Whole Foods in my neighborhood was out. I gathered everything last night, at dusk, which is my serene time. And let me tell you, after that FBI agent showed up at my house, I haven't had a lot of serenity. The tree branch was from my favorite olive tree in the garden. I've been saving it for something special. I didn't have a lot of particulars about what all was going on with you and this Alex Hodder person, so my visualization wasn't quite as detailed as I would have liked, but I think I managed to work it all out."

"You visualized my situation?" I was touched. My mother and I were so very different, and we'd been apart for so long, and I'd been so independent for so long, it hadn't occurred to me that she ever worried about me.

"Of course," Lynda said, tenderly brushing my cheek with the side of her thumb. "I'm your mother, silly girl. I visualize you every night, the last thing before I close my eyes to go to sleep. Didn't you know that?"

I shook my head, too touched, for a moment, to say anything. "How did you visualize me last night?"

She thought about it. "You were laughing, like you did when you were a baby. Silvery peals of laughter. You weren't troubled or worried. You were happy. Healed. Whole. And, sweetheart?"

"Yes?"

"You weren't dressed like one of the Beverly Hillbillies."

I looked down at my overalls and paint-spattered Chuck Taylors. "Gotcha. I'll try and do better next time."

She gave me an air kiss, and linked her arm through mine. "As part of the visualization, I went shopping. Wait until you see what I bought you."

We were headed up the stairs, each of us carrying one of Lynda's suitcases, when we heard a door open behind us.

Thump. Drag. Thump. Drag. Ella Kate's walker, and then her head, emerged from her doorway.

She stood in the hallway and sniffed, suspiciously.

"Dempsey!" she called.

"Right here, Ella Kate," I said, leaning over the banister so she could see me.

"I seen that woman gettin' out of that fancy Cadillac," she announced. "And I heard some kinda heathen humming, and then I smelled smoke!"

"It's all right, Ella Kate," I said with a laugh. "My mom is here. For a little visit."

The old woman's eyes narrowed. "That one. Lynda. Spelled with a *y* instead of an *i*. She's the one who run your daddy off, ain't she?"

Lynda hung her head over the banister and gave Ella Kate a friendly wave. "Hi, Ella Kate. I hope we didn't disturb you. I was just doing a little purification smudge."

"Smudge," Ella Kate said. "I'm old, but I'm not ignorant. I know that mary-ju-wanna stuff when I smell it. You better take that weed of yours right back to California where you came from, unless you wanna get them FBI agents back here with a pair of handcuffs."

"No, no," Lynda said, laughing. "It's nothing illegal. Just herbs. Sage. Rosemary. Cedar. It's all very healing. I heard you've been a little under the weather lately."

"Under the weather," Ella Kate sniffed. "I got a broke hip and breast cancer. I guess some people might call that under the weather. I call it sick and dying." She fanned her hand in front of her face. "Herbs, my aunt Fanny." She looked up at me meaningfully.

"She ain't fixin' to stay, is she?"

Lynda looked at me expectantly.

"Afraid so, Ella Kate," I said. "She's here for the duration."

55

I spent Friday getting Lynda settled in.

When I woke up Saturday morning, the sun was shining brightly through the windows of Norbert's old room. I sat up on the sagging mattress, and yawned and stretched. The first thing I noticed was, for the first time in a long time, I didn't have a knot of dread in my stomach. The second thing I noticed was the strong scent of fresh-brewed coffee.

I jumped up and headed for the shower. Maybe there was something to this purification and visualization thing after all. Here I was. Whole. Happy. Healthy. And I had my mother to thank for it. Didn't I?

After my shower, I padded back to my new room, where I found just how far Lynda's visualization project could go. She'd made up my bed, and laid out a new set of clothing for me, consisting of a pair of white cashmere leggings and a midriff-baring, off-the-shoulder pink cashmere sweater. Being Lynda, she'd thoughtfully accessorized the clothing with a filmy pink-and-orange silk scarf, oversize pink hoop earrings, and a pair of pink crocodile Miu Miu flats. She'd even provided me with what she thought of as proper undergarments: a pale pink lacy push-up bra, and the tiniest pink lace thong panties I'd ever seen.

The outfit would have been perfect for a well-dressed high school girl's trip to the mall. I hesitated, and then gamely struggled into the ensemble, which was clearly meant for someone a size smaller. She was my mother, and she meant well, didn't she?

When I got downstairs, Lynda was sitting at the kitchen table, a pair of needle-nose pliers in one hand, a thin circlet of gold wire in the other. She was dressed in pale yellow yoga togs, and a jeweler's magnifying headset rode low on her forehead as she painstakingly threaded a small ivory-colored fragment onto the wire.

"Mom?"

She looked up, taking in my new outfit, and beamed. "Don't you look adorable! I hope you don't mind. I saw those things at a little boutique in Malibu and they just screamed, 'Dempsey.' You like?"

"Oh, sure," I lied, trying to suck in my now-bared tummy.

She went back to work, and I wandered over to the coffeepot. I poured myself a cup of coffee, and hesitated before adding a dollop of half-and-half. I wouldn't have pegged my mother as an early riser, but she'd obviously been up and busy for some time. The plywood countertops were littered with small baskets. Each held a different color and variety of bead, jewel, or unidentifiable chunk. A black plastic tackle box was open, and tools and gold and silver jewelry findings glittered from their individual compartments. A pan of muffins sat on top of the stove and the scent of cinnamon wafted through the room.

"Help yourself," Lynda murmured. "Apple oat bran. And don't worry. They're vegan."

"Thanks anyway, but I'm not," I said. I picked up a muffin, sliced it in half and buttered it, and popped a piece in my mouth. "Yum," I said.

"Organic Yakima Valley applesauce. No sugar added," she said meaningfully. She slid a small gold hook onto the end of her necklace, made a looping knot, and snipped off the excess wire.

"There," she said, holding the necklace up for inspection. "What do you think?"

I walked over to get a closer look. The piece was threaded with a variety of off-looking dirty ivory chunks, interspersed with what looked like beads of semiprecious turquoise, coral, and jade. The beads were strung in graduated size, with a walnut-size object hanging from a pendant in the middle.

"It's different," I said, touching the beads with my fingertip. "What are these ivory-colored things?"

"Rattlesnake vertebrae," she said brightly. "Aren't they amazing?"

I jerked my hand back quickly. "What about the thing in the middle? It's not—"

"A tiny little snake skull," Lynda said, cradling the thing reverently in her hand. "Have you ever seen anything so awesome in your life?"

"Uh, no," I said, moving over to the sink, where I proceeded to wash my hands with soap and scalding water. "How do you happen to have a rattlesnake skeleton? Did they let you on the plane with that thing?"

"Oh, I didn't bring it with me," Lynda said brightly. "I found it on my walk this morning. I was actually hoping to find some headlight glass or metal fragments. I thought, this is the South, they love to crash cars down here. But I walked for at least two miles, and all I found were some mashed-up beer cans and discarded condoms."

"You didn't—"

She wrinkled her nose. "What kind of freak do you take me for? Of course not. Latex is not my medium at all. I was really pretty bummed out when I got back here. But then, just as I was coming up the drive-way, I spotted something off in the shrubbery. Something white, and I thought at first it was a bird's egg. Which would have been very cool. Very organic. But this! A snake skeleton. It just blew me away."

"Yeah," I said, shuddering. "It blows me away too, thinking that there was a rattlesnake right out here on the edge of the driveway."

"You don't have a snake phobia, Dempsey, do you?" she asked sternly. "I would hope no daughter of mine would be afraid of such a fascinating creature. Have you ever really studied a snake's skin? Really stopped to appreciate its beauty and symmetry?"

"Nope," I said, taking another bite of muffin. "Actually, I've never gotten close enough to any kind of snake to appreciate anything about it. When I even hear the word 'snake' I run the other way."

"Pity," Lynda said. She rummaged around in the materials spread out on the table until she found a small silken bag. She dropped the snake necklace inside and closed its drawstring.

"When did you start making jewelry from reptiles?" I asked.

"Oh, my work has been moving in this direction for some time now," she said, getting up and going to the refrigerator. She took out a small carton and poured herself a glass of muddy-looking glop.

"Wheatgrass juice," she said, smacking her lips. "Full of antioxidants. Would you like some? I brought plenty."

"No, no. I'm good with just the coffee. Which, by the way, is great. Thanks for making it for me."

"I remembered what a coffee fiend you always were," Lynda said. She began putting her tools and findings back in the tackle box.

"Lynda?" I said. "Will somebody actually buy a necklace like that?"

She smiled serenely. "I have a client in Santa Fe, as well as jewelry shops in Palm Beach and Beverly Hills who will buy every piece I can make. Last month? I did a bracelet from tiger's eye and bits of raccoon bone. Exquisite, if I may brag a little on myself. It sold for six, and if I'd had ten of them, I could have sold nine more."

"Six . . . hundred?" I asked incredulously. "For real?"

"Six thousand, silly," Lynda said.

"Where, uh, do you get something like raccoon bone?" I asked warily. "I mean, you don't actually kill them yourself?"

"Demspey Jo Killebrew!" Lynda said, putting down her empty wheatgrass glass. "Of course not. I would never kill an animal. I'm a vegan. If you ever came to visit us in California, you'd appreciate where we live. It's in a canyon. There are hawks and coyotes, and lots of wildlife. I'm quite the hiker. I pick things up myself, and then I have a nice network of people who know the kinds of things I'm always look- ing for."

"So, you're sort of a bounty hunter?"

She rolled her eyes. "I'd forgotten what a concrete thinker you are. Like your father, I suppose. And no, I'm not a bounty hunter. I'm an artist. Did you happen to see that piece about my spring collection in the January issue of *Vogue?*"

"Sorry," I said. "*Vogue,* huh? I had no idea your jewelry was such a success." I gave her a quick hug. "I'm proud of you, Mama."

"I'm proud of you too, precious," she said, "but please don't call me that. Lynda is fine. Mother or Mom, if you must, but I really must ask you not to call me Mama."

"Sorry," I said. "I'd forgotten about your little phobia. Mother."

She gave me a weak smile. "Silly, aren't we? Now, how are we going to spend the rest of our day? I thought maybe we could take a drive up to Atlanta and do a little shopping. No offense, precious, but after you went to bed last night, I went through your closet. We're going to have to burn most of what's in there, and rethink your whole wardrobe and self-image. And my hairdresser gave me the name of a good salon in Buckhead, so I've booked you a cut and color."

"Lynda!" I said.

"My treat," Lynda said. "I insist."

Before I could issue a formal protest, my cell phone rang. I glanced at the readout screen.

GOVERNMENT AGENCY, it read. I flipped it open.

"Dempsey?" It was Jackson Harrell.

"Good morning, Agent Harrell," I said coolly.

"What happened to Jack and Cam?" he asked. "I thought we were all cool with everything. You fixed me lunch yesterday. Gave Cam your bathrobe."

I walk-trotted out to the front porch for a little privacy. "That was before I knew you'd dragged my mother into this thing," I said fiercely. "She's here, you know. Flew all the way in from California yesterday afternoon with a suitcase full of vegan vodka and wheatgrass and God knows what else. She slept in my bed last night, and right now, she's out in my kitchen making jewelry out of snake corpses, and planning an extreme makeover for me."

"Hey, don't put that on me," Harrell protested. "I'm just a pawn of the government. I can't help it if your mama is a bona-fide wack job."

"She's not a wack job," I said. "She's different, that's all. I love her to pieces, but I love her best when there's a whole continent between us."

"Well, now," he drawled. "That's what I'm calling about. Cam and I did some fine reconnaissance work yesterday, and we got everything all laid out just like we want it. What we need now is for you to take a little ride so we can show you the setup, maybe do a little rehearsal. If you and your mama aren't too busy."

"Leave my mother out of it," I said. "When did you want to go? She wants to take me shopping in Atlanta and get my hair cut and colored."

"Turn your head to the right," Harrell said.

I did as he suggested, and spotted the familiar sedan, parked at the curb, three houses down. A hand emerged from the driver's-side window and gave me a little wave.

"Now's good," he said.

I flipped the phone shut and went back inside the house.

"Who was that?" Lynda asked, rinsing out her wheatgrass glass.

I decided to just tell her the truth. Coming up with a convincing lie this early in the morning seemed like too much trouble.

"Remember that FBI agent who came to see you?"

"Ah yes," she said. "The Fascist Bureau of Investigation. And dear old Agent Allgood." She pursed her lips, and for the first time I realized she'd had a little work done since our last visit. A nip, a tuck, a little dose of Botox. Vegan Botox, probably. "Do you think that's her undercover name? I mean, really, Allgood? Such a cliché. It worries me that our government can't come up with anything more original."

"I don't know if it's her real name," I said. "But I doubt she considers herself undercover. Anyway, she and her partner need me to go with them."

"Why?" She held up the glass and dried it with a dishcloth.

"Because I've got a meeting set up for Monday with Alex Hodder," I said reluctantly. "And they're going to be secretly taping us."

"Hodder!" she said, outraged. "Why would you have a meeting with that scum? After what he told the media about you? That you hired hookers and bribed a congressman? A Republican, at that! I swear, Dempsey, I don't approve of violence, but if I knew where that dickhead lived, I would track him down and personally rip his head off with my bare hands."

"Lynda," I said, taking a step backward.

"I don't care," she said, tossing her blond ringlets. "I'm a mother, and a mother protects her young."

"That's very sweet," I told her. "But I'm nearly thirty, and I think I can protect myself. This whole thing is pretty complicated. And it's supposed to be a secret, so I really shouldn't have told you what's going on. I promise, I'll fill you in when I get back."

"But, our shopping trip," she said.

I grabbed my jacket from the hook by the back door. "Go without me," I suggested. "But if you buy me anything, you might get one size bigger."

"And your hair appointment," she wailed. "It's a very exclusive salon."

"Get yourself some low lights," I suggested. "Knock yourself out. I'll see you this afternoon."

56

I jogged down the block and slid into the backseat of the waiting sedan.

"Howya doin'?" Agent Harrell turned around from the driver's seat and offered me his big all-American smile.

"Great, just peachy," I said.

Camerin Allgood was in the front-passenger seat. "You sure do look pretty in pink," she said, barely supressing a smirk. "Love the shoes too. Are they new?"

"A gift from my mother," I said, pulling my denim jacket closer together in an attempt to hide my exposed midriff. "Could we just drop the fashion chat and get down to business? I've got a lot of stuff to do today."

"We've got everything set for the meet," Agent Allgood told me. "You haven't had any more calls from Hodder, have you?"

"No, thank God," I said. "Where is the meet, by the way?"

"You'll see," Harrell said.

We drove for about fifteen minutes, leaving the Guthrie city limits behind. It was a beautiful early spring morning. The trees were fully leafed out now, and dogwoods bloomed pink and white and pale green. We passed a fenced pasture, where cows were clustered around a feeder, and another, where a farmer on a bright green-and-yellow John Deere tractor made passes in the newly turned red Georgia soil.

After a while, Harrell turned the sedan off the state highway and onto a bumpy asphalt road called Graham's Crossing. After another mile, we pulled off the road and into the parking lot of a church. The sign out front proclaimed it to be the NEW MACEDONIA FULL GOSPEL CHURCH OF THE BRETHREN, PASTOR: THE REVEREND EDSEL RUCKER.

Another sign, one of those magnetic boards, said QUESTIONING LIFE? GOD KNOWS!

"A church? You want me to meet Alex Hodder in a church?"

"What's wrong?" Agent Allgood asked. "You don't like church?"

"I like church fine," I told her. "I just think it's . . . I dunno, sacrilegious? To take a blackmail payoff in a house of God?"

"You'll be doing God's work," Harrell said, getting out of the car and opening my door. "Bringing the evil to righteousness."

I stood for a moment and took in the scene. New Macedonia had seen better days. Its white clapboard sanctuary hadn't seen a paintbrush in years. The tiny steeple leaned precariously to the left, and in one of the church's two stained-glass windows there was a gaping hole covered with plywood. Foot-high tufts of weeds grew up through the crushed-shell parking lot, and the small plot of lawn between the parking lot and the church steps was overgrown and weed choked. Off to the left of the church was a tin-roofed pavilion with weather-beaten picnic tables beneath it, and behind that, a huge live oak tree's limbs were spread over a bedraggled cemetery, its modest concrete headstones broken and strewn about the weedy graveyard.

"Come on," Camerin Allgood said, tugging at my arm. "Let's take a look around. Get you acclimated."

The wooden steps were rickety and uneven. Harrell took a key from his pocket and fit it into the church door. It opened slowly, with a loud creak that echoed through the high-ceilinged sanctuary. A wave of musty air greeted us. It had been a while since anybody worshipped at New Macedonia.

Sunlight streaming in through the one stained-glass window revealed a sanctuary that was bare, but surprisingly beautiful in its simplicity. The floors were worn pine, and the walls were of whitewashed planking. A red-carpeted aisle bisected two rows of crudely made white-painted pews. Red leatherette hymnals were stacked at the end of each row of pews. There was a choir loft at the back of the sanctuary, reached by a perilous-looking set of stairs covered with more red carpeting.

Harrell walked rapidly to the front of the church, and I followed.

The altar looked like a stage, with two short sets of steps leading onto it from either side of the church. There was a tall wooden lectern in the middle, and a high-backed throne-looking chair off to the right of the lectern. A six-foot-tall wooden cross hung from the peaked ceiling.

Harrell bounded onto the altar and patted the wooden lectern. "Right here is where we've got the first camera," he said. "Doesn't matter where you are in this church, the way we've got it set up, you'll be in the camera's view the whole time."

I walked over to the lectern and looked it up and down. "There's a camera? Where?"

He touched the outdated microphone mounted to the lectern. "Right here."

"Seriously?" I leaned in close and examined the mike. It looked like any other, obsolete piece of audiovisual equipment you might find in a country church that had fallen on hard times.

"Come on," Harrell said, going down the altar steps and striding down the center aisle. I followed him, and this time we climbed up to the choir loft. The wooden stairs groaned under the weight of our footsteps, and I clung to the metal handrail, just in case.

A battered upright piano had pride of place at the front of the choir loft, and just behind it were a dozen rusting folding metal chairs. Hooks held faded and dust-covered red choir robes, and more hymnals were scattered about on the floor and chairs.

"There's a camera up here?" I asked.

"Oh yeah," Harrell said. "Can you guess where?"

I touched the brass library lamp on the top of the piano. "Here?"

"No, but you're close," Harrell said. He patted a stack of hymnals next to the lamp.

"For real? That's pretty slick."

"We got guys can put a camera in a rat's nostril and you wouldn't know it," Harrell said proudly.

I followed him back down the steps to where Cam Allgood was lounging on a pew near the front of the sanctuary. Harrell sat down beside her, and patted the spot beside him.

I climbed over their feet and sat down.

"So," Allgood said. "Here's how we want this thing to play out. When Hodder calls you, tell him you'll meet him here, New Macedonia, whatever, church, at three o'clock Monday. We've checked all the flights out of D.C. and Baltimore and he should easily be able to get down to Atlanta by no later than noon. He hasn't booked a flight yet, but when he does, we'll know about it. Even if there's a weather delay, or a screwup with his rental car, he can easily get to this church by three o'clock Monday."

"We'll give you written directions that you can give him," Harrell said.

"What if he tries something sneaky?" I asked.

"Like what?" Allgood asked.

I shrugged. "I don't know. He's a sneaky guy. I don't trust him as far as I can throw him."

"Relax," Harrell said. "We've got every contingency covered. Right now, there's an agent watching his house in Georgetown, and another keeping an eye on his wife."

"Have you got his phones tapped?" I asked.

"That's not something you need to worry about," Camerin Allgood said.

"What about the money?" I asked. "What if he doesn't bring the money? What if he tries to screw me out of it? He probably thinks he can. He thinks I'm an idiot."

"He went to three different banks yesterday afternoon," Harrell said. "Withdrew a hundred thou apiece from the first two banks, and at the third bank, he accessed a safe-deposit box, so we don't know, but we're assuming he took the balance of your cash from his stash there."

I felt the knot of anxiety gnawing in my belly. It was back, despite all Lynda's purification and visualization.

"What if he's got a gun?" I asked, my anxiety growing. "I mean, I don't think he's violent, but you never know. He sounded pretty angry on the phone."

"He can't get a gun past airport security," Agent Allgood said. "And we'll have somebody on his tail, from the minute he leaves the house in

Georgetown to the minute he lands in Atlanta and picks up a rental car to head down here. Our people know this guy, Dempsey. He's no gunslinger. You are in absolutely no danger whatsoever."

I swallowed hard. "So, what now?"

"You meet him here on Monday," Harrell said. "Get here a little early, say, quarter of. You'll have the golf scorecard, and an empty satchel, for the cash."

"And where will you guys be?"

"Around," Allgood said. "You'll be on camera, and we'll also have people in the vicinity, for backup."

"What if the cameras goof up?" I worried. "What if he figures out I'm wearing a bug?"

"You won't be wearing a bug," Harrell said. "If he wants to check you out, let him. He won't find a thing."

"I'm not letting him check me for bugs," I said indignantly. "I'm not letting that slimeball so much as touch me."

"Whatever," Camerin said lazily. "We've got microphones that will pick everything up, no matter what."

"Where?" I asked. "I need to know, just in case something happens."

"Nothing's going to happen," she said impatiently. "Can you relax? We know how to do our job, and if you'll just listen, we'll tell you how to do yours."

Allgood glanced at her watch. "Okay, let's talk specifics. You meet Hodder here in the church, on Monday. He'll want to take a look at the scorecard. That's fine. Let him look. But you make sure he has the cash. Okay? Get him to show it to you."

"Right," I said. "Show me the money."

"This next part is really, really important," Allgood said. "You need to get him to talk about what he's paying you for. Not just the scorecard, but what that scorecard means. You don't have to use the word 'bribe' or 'payoff,' or anything like that; in fact, don't say those words at all. It could spook him. But do try to draw him out about the trip to Lyford Cay. You know, kinda like you did on his phone call to you. So, let's do a little role-playing, all right?"

"What do you want me to say?" I asked impatiently.

"Oh," Allgood said, "we wouldn't dream of telling *you* what to say. But Jack and I are just gonna kind of give you an example of how *we'd* handle it, if it was us."

She got up and walked to the middle aisle of the sanctuary. Harrell went around to the back of the church, and strode purposefully up the middle aisle.

He looked around the church, walked over to the front pew, and looked underneath it as though he was searching for hidden cameras or microphones.

Allgood stood perfectly still, right in front of the lectern, her hands on her hips. "What are you looking for, Alex?" she said. "Bugs? Cameras? This isn't the movies. This is Guthrie, Georgia. It's just you and me, partner."

Harrell looked annoyed. He did it very well. Working with Camerin Allgood, he probably had a lot of on-the-job training. "Did you bring it?"

"Bring what?" Allgood asked.

"You know what," Harrell snapped. "Don't play games with me."

Allgood pantomimed reaching into the pocket of her jacket and bringing something out. It was actually a half-empty bottle of water. She held it up for Harrell to see. "You mean this?"

Harrell walked over and pretended to examine the pretend scorecard. "This doesn't even look like my handwriting," he said.

"It's yours," Allgood assured him, smoothly putting the bottle back in her pocket. "Now, let's talk about what you've got for me."

"It's all here," Harrell said. He reached into his jacket and brought out a folded-up newspaper, which he extended to her.

Allgood took the newspaper. She unfolded it, and carefully looked through it. "You know, Alex, if you hadn't thrown me under the bus the way you did, this wouldn't have had to happen."

"I don't know what you're talking about," Harrell said gruffly. "Are we done here? I've got a plane to catch."

Camerin Allgood pretended to pout. "You're kind of hurting my feelings, Alex. I'm taking all the heat for you, and yet you just want to walk away, as if none of it ever happened. You set me up, didn't you? Had me make all the arrangements for the hotel, the golf, the dinners, the hookers. Had me call the 'wakeboard instructor' to set up the session with Licata, and then, as if that wasn't bad enough, you had me book a 'massage' with a known hooker—and charge all of it to my company-issued credit card. That way, you'd look clean, no matter what happened."

"You knew perfectly well what you were doing," Harrell said. "What did you think we were really down in the Bahamas for—choir practice?"

That got me. I couldn't stop myself. I jumped up from the pew. "I thought we were going down to the Bahamas to talk to a congressman about energy policy," I said heatedly. "I spent weeks working on that position paper. And we never once talked energy policy to Licata. As far as the two of you were concerned, it was golf and tennis and expensive dinners and hookers and champagne—it was all just a big boondoggle."

Allgood and Harrell turned and stared at me.

I felt my face turn as pink as my cashmere sweater.

Allgood clapped her hands slowly. "Excellent, Dempsey. The perfect touch. I couldn't have said it better myself."

"Rehearsal's over," I said, and I turned and ran out of the New Macedonia Full Gospel Church of the Brethren.

57

The house was quiet when I got home, although Lynda's rented Escalade was still in the driveway. I went directly to my closet and was relieved to find that, despite her dire promises, Lynda hadn't gotten around to destroying my clothes. I snatched up Norbert's overalls, a faded T-shirt, and my Chuck Taylors and went to my new room to change.

My mood was definitely much darker than it had been in the morning. Seeing the location where my meeting with Alex was to take place, and actually anticipating how the meeting might play out, had not had the effect the FBI agents had hoped for. Instead, it had only heightened my anxiety and desire to be done with the whole nasty mess.

I struggled out of the too-tight cashmere togs my mother had bought me. I knew she meant well, but I couldn't help resenting her makeover campaign. Did she think that dressing me like Hannah Montana would really be an improvement over the Dempsey Killebrew look? Or did she unconsciously hope that making me look like a teenager would, by default, make her look and feel like a thirty-something?

It was all too much psychodrama for one morning. I should have gone looking for Lynda, to ask her if she'd postponed her shopping trip, or even to offer to go with her now. Instead, I headed downstairs, to the kitchen, determined to finish tiling the counter and backsplash.

I'd already laid out and cut all the tiles to the needed size with the tile saw Bobby had loaned me. I plugged in my iPod and opened the bucket of premixed mortar, slathering it on the tile pieces, troweling off the excess as Bobby had shown me, and then slotting each tile neatly into place.

The thick mortar mix reminded me of cake icing, and once I got the hang of applying it at just the right consistency, and using the tiny plastic spacer bits to achieve uniform spacing between the tiles, I got into my tiling groove. The music played and my neat little rows of white tiles grew, and I lost all track of time. I didn't stop until I'd scraped up the last bit of mortar mix from the bucket, only one row short of finishing the whole project.

Damn! Now I'd have to go buy another whole bucket of mix—just to finish that one last row of tile. I glanced up at the kitchen clock. It was already 4:00. I knew the hardware store closed at 5. I unplugged the iPod buds, grabbed my purse, and was scrabbling around inside it, looking for the car keys, when it dawned on me that I didn't have the keys, because the Catfish was still out of commission.

I went looking for Lynda to see if she'd give me a ride to the hardware store. I tried the dining room first. She wasn't there, but I knew she had been, because she'd set up her jewelry-making equipment on the dining room table. Bits of beads, glass, metal, and a basket of assorted unidentifiable stuff were strewn all over the tabletop.

I went into the parlor and was astonished by what I found. She'd been there too, and she'd somehow managed to move down most of the furniture that had been stored in Ella Kate's bedroom. She'd obviously found a stash of Dempsey Mills bedspreads, because she'd covered all the drab Victorian wool and damask sofas and armchairs with the white cotton bedspreads, cleverly pinning and tucking them into makeshift slipcovers. She'd pushed two large, tufted velvet ottomans together in front of the settee to substitute for a coffee table and centered a black-and-gold tole tray, painted with peaches and cherries, on top of the ottomans. The tray held a cut-glass bowl of bright green apples, on top of a stack of three red-leather-bound books, and a horn-handled magnifying glass looked like it had just been set down.

Lynda must have had a field day digging through the crates of family china, silver, and other doodads that were packed away in Ella Kate's room. She'd sprinkled an array of blue-and-white transferware vases and platters around the room. Two massive blue-and-white ginger jars, filled with glossy green sprays of magnolia branches, now stood on either side of the mantel. A trio of transferware platters stood atop a stack of leather-bound books on the table in the corner, along with a tall sterling-silver loving cup filled with artfully arranged pink dogwood blossoms.

The heavy velvet drapes that had hung at the windows were now piled in a heap in a corner of the room. She'd rolled up the oriental rug too, and the dark wood floors gleamed in the weak rays of afternoon sunlight that now streamed in through the undressed windows.

I was outraged that she'd had the nerve to invade my decorating territory, and chagrined by the seemingly effortless charm she'd managed to achieve in one brief afternoon.

For the first time, I was aware of low voices coming from the direction of the hallway. I walked toward the voices. They were coming from Ella Kate's room. As I grew closer, I heard Lynda laughing, and then her voice.

"Oh, come on now, Ella Kate. That's not a real word!"

The door to the bedroom was open. I looked in and saw my mother and Ella Kate, sitting on opposite sides of a card table they'd set up in front of the window beside Ella Kate's easy chair. Their heads—Lynda's blond one and Ella Kate's steel gray one—were bent over a Scrabble board. Shorty was curled up on a pillow on the bed.

"Sure is a word," Ella Kate said with a cackle as she scooped up more letter tiles from the tabletop. "You can look it up if you want to. Any fool knows it."

"Well, I've heard it before, but I don't think it's a proper word," Lynda said indignantly.

I poked my head in the doorway. "What's the word? Maybe I can be the tiebreaker."

Ella Kate gave me a calculating look. "Skeeter. S-K-E-E-T-E-R."

"I know how to spell it," I assured her.

Lynda turned her face away from Ella Kate's and gave me a secretive wink and nod.

"You mean skeeter, slang for mosquito, right?" I asked.

"What else?" Ella Kate demanded. "Even a Yankee knows what a skeeter is."

"Sorry, Lynda," I told my mother. "She's right. It's slang, but it's acceptable. I think you have to give her the points."

"That's thirty-three points for me!" the old lady crowed. She tapped the *R* tile. "See that? Triple-word score."

"I see it," Lynda muttered. She looked down at her own tiles, then back at the board. Carefully, she picked up four tiles and placed them in descending order, using Ella Kate's *S* tile as a launching pad.

"Squat!" Lynda said. "Ta-da!"

"Hmmph," Ella Kate said.

"Well, it's a word," Lynda insisted.

"Not a very nice one, though," Ella Kate opined. "Anyway, it's only fourteen points. I'm still winning."

"Don't care," Lynda said, picking up a pencil to record her score. "Besides, maybe you didn't notice, but my *Q* is sitting on a double-letter spot. So, actually, that's twenty-four points for me."

"This is getting pretty vicious," I said, looking down at the board. "How long have you two been playing?"

"Since lunch," Ella Kate said. "Your mama—"

"Don't call her—" I started to say, but Lynda gave me the nod, so I shut up.

"Fixed me homemade tomato soup with buttermilk in it. Best thing I ever put in my mouth," Ella Kate said. "Gimme some wheatgrass juice too, but I spit that stuff out. Tastes like mud, if you ask me."

"The secret for the soup is using fire-roasted San Marzano tomatoes," Lynda offered. "I saved you some soup. I even went out to the kitchen after you got back from your meeting to see if you wanted some, but you were so fixated on your tiling, I decided not to bother you."

"Sorry," I said. "I have a hard time stopping once I get started."

"Oh!" Lynda said, clapping her hands over her mouth. "I almost forgot. Dempsey, you were in such a hurry to get to your meeting this morning that you left your cell phone."

"You didn't answer it, did you?" I asked, horrified at the idea of her having had a conversation with Alex Hodder.

"Well, of course I did," Lynda said. "But don't worry. It was just a nice young man named Tee Berryhill."

"Her boyfriend," Ella Kate said knowingly.

"How nice." Lynda beamed. "Then I'm glad I accepted his invitation for tonight."

"What invitation?"

"To dinner," she said. "He and his father are taking us to the country club tonight. There's even a dance! Doesn't that sound divine?"

I hesitated. My relationship with Tee was teetering on the brink of something, but I wasn't sure what yet. A night out with him—dinner and a dance—did, in fact, sound good, if not "divine," but did I want to expose Tee and Carter to my flamboyant mother this early in the game?

"I can't wait," Lynda said enthusiastically. "A real country-club dance. It sounds so quaint. Your father and I used to go to lots of dances when we first started dating."

"You and Mitch?" I'd never seen my father dance. It was hard enough imagining him married to someone as outrageous as Lynda, harder still imagining him doing anything as adventurous as the frug or the booga-loo, or whatever the dances were that they did in their youth.

"Oh yes," Lynda said dreamily. "Mitch was a great dancer back then."

"He was a little pissant when I knew him," Ella Kate volunteered.

"I think he reverted back to his pissant ways after Dempsey was born," Lynda told her. "But believe me, he wasn't like that when we first met. He was funny and sweet, and so thoughtful! A real Southern gentleman. And sexy!" She grinned and fanned herself vigorously. "I have never had so much fun in bed in my life," she declared.

"But you got yourself a divorce from him anyways," Ella Kate pointed out.

"Well, you can't stay in bed all the time," Lynda said sadly. "We never should have gotten married. Although it was worth every minute of it, considering I got a beautiful daughter out of the deal."

She stood up and kissed the top of my head. "Our fellas are picking us up at six. Don't you think you'd better start getting ready?"

I showered first, and while Lynda was still in the bathroom, I stood in front of my tiny closet, surveying the possibilities. I'd packed away most of my business suits and dressy clothes from my lobbyist life—no need for them now that my working days were spent painting and scraping. That didn't leave a lot of possibilities for a dance. I'd already worn my long skirt and top to the country club on my last "date," with Jimmy Maynard, and, as it turned out, Tee. There was a long-sleeved charcoal gray knit sweater dress, but it looked more suited to a funeral than a dance. As I rummaged through the clothes, I came across my old reliable, a navy blue matte jersey Marc Jacobs cocktail dress.

It was sleeveless, with a deep V-neck, pin-tuck details at the shoulders and the set-in waist, and a flirty little ruffle at the hem.

Ah yes. Marc had seen me through half a dozen weddings and cocktail receptions in the past couple of years, and he'd never let me down.

I took it off the hanger and held it up to my shoulders while I checked myself out in the mirror, turning to and fro to get the full effect.

Just then, Lynda walked in. She was in her bathrobe, and her damp hair hung in ringlets to her shoulders. "Oh, sweetheart," she exclaimed, catching the fabric of the hem between her fingertips. "No, no, no. This isn't right for you at all. Wait! I've got just the thing in my suitcase."

I walked over to her suitcase, which was open, and closed it.

"Mom," I said firmly. "We have to talk."

She sank down on the bed. "About what?"

"About you. And me. And your effort to make me into you."

"What? No, that's not true at all," Lynda protested. "I just think—"

"You think I'm ugly, and my clothes are ugly, and that basically I'm wasting my time down here."

"I never said that," Lynda protested, grabbing my hand. "I think you're the most beautiful girl in the entire world. You know that, don't you?"

"I'm not a girl," I said gently. "I'm a woman. I'm nearly thirty. I've been dressing myself for quite some time now, and although not all the choices I've made in my life have been the right ones, they've been mine. I love you, Lynda, but you have got to give me some space."

Her periwinkle blue eyes filled with tears. She stood up and reopened the suitcase. "I knew it! You don't want me here. You resent me. You've resented me ever since you were a teenager. I told myself you were feeling abandoned, and I wrote it off to your father's influence over you. No matter how hard I try, you'll never let me make it up to you. So I'll go."

"No, wait," I said, flipping the lid of the suitcase shut again. "I'm not telling you to leave. I don't feel abandoned. It took me a while, but I finally realized years ago that you were doing what you thought was best for me when you sent me to live with Mitch."

I took a deep breath. "Maybe it was the best thing for me. I don't know. My childhood is in the past. Parts of it were good and parts of it sucked, but I got through it. That's all that matters."

She sniffed and dabbed at her eyes with a tissue. "You haven't said a word about all my hard work in the house today. You hate it, don't you?"

I bit my lip and decided to be honest. "Lynda, I love the way the parlor looks. I never would have thought to use the bedspreads as slipcovers, or to take down the drapes. And I can't figure out how the hell you got all that furniture downstairs. But the thing is . . . I'm feeling kind of territorial here. Birdsong is *my* project. The house is Dad's, I know, but the work, it's mine. I'm sorry to be so selfish about it, but right now, this run-down, crappy house is all I've got. So, yeah, I was kind of bent out of shape when I saw what you'd done."

"That sweet contractor of yours, Bobby? He dropped by and I roped him into helping me. We can put it back the way it was," Lynda said tearfully. "I had no right."

"Don't you dare," I told her. "It's gorgeous. Fabulous. I can't believe how much you accomplished in a few short hours."

She smiled tentatively. "I've had the most amazing surge of creative energy since I got here. I don't know what it is. After you left this morning, I decided it wouldn't be any fun to shop without you. I took another walk, and then I poked around in the basement, and I came up with just the coolest stuff—pecans, sweet-gum balls, arrowheads, old marbles and Coke bottle caps, and bits of broken china. I got so stoked, I made three necklaces in less than an hour. Wait until you see! I think they're the best work I've ever done."

"I can't wait to see them," I said.

"I made one just for you," she said shyly. "Now, you don't have to wear it. You're right, I have no business telling you how to dress or act, or any of that. I'll try to do better, okay?"

"Okay," I said. "Can I see the necklace?"

"Sure you want to?" Lynda asked. "It's kind of a departure for me."

I held out my hand. "Give."

She went to the dresser, opened the top drawer, and brought out a little gold silk pouch. Lynda sat down on the bed beside me and, after a moment's hesitation, dropped the necklace into my open palm.

I'd been expecting one of my mother's usual bizarre combinations of broken glass, twisted metal, maybe even a fossilized bird's egg or raccoon tooth. But what she'd made for me was unlike anything I'd ever seen before.

A long, slender golden chain, maybe twenty-four-inches, held half a dozen charmlike tokens. Some were gold, others were silver. The center pendant on the chain held a tiny diamond-studded platinum woman's watch face, suspended from a bit of platinum chain. Beside it was a pale green cat's-eye marble. There was a small, scrolly, golden, heartshaped locket, and an intricately worked brooch that seemed to represent some sort of fraternal symbol with a small red stone in the middle. Another charm was a stud of some sort, with a pearl in the center, and the last one was a simple, worn gold band.

"Oh, Lynda," I whispered. "It's . . . exquisite."

She smiled. "Well, it's much more sentimental than anything I've ever done before, but then, I don't think it's too terribly self-indulgent, considering who I made it for, and what it represents."

"Represents?"

"This," she said, pointing to the watch face, "was your great-grandmother's watch."

"Olivia?" I asked.

"No, it was Olivia's mother's watch," Lynda said. "This little marble belonged to your grandfather Dempsey, when he was a little boy. Now, the locket, that was Olivia's. Open it up, why don't you?"

With a fingernail, I pried open the locket. Only one side of the locket held a photograph, the other held a lock of pale gold hair. I looked closely, then up at Lynda. She nodded.

"Your father's baby picture," she said. "And that's Mitch's first curl."

She touched the brooch. "This was your great-uncle Norbert's Masonic stickpin. I hope you don't mind that I cut off the pin part. And the ruby's real, by the way."

"It's, just . . . stunning," I said.

"The pearl was your great-great-grandfather's shirt stud. Again, real," she said. "At one time, honey, the Dempseys were totally loaded."

"That's what I've heard."

The gold ring was so small, I could only slip my pinkie halfway through it. "And this?" I asked, knowing the answer already.

She sighed. "Olivia's wedding ring."

I stood up and put the necklace around my neck. Lynda took me by the shoulders and turned me around, to fasten the catch.

"I love it," I declared. "I may never take it off."

"I'm so glad," Lynda said softly.

"But, Mom, where did you get all these things? I've gone through just about every closet, drawer, and cupboard, and I've never found anything remotely like these things."

"Ella Kate gave them to me," she said simply. "But you can't say anything to her about it. She made me swear not to tell."

"Ella Kate! But she hates my guts. Most of the time she won't even speak to me. Did she know you were going to give this to me?"

"It was her idea," Lynda said. "She's not such a bad old girl. She told me about how you saved her life. Hers and Shorty's. I think this is her way of thanking you." She laughed. "In case you haven't noticed, Ella Kate's sort of short on sweet words. But don't let her fool you. She's very fond of you, Dempsey Jo. She's been saving these things, bits and bobs, she calls them, all these years, for somebody special. As far as she's concerned, you're the last of the line."

I turned and gave her a hug. "Lynda? Will you do one more thing for me?"

"Anything," she said.

"Drop the Dempsey Jo, will you?"

58

When the doorbell rang, I licked my lips nervously. Stop it! I told myself. It's just Tee and Carter. So what if they are about to meet your mother for the first time? This is just a little dinner and dance at the country club. And even if they all hate each other, Carter and Tee are far too genteel to do anything except feign their absolute delight. I ran into the downstairs bathroom and checked my makeup. It was fine, although my cheeks were a little too pink from excitement. I pulled the hem of my dress down and the neckline up. Was Marc too risqué for the conservative crowd at the Pine Blossom Country Club? I glanced down at my watch. Too late to change now.

I forced myself to walk slowly to the front door. I could see Tee standing there, through the sidelight. He wore a dark suit, white dress shirt, and a wine red silk tie. He was dressed more formally than I'd ever seen him before, and it made him look blonder and taller and grown up. And handsome. Oh, God, how had I never noticed how fine looking a man was T. Carter Berryhill? My stomach did an un-grown-up flutter, and I silently cursed myself for being such a giddy little mall girl. He caught sight of me peeking at him through the glass, and gave me a flirtatious wink.

"Are those our dates?" Lynda called. I turned around to see her floating down the stairs. No need for me to have worried about my own appearance. There was almost no chance anybody would notice me tonight—not with Lynda in the same room.

She was wearing a tangerine silk sheath halter dress with a plunging V-neck. Its hem fell demurely at midcalf, but it was slit up both sides to midthigh. Her tanned legs were bare, and she wore impossibly high-heeled gold lamé sandals with skinny straps that crisscrossed her ankles.

She'd twisted her hair up in a messy topknot skewered with a jeweled butterfly clip. Gold-beaded chandelier earrings brushed her bare shoulder tops. My mother looked like an exotic bird that had just flown in from some unnamed tropical rain forest.

Tee rang the doorbell again, and I jerked the door open. "Wow!" he said, looking straight past me, and directly at Lynda, who had paused halfway down the staircase, as though for a photo op.

"Well, Dempsey," Carter said. He stepped around his starstruck son, took both my hands in his, and kissed them. "My dear, don't you look lovely tonight?" He nudged Tee in the rib cage. "Don't you think so, son?"

Tee managed to drag his eyes off Lynda and focus on me. He elbowed Carter aside, and brushed his lips across my cheek. "Hey, old man." He laughed. "Don't be trying to hit on my woman."

"You look amazing," he whispered in my ear.

"Hello," Lynda said. She'd finally managed to make it down the stairs. We all turned.

"Carter, Tee," I said dutifully. "I'd like you to meet my mom, Lynda, uh . . ." For a split second, I couldn't remember my own mother's last name. She'd dropped Killebrew right after she and my dad split up, and had gone back to using her maiden name, but then had taken her second husband's last name, but only for the duration of their three-year marriage. For a brief time, in my teens, she'd even eschewed a last name altogether, insisting on being called only Lynda.

"Lynda Hayes," she said, smoothly stepping into the void. Oh yeah. Hayes. She'd gone back to using her maiden name again. Duh.

My mother had all the social graces I'd momentarily lost. "So nice to meet you," she said, shaking Carter's, and then Tee's hand. "Dempsey has told me how much you've helped her with the house, and of course, with this whole distressing FBI situation. I can't thank you enough for coming to the rescue of our girl."

Rescue? I could feel myself bristling, but as always, Carter said just the right thing. "It's been our privilege to represent Dempsey," he told my mother. "And of course, to establish a friendship with such a charming young woman." His eyes twinkled as he looked from Lynda to me.

"And now I can see, as Dempsey assured me when we first met, that she does indeed look just as much like her mother as she does her Dempsey relatives. It seems to me that she's had the good fortune of inheriting the best of both sides."

Lynda's laugh tinkled girlishly, and after a few more minutes of small talk, we all trooped out to Carter's Mercedes. I'd grabbed a pashmina shawl from the coat closet before leaving the house, but Lynda merely shrugged off the subfifties chill of the early spring night.

"I'm not cold at all," she insisted when Carter offered to go back to the house for a wrap for her. "This is so refreshing after all that boring heat out in California."

I climbed into the backseat, and Tee went around and slid in beside me, casually throwing his arm across my shoulders, and pulling me closer. I could hear the murmur of Carter's voice coming from the front seat, giving my mother the condensed history and guided tour of Guthrie, Georgia.

"Your mom is really something, huh?" Tee said, his lips barely touching my ear. "How come you didn't mention she was coming to town?"

"I didn't know myself until she showed up," I whispered. "After Camerin Allgood took it upon herself to visit my mother to let her know about my noncooperation, Lynda decided to fly out here from California to see what kind of mess I'd gotten myself into."

Tee nodded thoughtfully. "Something tells me there're some, uh, unresolved issues between the two of you. Is that an accurate assumption?"

I sighed. "It's complicated. I love her, but she's just so . . . overpowering. So larger than life. I haven't even seen her in a couple of years. I mean, we talk on the phone. Sometimes. Then, all of a sudden, she sweeps into town and thinks she can fix me. With a new hairdo and a new wardrobe."

"But you're not broken," Tee said, his dark brown eyes crinkling with amusement. "And I, for one, happen to like your hairdo. And your wardrobe." He ran his finger down my shoulder, and I shivered. "Especially this part of your wardrobe. I like."

"You're sweet," I said gratefully. "But clueless. Anyway, I finally did manage to find the backbone to let her know tonight that I don't want to be made over. She was hurt, at first, but I think maybe we're making some progress with this whole mother-daughter thing." I fingered my charm necklace. "She made this for me today. All the charms have a family connection." I ticked off the meaning of the baubles as I touched them. "And here's the funny part, Tee. Ella Kate gave her all these things. She told Lynda she's been saving them up. For family."

Lynda turned around then. "What's all the whispering about back there, you two? Some little lovers' secrets?"

I felt my face burn. Tee laughed easily. "Dempsey's just telling me about this awesome necklace you made for her. I had no idea her mother was such a talented artist."

Lynda beamed. "Not an artist, really," she said. "Just a tinkerer."

"Don't let her kid you," I said. "Lynda's jewelry is hot, hot, hot. She sells to shops in Beverly Hills, and even Palm Beach. And wait until you see the magic she worked in the parlor this afternoon. If I thought I could afford her, I'd try to hire her on as an interior designer for Birdsong."

Lynda blew me an air kiss, and turned around to resume her conversation with Carter.

"That was nice," Tee said softly, giving my hand an approving squeeze.

"I can play nice sometimes," I admitted, snuggling back against the warmth of his arm.

"You are playing nice, agreeing to be dragged along to this stupid dance," Tee murmured. "It was Dad's idea, and I couldn't talk him out of it. You and I will be the only ones there without a walker or a wheelchair."

"You're exaggerating," I said. "Carter's not exactly drooling in his tapioca, you know. And, don't forget Lynda. Mentally, anyway, she's younger than both of us."

"Oh, it looks just like I remember it," Lynda said as we walked into the entry hall at Pine Blossom. "Except, what happened to the little fountain out front?"

"You've been here before?" Carter asked, startled. "But it was my understanding Mitch hasn't been back here since his mother died years and years ago."

"Of course I have," Lynda said. "Mitch had absolutely no interest in coming down to Guthrie, but there was no way I was marrying a man—and having his child—without seeing his roots firsthand. I met Uncle Norbert, and some distant cousins back then, but it's been so long ago, it all seems sort of hazy now. So much has changed, especially with the mill closed, but then again, some things really are frozen in time, aren't they?"

"Frozen in time," Tee said, with a guffaw. "That's Guthrie, all right. And as for the fountain, it's been gone for years now. Right, Dad?"

"The fountain met its demise after Bunky Patterson backed into it with his banana yellow Coupe deVille and knocked the statue of Venus de Milo on her derriere," Carter said. "I believe that was shortly after he hit a hole in one at the member-guest invitational and proceeded to drink his way through an entire case of Budweiser. It was the second time that a member had unwittingly dethroned Miss de Milo, and at that point, the board wisely decided to widen the driveway and porte cochere and do away with the fountain. I believe that would have been sometime in the seventies."

The Pine Blossom Country Club dinner-dance was obviously the social event of the season in Guthrie. Every table in the dining room was full. The men were dressed in dark suits, the women in cocktail attire—or the Guthrie version of it, which mostly seemed to consist of black dresses and pearls, lots and lots of pearls. I even noticed a few mink coats thrown across chair backs. And yes—I did spot a few walkers and at least one wheelchair. The crowd was, as Tee had predicted, mostly middle-aged or older.

Heads turned as we walked to Carter's table in the main dining room, but Lynda took it all in stride, nodding and smiling to the barely disguised curiosity she was arousing among Guthrie's country-club set.

"This is so nice," Lynda said when we were seated, looking over the table, with its heavy damask cloth, silver candlesticks, sparkling crystal, and old-fashioned arrangement of roses and ferns. "Everything's so casual in California, it's a treat to get dressed up and go somewhere where everything is so special."

"Well, Tee and I are delighted that you agreed to be our guests tonight," Carter said, beaming at Lynda's approval. He lowered his voice. "And may I say that the two of you are undoubtedly the loveliest ladies in the room?"

Lynda giggled. I blushed. Tee squeezed my hand under the table.

We made it through the cocktail hour without incident. Lynda was thrilled to discover that the bar at Pine Blossom carried Stoli, and that the bartender in a backwater such as Guthrie could manage to mix a decent martini. She and Carter sipped their martinis and chatted away, Tee drank Bud on draft, and I myself welcomed the burn of Wild Turkey on the rocks.

When the waiter arrived to take our dinner orders, I held my breath. Lynda looked at the menu—which was heavy on all forms of beef, pork, and chicken—and frowned slightly. "The salmon—is it wild salmon or farm raised?" she asked.

The waiter looked dumbfounded. "It's just . . . salmon, I guess," he stammered. "They don't tell us where they get it."

"Hmm. What about the tuna?" she asked. "Is it dolphin safe?"

"Huh?"

She sighed. "All right. I guess I'll just have a large house salad. Dressing on the side. And another Stoli martini."

The band started setting up as our entrées arrived. "Check it out," Tee said quietly, cutting his eyes in the direction of the bandstand. "Mötley Crüe they ain't." The five band members were silver haired, and dressed in throwback prom tuxedos complete with matching ruffled peach shirts and bell-bottom trousers.

"See the drummer?" Tee said under his breath. "That's Bert Fleishman. Mr. Fleishman was my high school chemistry teacher. And we all thought he was ancient back then. Faye Fleishman, his wife, was the home ec teacher. I think maybe she makes all their gig outfits."

We were finishing our entrées, and the band was still tuning up, when someone tapped me on the shoulder. I turned to see Shirlene Peppers and Jimmy Maynard standing hand in hand beside our table.

"Jimmy," I blurted out. "You're wearing pants!"

"And a tie," Shirlene pointed out. "I'm tellin' ya, it's the second coming."

Jimmy Maynard was, in fact, wearing a natty blue blazer, charcoal slacks, and even the aforementioned tie, a yellow-and-red rep-striped affair. He looked only a little uncomfortable. Shirlene looked an absolute bombshell in a tight-fitting, short, candy apple red satin two-piece dinner suit, and rhinestone-encrusted silver lamé pumps that I was pretty sure were Manolos. Her long dark hair was down tonight, but I could see the gleam of diamond solitaire earrings that looked to be at least two carats apiece.

"Weeellll," Jimmy drawled. "I was gonna stick to my guns and wear my shorts. But then I got over to Shirlene's place, and seen what a knockout she was in that red getup of hers, and I said, 'Son, it's time to do the right thing.' So I went on home and dug some long britches out of the mothballs."

Shirlene patted his head affectionately. "Our little boy is growing up," she laughed.

Jimmy nodded in the direction of Lynda. "You didn't tell me you had a sister."

Lynda giggled appreciatively, and I made the introductions. "This is my mother, Lynda Hayes, who is visiting from California, and Lynda, this is Jimmy Maynard. Jimmy sells real estate, and he paints houses—my house in particular—as a hobby. And, Lynda, this is Shirlene Peppers. She's a lawyer here in Guthrie."

"County attorney," Carter pointed out. "And a mighty fine one too."

After that, Carter insisted that Shirlene and Jimmy pull up chairs and join our table. Somehow, Jimmy ended up beside Lynda, and Shirlene ended up beside Carter. The band started playing a tune I didn't recognize, something from the '40s big band era, I thought, and couples slowly drifted onto the dance floor.

When the second number started, another golden oldie, Carter managed to coax Lynda—with very little effort—onto the floor. They were quite a picture, the silver-haired Carter, with his erect posture and courtly ways, and my mother, fluttering and floating elegantly around the floor.

"Somebody's had some lessons," Jimmy said, never taking his eyes off them.

Tee leaned toward me. "Shall we join them?"

"Maybe something a little more upbeat," I begged off. "I haven't waltzed since seventh-grade cotillion."

"Baby, I hate to break it to you," Tee drawled, "but Dad's been dragging me to dances here at the club for years, and this is about as upbeat as it gets."

Nonetheless, the band did break into some beach music a few numbers later, and Tee and I had our first dance together. It was "With This Ring." We sang along to the band, and I managed to do a respectable shag, which, Tee said, only reaffirmed his opinion that I was totally the girl for him.

When we got back to the table, laughing and out of breath, Lynda and Jimmy were just getting up for the next dance. Carter, being Carter, asked Shirlene to dance, and Tee and I escaped out to the terrace.

I was glad of the cool night air, and gladder still for my pashmina, and the warmth of Tee's arms around me, as he expertly eased me behind a huge camellia bush. "Let's blow this pop stand," he said, nuzzling my neck. "I love the way you look in this dress, but I'm gonna love gettin' you out of it even more."

"Can't," I said, glancing around to make sure nobody was watching. "Remember? We came in your dad's car? Anyway, my mom's staying with me, remember?"

"She won't care," Tee said. "Your mom's having the time of her life." He pulled his cell phone out of his jacket pocket. "C'mon. I can call us a cab. We can be back at my place in half an hour."

He kissed me deeply, as if to seal the deal.

"Mmmm," I said, full of regret. "There aren't any cabs in Guthrie."

"Sure there are," he said. "Ace Ballou at Town and Country Cab. He's parked outside at the curb right now, just waiting to take home Guthrie's finest who are too drunk to drive and too old to walk home."

"Last I heard, your place had a tree on the roof."

"Your place then," he said. "It's after nine. Ella Kate will be asleep."

374 — *Mary Kay Andrews*

"Lynda's taken over my bedroom. I'm sleeping on Norbert's twin bed. And anyway, what do we tell everybody at the table? 'Sorry—we're going home to do the mattress dance?'"

He laughed at that one. "I don't give a damn what you tell 'em, as long as it's bye-bye. Hell, for that matter, we could go out to the Mercedes for a little while. I've got a set of keys—"

I gave him one long, deep, meaningful kiss, then pulled away. "Tempting, Tee. Very tempting. But we just can't. Not tonight. I'm getting cold, and people are going to start assuming we *are* doing the mattress dance out here if we don't go back to the table."

He grumbled, but allowed himself to be dragged back inside. Lynda and Jimmy Maynard were alone at the table, looking very cozy, with Jimmy's arm draped casually around her shoulder and their heads touching. Lynda was giggling at something he was saying as I sat down.

Carter and Shirlene walked up just then too, and I saw, at a glance, that Shirlene was not nearly as amused by Jimmy as my mother was. As Shirlene sat down, I stood up again. I tugged Lynda's arm.

"I'm going to the ladies' room," I announced. "Mom, want to freshen your makeup?"

She didn't even glance up at me. "No thanks," she said.

I tugged her arm again. "How about freshening mine? My hair's a mess, and you always could do it better than me."

She turned around to give me an annoyed look, but I shot her my look back, so, with a sigh, she excused herself.

"What's wrong with you?" she asked when we were in the ladies' room. "You never liked the way I did your hair. And your makeup is just fine."

I took my lipstick out of my bag and reapplied it anyway. "It's about Jimmy," I said, turning to her. "Lynda, you need to turn off the charm."

"What? We were just flirting. It's all very harmless."

"To you, maybe. But Jimmy's like a diabetic in a candy store. He can't resist a pretty lady. And the thing is, I'm pretty sure he and Shirlene are trying to get back together."

"Well, who's stopping them?" she said, a note of annoyance in her voice. "And what do you mean—back together?"

"They were married once. To each other. I don't think she ever really got over Jimmy. And he's just lately starting to realize what he's missing out on. Don't screw that up for them. Please?"

"Oh, for Pete's sake," she said, clearly exasperated with me. "I'm just trying to have a little fun. Why are you being such a Goody Two-shoes all of a sudden?"

"What about Leonard? Why don't you go home and have fun with him?"

She pulled a tissue from the container on the bathroom counter and began blotting her lips with it. "Leonard's not a whole lot of fun these days," she said. "Not since good ol' Ed showed up."

"Ed? Who's Ed?"

She arched an eyebrow. "ED," she whispered. "As in erectile dysfunction."

A tiny giggle echoed through the tiled bathroom. We both whirled around in time to see a woman emerging from the first stall.

Lynda bristled. "It's not funny."

The woman scuttled out of the room without even pausing to wash her hands.

And then we heard a toilet flushing, and the rustle of satin, and then an older woman, walking slowly on flat-heeled shoes, emerged from the second stall.

She looked from me to Lynda. "No, honey, you got that right. It sure as hell ain't funny."

59

"Dempsey?" Carter tapped me on the shoulder and held out his hand. "May I have the honor of this dance?"

The band was playing a slow song—"The Twelfth of Never"—and couples were drifting out onto the dance floor, including Lynda, who'd managed to drag Tee out of his chair.

I hesitated. "Carter—I'm a terrible slow dancer. I'll step all over your toes."

"Never!" he said, leading me onto the floor. He took my right hand in his, and gently touched the small of my back. "Just relax and follow me."

True to his word, Carter was a superb dance partner. In a moment, we were gliding around the dance floor, and if we weren't exactly Fred and Ginger, at least we weren't Fred and Wilma.

"I've been wanting to talk to you all evening," Carter said, his voice low. "But I can't seem to pry you away from my son."

"You've been pretty popular with the ladies yourself," I pointed out.

"Oh, women humor me because I'm so old," Carter said. "Anyway, I wanted to hear how it went on your trial run with the FBI today."

"You knew about that?"

"Oh yes. In fact, they dropped off the agreement from the U.S. attorney's office before they went over to see you."

"Does it look all right?"

He shrugged. "I think we've gotten the best possible deal from them that we're going to get. We didn't get everything I would have liked, but I'm satisfied now that the Justice Department will not pursue charges against you. And that we have it in writing."

"Thank God!" I said. "Now all I have to do is face down Alex Hodder, and get him to say just enough about his relationship with Tony Licata to land himself in prison."

"Can you do that?"

"We'll see," I said. "The agents make it seem very simple and cut and dried. The spot they picked for the meeting is a little church way out in the country. They've already got it wired for film and sound. So all I have to do is get him to talk about Licata and that weekend in Lyford Cay. The thing is, I just don't believe he's ever going to admit—even to me—that he instructed me to hire that call girl for Licata. Even when we talked on the phone he tried to tell me I'd 'misunderstood' his intentions. He's such a slippery slimeball."

Carter nodded thoughtfully. "I wouldn't worry too much about getting him to implicate himself. The simple fact that he is coming down here to pay you to hand over the only real hard evidence against him in this bribery scheme should be enough to prove a public-corruption charge against him. These people at Justice aren't stupid. They say and do some stupid things, yes, but they are not unintelligent. I have a feeling they probably have other evidence against Licata—and your Alex Hodder—that we don't know about."

"God, I hope so," I said fervently. "I truly cannot wait for this whole ordeal to be done with."

"After Monday, the worst of it should be in the past," Carter said. "Have you thought about what happens after that?"

"You mean a trial, that kind of thing?"

"I mean you," Carter said. He looked down at me and smiled. "What happens to Dempsey Killebrew after her involuntary exile is over?"

I guess I blushed.

"Will you listen to me?" Carter said, tsk-tsking. "I sound like a high school guidance counselor. I guess it comes with age, this compulsion to pry into other people's lives. Do as Tee does, my dear, and ignore me."

"You're not prying," I told him. "You're a friend. A good friend." I grinned. "Are you wondering if my intentions toward your son are completely honorable?"

He threw his silver head back and laughed. "Something like that.

You'll have to forgive a father for wanting to see his son happy. And may I say, you seem to make him very happy, Dempsey?"

"He makes me happy too," I said. "He's not like any other man I've known before. He's sweet and thoughtful, and honest and good. You've raised a fine man, Carter Berryhill."

"His mother did all the heavy lifting," Carter said. "I was busy building my law practice, but she made sure I did the things a father is supposed to do with his son, Boy Scouts, sports, hunting, that kind of thing. Sarah was really the one who made him into the man he is today."

"I have a feeling you did it together," I said.

The music ended, and Carter eased me off the dance floor and back in the direction of our table. "I'm sorry you never met Sarah," he told me. "I think she'd have liked you. And I know she would have loved knowing our son had found somebody as special as you."

I turned and kissed him lightly on the cheek. "Now you're going to make me cry."

"I'd be happier if I could make you stay," he told me.

60

After a Sunday taken up with driving Ella Kate to church and Sunday school, and afterward, working her way through an entire paperback sudoku book, Lynda had obviously gotten bored quickly with Guthrie and my life there. When I got downstairs Monday, at seven A.M., she was sitting at the kitchen table, sipping a tumbler of wheatgrass, dressed in a chic hot pink pants suit. Her suitcases were sitting by the door.

"Going somewhere?" I asked, trying not to look too hopeful.

"Home," she said, blotting her lips with a paper napkin. "Leonard called last night. He's missing me something awful, poor lamb. So I called the airline, and had my ticket changed. My flight leaves Atlanta at noon."

"But . . . I thought you two were . . . on the skids?"

"No! What gave you that idea?"

I poured myself a cup of coffee. With Lynda gone, I was going to miss having my coffee made for me in the morning. But I was confident I would be able to bear up under the burden.

"Well, you did. Sort of. I mean, Saturday night you said he's no fun since 'ED' came along, and I guess I assumed—"

"Leonard and I are soul mates," Lynda said earnestly. "You don't give up the kind of connection we have just because of something physical, like sex." She looked over the rim of her glass at me. "Someday, Dempsey, I hope you'll experience the kind of awesome, life-changing relationship Leonard and I have forged together. The sex part is just a little bump in the road right now. We'll get past that, because on a higher plane, spiritually I mean, we are perfectly in tune."

"That's great, Mom," I said. "You had me kind of worried Saturday night, with all that heavy flirting you were doing. I guess at your age, sex is kind of beside the point anyway."

Her eyebrows shot up. "My age? My age? My lord, what kind of junk do you young girls get into your heads these days? Sex is never beside the point! Sex *is* the point! I told Leonard last night that he either goes and gets the little blue pill, or I replace him with something less complicated—like, say, something that takes triple-A batteries."

"Lynda!"

"He got the message. That's why I'm leaving today instead of the end of the week. Although I do hate to leave you in the lurch."

"I'll be fine," I said quickly. "I'll miss you, but Carter feels sure that after my meeting today with Alex Hodder, the feds will be more than ready to cut me some slack. So you see—there's nothing for you to worry about."

She got up and rinsed out her tumbler, then put it in the dish drain. "I wish I believed that, precious."

"Why wouldn't you believe it? The feds even signed an agreement, promising not to prosecute me."

"It's not your legal predicament that has me worried anymore," she said. "Now that I've met Carter Berryhill, I feel confident you're in the best possible hands. It's your life that has me worried."

"What's wrong with my life?"

She pressed her lips together tightly. "You accused me of trying to make you over. I'm trying hard not to."

"So, it's not just about my clothes? Or this house?"

"Oh, Dempsey," Lynda said. "This is going to sound so California flaky to you, I know. But I don't care. I just don't want you to wait till too late to find your bliss."

"My bliss?" She was right. It did sound flaky.

"The thing that makes you absolutely certain you are in the right place, doing the absolute right thing, and with the right person beside you. Look at me! I was nearly fifty when I found my art, my real talent. My niche in life. And then Leonard and I found each other, and it all came together. I spent all that time searching, spinning my wheels, desperately unhappy. I couldn't raise you. Not properly. I was still raising myself all that time. I blamed your father for years, but really, it wasn't him. Well, okay, some of it was him—he can be such a rigid, unbending, cold—"

"Mom," I warned.

"Right. He is your father. Anyway, I don't want that for you, sweetheart."

She looked around the kitchen, got up, and ran her fingertips across the top of the island Bobby had built for me. "This room has such a nice vibration, Dempsey. It feels like it has a soul. Does it feel that way to you?"

"Actually, it does," I admitted. "It still needs a lot of work. But I love knowing that I laid the tile, and I stripped the floor, and I sanded the cabinets."

She nodded. "You put your heart into this room. You've put it into the house too, haven't you? I couldn't see that when I first got here. All I could see was the enormous job you had ahead of you. I was afraid this old white elephant of your father's would suck the life out of you. My therapist says I've done a lot of work getting past my past, but I guess the truth is, I still resent Mitch. And his relationship with you."

I put my arms around her neck. "Aww, Mom. That's sweet. But our relationship isn't all that great right now. Anyway, he's not you. He's not my mom. He can't fix my hair, or make me a gorgeous necklace, or restyle my parlor."

"Even when you don't want it restyled," she added.

"I wanted it. I just didn't know I wanted it," I told her.

Thump. Slide. Thump. Slide. Ella Kate and her walker were slowly making their way down the hallway. Shorty ran ahead of her, his nails clicking on the worn floorboards. I got down his bin of dog food and filled his bowl, which he attacked as soon as he entered the room.

"I'm gonna miss that old girl," Lynda said. "I know she's been a pain in the neck for you, but she's got spunk. The universe should have worn her completely down by now, but it hasn't."

"More like the other way around," I said wryly, bending down to scratch Shorty's ears.

"I'm proud of you, Dempsey," Lynda said quickly. "For stepping in and taking care of her."

"I didn't have much of a choice."

"Everybody's up mighty early around here," Ella Kate said, pushing her walker into the kitchen.

"Lynda's decided it's time to go home," I told the old lady. "I tried to get her to change her mind—"

"No you didn't," Lynda said. "You're just as glad to have me out of your hair as I am to go."

Ella Kate looked from me to Lynda. "You two have a fuss?"

"Not at all," Lynda said. "I came because I thought Dempsey needed me. It turns out I needed to see her more than she needed to see me. I was worried about her, but I can see now that she's made a real life for herself here in Guthrie."

"I have?"

Lynda stood beside Ella Kate and helped ease her into her wooden chair. "Don't you think she's worked wonders on this old house, Ella Kate?"

"I reckon," Ella Kate said. "You got any coffee left?"

I fixed her a mug and took it over to the table. She took a sip and nodded her approval. "Your mama makes coffee a lot better'n you do."

"She does everything better than me," I said. "But I'm trying to learn from her example."

Ella Kate thought about that. She jerked her head in Lynda's direction. "How many times did you say she's been married?"

I gasped, but Lynda threw her head back and gave a belly laugh. "Only twice," she protested. "I know lots of women who've been married more times than that."

"You married to this Leonard fella you're livin' with?" Ella Kate demanded.

"Well, no, but we've been together for six years," Lynda said. "That's longer than I've ever been with any man before. It's my personal best."

"Huh," Ella Kate said, shaking her head. She looked at me. "What about you and that Berryhill boy? You ain't studying shacking up with him like your mama does, are you?"

"Ella Kate!" Lynda protested.

"I knew Sarah Berryhill," Ella Kate went on, as though she hadn't heard. "Now that was a fine Christian lady. But once that breast cancer took ahold of her, she was just eat up with it. I believe that's the biggest funeral I've been to around here since Olivia passed. The Berryhill boy's a lawyer, ain't he?"

"His name is Tee," I put in. "And you know good and well he's in practice with Carter."

"I hear the son is runnin' the newspaper these days. I reckon he wadn't too good at lawyerin'. Not as good as his daddy, anyhow." Ella Kate looked at me plaintively. "You got any eggs and bacon in the house? I b'lieve I got my appetite back this morning."

"Tee's a fine lawyer," I said, skipping over the subject of breakfast. "But he loves journalism, and he wants to give back to this community. He's doubled the paper's circulation since he took over running it, you know."

"I don't take a paper these days, but if I did, it would be the Atlanta paper," Ella Kate said grandly. "Norbert always took the *Atlanta Constitution.* He liked to read the sports section. I like the Sunday funnies and Ann Landers. Does your boyfriend's paper have Ann Landers?"

"Ann Landers is dead, you know," Lynda said, apropos of nothing. She went to the refrigerator and took out a carton of eggs. She set the eggs down on the counter and grimaced as she brought out a package of bacon.

"Here," I said, taking the offending meat from her. "I'll fix her breakfast. I'm not trying to chase you off, but I guess you better get on the road before you get tied up in Atlanta traffic."

"You're right," Lynda said. She planted a kiss on my forehead. "Goodbye, sweetheart. Call me tonight and let me know how your meeting turned out."

"I will," I promised.

"Be strong," she said, hugging me. "I'm going to visualize you strong. And that snake in the grass Hodder, I'm visualizing him in prison.

"And you!" Lynda said, wheeling around to face Ella Kate. "You take care of yourself, will you? No more joyriding around in stolen cars. And look after my girl too, will you?"

"Huh!" Ella Kate said, trying to suppress a pleased grin. "You comin' back for the wedding?"

"Wedding?" My mother and I said it in unison.

"Wedding," Ella Kate said firmly. "I ain't fixin' to live under the same roof with anybody livin' in sin. It ain't right. I don't care if her mama does it that way. That's California. But this is Guthrie, Georgia. In Guthrie, we go to church and stand up in front of God and pledge our troth. And then we have cake and punch in the church parlor. And cheese straws. Gotta have cheese straws."

"Is there going to be a wedding?" Lynda asked.

"He hasn't asked me," I said, blushing.

"He's fixin' to," Ella Kate volunteered. "The boy's goofy over her. Anybody can see it."

"Well then," Lynda said, picking up a suitcase in each hand. "That settles it. I'll definitely be back for the wedding. And who knows? Maybe I'll even bring Leonard along. Wouldn't that just set your father's teeth on edge?"

"I'm not even engaged," I said weakly. But nobody was listening.

61

As soon as my mother zoomed away from the curb in her rented Escalade, I started wondering how I would fill the hours until it was time to leave for the New Macedonia Full Gospel Church of the Brethren and my come-to-Jesus meeting with Alex Hodder.

When the senior-services bus arrived to take Ella Kate to physical therapy, I waved her off and promised to take Shorty for a walk. It was a beautiful morning, full of the promise of spring. The dogwoods were in full bloom, and every house on the street seemed to flaunt frills of azaleas at the edge of bright green lawns. Shorty was happy to be out, he trotted along, barked at every squirrel and stray cat and baptized every fire hydrant and shrub on the block.

But with every step, the what-ifs haunted me. What if Alex didn't come? What if he did come? What if he didn't bring the money? What if something happened—with the hidden cameras, or me? What if, after all that had happened, I somehow managed to screw the whole thing up?

Back from the walk, I decided to fight the sense of dread settling over me by keeping busy. I did the breakfast dishes, and wandered around the house making a list of all the projects I still needed to complete. The bathrooms were at the top of the list. Much as I loved the big pedestal sinks and roomy old bathtubs, no amount of scrubbing was going to remove decades-old chips and rust stains from their porcelain surfaces. We needed proper showers, new tile, new fixtures, new plumbing. It wouldn't be cheap.

As I tallied up the potential cost of the work, I started to think about all the questions Carter and my mother had peppered me with. What *would* I do after the whole Hoddergate mess was settled? If it was settled.

Carter seemed to think the feds would be happy to let me walk away from any charges, considering my cooperation with the FBI. Could I go back to Washington? Would anybody hire me as a lobbyist, after my name had been so publicly dragged through the mud? More to the point, and to Lynda's question—did I even want to go back to my old life?

Up until now, I hadn't allowed myself to dwell on the "what next" scenarios. It was all I could do to get through the moment I was in, without wondering about the moments still to come.

My mother seemed to think I'd made a life for myself in Guthrie. That thought hadn't occurred to me. True, I'd found unexpected joy in fixing up Birdsong. Unexpected joy too with Tee Berryhill. Was this the bliss Lynda had talked about?

I didn't have time to ponder the questions. The doorbell rang, and when I got to the door, I saw Carter and Tee standing there, both of them grinning from ear to ear.

"Well, hello," I said, swinging the door open. "You two seem pretty pleased with yourselves."

Tee leaned in and kissed me—full on the lips. "We've got a surprise for you," he said.

"Goody," I said. "Lead on. I just love surprises."

Carter turned and gestured toward the curb. "There she is," he said.

And there she was. The Catfish. Her Georgia Bulldog red paint gleamed in the warm morning sunlight. Her chrome had been buffed to a high sheen. Her crumpled roof and busted-out front and rear windshields had miraculously been mended. All the dents and scratches and indignities she'd suffered from her brush with disaster were but a distant memory. As far as I was concerned, she was showroom perfection. She had new white-sidewall tires. She was a smoking-hot vision of vintage loveliness.

"Oh my God," I shrieked, covering my mouth.

I walked out to the curb and circled her, running my fingers over the new paint job and the smoothed-out body. Tee and Carter stood on the lawn, enjoying the spectacle I was making. "This is so awesome," I said, blinking back tears. Yes, I was crying over a car. Maybe I'd become a bona fide Southerner. The next thing you knew, I'd be frying chicken and drinking sweet tea. It was insidious.

"You like it?" Tee asked. I threw my arms around his neck and demonstrated just how grateful I was.

"I believe she does," Carter said, chuckling.

"She's beautiful," I said, releasing Tee from the neck lock. "How on earth did you get her looking like this? I bet Uncle Norbert himself wouldn't recognize her."

"Shawn is a very talented and hard-working individual," Carter said. "As it happens, he used to do work for your great-uncle Norbert. He was very familiar with the Catfish."

"I can't thank you enough," I said. "I was just about to call you and ask if I could borrow a car for my meeting today."

"The timing of your meeting figured heavily in my urging the mechanic to put a rush on things," Carter said. "He only called an hour ago to tell me she was ready."

Tee ran his hand over the front fender. "Pretty sweet, huh? You wanna take her for a spin?"

I bit my lip. "Wait a second. This must have cost a lot of money. All the body work, the windshields, the paint job. And those are new tires. What's all this going to cost?"

"There is no bill," Tee insisted. "No cash changed hands. Shawn's girlfriend needed a lawyer, we needed a car fixed. It all worked out."

"It's a zero balance," Carter said solemnly. He held up his right hand. "Scout's honor."

"Then I owe you the money you would have gotten in legal fees, plus my own legal fees," I persisted. "I want a bill, Carter. That's the only way I'll take the Catfish back. That was our deal, remember? The pink slip for legal fees."

"C'mon, Dempsey," Tee said, tugging at my hand. "Will you let it go, please? It's a gift. From us to you."

I shook my head stubbornly. "My mother taught me some manners. Candy or flowers or books are proper gifts from a gentleman. She never said anything about cars."

Carter chuckled. "She's got us there, son. Your mother told you the same thing when you started dating." He rolled his eyes. "When he was fourteen, young Romeo here bought his lady friend a pair of blue jeans for Valentine's Day. Sarah was horrified."

"Got 'em at the Belk's in the Macon mall," Tee admitted. "I spent a month's worth of my lawn-mowing money on 'em, and then Mama made me take 'em back."

"What was that young lady's name?" Carter asked.

"Lydia Dexter," Tee said promptly. "The love of my life till she dumped me for B. J. Johnson. He was the first guy in our class to get his driver's license, because he failed fifth grade. Once she saw that Toyota Tacoma of his, it was all over between us. I still can't believe it. Ditched for a Japanese pickup truck. I tell ya, I'm still traumatized when I think about it."

"Cars. It all comes down to cars," I muttered.

Carter cleared his throat. "Dempsey, I don't have a bill to give you because we don't always work that way in Guthrie. It was a pure barter situation. And I can't let you give me this car as payment for my meager legal services. My fees might add up to the cost of one of those tires. So you see, my dear, we are at an impasse."

Tee jingled the car keys in front of my face. "C'mon. You know you want to see how she drives. And how else were you going to get to your meeting?"

I snatched the keys from his hand. "This isn't over," I said. "I'll find a way to pay you back, Carter, if I have to show up at your office and clean windows to pay off my debt."

"The office," Carter said. "Now there's an idea. I have somebody who does windows, but I could use some help with my caseload. And I seem to remember you have a law degree."

"From Georgetown," I said. "Although I'm not licensed in Georgia."

"Interesting," Carter said, nodding. "We must discuss this, Dempsey, if you're serious."

"I'm serious about paying you back," I told him.

Tee glanced at his watch. "Okay, you can negotiate a settlement later. Right now, it's after noon. Let's go get some lunch." He glared at me. "My treat, or we don't go. It's a date. Remember dates?"

"It's been a long time," I told him. "You might have to refresh my memory."

He opened the door on the driver's side, and I slid onto the leather seat. He loped around to the passenger side, and as we drove off, Carter gave us a snappy salute.

"I just love your dad," I told Tee, returning Carter's salute. "He's like someone from another century."

"He thinks the world of you," Tee said.

I smiled. "We had a talk at the dance Saturday night. I accused him of wondering if my intentions toward you are honorable."

"I hope you told him they aren't," Tee said, throwing his arm across my shoulders and scooting over on the seat beside me. He nibbled on my earlobe. I tried to concentrate on my driving.

"He's worried that I'm trifling with you," I said, not daring to take my eyes off the road. "He seems to think things have gotten pretty serious between us."

"That old hound," Tee said, groaning. "He's about as subtle as a sledgehammer. What did you tell him?"

I chose my words carefully. "He told me he's glad I make you happy. And I told him you make me very happy. He said he wished I could have met your mom. And then he said something, like, wishing I would stay."

"Stay?"

"Here. In Guthrie."

"What did you say to that?"

"Nothing. The song ended. 'The Twelfth of Never.' Kind of a dumb song, don't you think?" I held my breath, wondering what he would say to that.

He put his lips next to my ear and hummed a bar of "The Twelfth of Never."

"What if that song were still playing? What if instead of my old man, it was me you were dancing with? Johnny Mathis was always the king of the make-out song. What if we were dancing, right now, and I told you I've fallen in love with you. What if I asked you if you would stay? Right here in Guthrie. With me?"

I exhaled slowly. "I'd say I think I'm falling too. But I want the song to keep playing. Just a little longer, Tee. I'd say let's enjoy the right now. Let me get through this meeting with Alex Hodder. Let me banish the past before I try to figure out the future."

I shot him a quick, pleading look. "Please? Let me get through today?"

"And then you'll give me a straight answer? No more stalling? Yes or no?"

I nodded my head. "Absolutely."

"Then let's get some lunch."

62

I pulled the Catfish up outside the newspaper office, and leaned over
to kiss Tee good-bye.

"Call me as soon as it's over," he said. "And I mean as soon as it's
over."

"I will," I promised.

"And be careful," he said. "I don't like the idea of you meeting this
guy alone out in the middle of nowhere."

"I won't be alone, Agents Harrell and Allgood will be right there," I
reminded him.

"Yeah. That's what I'm worried about."

"See you tonight?"

"You better."

My cell phone rang as I was heading back to Birdsong, startling me
so badly I almost ran off the road. I dug in my pocketbook and brought
it out, glancing at the caller ID screen: GOVERNMENT CALLER.

This particular government caller happened to be Special Agent
Jackson Harrell.

"If you're done necking with your boyfriend, maybe we can meet
back at your place, for one last briefing," Harrell said.

I glanced in the rearview mirror and saw that the silver government-
issue sedan was right on my tail.

"You're following me?" I said indignantly. "That is so not cool!"

"For your own protection," Harrell said. "I'm just a servant of the
people."

"You're a damned peeping Tom is what you are. Why don't you follow Alex Hodder around?"

"We have been," Harrell said. "That's where Cam is right now. His plane just taxied up to the gate."

It was only one thirty. I swallowed hard and my stomach clenched. I glanced in the rearview mirror again, and Harrell gave me a little wave.

"Relax," Harrell said. "We're right on schedule. His plane landed all the way out at the E terminal, and unless he can sprint faster than ol' O.J. Simpson, there's no way he gets to the rental counter before two P.M, or to the church before three P.M."

"I'll see you at the house," I said, clicking the phone shut.

Harrell parked the sedan down the block from the house and loped up the street to meet me.

"Just takin' precautions," he said as he passed me on the sidewalk. "Go on inside. I'll double back around the block and cut through your backyard neighbor's yard. See you in five."

Ella Kate was back from physical therapy. She was sitting on the chair in front of her bedroom window when I walked past her door. "That colored FBI fella is back," she called out, putting down Norbert's army-issue World War II binoculars. "Wonder what he's up to."

"He's here to see me," I told her. "I'm meeting my former boss later today, and he wants to go over the plan with me. How was your physical therapy?"

She snorted. "That girl is more like a terrorist than a therapist. Had me workin' like a field hand. I'm flat wore out. This old boss—is this the fella been tellin' people you hired prostitutes for that crooked congressman?"

"He's the one," I said.

"You takin' a pistol to this meeting?"

"No!" I said. "Absolutely not."

"City girl," Ella Kate said contemptuously, picking up the binoculars again. "Well, I got Norbert's old Colt under my mattress if you change your mind."

"Thanks anyway," I told her, wondering how and when Ella Kate had spirited a firearm into her new sleeping quarters. God forbid it was loaded. Maybe I didn't want to know?

Shorty was barking frantically out in the kitchen, scratching at the back door. I opened it and let Harrell in.

He glanced down at the little cocker spaniel, who looked up and emitted a low growl.

"Don't bother trying to pet him," I told Harrell. "He's just like his owner. He plain doesn't like strangers."

I motioned for the agent to take a chair, and I pulled one up across from him. "You've had somebody watching Alex all weekend, right?" I asked.

"Never had him out of our sights," Harrell said. "He kept close to home, though. His wife went to some big charity gala Friday night, but he was a no-show. He didn't even play golf with his regular foursome Saturday morning. You've got him worried, all right."

"Not as worried as me. I feel like I want to throw up every time I think about this whole farce."

"It's no farce," Jackson said, dropping his casual demeanor. "This is the real deal. Hodder checked his suitcase at the airport. You don't do that for a down-and-back flight to Atlanta unless you don't want your carry-on searched in front of everybody by the TSA. He's got the money, we're certain."

He reached inside his jacket pocket and brought out a plain white business envelope, which he handed across to me. I opened it and pulled out an exact copy of Alex Hodder's golf scorecard from the infamous Lyford Cay outing.

"Wow," I said, gingerly turning it over and over to get a closer look. "Pretty decent forgery."

"Go ahead and handle it a little bit," Harrell urged me. "Your original was kinda beat up too. We want it to look like it's been kicking around for a while."

"You want me to give him this—instead of the original?"

"Yeah," Harrell said. "We've had the original fingerprinted, and the handwriting analyzed. It's got Hodder's fingerprints, and Licata's, which was a bonus. And it's definitely Hodder's handwriting. The boss doesn't want to risk him deciding to rip up the original once you hand it over to him."

I held the duplicate golf card in my hands, which were beginning to sweat.

"Got something else for you," Harrell said. He brought out a black plastic key fob with a Ford emblem in the center.

I looked up at him questioningly.

"Put it on the ring with the keys to the Bulldogmobile," Harrell said.

I went out to the hallway and got my key ring from my pocketbook and came back into the kitchen. He took the ring from me, and attached the fob to it.

"Okay," I said, tapping the fob. "A remote-control door-lock thing. Is this another example of my tax dollars at work?"

"It's your body mike," Harrell said. "You said you didn't want a bug on you, so this is what we came up with."

I gave the fob a closer look. It looked just like any other remote I'd ever seen. The silvery Ford logo looked real. It wasn't particularly thick.

"For real?" I asked. "This'll work?"

"Works like a charm," Harrell said smugly. "It's hypersensitive. Comes through clear as a bell. You can even leave it in your pocket if you want to."

"Where will it transmit to?" I asked.

"We'll have a team right across the road, in an old barn," Harrell said.

"Will you be there?"

"I'll be around," he said vaguely.

"Cam too?"

"Oh yeah. She's not missing out on this operation. She hung around the airport just long enough to see Hodder's plane land, and she's on her way back right now." He checked his watch. "I better get going too." He handed me another envelope. I opened it, and saw that it contained typed directions to the church.

"He should be calling you anytime now, to find out about the meeting place. Read him those directions, get him to repeat 'em to be sure. We don't want him getting lost."

"Okay," I said, looking up. "Just get me to the church on time, right?"

"Right," Harrell said. "You know what you're supposed to do, don't you?"

"Try to draw him out, get him to talk about Lyford Cay, and Tony Licata," I said. "Show him the golf scorecard, make him show me the money. Make it clear that I'm selling him the scorecard because that's his handwriting with the call girl's phone number on it. That's about it, right?"

"Just like we talked about the other day," Harrell said smoothly.

Harrell slid his chair away from the table and stood up. He extended his hand. "All right, Dempsey. Don't be nervous now. And don't be leaving your keys in the car. We need that to be with you just in case the mikes in the church don't pick up what you and Hodder are saying. This is gonna go just like clockwork. Don't you worry about anything. We got your back the whole way."

He was halfway out the kitchen door before another thought occurred to me. "What happens after he gives me the money?" I asked.

"You take your bag full of cash and get the hell out of Dodge," Harrell said, flashing a pearly smile. "We'll take care of the rest."

I took the stairs two at a time. I'd laid out my outfit earlier in the morning. It was my black Power Ranger suit. I was already wearing the Piaget watch. I got dressed, put on my high-heeled boots, twisted my hair up and back, and dabbed on some makeup—foundation, blush, heavy black eye liner, and mascara. At the last minute, I slipped Lynda's necklace over my head.

"Ready or not, Alex, here I come," I whispered.

The necklace charms tinkled merrily as I went downstairs, suitcase in hand.

"Dempsey?" Ella Kate called out from her room.

I stuck my head in her door. She carefully put the binoculars back in their case. She looked me up and down, taking in the dramatic makeup and the suitcase. "Don't you look a sight," she said.

I didn't know if that was a compliment or not, so I decided it was. "Thank you," I said.

"I see you're wearing that necklace your mama made you," she said. "She's a flighty one, your mama, but I believe she's got a good heart. Even if she is livin' in sin. I'll tell you something. Ever since she did that burnin' bush voodoo of hers, danged if I don't feel a good bit better."

"Really?"

Ella Kate nodded. "Your mama thinks I should go see another cancer doctor to get a second opinion about surgery. She says I'm too ornery to let cancer get the better of me."

My eyes widened. "Are you going to do it? Have surgery?"

"Ain't saying I will or I won't," Ella Kate said. "I'm just sayin' I'll study on it."

"I'm glad," I told her.

"Anyway, I know you got to git. But I got somethin' I want to give you."

The old lady was just full of surprises today. "Well, thanks," I said, hoping the presentation wouldn't take too long.

She reached into the pocket of her cardigan sweater and brought out a small box. It was covered in worn blue velvet, and had a tiny catch.

"Here," she said stiffly, pressing it into the palm of my hand.

I opened the catch. A small, gold, star-shaped pin twinkled from the blue velvet lining. I held it up to read the engraving. GUTHRIE UNITED METHODIST SUNDAY SCHOOL, it said.

"It's lovely," I said, lifting it from the lining and fastening it to the lapel of my jacket.

"My folks didn't have no money," Ella Kate said. "We were the poor relations to your kin, that's for sure. My daddy didn't have no diamond stickpins, or pearl shirt studs, and Mama didn't even have a real wedding ring, just a little tin ring Daddy give her. That pin there, that's the only prize I ever won in my life. Got it at church, for perfect attendance five years in a row at Sunday school, when I was ten years old. It's eighteen-karat gold. I know, 'cause I took it to Macon to the jewelry store at that mall and had 'em check it out. It's the real thing."

"Oh, Ella Kate," I said, feeling my heart melt. "I can't take your pin. It's too precious." I started to unfasten it from my jacket.

"No, now, I want you to have it," Ella Kate said. "I didn't think much of you when you showed up here at Birdsong. Still don't think much of your daddy, and his daddy, well, you know how I feel about that scoundrel. But you've been good to me and Shorty. Probably gooder'n I deserve. I don't know what's gonna become of you after you get this business settled with them FBI agents. Probably, you'll pack up and hightail it back up there to Washington, D.C. Probably, your daddy will sell this house, and turn me out. Carter Berryhill says that's his right. And he's a lawyer, so I reckon he knows the law."

"I wouldn't let him turn you out," I said quickly. "Anyway, we couldn't sell the house until it's finished. And it won't be. Not for a while yet. We'll figure something out."

"The Lord works in mysterious ways," Ella Kate said. "I've been prayin' on it, and that's what I know. I know my scripture verses too. And the scripture says no matter what happens, you are never alone. I keep that close to my heart, and you'd do well to keep it close to yours too. Either way, you keep that pin. You earned it. For perfect attendance. To me and Shorty."

I leaned down to hug her, but she turned her face back to the window. Probably hoping to spy some more skulduggery on the street outside.

"I'll be back in a little while," I told her. But she didn't turn around.

My cell phone rang as I was walking toward the front door. My heart nearly leaped out of my chest when I glanced at the caller ID readout: PRIVATE CALLER. This was it. We were rolling. I touched Ella Kate's Sunday school pin on my lapel. Be strong, I thought. Like that old lady in the front bedroom.

"Hello," I said, trying to sound cool.

"I'm here." Alex's voice was curt. "Tell me how to get to this meeting place of yours."

"Have you got the money?" I asked, fumbling in my purse for the directions to the church.

"Of course I've got the goddamned money," he snapped. "Now, can we get on with this? I've got a seven o'clock flight to catch, and I sure as hell don't want to spend the day driving around in the godforsaken backwoods of Georgia."

"You'd better get used to the backwoods. We're meeting at a church. It's the New Macedonia Full Gospel Church of the Brethren. Have you got a pencil?"

"A church? What the hell?"

"It's very private," I told him. "Away from prying eyes and ears. Now, write it all down. I don't want you and that satchel full of money getting lost on the way down here from Atlanta."

"Fuck," he said under his breath.

I read him the directions slowly, and even made him read them back to me.

"This is ridiculous," he said huffily. "You could have just met me up here at the airport. We could have met in the Waffle House and been done with it. I'd be back in D.C. in time for dinner. Why the hell should I have to go on some wild goose chase to get this taken care of?"

"Because this is the way I wanted it, Alex," I said, straightening my shoulders. "I'm the one holding the scorecard, and you're the one who needs it. Also, just in case you've forgotten? You're not the boss of me anymore."

I was backing the Catfish out of the driveway when my cell phone rang again: GOVERNMENT CALLER.

"Atta girl Dempsey," Jackson Harrell crowed. "Girl, you are one big ol' ballbuster. I didn't know you had it in you."

"You heard?" I glanced down at the key chain hanging from the ignition.

"Oh yeah," Harrell said. "We all heard you loud and clear. Everybody's in position here. Cam just called. She's five minutes out. When you get to the church, don't be lookin' around, trying to figure out where we are. We're here, okay? That's all you need to know. Just do what you got to do. Act natural. And give 'em hell."

Gravel crunched under the Catfish's new white-sidewall tires. New Macedonia Church looked no different than it had on Saturday. The parking lot was still empty. I pulled the Catfish up close to the church door, and tucked my key ring into the pocket of my slacks. My heart was already beating so fast I was sure Harrell and the rest of his agents—wherever they were hidden—could hear it as clearly as they'd heard my voice back at Birdsong.

It was two forty-five P.M. As I got out of the car, I spotted movement out of the corner of my eye. A stoop-shouldered black man, wearing a wide-brimmed straw hat and work-stained overalls, pushed an old-fashioned rotary lawn mower slowly across the church's grassy front lawn. Was this the pastor? What would he think of two strangers trespassing in his church? The old man worked slowly, back and forth across the grass. At one point, he turned toward me and tipped the brim of his hat, wiping perspiration from his face with a red bandanna.

The "pastor" was Jackson Harrell! I gave him a cursory nod and tried not to smile, but I did feel myself relax just the teensiest bit. I touched the Sunday school pin. Ella Kate was right about one thing. I wasn't alone.

I walked briskly up the front steps of the church, and when I got to the door, I saw that it was slightly ajar. The door creaked as I opened it wider.

Inside, everything was the same as before. The heels of my boots clacked noisily across the worn wooden floors. I walked up the center aisle, and looked slowly around the room, trying not to stare at the outmoded microphone on the lectern, or up at the choir loft, where I knew the second camera was hidden.

Finally, I took a seat in the front pew, sliding over a stack of hymnals so I could sit by the aisle. I took the key chain out of my pocket and stared down at it. "I'm here," I whispered. "Hope you guys are too."

I checked my watch. Ten minutes to go. I stood up and walked around the church, studying the stained-glass windows. The ruined one, with its crude plywood patch, depicted the peaceable kingdom, with a lion and a lamb resting together. The still-intact window showed a smiling, benign Jesus, his hands reaching out, the rays of the sun illuminating his head. There was a small brass plaque nailed to the wall beneath each of the windows: GIFT OF THE HENRY AND LOUELLA BRIGGS FAMILY and GIFT OF THE SUNSHINE SUNDAY SCHOOL CLASS.

I heard a car drive past on the road outside, but it kept going. A minute later, I heard the crunch of tires on the gravel lot. I clenched and unclenched my fists, rotated my shoulders, willed myself to stay calm and focused.

A car door slammed outside. Footsteps on the wooden porch. Now the creak of the door hinges.

Alex Hodder strode into the church. He wore a peach golf shirt under a blue blazer, and he radiated menace. "I'm here, goddammit," he said. "Let's get this thing done with."

63

"Hello, Alex," I said pleasantly. "Nice to see you too."

He walked rapidly toward me. I tried not to flinch, reminding myself that I was the one in control here.

As he drew closer, I was startled by the dramatic change in my former boss and mentor. He'd lost weight, at least ten or fifteen pounds. His jacket and slacks hung from his formerly athletic frame, and the flesh was stretched tight across his cheekbones and forehead, with deep pockets of dark skin sagging beneath his eyes. His hair was longish on the sides, and for the first time I noticed his receding hairline and definite bald spot—not to mention he was gray at the temples.

What had I ever seen in this angry old man?

He stretched out his hand, snapping his fingers impatiently. "Let's see it then. I didn't come all the way down here to chitchat."

I took a step away from him. "I don't see anything that looks like four hundred thousand dollars."

"The money's locked in the trunk of the rental outside," Alex said. "Did you think I'd just walk in some church with a suitcase full of cash?"

"That was our agreement," I said, trying not to sound nervous. Why would he leave the money in the car? Was he planning to try to double-cross me? I plunged my trembling hands in my pockets and clutched the key fob tightly.

"The scorecard," he said. "I want to see it. Right now."

I took the business envelope out of the inner pocket of my jacket, and my mother's charm chain jingled. I held the square of cardboard tightly in my fingertips and waved it in front of his face. "Here it is," I said. "But you're not touching it until I see my money." I put it back in the envelope, which I replaced in my inner pocket—the one closest to my heart.

"Christ," he muttered. "I don't believe this is happening."

"Believe it," I snapped. "I'm not enjoying this any more than you are. But we're not going any further until I see my money."

His face reddened, then he turned on his heel and strode out of the church.

Come back, I wanted to scream. But I stood motionless in front of the altar.

I heard the slam of a car trunk, and his footsteps approaching, even faster this time. He strode up the aisle with an inexpensive black roll-on suitcase under one arm.

"Here," he said, thrusting the suitcase toward me.

I laid the suitcase on the front pew, hoping the angle would be good for the cameras. My hands were shaking as I unzipped the top. I folded it back and blinked. It was that morning's edition of the *Washington Post.*

"What the hell?" I whirled around.

"Under the newspaper," Alex said, biting off the words.

I lifted the front page, and sure enough, was greeted with the sight of neatly wrapped stacks of cash. I picked up one of the bundles, which was banded with paper strapping, and fanned the bills. All twenties. I picked up another brick on the far side of the suitcase and fanned it. All fifties.

"There's two hundred thousand in twenties and two hundred thousand in fifties," Alex said. "Do me the courtesy of taking my word for it, okay? I don't have time to stand around here while you count each god-damned bundle."

"I should take your word for something?" I said, laughing bitterly as I put the bundle of bills back in the suitcase. "Trust you, is that what you're saying? You really do think I'm a moron, don't you, Alex? After the way you set me up? You had me plan that whole trip to Lyford Cay with Licata. Had me put all of it on my company credit card—including the golf and the hookers. You framed me nice and neat, and at the time, I did trust you. Look where it got me. I'm broke, jobless, unhireable."

"You're where you are right now because you're a stupid, incompetent twit," Alex said. "Don't ask me to feel sorry for you. You deserve everything you got—and more. Now give me the scorecard."

I hesitated. He'd shown me the money, after all. But I really hadn't gotten him to talk enough about why he was buying me off.

He held his hand out, snapping his fingers impatiently. "Come on. Hand it over."

I took the envelope out of my jacket and held it out.

He snatched it away from me, pulling the scorecard out of the envelope, which he carelessly tossed to the floor.

His head bent over the card as he read it. "Shit," he said, shaking his head. "I'd forgotten about this. Fucking Licata. He even cheats at golf. He took a four on the second hole? The weasel shot a six, and expected me to act like I didn't notice."

"He's a cheater?" I asked, incredulously, clutching and unclutching the key fob in my sweaty hand. "What about you? You and Peninsula Petroleum, and your other clients—you bought yourself a vote on that energy bill. Bought and paid for a United States congressman, with a trip to the Bahamas, fancy dinners, and hookers."

"You don't know what you're talking about," Alex said, shoving the scorecard in the pocket of his slacks.

"I'm talking about a bribe," I said heatedly. "You gave it and Tony Licata took it. And you tried to drag me down into your slime to save your own asses."

"You stupid, pathetic bitch." He spat out the words. "Don't you dare get all righteous with me about bribing a congressman. What the hell are you? A vicious little blackmailer! You say you're doing this because you need the money? Don't kid yourself. This is about revenge. The only reason you're doing this is because I wouldn't sleep with you. Tony Licata's an idiot too, but he was right about one thing. He said I should have fucked you, to keep your mouth shut." Alex laughed. "Hell, I told him, I got my standards. I'd rather fuck a pro than an amateur, any day."

I couldn't stop myself. I forgot why I was there. I forgot to be cool. Forgot to be calm. I even forgot I was holding the key chain. I hauled off and smacked Alex Hodder as hard as I could. The sound of flesh meeting flesh echoed in the high-ceilinged church. The key chain went flying into the air. It landed on the wooden floor. I watched, in open-mouthed horror, as the plastic key fob split in two and a tiny silvery disk inside went rolling across the floor.

Alex looked up at me, speechless with shock. He stared at the key ring on the floor. Was that the bug that had just rolled beneath a pew? Would he realize what it was? A fine stream of blood trickled down his cheek, which bore my red handprint. He swiped at his cheek, then looked down at his own blood-streaked hand.

"Stupid bitch." He said it quietly. Before I knew what was happening, he stalked over to the pew and snatched up the suitcase.

"No!" I screamed. "We had a deal."

"Did you think I'd just let you walk away with this kind of money?" He laughed and tucked the suitcase under his arm. "Fucking loser."

He turned and started for the door. With my money, and my future as ruined as my past.

"Oh, hell no," I said through gritted teeth. Maybe it was the Power Ranger suit, maybe it was the adrenaline. I'll never know. I launched myself onto Alex's back, locking my right arm around his neck.

Alex didn't go down, but he turned around, truly shocked by the assault. He grunted and shoved me backward, sending me sprawling on the floor, and in the doing, dropping the suitcase momentarily. "Crazy woman," he muttered, reaching again for the suitcase, lying inches from my feet. At that moment, I saw red. I kicked my wicked, pointed-toe boot high and hard and right at the sagging crotch of Alex's pants.

His high-pitched scream told me I'd scored a direct hit. He fell to the floor, clutching his wounded genitals with both hands. I scrambled to my feet and snatched the suitcase. Three more steps and I'd retrieved my key ring. Alex's moans echoed in the church sanctuary. I ran, as though the devil himself were in pursuit, straight out the door of the church. I threw the suitcase in the front seat, shoved the key in the ignition, and threw the Catfish into reverse. Gravel sprayed everywhere. I shifted into drive and stomped on the accelerator. Glancing into the rearview mirror, I saw, through the cloud of dust my departure had kicked up, Alex, standing silhouetted in the church doorway, his face contorted in pain and rage.

I was shaking and breathing hard, as though I'd just run a marathon. I didn't slow down.

64

I looked over at the suitcase, which had slid onto the floor of the Catfish when I'd gunned the engine during my great escape. Was it really possible that there was $400,000 in this cheap black bag?

I glanced backward, in the rearview mirror. Any moment now, I expected to see Alex Hodder's rental car bearing down on me, forcing me off the road or worse. Five minutes passed. And then ten. I sped on, back toward Guthrie's city limits. There was no sign of Alex's white Acura. My shoulders and arms were rigid with tension. My legs felt like rubber.

When I got to the Bi-Lo shopping center, I pulled into the parking lot and parked directly in front of the store, leaving the doors locked and the motor running. My heart pounding, I righted the suitcase and unzipped it. I lifted up the newspaper and stared down at the stacks of bills. I picked up a brick of the twenty-dollar bills, and sniffed. They weren't new bills, but they weren't too terribly old either. To my untrained eye, they looked very real. But I wouldn't have bet on it. Alex Hodder was a cheat and a crook, and I now knew that he was capable of all kinds of treachery.

I patted the stacks of bills one last time and zipped up the suitcase. And then I tenderly fastened the seat belt around my ill-gotten gains and headed for home.

I was pulling out of the Bi-Lo parking lot when my cell phone rang. "Hello?"

"Is this Dempsey Killebrew?"

It was a woman's voice, with a faintly Midwestern accent, but not one I could identify.

"Miss Killebrew, this is Sharon Douglas. I'm the U.S. attorney for the Northern District of Georgia."

"Oh. Hello."

"I can't really talk right now, but I did want you to know that I was with our team in the barn today, listening and watching everything. You did a great job. You were magnificent."

I gulped. "Well, thanks. I guess. What about Alex? Did you arrest him yet?"

She laughed. "We like to think we work fast, but not that fast. No, he finally managed to limp out to his rental car and leave."

"Do you think he's looking for me?" I asked, my pulse racing.

She laughed. "No, I don't think Mr. Hodder wants to see you again anytime soon. Agent Allgood is following him. He made a stop at a convenience store, and bought a bag of ice. I imagine that's for his, er, injury. Now it looks like he's headed in the direction of the airport."

"But . . . what if he tries to get away? Tries to leave the country or something?"

"He's not leaving the country," she assured me. "Why would he? He thinks he's got this thing licked. By now he's probably destroyed what he thinks is the only credible evidence against him. Right now, he's probably on the phone, booking a table at the Monocle for a late dinner."

"When will you arrest him?" I demanded. "Look, I've had this thing hanging over my head for weeks now. My life has been put on hold, my nerves are shot—"

"What?" I could hear the low buzz of other voices from her end of the line.

"Look, Dempsey," she said hurriedly. "I've got to go now. I've got a conference call in five minutes. We've still got a lot of loose ends to tie up on this thing. You don't just bring a public-corruption charge against a prominent businessman and a sitting U.S. congressman without a lot of preparation. Now, don't you fret. We've got Alex Hodder and Anthony Licata. We've got them both, cold, dead to rights, thanks in large part to you. If I were you, I'd go have a nice dinner out and celebrate."

"But, the money . . ."

She wasn't listening. "Oh, and Dempsey?"

"Yes?"

"Off the record? We all gave you a standing ovation when you slapped the snot out of that slimebag. And then, when you kicked him in the, uh, family jewels? Off the record, let's just say you struck a blow for women everywhere. Good job, girlfriend!"

I dragged the suitcase up the front steps of Birdsong, and into the hallway. Ella Kate's door was open, and when I looked in, I saw that she'd fallen asleep in her chair, the binoculars draped across her chest. Shorty was sleeping too, on a pillow on her bed, snoring lightly.

I looked down at Alex's suitcase, wondering what to do with it now. How would I keep it safe till the federal agents came to claim it? After a moment, I carried it upstairs and shoved it under my bed.

Downstairs, I went out to the kitchen and poured myself a very tall tumbler of Jack Daniel's. I cracked open a tray of ice cubes, and packed them into the glass, topping the whiskey and ice with two inches of water. I took a sip and then another.

When I'd finished my drink, I called Tee.

"Hey," I said softly.

"Hey you," he said. "How'd it go?"

"It went," I said. "He didn't pull a pistol, and he didn't try to pay me with counterfeit bills. At least, I don't think they're counterfeit." I didn't bother to tell him about my kick-boxing prowess. Maybe later.

"Great!" he exclaimed. "Should I turn on the news at six to watch footage of them slapping handcuffs on the sumbitch and hauling him off to jail?"

"Not just yet," I said. "The U.S. attorney for the Northern Georgia District called me."

"What's her name? Sharon something? She was just appointed last year. Supposed to be a real reformer-type prosecutor."

"Sharon Douglas," I said. "Yeah, she called to congratulate me, and to tell me not to expect any arrests just yet."

"Why the hell not? You did what they asked, right?"

"She said I was 'magnificent,' whatever that means. I guess they want to make sure they've got all their *i*s dotted and their *t*s crossed. She did assure me they've got both Alex Hodder and Tony Licata dead to rights. Her words, not mine."

"You don't sound very happy, Dempsey," Tee said. "What's the matter? This is the best possible outcome, right?"

"It is," I agreed. "But . . . it's weird. I just feel . . . kind of empty."

"Kinda like the day after Christmas, huh? You wait all year for that one day, tear through all your gifts and candy in an hour, and then the day after, you're wondering, what's so great about Christmas?"

"Something like that," I said. "Probably, I'm just tired."

"Pour yourself a stiff drink."

"I did. Now I just feel empty and . . . buzzed."

He laughed. "Take it easy, okay? I'll pick you up at seven, if that's all right. It's our night, remember?"

"I'll be ready," I promised.

"Dress warm," he said. "I've got a plan."

The late-afternoon sun made warm butterscotch-colored puddles on the front porch. Jimmy Maynard was dragging his extension ladder from one side of the house to the other. He was back to his usual penny loafers and madras Bermuda shorts.

"Jimmy," I said, my hands on my hips. "Don't you have anything better to do than paint my house?"

He propped the ladder up against the porch rail, and wiped his hands on a rag. "Well, now, Dempsey, funny you should mention that. I'm gonna be working double time around here this week, 'cause I gotta finish this job up before I move on to my next one."

"Jimmy," I said. "You don't paint houses for a living, remember? You're supposed to be in the insurance and real estate business."

He nodded. "Oh yeah. Now I remember. Actually, I got just one more painting job after Birdsong, and then, I swear, Jimmy is putting the brushes away for good."

"Who's the next recipient?"

He scuffed the toe of his loafer in the grass. "Shirlene."

"Should I read anything into that?" I asked teasingly.

"Aw, hell, I reckon so," he said. "You know what that damned fool gal went and did?"

"I can't imagine."

"She made me an offer I couldn't refuse. Said if I'd paint the outside of her house and get it ready to sell, she'd not only give me the listing, she'd give marriage to me another shot. You b'lieve that? I think she needs to have her head examined, don't you?"

"No," I said, throwing my arms around him and giving him a hug. "I think she's brilliant. I think she's the smartest lady I ever met. But here's what I want to know."

"What's that?"

"Why are we standing here when you've got a house to paint?"

"You like to paint?" he asked. "You're kinda dressed up for it."

"Be back in a minute," I told him.

And in five minutes, he had me up on a stepladder, cutting in around the edges of the parlor window with a bucket of dill pickle green paint. He'd sanded the old wood smooth, and as I brushed on the new green paint, I began to see why Jimmy loved his work.

New paint was about hope. It was about believing that underneath the dirt and the crud and the hurt, it was possible to find something solid and substantial. Something worth saving. And when you found something good, wasn't it right to try to fix it?

From four feet above me, Jimmy started whistling. After a few bars, I found myself whistling too. After an hour, we moved our ladders again and started to save a fresh patch of wall.

I only stopped painting when I realized the shadows were obscuring my ability to see where I was going, and it was almost dusk. "We're runnin' out of daylight," Jimmy announced, climbing down from his ladder.

We folded the drop cloth and stowed it in the back of his Jeep, then washed the brushes and put the paint cans in the corner on the front porch. Then Jimmy, still whistling, climbed in the Jeep. "Be good now," he admonished. "Or if you can't, at least be good at it."

It was almost six by the time I showered and dressed and came downstairs. Ella Kate was standing at the stove, stirring what looked and smelled like beef stew. "I've done cooked," she said, gesturing toward the pot. "There's enough, if you want some. I got corn bread too."

It wasn't the most gracious dinner invitation I'd ever had, but coming from Ella Kate, it was positively effusive.

"Thanks," I told her. "It smells wonderful, but I've got a dinner date."

She got a spoon from a drawer, and dumped some in a bowl for herself, and another helping in Shorty's bowl. She cut herself a generous wedge of corn bread, and slathered it with butter, remembering to break off a corner for Shorty.

"Going out with the Berryhill boy?" she asked, raising an eyebrow.

"Yes, ma'am," I said, bending over to scratch Shorty's ears.

"How'd your meetin' go today?" she asked. "I was watching CNN, till I dozed off, hoping I'd get to see them two crooks gettin' locked up in the jailhouse."

"It went pretty well," I said. "They haven't arrested Alex Hodder or Tony Licata yet, but I have it on good authority that it won't be long now."

"I seen you outside painting," she said, making it sound ominous. "Won't be long now."

"There's still a lot more to do," I told her. "I've been pretty distracted with all this FBI stuff lately, but now that that's over, I can't wait to get back to work on the house again."

"Huh," she said sourly. "There's a big ol' wet spot on the ceiling in my room. I believe that upstairs shower is leaking again. And I seen some little-bitty bugs flying around on the right side of the porch when I was comin' in the house today. Might be one of them termite swarms."

I laughed. "Bobby says this house is made of heart pine. He says these old boards are like iron, and not even the toughest termite could chew through them. But I'll have him take a look next time he comes."

The doorbell rang then, and I went out to meet my date.

ee was dressed in a pair of blue jeans and a plaid flannel shirt. The temperature had dropped a good twenty degrees just since sundown.

"Hey, you," he said, kissing me. "You ready to go?"

"Yep," I said, turning around. "Do I look all right? You said to dress warm."

I'd put on a pair of khaki slacks and a soft turquoise cotton-knit sweater, along with a pair of turquoise leather flats that Lynda had brought me from California.

"You look great," he said. "But then, I think you look great in everything, including your dead uncle's overalls."

And then he did a mincing pirouette of his own. "What about me? How do I look?"

"Fabulous," I said. "But then, I think you look fabulous in everything too."

We walked out to the Mini Cooper and drove off.

"You still haven't told me where we're going," I told him.

"No place fancy. I thought we might have a picnic."

"I love picnics, but in the dark?"

"This is sort of an indoor picnic," Tee said. "At my place."

"Okay," I said, deciding to give him the benefit of the doubt.

We pulled into the drive at Carter's house, and walked down the path to Tee's place. I hadn't actually been there since the night before the storm. The tree that had smashed through his roof had been cut up into logs that were stacked neatly near the back door to Carter's house. The back-porch lights shone on the little house, illuminating a bright blue tarp covering the roof.

"Bobby Livesey's supposed to start working on the roof sometime this week," Tee said, opening the pottery shed door. "The tarp keeps things pretty dry, but it does get kinda chilly at night."

I stepped inside. Dozens and dozens of lit candles cast a cozy glow on the old brick walls. There were candles in Mason jars, candles in silver candelabra, candles in dime-store votive glasses, and candles in brass candlesticks. Except for the bed most of the furniture was pushed to the sides of the room, and covered with more tarps. But in the middle of the room, a large oriental rug had been laid with a red-checked picnic cloth. The cloth was set for two, down to gold-rimmed china, cut-crystal wineglasses, silver flatware, and a small arrangement of white roses that had been poked into a silver teapot in the middle of the cloth.

I turned to Tee. "You did all this? For me?"

"You like?"

I wrapped my arms around his neck and showed him just how much I loved his idea of a picnic.

"This is the sweetest thing any man has ever done for me," I told him, laying my cheek against the warm flannel of his shirt.

"I'm just glad I didn't burn the place down," he said, pulling me closer. "Fire trucks really would have ruined the ambience."

"Nothing could ruin this," I said. "And, did you say something about dinner?"

"I did," he said, taking me by the hand and showing me the sofa cushion that was my designated seat for the evening. "Be right back," he said, disappearing into the tiny kitchenette.

A moment later, he was back, carrying a large black-and-gold tole-painted tray. A roast chicken had pride of place on the tray, and I could see a cut-glass dish of potato salad, a small dish of deviled eggs, a plate of grapes and sliced apples, and a plate with two chocolate-frosted cupcakes.

"Tee!" I said. "Did you fix all this food yourself?"

He did another exaggerated pirouette. "No. But I paid the lady who caters all the fancy parties in town to fix it. That counts, right?"

"Absolutely."

He set the tray down, went out to the kitchenette, and came back with a tarnished silver champagne bucket—complete with a bottle of iced-down Mumm's.

"Sorry," he said, plopping down on the cushion beside mine. "I just unearthed the champagne bucket from Mom's silver cabinet down in the basement. I didn't have time to actually polish it."

"It's beautiful. The whole table is beautiful. I am totally impressed," I said.

"All this stuff was kinda shoved in boxes down in the basement," he said, popping the champagne cork. "I think Dad felt kind of overwhelmed by trying to keep up with polishing and cleaning it after Mom died, so he packed it all away."

"Your basement sounds a lot more promising than the one at Birdsong," I said. "All I've found in our basement is what looks like thirty years' worth of back issues of *Mechanics Illustrated* and *Field and Stream*, along with cartons and cartons of old business files from Dempsey Mills."

He poured both of us glasses of champagne, and I was too overwhelmed by his thoughtfulness to point out that we were drinking out of red-wine glasses that were just the *teensiest* bit dusty.

We clinked glasses. "To us," Tee said. "And death to our enemies!"

"Or at least jail," I said, taking a sip of the champagne.

"You still sound kind of conflicted about all this business with Hodder and the FBI," Tee said, frowning. "What's that about?"

"I don't know," I admitted. "I really thought I'd be so relieved, once I got out of that church, knowing I'd done what the feds wanted me to do, and that I was finally off the hook. But I don't know. I felt sort of . . . dirty. Because I'd stooped to his level."

"You couldn't stoop to his level, Dempsey," Tee said. "He's scum. He put you in a bind, and you did what you had to do to get out of it. Stop beating yourself up and comparing yourself to him."

"I'm trying. But you should have seen the look on Hodder's face, Tee, when he walked into that church. He was beyond pissed. Murderous. That's the best way to describe it."

"Well, yeah. You had him over a barrel, and he knew it. He was busted, unless he dealt with you. And let's face it, he was handing over a big old wad of cash to you. I'm sure as far as he was concerned, you were the real criminal in the room."

"He made that point," I said ruefully. "Called me a stupid, pathetic bitch."

Tee shrugged and bit into a deviled egg. "Consider the source. Hey, speaking of the cash, what did you do with the money?"

"It's in the suitcase, under my bed. I get the willies thinking about it. I guess Jackson Hodder or Camerin Allgood will be along to collect it as evidence in the next day or two."

I hesitated, and then went on. "Alex said . . . he said the only reason I was turning on him, you know, blackmailing him, was out of revenge." I chewed on the inside of my cheek. "He said I wanted revenge because he wouldn't sleep with me. He even said Licata told him he should have, uh, slept with me to keep me quiet. But then Alex said he'd rather, uh, sleep with a pro than an amateur like me."

Tee's face reddened. "Lying sociopath son of a bitch."

"I hauled off and slapped him as hard as I could," I said. "I forgot I had my keys in my hand. Tee, I slapped him so hard I drew blood. Also, I, uh, kinda kicked him in the nuts."

"Good for you!" Tee said, chuckling. "I'd pay to see the film of that."

I shuddered at the mention of film. Were a roomful of federal agents even now sitting around, watching me bust Alex Hodder across the chops? Not to mention the footage of me kicking him in the nuts?

"It did feel kind of good," I admitted. "In an awful way."

Tee busied himself fixing me a plate, slicing off some of the chicken, adding a deviled egg and some potato salad.

"So," he said, trying to sound offhanded. "Not to put you on the spot or anything, but have you had some time to think about what we talked about earlier?"

I took another sip of champagne. "A little bit."

He handed me the plate. "Look, Dempsey. I promised myself I wasn't going to pressure you to stay here. Tonight was just going to be about us. And our future together. But that was before I heard the crap that asshole Hodder tried to lay on you. I don't know who you were before you came to Guthrie, but I don't believe you were anything like what Hodder accused you of being."

"I was an idiot," I whispered, blinking back tears. "And remember— I told you in the beginning, I did have a crush on Alex. I guess maybe I turned a blind eye to what he was doing. God help me."

Tee put his wineglass down so abruptly it sloshed champagne onto the cloth. "I'd like to get my hands on that guy. He used you! He saw a young, vulnerable girl, and he manipulated you." He reached over and cupped my chin between his hands. "You are nothing like the person he described."

"You only see what you want to see," I said. "You don't really know what I'm capable of doing."

"No," he said. "I see you as you are. Today. Here's what you're capable of, as far as I can see. You took a run-down ruin and made it into a home. You finally stood up to your father. You dealt with your mother. You inherited an irascible old lady and her dog, and saved both their lives. And you not only stood up to a crook, you brought him to his knees. You've become a part of this community, Dempsey. You can't leave now."

He let go of my face and took a sip of champagne. "Wow, big speech, huh?"

"Wonderful speech," I told him. "I think maybe you missed your calling by not going into politics."

"Politics!" He made a wry face. "I'd rather write about the rascals than become one of 'em."

"Guthrie's not such a bad place," I said slowly. "But I do wish there was a Starbucks. Or maybe just a Whole Foods."

"It ain't Camelot. But Guthrie is a good place, with good people. You go back to D.C., and what? Pick up where you left off?"

I shook my head. "No, there's no going back there, even if I wanted to."

He leaned forward, so that our foreheads were almost touching. "What do you want, Dempsey?"

If he'd asked me that question earlier in the day, especially right after

I'd left New Macedonia church, I probably couldn't have told him. But as improbable as it seemed, I'd found some answers in the few short hours since then.

The words just seemed to tumble out. "I want to finish what I started. There's so much left to do at Birdsong, and we're almost out of money. Mitch says old houses hemorrhage money. He wants the place sold as soon as possible. But, even if I could sell it, what happens to Ella Kate? It's her home. And Shorty's. I can't just put her out on the street, like a broken piece of furniture. If I had a job, maybe I could buy Birdsong from Mitch myself. He did promise to split any profits with me. Who knows, maybe he'd let me make payments or something."

He nodded, his face serious. "So, what's the answer?"

I chewed on a grape. "You know of any openings in this neck of the woods for a disgraced junior lobbyist?"

"Hmm," Tee said. "No, but I do happen to know of a firm that's looking to hire a feisty, energetic young attorney for a general practice."

"That sounds vaguely interesting. Maybe you could give me a referral?"

He leered at me over the top of his wineglass. "I could give you more than that. A lot more."

"Be serious," I told him.

"I'm serious as a heart attack," Tee said. "Just think about it. I'm not ready to totally give up practicing law, but running the newspaper is taking up more and more of my time. And Dad's got more work than he can handle. He's been talking about trying to slow down a little. Come work for us. If not for me, for Dad. You love him, he loves you. It's a no-brainer. Just think, we'd be Berryhill, Berryhill, and Berryhill."

He kissed me deeply, as though that would seal the deal.

"Hey," I said, pulling away. "Was that a merger offer or a marriage proposal?"

"Both," he said, pulling me back into his arms.

"Uh-uh," I said. "Berryhill, Berryhill, and Killebrew."

He stood up, gave me his hand, and pulled me to my feet. "Agreed," he said, pulling me toward the bed. "Now, can we finish these negotiations a little later?"

It was later, much later, in fact, that we hashed out all the details of the merger proposal. I'd drifted off to sleep, with Tee's arms wrapped securely around me, when I heard my cell phone ringing. Terrified that it might be a call about Ella Kate, I stumbled, naked, toward the chair where I'd left my pocketbook.

I grabbed the cell phone.

"Hello," I said breathlessly.

"Dempsey?" It was FBI Special Agent Jackson Harrell.

"Jack?" The room was near freezing. I groped around in the dark for something to wrap around me, and managed to come up with the checkered tablecloth. "What's wrong?"

"Wrong?" He was crowing. "What could be wrong?"

I held the phone away and looked at the clock at the bottom of the phone's readout screen. "Jack, it's nearly midnight. Are you drunk?"

"Drunk, hell no," he said indignantly. "I just thought I'd share a little good news with you, is all. Are you near a television?"

I looked around the room and saw Tee's tiny flat-screen television, and then I remembered. No electricity.

"No," I said impatiently. "There's no TV. Why? What's happening?"

"Well, that's too bad," Harrell said. " 'Cause if you did have a television, I'd tell you to turn on CNN so you could watch your buddies Alex Hodder and Tony Licata doing the perp walk."

"They've been arrested? When? The U.S. attorney said it might take a while."

"She meant hours, not days," Harrell said, chuckling. "We had agents waiting for Hodder when he got off the plane. And by the time they'd escorted him out to the main terminal, what do you know? Somebody had leaked the news to the press. Your friend Shalani from the *Post* was there, front and center. I think you'll be seeing a story tomorrow or the day after, clearing your name. Girl? You shoulda seen Alex Hodder trying to walk with his jacket pulled over his head. And he's still limping from that nutcracker you put on him. I tell ya, Dempsey, it was a beautiful sight."

I yawned despite myself. "That's good, Jack," I said sleepily. "It's fantastic. Thanks for letting me know. I'm sure I'll see the footage in the morning. Good night, Jack."

And then I remembered that suitcase under my bed at Birdsong.

"Oh, yeah. Jack, wait," I said. "What about the suitcase? Will you be sending a U.S. marshal or somebody to pick up the money?"

There was a long pause. I could hear voices in the background, and then static.

"Money?" Harrell said. "What money? Good night, Dempsey. See ya around."

Recipes

Ella Kate's Beef Stew

¼ cup all-purpose flour

1 tsp. salt

1 tsp. cracked black pepper

2 lbs. beef chuck roast trimmed of fat, cut in 1-inch cubes (or precut stew meat)

2 to 3 T. vegetable oil

4 cups beef broth or beef stock

1 bay leaf

2 stalks celery, roughly chopped

1 large onion, roughly chopped

5 medium-size red potatoes (skin on), cut in eighths

1 cup baby carrots, roughly chopped

1 T. GravyMaster

2 T. cooking sherry

Place flour and seasonings in large Ziploc bag, add cubed meat, close, and shake to coat. Heat oil in large, heavy-bottomed lidded pot such as Dutch oven, add meat, and cook over medium heat, turning until meat is browned on all sides. Add beef broth, and bay leaf, cover pot tightly, reduce heat, and simmer on stovetop approx. 1½ hours, or until meat is fork tender. Add vegetables to pot and return to simmer for additional hour. When vegetables are tender, remove meat and vegetables from pot with slotted spoon. Whisk in GravyMaster and cooking sherry. If gravy needs thickening, you may whisk 2 T. of flour into 2 T. water. Over medium heat whisk thickener into gravy, stirring constantly till smooth. Check seasonings and add salt and pepper if needed. Return meat and vegetables to gravy to heat through.

Lynda's Fire-roasted Tomato Soup

8 generous servings

½ *stick (¼ cup) butter (or 4 T. olive oil for vegans)*
1 *onion, finely chopped*
1 *cup baby carrots, finely chopped*
3 *T. minced garlic*
Two 28-oz. cans fire-roasted San Marzano tomatoes
1 *bay leaf*
¼ *tsp. red pepper flakes*
½ *tsp. dried thyme*
¼ *tsp. dried basil*
Salt and pepper to taste
1 *T. sugar*
6 *cups low-salt chicken broth (or 6 cups vegetable broth for vegans)*
Optional: buttermilk or low-fat sour cream stirred in before serving,
    chopped fresh basil leaves

Melt butter in heavy-bottomed soup pot over medium heat. Sauté onions, carrots, and garlic until translucent. Add canned tomatoes with their juice, and all seasonings and chicken or vegetable broth. Cover and simmer 40 minutes. Remove bay leaf. For smooth soup use immersion blender or let cool completely before pureeing in food processor or blender. Reheat and swirl in 1 T. buttermilk or low-fat sour cream. May be garnished with fresh basil.

Dempsey's Egg Salad

4 generous sandwiches

8 eggs, hard cooked
1/4 cup finely chopped celery
1/2 cup mayonnaise (preferably Duke's)
1/4 cup sweet pickle relish
1 tsp yellow mustard
Salt, pepper, celery salt

Peel and roughly chop hard-cooked eggs. Toss in celery. Fold in mayonnaise, relish, and mustard. Season to taste with salt, pepper, and celery salt.

For sandwiches use multigrain bread; add lettuce and red pepper rings.

The Fixer Upper

~

MARY KAY ANDREWS

A READER'S GUIDE

Questions for Discussion

1. Dempsey is one tough cookie! Strong and independent, she weathers a major life upheaval without much hysteria and lets on to relatively few people what she is going through. What attitudes does she adopt and behaviors does she engage in to help her get through it all? How would your coping mechanisms compare to Dempsey's were you to find yourself in a similar situation?

2. Consider the level of support that Dempsey gets from her parents and friends. How do you think your family and friends would react if you were in a professional and legal predicament like Dempsey's? When support is offered, how does Dempsey respond?

3. When Dempsey's father sets her up at Birdsong, do you think his motives are entirely selfless? In what ways—financially, emotionally, otherwise—does it benefit him to have Dempsey go to Guthrie? Discuss his motivations. How does the dynamic of their father/daughter relationship compare with your own or with those of your loved ones? What is a "daddy's girl"? How can a daddy's girl grow up to be her own woman?

4. Bobby Livesey plays a huge role in the transformation of Birdsong. In what ways is Bobby also pivotal in Dempsey's personal transformation?

5. What is your take on Ella Kate's relationship with Dempsey's grandmother? How might their relationship be received differently today?

6. What do you think Dempsey sees in Jimmy Maynard initially that allows her to be open to his flirtations? Why are smart women attracted to bad boys? What is the difference between a bad boy and a truly evil man?

7. Agent Harrell tells Dempsey her mother is a "bona-fide wack job." Do you get the impression that deep down Dempsey agrees with this assessment? In what way is Lynda's presence in Guthrie a help to Dempsey? A hindrance?

8. Several characters in the book appear one way at first, but our perception of them changes over the course of the novel. What events in particular caused you to sympathize with Ella Kate? How does Jimmy Maynard redeem himself in your eyes over the course of the novel? How do Dempsey's relationship with and opinions of Lynda evolve over the course of her visit? How did yours?

9. Agents Allgood and Harrell at first appear to be out to get Dempsey, but in the end they are rooting her on in her revenge plot. What is the turning point in this relationship? When does Dempsey transform from villain to victim in their eyes? Do you get the impression that Dempsey and Allgood could be friends under different circumstances? How are they alike?

10. When we meet Tee Berryhill, he seems like a knight in shining armor and the perfect mate for Dempsey. Why do you think she remains resistant to his advances for so long? What turns her around on him? Have you ever been pursued so relentlessly? If so, how did you respond at first? If not, put yourself in Dempsey's shoes and discuss how you would react.

11. Do you think Alex Hodder acted maliciously and set out deliberately to frame Dempsey from the start? At any point in the novel were you able to sympathize with Alex on some level in his profes-

sional or personal life choices? What figures in present-day political life come to mind when you think of Alex Hodder?

12. What factors contributed to Dempsey's naïveté in her dealings with Alex Hodder? What warning flags should Dempsey have seen, and what caused her to miss them? What do you think Dempsey learns from her ordeal?

13. Have you ever been screwed over by an employer or superior? If so, did it come as a shock and how did you react? Now that you've seen how Dempsey took care of her tormentor, how would you get the revenge of your dreams?

14. Discuss the renovation of Birdsong. In what ways is a project of this magnitude appealing to you? What most impressed you about Dempsey's work on the house? What decorating choices did you admire or disagree with? How is the transformation of Birdsong a metaphor for the changes that occur in Dempsey's life? How does the experience of fixing up Birdsong prepare Dempsey for what lies ahead?

15. How do you imagine Dempsey's future life in Guthrie to be? Will she be content? What aspects of living there will pose the biggest challenge for her? Bring the most pleasure? How do you imagine her working relationship with Carter Berryhill to be different from hers with Alex Hodder?

Ten Tips for Fixing Up a Fixer Upper

1. Look before you leap. Even if the house of your heart oozes charm out the wazoo, pay for a professional inspection before you sign on the dotted line—because sometimes, beneath all that ugly-duckling peeling paint, you find a swan, and sometimes you just find rot. Better to know ahead of time.

2. Be ruthlessly realistic when it comes to your fixer-upper abilities. If you and your partner both hold down full-time jobs and are raising a family, how likely is it that you'll truly be able to do it yourself? Ask around in the neighborhood for recommendations for experienced, qualified contractors. Look at the contractor's work; talk to past clients. Check to see if he's licensed, insured, and bonded, not to mention informed about local building codes.

3. Guesstimate a budget for your anticipated restoration/remodeling. And then quadruple it.

4. Prioritize. Pretend the house is in the emergency room and you're doing triage to stabilize it. This means start with the roof. If it leaks while you're trying to do Sheetrock, you can kiss that money good-bye. And how about the foundation? Mechanical systems—plumbing, electrical, heat and air—come next. Only after you've gotten the systems figured out and up to current code standards do you get to start on the fun, sexy stuff like paint, wallpaper, and fixtures.

5. Kitchens and baths eat up money like no tomorrow. Take a good hard look at your existing kitchen and bathrooms. Can they stay in

the same location? You'll save money if you don't have to go to the expense of moving water and plumbing lines. Are any of the fixtures salvageable? Maybe you'll be able to keep that adorable clawfoot tub in the bathroom, but it's likely you'll want to replace the outdated toilet with a new low-flow model.

6. Old homes like Dempsey Killebrew's Birdsong are notorious for lack of energy efficiency. Don't forget to budget money for insulation as well as possibly replacing drafty windows and exterior doors

7. If your old home is in a historic district, you'll probably need to follow guidelines for historic preservation regarding any exterior changes to your home. In some cases, you may qualify for tax breaks for following historic preservation guidelines.

8. Once you've got your patient's condition stabilized, it's time to concentrate on the fun stuff. Like paint. Don't rely on those tiny paint cards you get at home improvement stores. Buy the smallest-size paint can available and paint on different places on the walls. Try darker and lighter values of the same color, and give yourself a day or two of evaluating before buying.

9. The devil is in the details. Nothing looks worse in an old home than shiny new appointments. Haunt salvage shops, Craigslist, antique stores, and junk shops for period-appropriate light fixtures, door knobs, cabinet pulls, and hardware.

10. Educate yourself about old homes. Read shelter magazines, take historic home tours, and tour local house museums to see authentic period architecture and design.

Jimmy Maynard's Beer-braised Barbecued Ribs

6 servings

2 racks of ribs
Your favorite dry rub for steak or pork
2 onions, sliced thin
1 bottle dark beer

Line 9 x 12 baking pan with aluminum foil.

Let ribs reach room temperature—approximately 2 hours. Apply generous amount of dry rub. Let stand for an hour to absorb spices.

Line bottom of pan with sliced onions and set ribs atop onions. Pour beer over meat. Cover pan tightly with foil. Bake at 250°F for 2½ to 3 hours, or until tender. Remove from pan, and finish on grill over white coals. Cook to desired color, 6 to 8 minutes on each side.

May brush with barbecue sauce immediately before removing ribs.

BOOKS BY
Mary Kay Andrews

Inquisitive Atlanta cleaning lady—and former cop turned part-time P.I.— Callahan Garrity is on a course for adventure as she investigates mischief and murders in this original and witty mystery series by Mary Kay Andrews.

EVERY CROOKED NANNY

HOMEMADE SIN

TO LIVE AND DIE IN DIXIE

HAPPY NEVER AFTER

MIDNIGHT CLEAR

STRANGE BREW

Mary Kay Andrews Titles Are Available in Paperback and eBook Wherever Books Are Sold

For the perfect warm weather getaway, don't forget to pack the latest from *New York Times* bestselling author **MARY KAY ANDREWS!**

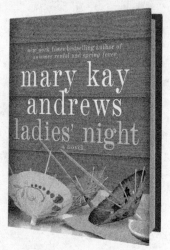

"An engaging and satisfying tale of life, loss, and love."
—*Booklist*

Mary Kay delivers a delicious escapist novel about small towns, old flames, and deep secrets.

"This warm weather treat has a lot going for it, not least the sunny forecast that summer love can blossom into a four-season commitment."—*Publishers Weekly*

MARYKAYANDREWS.com
facebook.com/marykayandrewsauthor

ST. MARTIN'S PRESS   St. Martin's Griffin